AMBER
MOMENT

0223-SLAT

AMBER MOMENT

Marion Marshall

0223-SLAT

Library of Congress Number:		98-87831
ISBN#:	Hardcover	0-7388-0121-6
	Softcover	0-7388-0122-4

This book was printed in the United States of America.

To order additional copies of this book, contact:
Xlibris Corporation
1-888-7-XLIBRIS
www.Xlibris.com

CONTENTS

FOR MY LATE HUSBAND, CLYDE WAYNE, WHO WAS,
WHO IS, AND WHO WILL ALWAYS BE MY INSPIRATION.

CHAPTER ONE

TEXAS, 1880

The Texas sun was warm and brilliant as she raced her horse through the tall grass. It waved before her like a green sea, rippling and dancing in the light breeze that stirred the heat of the June afternoon. The wind in her face lifted the mass of golden waves from her shoulders and left it trailing behind her, sparkling in the sun like a cape of sunbeams.

"This is wonderful, Sheik," Amber McCandless shouted against the wind. "I had almost forgotten how good it feels to ride so fast. There were few places in Boston where I could ride so freely."

Finally she eased the big horse into a sedate walk to allow him to regain his breath and looked around happily. As far as she could see in any direction lay acres of grassland on which fed her uncle's herd of Texas longhorns.

Amber looked toward the northwest and squinted through the sun at the peak of Guadalupe rising above the land at the point where the New Mexico territory began and her uncle's enormous ranch ended. The McCandless ranch lay between the Pecos River on the west and the Colorado River on the east, covering several thousand acres of West Texas cattle country.

To the east lay the silver ribbon of railroad tracks that kept McCandless, Texas in touch with the rest of the world. The railroad was new to Amber. It had been built during the time she had lived in Boston with her grandparents after her father's death. When she had left Texas twelve years earlier the only method of getting cattle to market was to drive them down the Chisholm Trail.

It had been on one of those cattle drives that her father was killed, bringing to an end her life in Texas. Shortly afterwards her mother had taken her and moved back east to live with her mother's parents. Her grandparents had died within months of each other when Amber was still in school, leaving Amber and her mother alone in the big house until her mother was stricken ill a few weeks ago. Thinking about her mother brought sadness to Amber's mood and she shook herself to get rid of the heavy feeling of loss that still came upon her whenever she thought of her mother.

She supposed she should be thankful that her mother's illness had been a short one. Althea McCandless had died without much suffering, but only a short time had passed so Amber still felt the numbing loss.

The easy gait of the horse made it easy for Amber to become lost in her thoughts. Her mind drifted back to a day the previous month when Mr. Swanson, the family's attorney for many years, told her the surprising condition of her finances. Amber had long suspected her grandparents had lived in a manner beyond their means, but it came as a shock to learn they had left nothing at all. Everything had been heavily mortgaged so that Amber had been forced to sell even the grand old house to pay off their debts when her mother died.

Althea McCandless had left Texas with only what she could carry, but Amber remembered the letters that arrived with regularity from Texas all those years. Althea had thrown them away unopened, forbidding Amber to discuss her uncle.

That was the strange part, Amber mused as she absently patted the horse's silky neck. She only knew that when her father died, her mother took her back East and forbade her to speak of her uncle or write to him.

Her brow wrinkled as she tried to remember her mother's words shortly before her death. Althea had said something strange and unsettling. She had asked Amber to promise that she would never return to Texas, no matter what. When Amber questioned her mother, asking Althea McCandless to explain her strange behavior all those years, her mother murmured something about a diary, but died before she could explain further.

Amber's search for the diary had turned up nothing, but she felt little regret at having broken that promise. It was a promise she did not understand and one that had become impractical upon learning her true financial picture.

It had been a great relief when Mr. Swanson informed her of the huge trust fund Owen McCandless had established for her. The terms were simple; on her twenty first birthday she would receive one half of *Sierra Vieja*; the land, the cattle, the sulfur mines, the railroad contracts, everything. The only stipulation was that she had to live in Texas to claim it.

With her mother gone and her education completed, the only thing holding her in Boston had been Larkin Prentiss. Even now her nose wrinkled in disgust at the thought of him. How naive and trusting she had been, she thought angrily. She had thought her future was assured when Larkin proposed marriage on her eighteenth birthday. Funny how the love she thought would last forever had dissolved into vapor when he realized she would have to leave Boston.

Larkin had been thrilled to learn of her inheritance until he realized it meant giving up the wealthy friends he had accumulated over the years. Amber learned quickly that his love for her wasn't deep enough to endure living in the southwest, which he considered to still be under the control of roaming bands of wild Indians.

So she had given him back his dainty diamond ring, packed her trunks, and caught the first available packet for Galveston. Even now the thought of his shallowness still hurt.

Amber drew a deep breath and looked about once more, breathing in the smell of fresh air and open skies. God, it was good to be back in Texas! To finally be home. She had not realized how deep her love for this great sprawling land went until she stepped off the stagecoach two days earlier and saw the familiar sight of McCandless.

The black Arabian tossed his head and snorted, pulling her from her thoughts. Amber loosened her grip on the reins, allowing the animal to break into a swift gallop. Sheik had been a gift from her uncle upon her arrival at the ranch and she had fallen in love with him immediately. He was a pure-bred Arabian gelding, brought all the way from the Middle East just for her.

Despite Larkin's betrayal fresh in her mind, Amber had to admit to a certain attraction for the handsome sheriff of McCandless whom she had met upon arriving in town. Steven Riker was everything Larkin wasn't; self assured without being arrogant, handsome without being flashy, friendly without being pushy. Yes, she thought cheerfully, Steven Riker had definite possibilities as a beau. And although he had not come to call on her yet, she felt sure he would, and soon.

An approaching rider put Steven Riker into the back of her mind as she directed her attention to the stranger who was riding toward her. She glanced around uneasily, realizing that she was miles from any assistance, but the approaching cowboy halted his mount a respectful distance from her and smiled.

"Howdy, ma'am," the man said with a polite tip of his hat. "Sorry to bother you, but I think I must be lost. I'm a stranger to these parts and I wonder if you could tell me how to get to McCandless."

"The ranch or the town?" Amber asked cautiously.

"The town, ma'am." The cowboy's manner was polite and he made no effort to move closer. It made Amber relax a little.

She smiled and turned in the saddle to point toward the north. "It's directly north of here about ten miles. You can't miss it," she told him.

The cowboy nodded and tipped his hat again, smiling pleasantly after glancing over his shoulder in the direction she had indicated.

"Much obliged, Miss...'"

"McCandless, Amber McCandless," Amber replied.

"McCandless? The same McCandless the town is named after?" the lanky cowboy asked in surprise.

Amber nodded, smiling. "Yes. The town is named after my father and my uncle. They founded it more than thirty years ago."

"Well, thank you for the directions, Miss. I best be getting on if I'm gonna make it before nightfall," he said in a Texas drawl. After tipping his hat once more, he rode away in the direction Amber had instructed.

Amber watched him for a moment before turning the Arabian around and heading back in the direction they had come.

***

As the girl on the black horse disappeared into the distance, the cowboy urged his horse into a gallop and headed for a stand of cottonwoods a short distance beyond the spot where he encountered her. Within moments he reined the horse to a halt and grinned at the man who waited for him beneath the trees.

"Did you get a good look at her, Morgan?" he asked.

Morgan Devereaux nodded, watching the girl on the black Arabian as she rode swiftly across the prairie. "Was that her?" he asked in a quiet voice.

The cowboy nodded and grinned again. "Yep, that was her. Miss Amber McCandless in the flesh. Quite a looker, ain't she, boss?"

Morgan nodded, watching the girl until she was only a speck on the horizon.

"The only thing that interests me, Jase, is her name. She's the chance I've been waiting for, the chance to get Owen McCandless where it hurts. Now that she's here, it won't be much longer," he said in a cold, ominous tone.

"You're sure this is the best way, Morgan?" Jase asked cautiously.

He had known Morgan for a couple of years now but he had

never heard him speak so coldly or look so dangerous before.

"It's the only way," Morgan said curtly.

CHAPTER TWO

Amber's arrival at the ranch did not go unnoticed by the cow-hands gathered around the corral. As she cantered into the ranch yard and sprang down from the Arabian, the men lost interest in the job of breaking new cow ponies to ride, to gawk at the slender girl as she led the horse into Owen McCandless' private stable at the side entrance of the enormous barn.

The girl seemed unaware of the approving stares of her uncle's hired hands. She was more concerned with the immediate job of unsaddling and brushing the big horse. She led him to his sizable private stall, took off the saddle with practiced ease, then hung it and the damp blanket on the side of the stall to dry. She took a moment to dish up a bucket of grain from a barrel nearby and put it into the feed bin in one corner of the stall before taking down the curry comb and beginning to groom the animal.

'Always take care of your horse, Amber, and he'll take care of you,' Price McCandless had taught her. It was a lesson she had never forgotten.

Sheik turned his head and nudged the girl with his shiny muzzle, rousing her from her thoughts. His intelligent black eyes surveyed her quietly as though trying in his own way to comfort her.

Amber smiled faintly and rubbed his shiny coat, brushing down across his sleek sides to the powerful muscles in his front legs. It must have cost her uncle a fortune to have him shipped all the way from the Middle East. His thoughtfulness made her eyes mist with love.

"Well, how was the ride?" came a deep masculine voice from the doorway.

Amber's head snapped up and a smile quickly flashed across her face at the familiar sight of Cooter Jackson, her uncle's friend and head wrangler for many years.

"It was wonderful, Cooter," she said happily. "Sheik is magnificent. He runs like the wind."

"He should, for what he cost," the old cowhand grumbled with a smile that offset his gruff tone of voice.

Cooter had been with Owen McCandless for more than twenty-five years. He was getting along in years now. His sight and hearing weren't as good as they once were and his once strong body was now often crippled by arthritis.

He came into the stable while Amber noted with dismay the noticeable limp that slowed his progress. His weathered face was wrinkled but the eyes set amid a maze of crows-feet were startlingly blue and alert.

"But I guess he's worth it if he makes you happy," he conceded with a teasing grin.

Amber squeezed his arm affectionately before returning to the task of grooming Sheik. "He is beautiful, isn't he, Cooter?"

The old cowboy nodded as he reached into the stall to rub the animal's shiny back. "He is that, Miss Amber. Your uncle sure knows his horseflesh."

Then his eyes took on a more somber glint as he directed his full attention to the girl. "It means an awful lot to him to have you back here, Miss Amber. He's missed you more than anybody knows."

"I'm glad to be back, Cooter. This is my home, where I belong. I never wanted to leave it. I've never understood why we had to leave after Papa died, or why Mama never answered any of Uncle Owen's letters."

"Your mama did what she thought was best, Miss Amber. You cain't fault her none for that. And just look at you now, why, you're just about the prettiest little thing in Texas. Who'd ever thought you'd turn out to be such a beauty? You look more like you mama every day," Cooter told her fondly.

"Do you really think I look like my mother?" Amber asked while she brushed the horse's sleek sides. She had always admired her mother's grace and beauty, but had never considered herself in the same way.

Cooter nodded with a grin. "You sure do, Miss Amber. I never thought I'd ever see a woman as pretty as your mama but I do believe you out-shine her. You've got her hair and those eyes, I've never seen eyes like that except your mama's. Yes sir, you've turned out to be quite a looker, Miss Amber."

"Do you think my father would be proud of me, Cooter?" she asked wistfully, her hand pausing in mid-air to await his reply.

The old cowboy's eyes took on a faintly bleak glow as he glanced away from her for a moment. "He sure would, Miss Amber. If your daddy was still alive, he'd be bustin' his buttons with pride. It's a damned shame he ain't here to see how you've turned out."

Amber's eyes grew misty as she cleared her throat in an effort to keep her voice steady. "You still miss him too, don't you, Cooter?" she asked softly.

"Your daddy was the finest man I ever knew, Miss Amber. He was the most honest, hardest workin' man that ever came to Texas. And he loved you and your mama more than anythin' in the world," he said gruffly.

"Isn't it a shame, Cooter, that Uncle Owen is the only McCandless left? I mean, there was my daddy and his older brother, the one that died before I was born. Now Uncle Owen is all alone except for me," she said sadly, still brushing absently at the Arabian's legs.

"Well, Miss Amber, I wouldn't worry too much about your Uncle Owen. There ain't nobody in this world stronger than Owen McCandless. Sure, he's been real lonesome since you and your mama went back east, but I don't think he's wasted much time over the years mournin' his losses."

Amber failed to note the sarcasm in his voice and stood staring at him wide-eyed and confused. "That's a terrible thing to say, Cooter."

His eyes softened a moment later and he reached out to pat her arm fondly. "Anyways, that's all in the past now, Miss Amber. You're here and that's all that matters."

The confusion faded from the girl's beautiful face as she nodded with a smile. "Yes, that's all that matters, Cooter. I'm home and I'm Uncle Owen's family. What more could he need?" she added with a teasing lilt in her voice.

"Nuthin' as far as I can see," the cowhand agreed with a smile that didn't quite reach his eyes.

He took the curry comb from her and hung it in its place on the stable wall, then limped alongside her as they walked from the cooling shade into the sun outside. He left her in a few strides and paused to watch her hurry toward the house. His wrinkled brow furrowed in thought as he studied her disappearing back, then he shook his head.

"I'm afraid, Missy, that you've got a lot to learn and it ain't gonna be a pleasant lesson," he said aloud.

***

Amber swept into the house with a sunny smile. Pausing to pick up an inviting red apple from the bowl on the credenza in the front hallway, she took a bite and scampered down the hall, chewing.

The house was a grand structure built in 1855 by Owen's own hands. It was a rambling ranch house two stories high with a wrought iron railing running the length of the balcony that graced the front of the house. *Sierra Vieja,* the ranch and house were called, or old mountain, so named because of the mountain range that extended along the Mexican border northward toward the New Mexico territory. The name had always had a certain romantic ring to it for Owen, for it was here he had planned to bring his young bride. He never had, for the young lady fell in love with another man and married him instead, leaving Owen with a houseful of shattered dreams.

Nevertheless, *Sierra Vieja* was home and over the years Owen had built it into a showplace of wealth and social position. Those grand old walls had been visited by kings, governors, senators, cattle barons, railroad financiers, judges and mayors. There had been a succession of women as well, but none ever stayed more than a few days before she was asked to move on, always with a generous check in her bag for her services..

The house was sparkling white, standing out on the horizon like a beacon. It contained eighteen rooms, running water and an assortment of expensive imported furniture sitting on elegant Oriental rugs brought overland from San Francisco on Owen's own stagelines. *Sierra Vieja* was an oasis in the Texas prairie, a gathering place for the state's wealthiest and most powerful men.

Still, the house at *Sierra Vieja* lacked the things needed to make Owen McCandless a happy man; the woman he had lost and children of his own.

Amber paused to tap lightly on Owen's office door, but did not wait for an invitation before opening it and breezing inside. She was home again at *Sierra Vieja*. It was as though she had never left it when the door swung open and her uncle raised his head from the stack of papers on the desk he was seated behind and smiled widely.

"Well, there you are," Owen McCandless boomed in a hearty voice as the girl entered the room and closed the door behind her. "How was the ride?"

"It was wonderful, Uncle Owen. Sheik is the most magnificent animal I've ever ridden. How can I thank you for such a marvelous gift?" Amber replied cheerfully.

"Just knowing you're enjoying him is all the thanks I need," Owen replied in his deep voice, his face bathed in smiles at Amber's happiness. "Does the ranch look the same after all these years?" he asked, leaning back in his plush chair to survey her.

"I can't tell its changed at all. But I was only seven the last time I saw her."

"The land hasn't changed much, Amber, just the improvements I've made on it," Owen said proudly.

He tapped the stack of papers he had been looking over when she entered and smiled again. "The railroad is new. It's only been around a few years. It makes things a good deal easier at roundup time, I can tell you. Now all we have to do is take the herd into town and load it on stock cars. The railroad does the rest."

"What about the land the tracks run through? What became of all the small ranchers in that area?"

Owen nodded and paused to take a cigar from the gold case on top of his desk and lit it before responding to her questions. "I bought them all out years ago, princess. Cost a great deal of money too but it was well worth it. I've more than recovered my expenses since the railroad has come over that land."

Amber nodded in understanding, her golden head shimmering in the sunlight that streaked through the bay window behind her uncle's desk. She took a moment to look around the familiar room and then sighed with contentment. "I can't tell you how glad I am to be home, Uncle Owen," she said happily.

Owen shifted in the big leather chair and drew on his cigar, exhaling a gray plume of smoke into the air, then smiled affectionately at her. "You can't be more happy than I am to have you here once again, princess."

"Uncle Owen," Amber began hestitantly, trying to find the words to ask the question that had been on her mind for a very long time. "Why did my mother take me away after Papa died? And why did she refuse to open your letters all those years?"

Owen met her curious gaze over the smoke of his cigar without blinking. "It was some silly misunderstanding, princess. It didn't amount to anything really, just one of those silly things that got blown out of proportion. But your mama was one stubborn woman. She could hold a grudge longer than anybody I've ever known."

Amber studied him silently for a moment. She knew how determined her mother could be once she made up her mind about something. Since Owen's expression was frank and candid, she had no reason to doubt him.

"Uncle Owen, my mother mentioned something about a diary shortly before she died. I looked and looked, but I couldn't find it. Do you have any idea what she was talking about or where it might be?" she asked.

Owen's brows rose momentarily. He cleared his throat as he tapped the cigar into the ashtray. "Princess, your mama was a very sick woman at the end. She was probably remembering something from her childhood. I doubt there was a diary. If there was, I don't know anything about it."

He smiled widely then to disspell the somber mood that had invaded their conversation. "Listen to us, will you? We should be celebrating your homecoming, not talking about such sad things. Now tell me about your ride."

Amber nodded in agreement, eager to put those painful memories away, and broke into animated conversation about the wind and sunlight, and the performance of the Arabian gelding. Owen smiled and nodded from time to time as she talked, pausing occasionally to draw on the cigar and flick the ash into a crystal ashtray on the desk top.

Owen McCandless was an impressive looking man, tall and powerfully built with massive shoulders and a thick neck, his skin burned to a deep bronze from years of the relentless Texas sun. He was well over six feet tall with once dark hair, now graying at the temples, which gave him a sophisticated air. His still handsome face was lined from years of hard work and his blue eyes were clear and contained a shrewdness that was difficult to overlook. He was fifty-five years old now, but the agile way he moved belied his advancing age. He still considered himself a young man, and a better man than any of the younger cowhands he employed. He was a proud man; proud of his looks and proud of his accomplishments.

Everything he had been through to make himself a rich, powerful man had been for Amber. When he was gone, she would be an immensely wealthy young woman so he would have to groom her carefully on how to deal with that wealth and the power that came with it. He would take great pleasure in teaching her the operation of the ranch during the coming years. For the first time in twenty years, Owen felt that life had something worthwhile to offer him.....

"Are you listening to me, Uncle Owen?" Amber asked, puzzled at the distracted expression on his face.

"Of course I am, princess. I was just thinking how much more like a home this old house seems with you here."

Amber smiled, her eyes glowing with affection. "I've missed this house so much, Uncle Owen, and you. I promise never to leave either of you again."

Owen crushed out his cigar and pushed his chair back from the desk as the girl bounced from her seat and rushed around the desk to give him an impulsive hug. Owen returned the brief embrace with affection then reluctantly pulled away from the slender arms wrapped around his neck.

"You better get upstairs and change for supper, princess," he suggested gruffly.

Amber smiled after glancing at her reflection in a heavy mirror that adorned a spot in the center of the far wall of the room. She reached up to smooth her tumbled hair and grimaced at her dusty clothing and boots.

"I suppose you're right, Uncle Owen. I must smell a good deal like Sheik. I'll hurry down. Something smells wonderful and I just realized that I'm starving."

Owen smiled and gave her a mild swat on the rump as she moved toward the doorway. Before she reached it, the double doors swung open and the ranch foreman burst inside.

"Mr. McCandless, I've just come from the east range. We got five miles of cut fence and a couple dozen dead cows. Somebody's poisoned the water hole too," he blurted out, gasping for breath from the long hot ride.

Owen came to his feet with surprising speed for a man his age and strode around the desk in two long strides. Then he remembered Amber and stopped to lean back against the desk. "You're forgetting your manners, Wade," he growled. "I don't believe you've met my niece. Amber, this is Wade Harding, my foreman."

"Miss McCandless, please excuse my manners. I didn't know the boss was busy," he stammered.

"It's nice to meet you, Mr. Harding. If you will excuse me, I must run up and change for supper," Amber told him in a warm, friendly tone, then swept past him through the doors.

Harding's eyes followed her, taking in the curves of her slender body and the tantalizing way her hips swayed in the fitted riding dress.

"Close the door, Wade, and put your eyes back in their sockets," Owen grunted, his eyes narrowing and taking on an ominous gleam.

Harding swallowed, turning to close the doors behind him, then moving further into the office. "Sorry, Mr. McCandless, I didn't mean to stare."

"See that you keep your distance from my niece, Wade, if you value your job here."

"But, Mr. McCandless, I didn't mean anythin'..."

"I know exactly what you mean, Wade," Owen cut in sharply. "And I'm warning you. My niece is a lady and you will treat her like one. Is that clear?"

"Of course, Mr. McCandless," the cowboy stammered, wondering what he had done that was so terrible.

"Now tell me about the trouble in the east range. Cut fence and a poisoned water hole?"

"Yes sir," Harding replied in a relieved tone. He fidgeted with his hat and found it difficult to look his boss in the eye. There was something unsettling about Owen McCandless, something that always made him nervous but he didn't dwell on it. He had a good job here and he wanted to keep it. "About two dozen dead cattle, sir. Looks like Devereaux's work again."

Owen's meaty fist slammed down onto the desk top with a

sharp bang that caused Harding to jump. Owen's face had paled
beneath the deep tan and his eyes had narrowed to slits of ice cold,
blue fury. "That son-of-a-bitch! What does he want from me?"

He turned away for a moment to regain his composure. He
took a few deep breaths and turned back to his foreman.

"Send one of the men into town for the sheriff, Wade. I know
it's probably a waste of time, but I want Riker to know about this.
He must have a catalog of my complaints about that bastard by
now," he said in a more controlled voice.

Harding spun about, took a step toward the door, then paused
to look back at Owen, his eyes puzzled. "Don't it strike you as a
bit odd, Mr. McCandless, that Devereaux ain't cut anybody else's
fences or poisoned their water holes? Last week it was the Austin
stage his gang held up and the week before that he ran off the
supply train for the mines. It's almost like he's got something personal against you."

Owen didn't reply and after a moment Harding shrugged and
left the room. Behind him, Owen's fist came down on the desk
again in frustration. He hated to admit it, but it was beginning to
look like Wade was right. For weeks now he had been plagued by
Morgan Devereaux and his band of outlaws.

The incidents were never serious, no one had been gravely
injured, but the man was a constant source of irritation. Cutting
fences, running off herds, holding up stages when there was no
money aboard, terrorizing the men at the sulfur mines, burning
down line shacks and taking stray shots at out-riders. And for what?
Why? What was the purpose? He didn't even know Morgan
Devereaux.

CHAPTER THREE

Steven Riker arrived while Amber and Owen were still having supper. Quincy, Owen's colored butler, led him into the dining room and Owen rose to greet him with a smile.

"Steven, good of you to ride out so late in the day. Have a seat and join us," Owen invited as he indicated a chair next to him at the long dining table. "You remember my niece."

"I certainly do, Mr. McCandless. How could I forget such a lovely young lady?" Steven said with a friendly smile as he reached across the table to lightly kiss the back of Amber's hand.

He took the chair Owen had indicated and paused to let Quincy take his hat before turning to his host with a smile. Amber was seated directly across the table from him, making it an effort to keep his eyes focused on Owen.

Who would have imagined that a tough old Texan like Owen McCandless had a female relative like this glorious creature?

"Won't you join us in a bit of this delicious roast chicken, sheriff?" Amber asked in a soft voice.

"No, thank you, Miss McCandless," Steven declined politely. "I've eaten already but please, don't let me interrupt your meal."

Amber's cheeks dimpled with a smile before she returned to her supper. She glanced upward occasionally at the sheriff and was impressed by what she saw.

His clothes were immaculate and his black boots, she had noted, were polished to a rich gleam. He was obviously a man who took pride in his appearance. He was dressed in a dark gray broadcloth suit, complete with silk vest and a crisp white shirt. He was attractive, no doubt about it, and she felt a blush warm her cheeks when she glanced up to find those deep blue eyes fixed on her. Obviously, he felt the same about her.

"I understand you've had another visit from Devereaux and his boys," Riker remarked, directing his attention to the real purpose of this visit.

Owen nodded, but took a sip of the deep red wine from his glass, giving himself a moment to consider his reply before answering. "It appears so. Wade tells me he discovered five miles of cut fence and a poisoned water hole this afternoon," he grunted finally.

"This is becoming a habit, isn't it, Mr. McCandless? This makes about the sixth or seventh incident you believe Devereaux's responsible for."

Owen's face bore a distinctly annoyed expression as he surveyed the young sheriff. "I don't need a list of the offenses, Riker. I need action."

Amber stopped eating to stare at her uncle in concern. She had never heard him speak so sharply to anyone and her eyes flashed to Riker's face. Surprisingly, the sheriff did not seem offended by Owen's caustic remark. He sat calmly swirling the contents of his wine glass in one hand while he met Owen's level gaze.

"Mr. McCandless, you know I'm doing everything possible to round up Morgan Devereaux and his men. I've raised the reward on him to five thousand dollars like you asked. Unless someone comes forward with some information, there isn't much I can do."

"Then look harder, damn it!" Owen growled. Then remembering his manners, he turned quickly to Amber with an apologetic expression to add, "I'm sorry, princess, I forgot myself for a moment. Please forgive my language."

Amber smiled briefly and took a sip of wine while she studied the two men. There was an uneasiness in her uncle she had never seen before and it concerned her to see him upset.

"Who is Morgan Devereaux?" she asked.

Owen and Riker exchanged glances before Owen reached to

pat her hand. "Nobody for you to be concerned about, princess. Steven and I should wait to discuss this matter privately."

"I'd rather know about it, Uncle Owen," she insisted. "If it concerns you, then it concerns me, as well."

"Morgan Devereaux is an outlaw, Miss McCandless," Steven Riker explained slowly, ignoring the displeasure on Owen's face. "He's a gunslinger, a renegade that's been seen in this area. Your uncle believes he's responsible for several attacks on McCandless property during the past few weeks."

"It's nothing, really," Owen interjected. "Nobody has been seriously injured and no real damage has been done except for the money it's cost me. The man's more of an irritation that anything else."

"Why would this man do such things?" Amber inquired.

Owen shook his head wearily and shrugged his shoulders with a sigh. "That's the thing that puzzles me, princess. I don't know. I don't have an explanation for any of it. I don't know Devereaux. Yet he's singled me out for some reason."

"I've heard that he could be working for Welch Mandell," the sheriff remarked casually.

Amber watched with growing alarm as her uncle's hand shook when he set down his wine glass. Owen's face had paled beneath the tan and he touched his tongue to his lips and swallowed before acknowledging the sheriff's remark.

"Welch Mandell! Are you certain of that, Steven?"

Riker nodded and sipped at his wine. "Sure enough. You know Mandell?"

"No, I only know who he is," Owen replied harshly. He pushed his plate away and snapped his fingers impatiently. A moment later Quincy appeared with a cigar case and a lighted match. Owen quickly selected a cigar and lit it, drawing deeply and exhaling while he nodded briskly. "Everybody in Texas knows Mandell. He's a murdering, black-hearted renegade."

Riker nodded in agreement. "I understand he's one of the fastest men alive with a gun. Could be he's the one who taught Devereaux. At least, that's what I hear."

"What else do you hear, Steven?" Owen asked gruffly, his cold blue eyes studying the sheriff intently.

Riker shrugged and swirled the glass of wine once more. "I hear Devereaux and Mandell go back quite a way. Rumor has it Mandell raised him. If they're around here, it would certainly explain the rash of robberies in the area lately."

"But does it explain why this man is harassing my uncle?" Amber asked.

"No, Miss McCandless, it doesn't. It's not like Mandell to bother with cutting fence and killing cattle. He's usually more interested in stealing them."

"Amber, if you will please excuse us, dear, I would like to discuss this matter with the sheriff in private," Owen said stiffly.

Amber started to protest, but something in her uncle's eyes stopped her. Owen looked decidedly uncomfortable, so she nodded as she rose to her feet. "Of course, Uncle Owen. If you will excuse me then, gentlemen, I shall go to my room," she said in a puzzled voice.

Both men rose to their feet and Owen leaned down to kiss her on the cheek. Steven took one of her hands in his and kissed it lightly, his eyes remaining locked with hers.

"Miss McCandless, if you would do me the honor of accepting my invitation to a barn dance this Friday night, I should be very flattered," he said in a smooth, friendly tone.

A faint blush stained Amber's cheeks as she smiled. She looked at her uncle expectantly. "May I, Uncle Owen?"

Owen's heavy brows were pulled into a frown but he reluctantly nodded.

"Thank you, Mr. Riker, I shall be pleased to accept your invitation," Amber replied to Steven with a smile.

"Then I shall pick you up around six o'clock Friday evening."

"I look forward to it, Mr. Riker," Amber replied with a dazzling smile.

She paused to place an affectionate kiss on her uncle's cheek before leaving the room. After her footsteps had died away on the carpeted staircase, Owen turned to the sheriff with a scowl darkening his features.

"Who the hell do you think you are, Riker, to just waltz in here and ask my niece out without checking with me first?" he demanded angrily.

Steven again took his seat and reached to fill his wine glass from the crystal decanter on the table. He took a leisurely drink from the glass, all the while observing the older man's glowering face.

"I'm the man who's going to take care of Devereaux for you, Mr. McCandless. Besides, your niece is not a child. I hardly think she needs your permission before accepting my invitation to a perfectly innocent dance."

Owen leaned forward until his face was only an inch from the young sheriff's, the cold blue eyes blazing with anger. "Now you listen to me, you young whelp!" he said coldly. "Whatever ideas you have about Amber, you just put right out of your head. She's off limits to you, do you understand me? She's not like the whores that occupy your saloon in town. She's a lady. She knows nothing about men like you."

Steven chuckled softly as his eyes met Owen's in a level, unwavering gaze of confidence. "Take it easy, Mr. McCandless. I have only the most honorable intentions toward your lovely niece. I should think you would rather Amber be attracted to me than some twenty dollar a month cowhand. I have a great deal to offer her."

"Like what?" Owen growled as he settled back in his chair and drew on the cigar.

"Like ambition for one thing. I'm not unlike you in that respect, Mr. McCandless. I'm an ambitious man. Someday I intend to own a good portion of this state."

"Not through my niece, you won't," Owen assured him scornfully. "I see what you're up to, Riker, and it won't work. My niece is too damned good for you, or anyone like you, and don't you ever forget it."

"I think we should let Amber use her own judgment. "

"Amber will do what I tell her," Owen snarled. "I'll pick a husband for her when the time comes and it won't be you."

Steven merely sipped at his wine and smiled confidently in a manner that made Owen's blood boil with anger. The young sheriff was much too cocky to suit him.

"Don't be so sure of that, Mr. McCandless. I think you underestimate me. I think I am exactly the kind of man you want her to marry. I'm ambitious. I'm smart, and I'm greedy; three sterling qualities for the husband of a young woman who will someday own most of West Texas."

Owen snorted in contempt and drew on the cigar again, exhaling a plume of gray smoke toward the ceiling. "I made you the sheriff of my town, Riker, and I can just as quickly replace you. I'd keep that in mind, if I were you."

"So you did," Steven agreed. "But perhaps I should remind you just how much money I've made for you since you put me in this office. The saloons are bringing in hundreds every week from the railroad people, not to mention the miners. When you analyze it, those men are working for nothing. The wages you pay them for working in your sulfur mines, I'm making back with the games and the whores in my saloon. I think you'd have to look pretty far to find another man with my abilities."

"It's not your abilities at making money for me that I find objectionable," Owen pointed out sourly. "It's the abilities you use upstairs with the whores that worries me. I'm warning you, Steven; if you lay so much as one finger on my niece, I'll kill you. You've got my word on it."

The men stared at one another in strained silence for a long moment before Steven laughed softly and raised his glass in a toast. "I think we understand each other perfectly, Mr. McCandless. Shall we drink to our partnership?"

After a moment the frown eased from Owen's face and he lifted his glass to touch Steven's with a crystal tinkle. "Just so you re-member who's working for whom, Steven."

"You're the boss, Mr. McCandless," the sheriff assured him with an easy smile. "I'm not likely to forget that."

"Good, see that you don't. Now, let's get down to business about that goddamned gunslinger. I want Devereaux's hide, Steven, and I want it now. Do whatever is necessary to find him. Pay off as many people as you need, but I want that son-of-a-bitch!"

"And if he *is* working for Welch Mandell?"

"So much the better," Owen growled. "Get Devereaux and you may flush out Mandell in the process. That should put a real feather in your cap. How would you like to be the man who killed both Devereaux and Mandell? You'd be the most famous lawman in the United States."

Riker laughed again softly, his eyes narrowing with anticipation at that prospect. "A man who managed to rid Texas of those two might even be considered worthy of becoming the husband of its wealthiest young woman. Wouldn't you say, Mr. McCandless?"

"Perhaps, Steven, perhaps," Owen replied with a sly smile. "Just perhaps my opinion of you would improve if you were able to pull that off."

Riker again lifted his glass to touch Owen's in a cold clink of questionable alliance. All that stood betweed him and becoming one of the most wealthy and powerful men in the nation was one man....Morgan Devereaux.

CHAPTER FOUR

When Owen's head housekeeper, Hannah Upton, announced early the following morning that she was going into McCandless for supplies, Amber jumped at the chance to accompany her. Making a mental list of the things she wished to purchase in town, she breezed into Owen's study to tell him she was going with Hannah.

Owen glanced up from an official looking document on his desk and nodded agreeably. "Of course, princess, I think that's a fine idea. By all means, buy whatever strikes your fancy. Just tell Roscoe to put it on my bill," he told her in a distracted manner.

"Thank you, Uncle Owen."

She planted a brief kiss on his cheek and hurried from the room.

The ten mile ride into McCandless was pleasant for Amber quickly learned that Hannah possessed a grand sense of humor so before they arrived in town, they were the best of friends.

Hannah pulled the buckboard to a halt in front of Roscoe's General Store and Amber bounced down from the seat. Alighting onto the hard packed dirt street, she smoothed her skirt and paused for a moment before following Hannah inside to take a long look at the town she remembered so well.

McCandless, Texas was a quiet, sleepy frontier town. Amber surveyed it with a fond smile. McCandless hadn't changed a lot in the twelve years she had been away. It was a bit larger, but she had expected that with the coming of the railroad. She remembered the friendliness of its people for everyone knew everyone else in McCandless. They cared what happened to each other. Amber had missed that personal concern for others that did not exist in Boston.

Finally she followed Hannah into the store. Floyd Roscoe was exactly as she remembered him; big, raw-boned, with a chest length chestnut beard and a full mustache, his ruddy face softened by the beaming smile he reserved for his special customers.

Roscoe was one of McCandless' original pioneers for he had come to this part of Texas shortly after the McCandless brothers in the early 1840's. His ruddy face broke into a wide, toothy smile at the sight of Amber. He came from behind his counter to extend a large, brawny hand in greeting.

"Well, well, Miss Amber, just look at you," he boomed in a hearty voice. "Just look how pretty you've turned out. Who would have ever thought that such a skinny little thing with pigtails would ever have grown into such a beautiful young lady!"

Amber's face dimpled with a faint blush as she returned his friendly greeting. Being in this store again brought back such pleasant memories. Her bright golden eyes darted to the counter to spot the tall canisters of candy that had so fascinated her as a child. Not once had she ever left Mr. Roscoe's store without a stick of candy in her mouth, even when her father had no money to pay for it.

Those were the days before the McCandless ranch had flourished and became the largest cattle ranch in west Texas. In those days, Floyd Roscoe was just getting his business started, struggling to gain a foothold in the prairie, just like her father and uncle. "Mr. Roscoe, how nice it is to see you again," she told him with a bright smile. "I see you still have those heavenly peppermint sticks."

"Indeed I do, Miss Amber, just help yourself."

Unable to resist a giggle, Amber crossed the plank floor and lifted the top off one of the canisters to select a piece of candy. Nibbling on one end of it, she turned again to the burly store owner and smiled.

"The only difference is that now I'm able to pay you for it," she told him in a teasing tone. "If I were to add up all the peppermint sticks I ate without paying for them, Mr. Roscoe, I'd owe you a small fortune."

"Well, you just pick out anything you want, Miss Amber," Roscoe told her with a hand extended toward the tables stacked high with merchandise that covered the interior of his store. "I've got most anything you might need. If you need any help, you just let me know."

Amber smiled and began investigating the piles of clothing. She hummed softly under her breath as she paused to inspect a table of hand-tooled boots but decided breaking in a new pair was too painful and the old worn ones she had found at *Sierra Vieja* would do just fine.

It was several minutes before she realized someone else had entered the store and glanced up to see a man walking toward her.

The man came to a halt a few steps away and was watching her in a pleasant manner. He did not smile but did not seem threatening in any way as Amber turned away from the rack to give him her full attention.

The man was considerably taller than she, perhaps six feet three inches. He was strongly built with broad shoulders, a wide chest and long arms. His thumbs were hooked in the black leather gunbelt that was resting around his waist, secured to his left thigh with a leather thong.

She was looking up into the face of the most incredibly attractive man she had ever seen. His raven black hair was neatly combed beneath the black Stetson hat, on which sparkled a hatband made of silver conchos. His face was tanned and flawless, his nose slightly angular though not to the point of being unattractive. His lips were full and possessed a sensual quality that made it hard for Amber to tear her eyes away. It was those remarkable eyes that held her spellbound, however. They were coal black in color, large and fathomless, fringed by thick dark lashes.

He was not the typical cowboy of the region. Instead of chaps and rough work shirts, he was dressed in a royal blue, long sleeved shirt and a black leather vest. His lean, muscular legs were encased in a pair of black trousers that fit him like a glove.

She judged him to be in his late twenties or possibly early thirties. He was clean shaven and she noted the pleasant aroma of bay rum, light and understated.

"Miss McCandless?" he inquired politely.

After a long moment, she recovered her voice. "Yes, I 'm Amber McCandless." she answered, feeling a blush creep into her cheeks for she knew the man must have observed the bold way she had been staring at him.

"I have a message for your uncle. I wonder if you might give it to him," the stranger told her in a matter of fact tone while his ebony eyes continued to regard her solemnly.

Amber nodded, wondering as she did why she suddenly felt so flushed.

There was something unsettling about this man, something unusual and a little dangerous, but she was at a loss as to what it was in his manner that gave her this impression. Certainly nothing he had done or said was out of line or menacing in the least. No, it was something else, something about the way those coal black eyes pierced into hers without revealing anything about his thoughts that made her suddenly feel almost vulnerable. She wondered why he seemed both intriguing and dangerous at the same time. The combination made her pulse race.

"Yes, I would be happy to," she replied in a shaky voice.

The man reached into his vest to produce an envelope that he handed to her, noting with amusement the way the girl's hand trembled slightly as she reach to take it from him. She seemed almost shy and uneasy, not at all the way he had perceived Owen McCandless' niece to be. Jase McCally had been absolutely right about her beauty. She was without a doubt the most beautiful girl he had ever met.

He continued to study those clear golden eyes. They were like crystal candles lighting the way into her thoughts, he noted with a sardonic half-smile. He wondered if she was aware of how clearly those astounding eyes revealed her innermost thoughts, then decided she wasn't. If she knew how easily he could read her, she would have done a better job of concealing her curiosity about him. Then he reminded himself sternly that she was, after all, a McCandless.

"Thank you, Miss McCandless," he said curtly and turned on his heel, suddenly anxious to put distance between himself and the girl.

Amber watched him stride toward the open doorway in speechless wonder. Then remembering he hadn't given her his name, she clutched the envelope in one hand and hurried after him.

"Excuse me," she called.

The man halted and swung about to face her once more, his dark eyes stabbing into hers, and though he gave the appearance of being completely at ease, Amber had the distinct impression that beneath that casual pose steel muscles lay coiled and ready to strike.

"Who shall I say gave this to me?" she stammered breathlessly, wishing she could tear her eyes away from his. "Mr.....er,..er?"

For the first time a smile appeared on his lips and Amber was astonished at the transformation that took place. If she had thought he was handsome before, he was a thousand times more attractive now. His dazzling smile had lessened the seriousness around his mouth, revealing twin rows of perfect ivory teeth that were a flash of brilliance in his deeply tanned face.

"When he reads the message, he'll know who sent it," he told her dryly with an undercurrent in his voice that Amber could not grasp.

She stood holding the envelope tightly, staring at him with wide eyes, trying to think of something else to say so he would not walk away, but after a final flashing glance at her confused face, the man turned on his heel and walked out the doorway and down the boardwalk.

Amber remained in the same spot, listening to the jingle of his spurs as his footsteps receded into the noise of the street, wishing fervently that she had been able to learn more about him.

After a few long moments she turned back to her shopping with a sigh of regret. The most exciting man she had ever met in her life and she had let him get away without even learning his name.

CHAPTER FIVE

After taking time out for lunch at the McCandless Hotel, and securing the services of a dressmaker that Hannah recommended, Amber and Hannah set out for the ranch. Having not been able to find suitable dress fabric in Mr. Roscoe's store, she had decided to have the dressmaker alter one of her finer Boston creations into a more appropriate garment for the dance. An appointment had been made for the following day.

During the ride back to the ranch Amber could not keep her mind off the handsome man who had approached her, or the letter she carried in her bag.

She scrambled down from the seat and flew up the walk into the foyer of the big house. The heavy double doors closed with a bang behind her as she scurried down the hallway to Owen's study to deliver the mysterious message. She flung open the doors without pausing to knock and approached the desk with a cheery smile. Behind the mammoth desk Owen McCandless looked up from his ledgers and a wide smile broke across his face at the sight she made as she hurriedly sank into the leather chair opposite him and dug into her bag for the envelope.

"Well, I trust you had an enjoyable morning," Owen observed with a smile while he studied her golden head bent over her search.

"Uncle Owen, the most remarkable thing happened in town," she told him, excitement making her voice rise slightly. "I met the most mysterious man in Mr. Roscoe's store and he gave me something for you."

Owen's heavy brows arched in surprise as he reached across the desk to take the envelope Amber was holding out to him. He turned it over in his hands, looking for a postmark or address of some kind and was further intrigued to find only the blank sides of the plain white envelope.

"Oh really? Who was this mysterious man?" he asked with a teasing lilt in his voice, glancing at her across the desk.

Amber's golden brows furrowed into a frown as she shook her head with a sigh. "That's what is so mysterious, Uncle Owen. He didn't tell me his name. He said you would know who sent the message when you read it."

"That is a bit mysterious, isn't it?"

Owen took a silver letter opener from the top drawer of the desk and slit the envelope open. Laying aside the opener, he drew a single sheet of paper from inside and unfolded it, still smiling at Amber's urgent curiosity.

Slowly the smile on his lips faded and the color left his face as he read the message. Amber thought she saw his hands shake before he refolded the sheet of paper, put it inside the desk drawer, and then clasped his hands on top and smiled at her again.

"Tell me, Amber, what did this man look like?" he asked in a calm, but obviously forced tone.

"What does it say, Uncle Owen?" she asked in alarm, for she could see he was more concerned than he wanted her to know.

Owen's massive shoulders moved in a noncommittal shrug while he fought to keep his voice controlled. He intertwined his fingers on top of the desk, each hand gripping the other so tightly the knuckles were turning white in his effort to still their trembling.

"It's a personal joke, Amber. Nothing important at all," he told her. "Do you remember what this man looked like?"

She gave a disappointed nod while she resisted the urge to inquire more about the message. It was obvious from Owen's nonchalant attitude that he did not intend to reveal what the message contained and she felt a keen pang of regret.

"Of course, Uncle Owen. I'm not likely to forget him."

"And why is that, Amber? Did this man frighten you or threaten you in some way?" Owen demanded sharply.

Surprise flashed across Amber's face, making him regret the

harshness of his words. The last thing he wanted was to alarm her so he took a long breath and paused to regain his composure so that he would be able to maintain an outward calm.

"No, of course not. He was quite pleasant actually," she said in a puzzled voice while her gaze searched Owen's pale face. "He didn't say all that much really. He asked if I was Miss McCandless and if I would deliver this message to you. I asked his name and he said you would know who he was when you read his message."

"That's all he said?"

"Yes, that's all."

"Why did you say you weren't likely to forget him?"

A faint blush crept into Amber's cheeks. She looked away for a moment so her uncle would not be able to see the excitement in her face. For some strange reason, she wanted to keep her thoughts about this man private for a while longer, at least until she had a chance to determine why she had felt so flustered in his presence.

"I only meant that he was a very attractive man, Uncle Owen," she said carefully.

"Describe him to me, Amber," her uncle commanded in an urgent tone that alarmed her a bit.

"Well, he was tall and quite dark," she began hesitantly, her lips pursing as she tried to put her impressions of the stranger into words. "He was very handsome...."

"You said that already," Owen pointed out dryly. "How old was he, what color was his hair?"

"He was probably in his late twenties. His hair was black, really black, and so were his eyes. His eyes were remarkable, Uncle Owen. I've never seen anyone with eyes like that before. It was like he could see right through my skull and tell what I was thinking," she said in a subdued tone, keeping her face averted from her uncle's penetrating gaze.

Owen's hand shook as he reached for a cigar from the gold case atop his desk. His mind raced furiously as he held a match to the cigar and drew deeply, filling his lungs with the pungent smoke.

"You have never seen this man before?"

Amber shook her head. "No, Uncle Owen, I'm certain I have never seen him before."

Her curious gaze made Owen uncomfortable, but he was unable at the moment to think of anything light to dispel the mood. It was with a great deal of effort that he managed to put a smile on his face while flicking the ash from his cigar into the crystal ashtray on the desk. "Well, no matter, princess. As I said, it was a joke, nothing more."

"I don't understand, Uncle Owen, why a simple joke would upset you," Amber pointed out quietly. Her eyes searched Owen's still slightly pale face for a clue to the mysterious message, but there was nothing in that clear blue gaze that gave any indication as to what the envelope had contained.

"It just came as somewhat of a surprise, princess. You see, I haven't heard from this man for quite some time and I'm just a bit startled at the method he chose to make his whereabouts known," Owen lied skillfully.

"Then this man is a colleague of yours?"

Owen slowly exhaled and sent a plume of aromatic smoke into the air. "I think the term, acquaintance, is probably more accurate. A very slight acquaintance. As I said, it's been quite a while since I've heard anything about him."

"What's his name? Will he be coming to the ranch ?"

Owen's blue eyes narrowed slightly before he could put a smile on his lips. Shaking his head and taking another pull on the cigar, he avoided her eyes while he flicked away the ash.

"No, I don't think he'll be calling on us anytime in the near future," he said dryly. "Now, why don't you run out and bring in those packages and show your old uncle what you bought in town?"

"I'd rather discuss why this message has upset you."

Owen forced a smile as he reached to pat her hand. "I'm not upset, princess, not at all. Just surprised, that's all. There's nothing for you to be concerned about. Now, will you please send Quincy in here on your way out? There are a few matters I need to discuss with him."

The sunlight from the large window at the side of the room cast brilliant golden beams from her shiny head as she nodded with a cautious smile. She glanced back at her uncle, relieved to find that he seemed his old self; smiling and relaxed. Whatever the strange message was, it was surely as Owen had said; just a joke that had startled him for a moment, nothing more. With that thought in mind, she tried to shake off the uneasiness that gripped her as she moved through the house on the way to retrieve her parcels from the buckboard, pausing to inform Quincy that he was needed in the study.

***

"Sit down, Cooter," Owen said sharply as the old wrangler limped into the study a few minutes later.

Quincy had located him in record time after receiving Owen's command to find the old cowhand and send him to the house right away. Cooter now sank into the immense leather chair across the desk from Owen and settled himself as comfortably as possible. He had been in this same chair many times over the years but he had never grown accustomed to the wealth and power he saw so clearly reflected in this room. He was much more comfortable with his horses and the stables. Here, in Owen McCandless' house, he always felt ill at ease and out of his depth.

Having been with Owen for better than twenty five years, he was considered more a member of the family than a hired hand. Owen occasionally asked his advice so he assumed that was why he had been summoned. He studied Owen in silence for a moment. Knowing the man as he did, he quickly noted the slight tremor in Owen's hand as he flicked away the ash from his cigar. There was also a paleness beneath Owen's weathered tan that was totally out of character. Owen McCandless was a man who rarely displayed any outward concern as he was doing now.

"What's on your mind, Owen?" he asked curiously.

"This..." Owen grated as he flung open the drawer and whipped out the sheet of paper he had put there only a few minutes before. "Take a look at this, Cooter. Tell me what you make of it."

Cooter reached forward and took the folded paper, then settled back in the chair to smooth it out and glance over the contents. After a moment, he looked back to Owen's face in confusion and shook his head. "It's a wanted poster."

"I know that," Owen growled impatiently. "Look whose picture is on it."

Cooter glanced down at the paper again, then shrugged. "It's a wanted poster of Morgan Devereaux. So?"

Owen slammed the desk drawer shut with a bang and snorted in disgust. "Of course it's Devereaux, you old fool. Look at what's written at the bottom."

Again Cooter dropped his gaze to the poster in his lap and studied the face that stared back at him. It was Morgan Devereaux all right, there was no mistaking that piercing pair of eyes. 'Five thousand dollars reward..dead or alive,' he read to himself. Dead or alive! That'll be the day..when they bring in Morgan Devereaux! He was only the fastest man with a gun in Texas, with the possible exception of Welch Mandell, Cooter thought dryly. It was moments like this that made the struggle of having Price teach him to read and write worth the effort.

Then he glanced at the bottom of the poster, just below the picture itself to find the words *Your niece is very beautiful, McCandless. I'm sure you must be very proud of her* written in a neat, concise hand with black ink. There was no signature and after a moment of staring at the message, Cooter raised his head in wonder.

"You ain't tryin' to tell me that you think Devereaux sent you this message?"

"Who else?" Owen growled with a scowl of disgust.

Beneath the impatience he saw in the man, Cooter also sensed the unmistakable signs of worry. "Why would Devereaux send you a message like this? It don't make any sense."

"It's a threat, Cooter, plain, open and right to the point. That black-hearted son-of-a-bitch is threatening Amber. Can't you see that?"

Cooter glanced back to the wanted poster in his lap to study the written message again. After a long pause he again raised his head to give Owen a questioning gaze. "Now, why would he do a thing like that? He don't know Miss Amber. Why would he want to hurt her?" he asked skeptically.

Owen's graying head wagged from side to side in confused concern, his eyes reflecting the worry that was building steadily inside him. He pulled on the cigar again, exhaling slowly before he directed his attention to the old cowhand's question.

"I'm sure it's not Amber herself he's after. It must be me, but why? What have I done to this man? Who the hell is he anyway?"

"Maybe you're wrong about this, Owen," Cooter pointed out. "How do you know Devereaux wrote this or sent it, for that matter? Maybe it's just somebody's idea of a joke."

"No, no, it's no joke," Owen contradicted with a scornful glance at Cooter. "It was Devereaux himself that gave this to Amber to deliver to me. The arrogant bastard walked right up to her in town, in broad daylight, in Roscoe's store and spoke to her. She described him to me. It was him all right. No doubt about it. Every lawman in West Texas is looking for that cutthroat gunslinger and he has the guts to parade right through my town and approach my niece!"

Cooter nodded solemnly. "Does Miss Amber know who he was?"

Owen waved one large hand in an impatient gesture toward the ceiling and chewed the end of his cigar thoughtfully. "No, of course not. I certainly don't want to alarm her, Cooter. She's only been home a couple of days. The last thing in the world I want is for her to know she has been face to face with the most notorious gunslinger in the territory. Such a scare might do her irreparable harm."

Cooter's heavy brows raised in mild surprise. Somehow he felt it wasn't Amber's delicate nature that was giving Owen such con-

cern. It was far more likely that he was afraid the girl would catch
the next train East and be gone from his life for good.

"I don't think you're givin' the girl enough credit, Owen. Miss
Amber comes from good stock. I doubt she's goin' to curl up and
faint if she was to learn she was so close to an outlaw. She *is* Price's
child."

Owen leaned forward slightly, his eyes narrowing to slits and
his firm jaw twitching from the anger that flared inside him. "I
told you, Cooter, twelve years ago, that I did not want my brother's
name mentioned in this house," he ground out ominously through
stiff lips.

The old cowhand met those cold blue eyes evenly and stared
back without flinching. "So you did, Owen," he agreed. "And I
wouldn't do it now if it weren't for the fact that you're
underestimatin' your niece. You made the mistake of
underestimatin' Price twenty years ago and you underestimated
Althea twelve years ago when Price died. I should think you'd have
learned somethin' from that by now."

"Shut your mouth, you old fool!" Owen warned coldly. "You're
over-stepping your limits."

"Maybe so, but then I ain't one of your mealy-mouthed cronies, Owen. I ain't afraid of you and I ain't afraid to tell you the
truth. We've been through far too much together, you, me, and
Price, for me to start sayin' just what you want to hear now."

Owen glared at him for several long tension filled moments,
then he sighed heavily and gestured with an outstretched hand. "I
know that, Cooter. Sorry I snapped at you. You're the only man
left who isn't afraid to tell me off when I need it. I'm just so
goddamned worried about Amber. I don't know what to do, Cooter."

Cooter stared at Owen's tight, concerned face and allowed a
brief smile to touch his lips. At moments like this, it was almost
like seeing the Owen McCandless he had known twenty-five years
ago. Before the obsession to become the most powerful man in
Texas had taken over his life. It almost gave him a twinge of re-

morse for the pain he saw in Owen now. Then he remembered a promise he had made many years before.

"Tell her the truth. Let her decide what's to be done."

"I can't do that!" Owen snapped, his voice almost becoming a shout before he realized he might be overheard. Continuing in a more controlled tone he said, "I don't see any need to frighten her, Cooter. No, I have another alternative in mind. I can send her to El Paso for a few days until Riker can round up Devereaux and his gang. She'll be safe there."

"Riker's been huntin' Devereaux for weeks. He ain't caught him yet and I don't hold much hope that he will in the near future. If you send her away, it may be for quite a spell."

Owen nodded absently, drawing deeply on what was left of the cigar, then flicking the ash away. "I realize that, but with this maniac running loose, I don't see any other way. No, my mind's made up, Cooter. I'll send her to El Paso to stay with my old friend Judge Davis and his family until this thing blows over. Either Riker will get Devereaux or the man will get tired of harassing me and find greener pastures elsewhere. Either way, Amber can come home in a few weeks, a month or so at the most, and in the meantime she'll be safe from this renegade."

His strong voice rang with authority and Cooter shrugged.

"You do what you think is best, Owen. You know I'm behind whatever decision you make one hundred per cent. But you're gonna have to come up with a pretty good story for sendin' her away."

"I'll think of something, Cooter. Right now, I want you to go into town and make arrangements for Amber to catch the noon stage tomorrow for El Paso. Send Judge Davis a telegram and let him know she's coming. I'll convince her to take this trip at dinner. I will have thought of a reason by then, I'm sure," Owen said confidently.

Cooter rose to his feet and ambled toward the door, pausing once to glance back and nod agreeably. "Right, Owen, I'll go into town right now and make the arrangements. And good luck when you tell Miss Amber she's got to go away for awhile. I have a feelin' you'll need it."

He passed through the double doors and into the hallway, pausing long enough to pull the doors closed behind him. Owen leaned back in his chair, selected another cigar, and lit it thoughtfully. Dinner was only a short time away and at the moment he had no idea what he was going to say to Amber to persuade her to take this trip.

CHAPTER SIX

"Well?"

"It went just like we figured, Morgan. She'll be on the noon stage for El Paso tomorrow. I've just now come from the stage office."

Morgan Devereaux leaned back in the straight-backed chair and smiled. He poured whiskey into two glasses and slid one across the narrow table to his friend.

It was dark; long shadows filled the corners of the small house on the outskirts of McCandless. Still, there was plenty of light from a pair of lamps set around the room to fully illuminate the worried face of the man who sat opposite him at the table.

"You've done your job well, Cooter," Morgan said, his husky voice firm and friendly. "What about guards?"

"There won't be any except the usual one, that is. No extra guards, unless he changes his mind before tomorrow."

"No matter. If he does, I'll be ready."

"You should've seen his face, Morgan. He looked like a sick cow when he handed me that poster of you. It made waitin' all these years almost worthwhile," Cooter said with a tight grin while he swirled the liquid in his glass. "I don't know if he was more pissed off because he thought you were threatenin' Miss Amber, or if it was because you walked right through his goddamned town in broad daylight and made a fool out of that son-of-a-bitch Riker. Either way, it gave me a real warm feelin' right here."

Cooter rubbed his stomach with a grin while studying the dark, veiled face of the man across the table. He had known Morgan Devereaux for almost fifteen years and he was still unable to read him. The man was a paradox; sometimes open and friendly, sometimes cold and dangerous, as he appeared now.

That was what hatred did to a man, he thought silently. He should know; he'd carried around a load of it himself for quite a while now. Funny, but now that the time was approaching when he would at last get to see Owen McCandless brought to his knees, he didn't feel the satisfaction he'd anticipated. Glancing at Morgan's dark face, he wondered if the gunman felt the same.

When Morgan didn't reply for a time, Cooter stirred uneasily in his chair and cleared his throat. "Morgan, about Miss Amber, you won't forget your promise?" he asked worriedly.

Morgan tossed back his drink and poured another as he shook his head. "I won't forget, Cooter. I gave you my word the girl wouldn't be hurt."

"If I cain't trust you, Morgan, I don't reckon there's a man alive I can trust," the old cowhand said with an audible sigh of relief. "Miss Amber cain't help bein' his niece."

A bitter snort ripped from Morgan's throat as he eyed the older man skeptically.

"She's a McCandless, isn't she? Don't tell me about being a McCandless, Cooter. That's a lesson I learned well and one I'll never forget."

"I don't want you forgettin' that Miss Amber is a lady," Cooter said sharply. "She ain't to blame for what her uncle's done. She's more of a victim than she knows. Don't you go takin' out your hate for the old man on her."

Morgan's black eyes locked with the old cowboy's gaze in a mocking glance that for a moment, allowed Cooter to see the contempt behind those unpenetrable ebony pools.

"I gave you my word, Cooter," he reminded his companion quietly. "It's him I want, just like you. No harm will come to the girl. We just have to make McCandless believe it will if he doesn't live up to his end of the bargain."

"No need to fret about that," Cooter said confidently, holding out his glass for a refill from the bottle between them. "He'll sell his soul for Miss Amber. I'd stake my life on it."

"We'll know soon enough, won't we?"

Cooter nodded and sipped the raw whiskey. He was silent for a moment while his thoughts drifted back to the past. "You know, Morgan, he'd be a different man if Amber's mother hadn't fell in love with Price. We wouldn't be doin' any of this; there'd be no need."

"I'm not interested in what could've been, Cooter, only in what was. McCandless has spent the past twenty years caring about nobody but himself, getting what he wanted, no matter what it took, and it's time he paid for it," Morgan reminded him curtly.

The coldness in the younger man's voice made Cooter shiver. He quickly swallowed the remainder of the whiskey in his glass. As much as he wanted to see Owen pay for his sins, he almost felt sorry for him.

"You're right, Morgan. If I didn't know that, I wouldn't be here. I have a stake in this too."

Morgan nodded, his black hair shimmering in the light from the lamp at the end of the table. The hat he had worn earlier in the day, when he approached Amber McCandless lay beside him, the silver conchos gleaming as they reflected the dull light.

He looked much younger without the hat, somehow. His ebony hair fell over his forehead and he absently raised a hand from time to time to push it back from his eyes. He was only thirty, but he felt much older. Orphaned at ten, raised by the outlaw king Welch Mandell, he had become the most notorious gunfighter in the southwest. His speed with the six gun cradled on his hip was unparalleled. It was a reputation he had earned justly.

For almost twenty years Morgan had practiced his craft diligently, spending hours every day developing his speed with the six-gun; hundreds of hours spent with Welch, drawing and firing, again and again until his arm ached, his eyes burned, and his head pounded from the concentration Welch demanded.

Raising his head a bit, he glanced at the weathered old cowboy and asked, "He still doesn't know why, does he?"

Cooter shook his grizzled head with a tight smile. "Not a clue, Morgan. He cain't figure out why a man he's never seen would be doin' this to him."

Morgan's black eyes narrowed to flinty slits, his jaw tightening with a menacing quality that made Cooter glad Morgan was his friend, not an enemy.

"The murdering son-of-a-bitch! He doesn't even remember." Then he smiled slightly, a frosty mirthless smile that curled his lips but did not reach his eyes. "But he will."

Cooter shivered as he reached to refill his glass from the whiskey bottle. "There's lots of things Owen don't remember, Morgan. He's got a knack for forgettin' what he wants to. I doubt you could prod his memory with a picture," he said quietly.

Morgan's eyes locked with the old cowhand's, piercing into Cooter's uneasy thoughts. He knew Morgan well enough to know his anger was directed at Owen, not at him, but whenever those coal black eyes burned into his, it made him very uncomfortable.

"I'll do better than that, Cooter," Morgan promised, his lips curling in a contemptuous sneer. "Before I kill him, I'll make sure he remembers what he's done to you and me and Welch. And if you're right about the girl, her too."

"I'm right about that, Morgan. I'd stake my life on it. She's got to see the truth before he destroys her too."

Morgan raised an eyebrow at the urgency in the older man's voice. "The girl seems to trust you, Cooter, why haven't you told her before?"

Cooter shrugged helplessly and sighed. "Because she'd never believe me, Morgan. She has to see for herself what Owen McCandless is."

"What makes you so sure she'll believe me?" Morgan asked while he continued to regard Cooter thoughtfully.

"You're the proof, Morgan. You're livin' proof of what he's done. She'll have to believe you."

"And if she doesn't?"

Cooter shrugged again and Morgan saw a weariness come into the old man's eyes. "Then I've done all I can to protect her. If she refuses to believe the truth, then I'll have no choice but to kill Owen myself."

A slight grin touched his lips at the gleam that flashed through Morgan's ebony eyes. Unable to read the younger man, he could only guess at what it meant. "But I doubt I'll ever get the chance. You're better at that than me, so I'll leave it up to you. By rights, you've got first crack at him."

"How have you managed to work for him all these years, feeling the way you do?" Morgan asked curiously.

"I had to," was Cooter's answer. "If I aim to keep my word to Price, I have to be in a position to know what's goin' on and I cain't do that from the outside."

"You're a good man, Cooter. And a loyal friend to me and Welch. We won't forget it. Now you better head back to the ranch. Don't worry about anything; it's all under control. By this time tomorrow you'll be seeing McCandless start to squirm."

A broad grin flashed across Cooter's face as he climbed to his feet. He paused a moment to finish his drink, then limped toward the door. He halted with one hand on the knob and turned back to Morgan.

"It's been a long time comin', Morgan, and I'm goin' to enjoy every minute of it. Just remember, Welch promised Miss Amber wouldn't know I'm involved in this until it's over."

Morgan nodded in agreement. "Welch gave his word and I gave you mine, Cooter. She'll never know you had anything to do with us until you choose to tell her. She won't learn it from either of us," he assured the old cowboy.

"Tell Welch,....well, just tell him thanks."

"No thanks are necessary, Cooter. Welch promised to help you keep your word to the girl's father; that's what he's doing."

"Just don't make me sorry, Morgan. Make sure no harm comes to Miss Amber. If you hurt one hair on her head, you'll have to kill me too," Cooter promised in a soft, sincere voice.

A slight smile curled the gunman's lips as he nodded in acknowledgment. "It won't come to that, Cooter. Goodnight."

"'Night, Morgan, and good luck."

Having said that, he moved into the darkness beyond the lamps and a few moments later Morgan heard his horse canter out of the yard. Morgan tossed back the remainder of his drink and blew out the lamps, pausing to pick up his hat as he slipped silently toward the door.

CHAPTER SEVEN

The heavy stagecoach lumbered along through the dreary June afternoon. It was hot and stuffy inside and Amber grimaced in irritation as a trickle of sweat ran down the back of her neck. Had she realized how uncomfortable this trip was going to be, she would have dressed more appropriately. As it was, she was thoroughly out of sorts. Not only was she hot and sticky due to the closeness of so many bodies stuffed into such a small space, but she was still seething at her uncle's shuffling her off on this ridiculous journey.

She sighed and edged closer to the door of the stage. The medical drummer seated next to her was sound asleep and leaning heavily on her, making her even more uncomfortable. Not only was his head resting on her shoulder, but he reeked of alcohol, making Amber wonder if he sold as much medicine as he drank.

They were five hours out of McCandless on the road to El Paso. They had forded the Pecos River a short time before and Amber looked out the window at the passing countryside. In spite of her discomfort, she felt a thrill of anticipation as the plains opened up before her. She took a deep breath and forced a smile to her lips in an effort to improve her spirits. There was something about this country that always seemed to bring out the best in her, she thought with a growing degree of cheerfulness.

She had never been to El Paso, but knew that very soon now the Pecos Valley would gradually begin to change into the mountainous regions of the Davis Mountain range. Already she could see the foothills looming ahead when she peered out the window of the coach.

Before the stage reached El Paso they would pass through some very rough country. Amber hoped the mountains would at least bring some respite from the heat, as the heavy stage lurched through a series of pot-holes in the road. If the route did not improve considerably, her entire body would be black and blue when she finally reached her destination.

Seated across from her were two young ladies in their mid-twenties, dressed in the latest fashion, complete with great feathered hats and capes of soft velvet that rested on their shoulders to prevent the dust from smudging their clothes.

Amber studied them from beneath her thick, dark lashes, for she did not want to stare. Both women were obviously more accustomed to saloons than stagecoaches, she decided on the basis of their make-up and scandalously fitting dresses which cinched their waists and pushed their bosoms high above the neckline.

Amber had never had occasion to study such women before. She found them fascinating instead of offensive, as did the other female passenger. Turning her eyes from the two saloon girls, Amber studied the somewhat dowdy lady seated at the far end of her own seat beside the sleeping drummer.

Mrs. Appleton, she had said her name was. She was a heavy-set lady in her late forties, Amber judged, with graying hair pulled into a severe bun at the nape of her thick neck. Her face was set in a tight, rigid cast of displeasure that made Amber wonder if the woman ever smiled. It seemed doubtful, for she sat very straight, her lips thinned into tight, pale lines while her narrow eyes raked the two saloon girls with disgust.

Seated beside the unsavory young ladies was another gentleman, a gambler by trade, if Amber was correct. He was neatly dressed in a spotless black suit with a starched white shirt and string tie, but he possessed an oily air that made Amber a little uneasy. She was grateful that he was seated across from her so she wasn't any closer, despite the fact that her snoring companion's head rolled onto her shoulder every time the coach hit a bump in the road. Even if the drummer was a drinker, he didn't make her flesh creep like the gambler.

What an odd assortment, she thought with a smile; a gambler, a snoring drummer, a crotchety older lady with absolutely no sense of humor, two young women with unsavory backgrounds, and herself.

Deciding against passing the time in conversation with her companions, Amber turned her attention once more out the window. Settling back against the seat, she reached over to remove the snoring drummer's head from her shoulder with a grimace.

After making herself as comfortable as possible under the crowded conditions, Amber's thoughts returned to her uncle's reasons for sending her to El Paso. The previous evening came immediately to mind as she tried to analyze Uncle Owen's sudden and disturbing decision to go to Austin on business. His reasoning had been vague and she had sensed an uneasiness in him that still nagged at her.

He had sudden, urgent business that could not wait, he had told her after dinner, that might take several days to conclude. Therefore, he wanted her to go to El Paso to stay with some friends of his in his absence. Amber had tried to persuade him to let her accompany him to Austin, and when he would not be convinced, insisted on staying at the ranch until he returned.

Again he had been adamant; she could not possibly stay in the big house alone. Although Amber failed to see how she could possibly be alone with a house full of servants. No, she must go stay with Judge Davis and his family until he could take care of this business.

She shook her head. She had sensed uneasiness in her uncle and it gave her the distinct feeling there was more than he was willing to reveal.

Was it possible this sudden desire to send her away had something to do with the mysterious message she had delivered to him earlier? It had only been a couple of hours from the time she gave him that envelope that he had informed her of his need to go to Austin. Perhaps there was no business that needed his attention. Perhaps it was the handsome stranger who required his presence.

If that message was at the root of this stupid trip to El Paso, the very least Uncle Owen could have done was be honest with her. If he wanted her out of the way so he could feel more free to meet with the man who sent him that message, then he should have simply said so instead of sending her away on such a flimsy excuse.

She was not a child to be sent to her room whenever grownups wanted to discuss something in private, she thought irritably. If she was to inherit *Sierra Vieja* someday, she certainly had a right to be treated as an adult, and she had every intention of letting her uncle know it in no uncertain terms as soon as possible.

The thought occurred to her then that when the stage made its first stop, she would get off and catch the next one back to McCandless. Yes, she thought with a firm nod, that's exactly what she would do. If there was something going on that concerned her uncle then it concerned her too. She should be with him; facing their problems together like families were supposed to.

With her mind made up, she smiled to herself and directed her attention back to the Texas countryside that was passing outside the window. The stage had entered rougher country now and was starting to climb. The heavy vehicle slowed almost to a crawl as it made its way up a steep grade. Off to the north a few miles lay Owen's sulfur mines, and northwestward about seventy miles, was the New Mexico border beyond which lay the Badlands.

"How much further to the way station?" one of the dubious ladies was asking the gambler.

"About fifteen miles," the man replied, his face lighting up at the opportunity to talk. "We'll get there just about dark."

"That's good news," the redheaded saloon girl said with a sigh of relief. "I don't care for the idea of traveling through this Godforsaken country at night. The Badlands are too close to suit me. Who knows what could be lurking ahead waiting for us?"

"I'm sure there's nothing out there that could possibly be any more unpleasant than some of the things you've already seen," sniffed the older lady with a haughty sneer.

A hurt expression flashed across her pretty face, but she forced a smile. "Then you've never seen Welch Mandell, Mrs. Appleton," she said softly.

The mention of the outlaw's name snagged Amber's attention immediately. Remembering her uncle's reaction the night Sheriff Riker had brought up Mandell's name, she sat up straighter on the hard seat, her tawny eyes brightening with interest.

"I don't make a habit of consorting with outlaws," Mrs. Appleton snapped indignantly.

"Neither do I, ma'am," the girl replied, her clear brown eyes boring into the older woman's with frosty determination. "But I seen him once in Cheyenne. Take my word, he's not a man you'll likely forget."

"What's he like?" Amber interjected before Mrs. Appleton could make another caustic remark.

The girl turned to Amber with a smile, her pretty face brightening at the prospect of having a conversation with someone more pleasant.

"He's quite handsome actually," she replied eagerly. "He's a real gentleman, too. He's very tall and has sort of blondish hair, but it's not what he looks like that grabs your attention. It's something about the way he moves, like a panther about to spring. He gives the impression of danger, you know? I don't really know how to explain it."

"I think I know what you mean," Amber said seriously, for the image of the handsome stranger had flashed before her mind's eye.

"My name is Lucille," the girl was saying.

"Hello," Amber replied with a smile. "I'm Amber McCandless."

"And this is my friend, Nettie," Lucille said, indicating the other girl beside her with a gesture.

"You must be kin to Owen McCandless himself," Mrs. Appleton interjected. Her severe features had brightened with a smile when she recognized the name, but her obvious effort to be friendly struck Amber as patronizing.

She had seen other people turn to butter at the mere mention of her uncle's name and mostly it struck her as funny, but the mention of Welch Mandell dismissed the woman from her thoughts.

"Tell me more about Welch Mandell," Amber prompted.

"I can tell you one thing about him. His hideout isn't all that far from here," the gambler chimed in with an effort to join the conversation.

Amber's eyes widened in alarm. "Really?"

The gambler gestured toward the north and shrugged. "Somewhere in the Badlands, they say, just over the border. Just a couple of days ride from here. He could be watching us now for all we know."

"What would an outlaw like Welch Mandell want with this stagecoach?" Mrs. Appleton scoffed. "We're not even carrying a strongbox."

"He may not know that," the gambler pointed out with a sour expression.

"Of course he does," Lucille argued with a serious light coming into her dark brown eyes. "He has spies everywhere. There isn't anything going on in the whole state of Texas that he doesn't know."

"How can you be so sure?" Amber asked.

"Because I used to know one of his men up in Cheyenne. He told me that Mandell has more people on his payroll than the governor."

"There's only one man on his payroll that interests me," Nettie said with a sly smile and a gentle nudge at Lucille's ribs. "And that's Morgan Devereaux."

"Now there is one good looking man," Lucille agreed with a sigh.

"What does he look like?" Amber questioned eagerly.

"He's dark, about my height, maybe a little more slender," the gambler said.

Everyone's eyes turned to him in surprise. The man straightened up to his full potential like a rooster surrounded by a group of adoring hens and smiled. "I saw him kill a man in Tombstone last year. Never saw anything like it. He pulled that gun so fast you couldn't even see it move. Some say he's even faster than Mandell, and I don't doubt it."

The mention of Devereaux's name brought a sudden chill over Amber. This was the man Uncle Owen believed was causing him so many problems. Perhaps if she could learn more about him, she'd have some idea why he was tormenting her uncle.

"I still say he's the best looking man I've ever laid these two eyes on," Nettie sighed.

"Well, I just hope these two eyes don't see him until we get to El Paso," Lucille remarked. "You can bet that wherever Morgan is, Welch Mandell can't be far away and I'd just as soon not run into either of them out here in the middle of nowhere."

"I doubt that we have any reason to be concerned on that score," the gambler said comfortingly. "As Mrs. Appleton pointed out, this stage isn't carrying anything of value. There's no reason why Mandell or Devereaux would be interested in it."

"What else do you know about this Morgan Devereaux?" Amber persisted with an eager glance at the girls.

"Not much I guess, when I really think about it. I did hear that Welch Mandell raised him and treats him like a son. Other than that....."

Nettie's voice faded away into silence when the driver on top of the coach suddenly began to call to the horses to slow down. Amber couldn't imagine why he wanted them to slow any more for the coach was barely creeping along as it was. Within a few moments the vehicle came to a complete halt and Nettie stuck her head out the window in an effort to see what the problem was.

When her head came back inside the coach, her face had paled and her eyes were wide with surprise.

"Nettie, what is it? What's going on out there?" Lucille demanded impatiently.

"You'll never believe it. We were just talking about him!" Nettie exclaimed.

"Who? What on earth are you babbling about?" Mrs. Appleton

asked as she pulled aside the curtain on her side of the coach to peer out.

"It's him! It's Morgan Devereaux! He's holding up the stage!" Nettie cried.

Amber gasped in disbelief and leaned across the drummer to join Mrs. Appleton at the window of the coach. Her breath froze in her throat. For an instant she thought her heart had stopped beating as she stared out into the bright sunlight at the band of men who had surrounded the stage.

There were six men on horseback holding guns on the driver and shotgun guard. But Amber's shocked eyes were focused on the man who was obviously the leader of the group. She blinked a couple of times to be certain her eyes were not playing a grotesque trick of some kind. The leader of this band of outlaws was the same man she had spoken with in McCandless only yesterday.

Her mind reeled from the realization. The handsome, mysterious stranger who had given her the message for her uncle was Morgan Devereaux!

"We're not carrying a strongbox, Devereaux," the driver was explaining from his perch atop the stage.

"You're carrying something a lot more valuable," was Morgan's curt reply. "Tell the passengers to get out."

The driver climbed down from his seat and opened the door next to Mrs. Appleton. His face bore an apologetic expression as he extended his hand inside to help the ladies climb out.

"Sorry, folks. You'll have to get out."

"This, sir, is an outrage!" Mrs. Appleton spluttered as she lumbered out of the coach.

"Line up alongside the stage and shut up!" Morgan ordered, his eyes locking with the dowdy older woman's in a gaze that left no doubt as to his authority.

Mrs. Appleton clamped her lips together with an air of indignant outrage and stood glaring at Morgan, but he had already put her out of his mind as the other passengers began to line up beside the stage.

The two saloon girls followed Mrs. Appleton, then the gambler, then the drummer who was finally roused from his nap by the driver's insistent prodding, and finally Amber.

She paused outside the coach to smooth her rumpled skirts and brush the dust from the short cape that covered her shoulders, stalling for time to recover her composure before bringing her face up to deal Morgan a scathing glare of contempt.

She discovered that those black, disconcerting eyes were focused on her, singling her out of the group to be surveyed with cool appraisal. She felt foolish and angry with herself for those disturbing thoughts she had allowed herself the previous day. In spite of his physical appeal, the man was a common outlaw. She felt a keen pang of disillusionment.

Time seemed suspended in those few tension filled moments as Amber and Morgan stared at one another. No one moved or made a sound while they waited. The only sounds that broke the eerie silence was the jingle of the horses' bridles as they shifted positions around the stage.

"What is it you want, Devereaux?" the guard asked, careful not to make any sudden movements. "We're not carrying any gold."

The man's question finally drew Morgan's attention from Amber. He lifted his head slightly and shifted his eyes to the driver, who stood beside the passengers, his hands raised into the air in a sign of compliance.

"Do what you're told and nobody will be hurt," Morgan said in a matter of fact tone that made Amber wonder how many times he had done this sort of thing.

He certainly seemed at ease, she thought angrily. There was no urgency in his manner, as though he had all the time in the world to rob them and was in no hurry.

He was immaculately groomed, his handsome face clean shaven. The thing that stood out most about Morgan Devereaux, however, was the cool confidence he exuded, in the way he moved, in his manner, as if he were quite pleased with himself and felt no need to prove anything to anyone else.

In contrast to his clean, well dressed appearance, his companions didn't appear to have bathed in recent weeks or changed clothes either. They shared one common factor, however, they looked dangerous and menacing with their guns drawn, and their eyes all revealed a hunger that made Amber shiver despite the heat.

"What I want is very simple," Morgan was saying to the driver in that same cool baritone that had aroused Amber's curiosity the previous day. "I want the girl, Miss McCandless."

Amber realized with a shock that he had spoken her name. When she raised her eyes back to his face, she saw he was watching her for a reaction. There was no discernible expression in his eyes. They simply bore into hers with a piercing quality that was difficult for Amber to return. She ran her tongue over her dry lips and opened her mouth to speak, although it took several attempts before her throat opened up enough to allow her voice to filter out.

"What is it you want with me, sir?" she asked at last, trying desperately to keep her voice steady.

"I'm conducting business with your uncle," Morgan replied. "You'll be staying with me until it's settled."

"Now just a minute, Devereaux," the stage driver broke in. "I can't just let you take Owen McCandless' niece off my stage. That old man will have me hung."

Morgan's eyes darted to the man's pale face momentarily, but returned to Amber's startled features before he acknowledged the protest. "He's good at that," he said dryly. "He should be. He's had enough practice. Anyway, that's your problem."

He motioned behind him and one of his men brought up a riderless horse and handed Morgan the reins.

"Miss McCandless, mount up."

"I most certainly will not!" Amber cried indignantly.

Morgan moved his horse forward until he was directly in front of her. She had not moved, for his coal black eyes held hers in a trance-like stare. "Miss McCandless, listen to me well. I'm only going to say this once. If you're not on this horse in one minute, I'll start shooting these people. If you do what you're told, they'll be allowed to get back into the stage and continue on to El Paso. Either way you're coming with me. Now make up your mind."

Amid the horrified gasps of the other passengers, Amber heard only the sound of his voice, soft and calm on the surface, but cold as ice beneath. His eyes were still locked with hers in an unwavering ebony stare that suddenly chilled her right down to the marrow of her bones. There was no doubt in her mind that he meant exactly what he said and she had only a split second to decide.

"There is no need to harm anyone," she said in a shaky voice. "I'll do as you say."

"I thought you would," he replied with a mirthless smile that barely curled his lips. "Get the others aboard and pull out," he instructed the driver curtly.

The other passengers scurried to get back into the coach and the driver climbed back onto his seat. Morgan unceremoniously leaned over, caught Amber's arm, and lifted her onto the extra horse. Then he moved his own horse close to the coach and reached inside his vest to produce an envelope which he handed to the driver.

"See that McCandless gets this. Leave it at the first way station and have it sent back. Remember, do just what I've told you. If the law tries anything, McCandless will never see his niece again...alive at any rate. Any questions?"

The driver and the guard shook their heads in unison as Morgan smiled briefly and backed his horse out of the road. He reached to take the reins of the horse Amber had mounted as the heavy coach began to roll.

Amber's heart sank to her toes as it lumbered out of sight behind an outcropping of rocks and she was left in the dust with the bandits. Her frightened mind could not fully comprehend what was happening. Surely the stage driver did not mean to drive away and leave her at the mercy of these outlaws. Frightened tears burned her eyes as the carriage began moving away.

Once the stage had disappeared, the bandits put away their

guns and gathered around Morgan, staring at her with open delight.

"Let's get started. It's a long ride," Morgan said curtly.

His men turned away from Amber reluctantly and urged their mounts into a canter. Amber's horse turned to follow, but Morgan retained a firm grip on the reins until she turned to stare at him in alarm.

"Miss McCandless, it looks like you and I might be together for some time. I want to make one thing clear to you right now. If you do what I tell you and don't give me any trouble, you'll be home with your doting uncle in a few days. If you don't...I'll kill you. You'll stay alive only as long as you're of use to me. Do you understand?"

Amber's face went chalky white as he spoke. She felt as though her heart was going to burst through her chest from the furious way it pounded. She was suddenly bathed in cold sweat, chilled as though it were the middle of winter.

She sat without moving for a long moment, her eyes wide with fear as she stared into his calm, expressionless face. He had spoken quietly as if discussing the weather instead of having made a threat to her life, but there could be no doubt that he was sincere. She was absolutely certain that he would not hesitate to kill her if she failed to do as he said.

She had never known fear like she felt in that instant as she stared into those cold black eyes. It took all her strength to nod that she understood him. Speaking was impossible, for her voice was paralyzed with fear.

Satisfied that she understood the fragility of her position, Morgan turned his Appaloosa toward the mountains. Amber's mount followed docilely, breaking into a swift gallop at Morgan's urging, causing her to clutch the saddlehorn for support.

Slowly her heartbeat resumed a near normal level and she tried to think logically. She had been kidnapped right off the stage by a man who intended to ransom her from her uncle. She knew now why her uncle had insisted she go to El Paso. That message she had inadvertently delivered to Owen must have contained some kind of threat to her. Why hadn't he told her the truth, she wondered tremulously. He must have been desperate to protect her. How ironic that the very stage he put her on for safety was stopped by this terrible man.

Amber glanced at her captor as they rode briskly through the rocks and scrub brush. He didn't appear to have a care in the world, she thought fearfully. How callous and cruel Morgan Devereaux was to cause her such anguish. And what possible reason could he have to torment her uncle? One thing was certain; before she left his dubious company Amber intended to find out..and stop him if she could.

CHAPTER EIGHT

After two hours of hard riding, moving ever deeper into the mountains, Morgan stopped his gang to give the horses a chance to rest. By this time, Amber's body had begun to feel the strain of the hard saddle and the uncomfortable clothing.

At least the sun would be setting soon and the air would get cooler. Perhaps that would ease her discomfort. Morgan had not said one word during the first two hours of riding. Indeed, it was as though he had forgotten her. They had ridden in stony silence, each occupied by their own thoughts, but now Morgan dismounted and walked around to where she sat, rigidly looking straight ahead.

He did not speak as he reached up, lifted her down from the saddle, and stood her on her feet in front of him. A sudden wave of dizziness washed over her and she weaved unsteadily. She felt his hand grasp her arm just above the elbow as he caught her. She leaned against him for a moment until the unfamiliar faintness faded. When she regained her composure, she jerked her arm free of his supporting hand and looked up into his face.

"I don't need your help, thank you. I'm quite all right."

His coal black eyes regarded her thoughtfully as he moved back a step. He pointed to a flat rock, indicating he wanted her to sit down. Amber stalked as confidently as possible to the rock and plopped down on it and began to smooth her rumpled skirts, avoiding any eye contact with him or the others.

A grin touched his lips as he walked to his horse and took his canteen from the saddle. He handed it to Amber silently, then went back to remove a neatly rolled bundle from behind his saddle and once more walked to where she sat drinking gratefully. She replaced the cap and wiped her lips with the back of her hand, her tawny eyes watching him warily all the while.

The other members of Morgan's gang had dismounted and were now resting on rocks nearby, talking quietly among themselves, glancing occasionally in her direction. Amber could feel their eyes on her, but she made a concentrated effort to ignore the creepy way they made her feel, as though she were the prize in some grotesque game.

She looked upward to find Morgan standing before her holding the bundle. "Miss McCandless, I brought you some clothes. You must be getting pretty uncomfortable by now."

"How thoughtful of you," Amber said sarcastically while she stared at him.

There was a snicker of amusement from the men, but it didn't seem to bother him. How could anyone tell, Amber wondered, what he thought or felt. Those dark impenetrable eyes reflected no emotion as he continued to study her, only a steady ebony gleam that revealed nothing.

"I bet her pretty little ass is blistered by now," one of the men suggested in a high pitched nasal voice that made the hair on the back of Amber's neck rise.

Morgan's head did not move, only his eyes as he directed his attention to the man who had spoken. "Patch, watch your mouth. I won't tell you again."

Again, Amber was stunned by the effect his quiet, level voice had on others. He had not raised his voice, but she could feel the steel beneath his words. She risked a glance at the man Morgan had called by name.

Patch was aptly named, for he wore a grimy black eye patch that covered the right side of his face. The lower portion of his face was covered by a scraggly beard. His clothes were covered with grime. He met Morgan's steady stare for a moment, his good eye blazing with icy scorn, but Amber saw his bravado wilt under Morgan's unwavering gaze.

"I didn't mean nothin', Morgan," he said finally in a whiny voice.

Morgan dismissed Patch then and looked back at Amber. "There's a small cave behind that big rock," he said, indicating a spot off to his left. "Take these and put them on." Then, noting the apprehensive glance she shot his companions, he added, "No one will bother you. Just remember what I told you earlier."

Amber rose stiffly, snatched the bundle from him and marched off toward the spot he had indicated. As she disappeared behind the rock, she could hear the comments from the outlaws.

"Good God, Morgan, you didn't tell us what a looker she was," one of the men exclaimed.

"Damned if she ain't the prettiest thing I've seen in a while," another agreed.

Morgan listened to their comments silently and when they had finished, he studied each one for a moment. Perhaps he should have prepared them better. His dark eyes settled on Patch's sullen face, noting the way the man looked away. There was one he'd have to watch carefully.

None of these men had any scruples, he knew. Between the five of them, there was a combined reward of over fifteen thousand dollars being offered to anyone foolhardy enough to think he could collect it. But Patch was the most dangerous of the lot. Wanted for murder in three states, Patch was also the newest member of the band and though he had a healthy regard for Morgan's authority, he still wasn't quite convinced he couldn't take Morgan, if he got the right opportunity.

Morgan trusted the other four as little, but they had been with him long enough to know they better do what he said. He smiled inwardly as he remembered the last time one of his men questioned his authority. The result had made believers of the rest and he'd had no problem for almost a year. He'd learned early that in order to control men like these, he had to be tougher than any of them, and not be afraid to show it.

Welch had taught him that when you run with wolves you have to be the leader of the pack Watch your back, don't trust anybody, and the first time one of them even hints that he'll cross you, you kill him. That's how you stay in control. That's how you stay alive. It was a lesson Morgan had learned well.

"Maybe I better remind you again," he told the men. "The girl is strictly business. She is off limits to you. If you don't think you can remember that, you better speak up now because the second one of you forgets it, I'll kill you. Everybody got that?"

The men all nodded, murmuring their agreement. Watching the way Patch avoided his eyes, Morgan had the gut feeling the man would prove to be trouble. He'd have to keep a close eye on Patch.

"It ain't like you to be selfish, Morgan," one of the men pointed out with a grin. "You've always shared with us before."

"There was never a McCandless involved before," Morgan said curtly in a manner that ended the discussion.

He drank from his canteen and replaced the cap just as Amber came back into view. Gone were the hot, stuffy traveling clothes. In their place was a denim riding skirt and a long sleeved cotton shirt with the sleeves rolled up above her elbows. Her hair had come loose from its chignon in the process of changing and now hung softly around her shoulders. She had also discovered in the bundle a pair of worn boots that while scuffed, were an almost perfect fit.

Morgan Devereaux had done a remarkable job of judging her size from only a few minutes in her presence, she thought sourly. While she had been admiring his physical attributes, he had been deciding what size boot she wore. Somehow, that knowledge did not set well.

The procession headed out once more, still northward, deeper into the mountains that lay between Texas and New Mexico. From the conversation on the stage, she knew they must be nearing the Texas border. Devereaux must be taking her to Welch Mandell's hideout in the Badlands.

Morgan rode easy in the saddle beside her, one hand resting on the saddlehorn, the other loosely holding the reins. He gave the appearance of being completely at ease, but still, Amber was certain that beneath that calm, controlled exterior the man was alert and constantly on guard.

She sighed in frustration, lifting the mass of hair from her neck.

"I don't suppose you thought to include a hair ribbon, did you?" she asked. "I seem to have lost my hair pins,"

When Morgan turned to look at her, one glance at his face was enough to convince her that he was not in the mood for polite conversation. Regardless, she was determined to get him to talk. If she could, maybe this cold, scared feeling in the pit of her stomach would ease.

She was surprised when he suddenly smiled. It wasn't really a smile, rather more of a slight upward movement at the corners of his mouth.

"Here," he said as he untied the gray silk bandanna from around his throat and held it toward her. "I didn't think about hair ribbons."

Taking it, Amber quickly tied her hair up into a make shift chignon to keep her hair off her neck.

"Am I correct in assuming you're taking me to your hideout until my uncle pays the ransom?" she asked finally in a shaky voice, in an effort to break the unbearable silence.

He nodded without speaking, his gaze remaining locked with hers. He smiled to himself. She had demonstrated remarkable spirit so far, he thought grudgingly. She had not cried nor whined even once. He admired that. He had scared her silly back at the stage, which was his intention. The sooner she realized just how precarious her position was, the easier it would be to control her. This girl was no gilded lily. In that respect, his first impression of her had been wrong. She had shown more spunk than he had expected, certainly more than a typical rich, spoiled girl would have. It made him wonder if Cooter wasn't right about her.

Not that it really mattered, he reminded himself. Spirited or meek as a lamb, it made no difference. She was merely a pawn in a much larger game, a tool, and it was best if he remembered that.

She was Owen McCandless' niece. She had been raised by a
loving family. She had gone to the best schools money could buy,
while he had been educated by a tutor Welch had hired to come to
the Lair. She'd grown up with all the things he had been cheated
of. Doubtless, she did not know the meaning of revenge or retri-
bution. His lips curled into a brief smile as he studied her innocent features. She would...and soon.

Still, the naive quality in those clear, amber colored eyes disturbed him. Was it possible she was as innocent as she appeared?
She was a McCandless, wasn't she? Manipulating people to get
what she wanted was the thing a McCandless knew how to do
better than anything else. The fact that she was a female wouldn't
have any bearing on that cold, calculating ability. If anything,
being a woman could only make her better at it.

"Why are you doing this to me?" she asked suddenly.

Roused from his private thoughts, Morgan stared at her for
another moment before speaking. If nothing else, the girl was direct.

"I thought you'd already figured that out," he replied.

"I suppose it's for the money. How much are you asking my
uncle for my return?"

"Fifty thousand dollars."

Amber's eyes widened in shock, her lips opening and closing
silently for a few seconds, while she stared at him in disbelief.
"Fifty thousand dollars!! You must be insane! Nobody has that
kind of money lying around! It could take weeks to raise it."

"I've got plenty of time," Morgan said with a sardonic grin.

His dark eyes flicked over her lazily, taking note of the soft
curves of her body and the swell of her firm breasts against the
shirt. He took particular note of her creamy complexion, her cheeks
taking on a pink tinge as she realized he was assessing her, and her
red lips that had parted in breathless amazement.

"Suppose he can't raise the money," Amber stammered, in an
effort to direct his attention back to the conversation and away
from her body. His bold stare made her heart pound with fear.

Morgan's ebony eyes mocked her stumbling attempt to distract him. He decided to let it go for the moment. "You better hope he does."

"If he doesn't, what will happen to me then?" she persisted, not at all sure she wanted to know.

"Then I'll have to decide what to do with you."

"Why you?" she asked apprehensively.

"I captured you. I decide. That's how it works."

"Will you kill me?"

Again, she saw his eyes sweep over her in a cool, appraising glance that made her feel warm and weak. Forcing herself to return his stare, she waited anxiously for his reply.

"Maybe," was his nonchalant answer. "Maybe I'll give you to my men for entertainment. Maybe I'll keep you for myself. I'll make that decision when the time comes."

Amber sucked in her breath in a horrified gulp while her frightened eyes betrayed her grim determination not to show him how badly he scared her. She stared at him wordlessly while her mind tried to devise some reply. His eyes rested on hers, his jaw set, and his face calm. At last she touched the tip of her tongue to her dry lips and swallowed.

"How do I know that you'll let me go if my uncle should be able to raise the money?"

When he ignored her question, Amber's chest felt as though her lungs were paralyzed while she and Morgan stared at each other silently.

"You don't intend to give me back, do you?" she asked in a soft, trembling voice, her eyes huge in her pale face. "You know my uncle can't raise that much cash. You never intended for him to."

"I've gone to a great deal of time and effort to make sure he couldn't," Morgan replied dryly.

"Oh, my God!" she whimpered softly. "That's why you've been doing all those things, cutting fences and stealing payrolls. You knew how much it would cost to keep replacing those things so now Uncle Owen won't have the money to pay my ransom."

"Very perceptive, Miss McCandless," Morgan said, with a tight, grim smile.

"But why?" Amber cried. "Why are you doing this to us? I've done nothing to you! I don't even know you! Why do you want to hurt me?"

Morgan's black eyes regarded her steadily beneath the Stetson that shadowed his face, giving him an even more menacing quality.

"Hurting you is not my objective. You're merely the means of pushing Owen McCandless into making a mistake."

"What do you mean?" Amber whispered through stiff lips.

Morgan's broad shoulders moved in a slight shrug as he shifted in the saddle, amid the squeak of protesting leather. " I mean to kill your uncle. On my terms, when I'm ready. Keeping you as my guest merely insures his cooperation."

"Why? What could Uncle Owen have ever done to you?" Amber cried, her voice rising with fright.

A coldness touched Morgan's face, a hatred so deep and bitter it burned through the veil he kept over his emotions, allowing Amber a chilling glimpse beyond those stabbing black eyes into his anguished soul, but only for an instant. Then he recovered that lock over his feelings and veiled his eyes again.

"Let's just say that I owe him something," he said in a low, savage voice.

The burning intensity that leaped at her from the granite expression on his face sent a shiver of fear, such as she had never experienced, through Amber's slim body. There was a coldness in his eyes now, a merciless rage that boiled in him just below the surface, held in check by the slimmest of threads. She was overwhelmed with fear.

Throwing caution for her own safety to the wind, Amber suddenly lurched forward, digging her heels into the sides of her horse and sending him crashing into Morgan's Appaloosa with a startled snort.

In the split second it took Morgan to regain control of his horse, Amber whirled her mount and, using the ends of the reins as a whip, quickly brought him to a dead run in the opposite direction. Leaning low over the animal's back to make herself as small a target as possible, she expected any second to hear gunshots. She kicked the horse viciously, urging him to top speed as they flew across the ground, dodging rocks and bushes, covering the same area she had ridden over just moments before.

When Amber's horse snorted in alarm, it had spooked the other outlaws' mounts. When they turned, they saw the girl streaking away. Patch yanked his rifle from the boot and brought it to his shoulder, but Morgan knocked it aside as he whirled the Appaloosa.

"Hold your fire, goddamn it!" he shouted over his shoulder.

He gave the Appaloosa his head and the powerful little horse stretched out, covering the distance between Morgan and the girl in record time. Within seconds, the Appaloosa had cut the distance to a few feet. As they left the brush and entered a small clearing, he drew alongside. Morgan caught Amber around the waist, dragging her from the saddle. She struck out blindly with all her strength, her fists flailing away at his face and shoulders while she kicked the Appaloosa in the sides in an effort to break Morgan's grip.

He reined the horse to a stop and dropped Amber onto the hard packed dirt at his feet. She fell squarely on her bottom, but scrambled up and ran for her horse, who had stopped a few yards away. She raced across the ground, her heart pounding with fear, praying with each gulping breath for the strength to outrun him to her horse.

Morgan leaped down from the saddle and ran after her, catching her in a few long strides. He grabbed her arm and spun her around, knocking her off balance. Amber's feet got tangled up with his and they both fell with a thud.

Amber struggled frantically, scratching, biting, kicking, and clawing while sobs of desperation choked her. Her flailing hand fell upon a short tree limb lying on the ground and she swung it with all her strength. She heard a thud, then a muttered curse, but Morgan maintained his grip on her arm. A second later, he ripped the limb from her grasp and flung it aside.

When the cloud of panic lifted enough for her to see clearly, she was on her back staring up into Morgan's furious face. He was on his knees astride her body, keeping his weight on her legs to subdue her violent kicking. He lifted one hand to his head and it came away bloody from the vicious blow she had landed with the limb. He had lost his hat in the struggle and now his rumpled hair hung into his eyes in raven waves.

He wiped the blood onto his thigh and raked his hair back with the fingers of one hand, keeping the other hand securely on Amber's upper arm. Amber was certain he was going to kill her when he rested the heel of his left hand on the butt of his pistol. He seemed to be considering it, but a moment later he took his hand from the gun and slapped her across the face instead.

Amber did not cry out, but turned face down in the dirt with a whimper. By the time the sparks had settled in her head from the blow, Morgan had gotten to his feet and retrieved his hat. Reaching down to pull her to her feet, he caught both her upper arms in his hands, yanking her forward until she was close enough to feel the heat from his body.

"You goddamned little fool!" he snarled. "If it weren't for a promise I made, I'd kill you right now. I'm warning you! Try anything like this again and a promise won't stop me."

"Go ahead! Shoot me! You're going to anyway!" Amber cried. "Why don't you just kill me and get it over with?"

Her voice broke at the end of the outburst and she blinked rapidly to keep tears of fear and frustration from filling her eyes. Her legs felt weak and her stomach churned furiously. For a moment, she thought she was going to vomit.

Morgan moved aside and pushed her toward her horse. Amber put one foot in the stirrup, but turned away suddenly and sank to her knees in the dirt, vomiting and coughing as the sick feeling returned to overwhelm her.

Morgan watched her silently, remembering a small boy who had vomited from fear and anguish. He whistled to the Appaloosa and took his canteen from the saddle when the animal trotted up beside him. He drew a handkerchief from his hip pocket, wet it from the canteen, then passed it silently to the girl who sat retching at his feet. Amber washed her face and tried to catch her breath, then climbed stiffly to her feet.

"You okay?" Morgan asked.

Amber nodded, unable to speak for the tight, burning feeling in her throat. Her hands shook so badly, she could hardly grasp the saddle horn. She closed her eyes, leaning against the horse for support while she gathered her strength. Then she felt Morgan's hands, one on her shoulder, the other on her bottom, as he lifted her onto the horse.

Amber weaved in the saddle for a moment, then regained her balance. Morgan took the wet handkerchief from her and placed it against the cut she had opened up at the base of his hairline, just to the side of his left ear. He took a long breath and mounted, took the reins of Amber's horse and tied them around his saddlehorn.

"Don't give me anymore shit, lady," he said coldly. "We'll be making camp in an hour. Keep your mouth shut till then."

Amber kept her head down to avoid the winks and cat calls from the outlaws as Morgan led her horse back to where they waited. She sat meekly while he tied her hands together and wrapped the rope tightly around her saddle horn. He did not speak, and she scarcely dared breathe until he was finished and they were under way again.

"That was some lick," Patch commented as he pulled his horse alongside Morgan. "You all right, boss?"

Morgan nodded, as he gingerly touched the swelling lump on his head.

"You know, boss, if you want somebody to take a little of the vinegar outa her, I'd be real happy to."

"Any vinegar that's to be taken out of her, I'll gladly do my-self," Morgan grunted with a glare at the grimy little man.

"I mean, it's a shame, boss, to waste that," Patch went on with a gesture to Amber. "We won't be back to camp before tomorrow noon, at best. We still got all night. Me and the boys, we been thinkin', ain't no sense in lettin' all that time go to waste. Hell, her uncle won't know the difference if we have a little fun with her before you give her back. What do you say, boss?"

Amber's breath caught in her throat as she waited for Morgan's answer. Had she made him angry enough to give her to those horrible men? She lifted pleading eyes to his impenetrable face while he weighed his decision.

He glanced at her once, his eyes raking hers coldly. Then he turned in the saddle, his left hand lifting the pistol from its holster with a single fluid motion. His right hand caught Patch by the shirt collar and yanked him forward, almost out of the saddle. The other men stopped, watching with mild amusement while Patch coughed and sputtered. Morgan rested the barrel of his pistol di-rectly under Patch's nose, the cold metal touching the man's grizzled face. Patch's good eye grew wide with alarm, his mouth working soundlessly.

"You want the girl, Patch?" Morgan asked softly. "You can have her. All you have to do is walk through me. What do you say?"

Patch shook his head violently. He wet his lips with the tip of his tongue and swallowed hard. "I don't want no piece of ass bad enough to get killed for it," he stammered.

"I didn't think so," Morgan said in an easy drawl. "I don't want to hear anymore about it. The girl is mine, do you all under-stand that?"

The question was directed to the group and they all hurried to assure him they were quite clear on the point.

"The next man who mentions it better be ready to fight me

for her." He looked at one of the men and said, "Lester, ride ahead and see if camp is ready."

Lester Rollins dug his heels into his mount's sides and dashed past in a hurry to do what Morgan ordered. Morgan let go of Patch's shirt and the little man sank back into his saddle with a gulp. Morgan holstered the pistol and urged the Appaloosa into a canter, pulling Amber's horse along.

"Thank you," she told him in a hushed tone when they were several yards ahead of the others.

"Don't thank me yet," he growled. "We've still got a long way to go and Patch is a determined man."

Amber stared at him, blinking rapidly while her mind filled with horrible visions. "You don't think he would really challenge you, do you?" she asked at last in a shaky whisper.

Morgan glanced over his shoulder at Patch, then to Amber's pale face. "I've got a hunch that I'm going to have to kill him before we get back to the Lair."

CHAPTER NINE

Morgan turned away, his mind already on other matters, but Amber continued to stare at him in astonishment. There was such coldness in his voice, such detachment as though taking the life of another man meant no more to him than stepping on a bug. Her frightened eyes darted to the pistol resting on his hip. The last rays of the sinking sun reflected momentarily off the tiny notches carved in the grips of the weapon, so many Amber was unable to count them.

Remembering his threat to her life if she made another attempt to escape, she wondered if being a female would slow down his actions if she put him to the test. She decided it would not.

Shortly, Amber saw through the darkening twilight the red glow of a campfire through the trees and in a few minutes they rode into a clearing. A fire burned within a circle of large stones and the smell of food wafted to her on the night air.

Another man, who'd been waiting for them to arrive in camp, approached Morgan with a welcoming grin. Amber's brows arched in surprise as she recognized him as the same one who had approached her during her ride only a couple of days before to ask directions to McCandless. She realized now that the man had probably been sent to learn her identity. She was filled with self recrimination to have fallen for his ploy.

"You're late," the man said as Morgan swung down from the Appaloosa.

"We ran into a slight delay," Morgan grunted after a meaningful glance in Amber's direction.

"Any trouble?" Jase McCally asked.

"Nothing I couldn't handle. Miss McCandless decided she

didn't like my company and made a break for it."

Jase noticed the swollen bruise at the base of Morgan's head and grinned. "Looks like she put up quite a scrap. How bad is it?"

He reached to inspect the wound, but Morgan brushed his hand away and handed him the reins of his horse. "Just a scratch. Take care of the horses, will you, Jase?" he said in a sour tone that made Jase grin again.

"Sure, Morgan. Supper's ready. Go ahead and eat. I'll take care of the horses."

Morgan walked around Amber's horse, reached up to untie her hands from the saddle horn, and started to lift her down from the saddle. Amber pushed his hands away, swung one leg over the horse's neck, and slipped to the ground. For a long moment they stared at each other without blinking, then Morgan stepped back and indicated a smooth rock beside the fire. "Go over there and sit down," he ordered.

Amber raised her head to send him a scornful glare before stalking over to the fire and taking a seat. Behind her stiff back, Jase nudged Morgan in the ribs and grinned.

"She's turning out to be more of a handful than you thought, ain't she, Morgan?"

"She's turning out to be a pain in the ass," Morgan replied stiffly with a glance in her direction. "I told Welch she'd be more trouble than she'd be worth. The men are already looking at her like a flock of goddamned vultures, especially Patch. I'll have to sleep with one eye open all night."

Jase studied Amber's gloomy profile by the firelight for a second and replied, "Can't say I blame them, Morgan. It ain't often the men get a chance to see a real lady, especially one that pretty."

"Lady, hell," Morgan growled. "Goddamned wildcat is more like it."

Jase chuckled softly as he took up the reins of both horses. "Well, Morgan, you're always saying you like a woman with spirit."

Morgan snorted and moved between the horses to take his bedroll from behind his saddle. Sticking it securely under one arm, he turned to take the one off the horse Amber had been riding.

"The only thing about her that interests me is her name, Jase. If I hadn't promised Welch I'd make sure nothing happened to her, I'd give her to the men as a gift. That would take some of the starch out of her sails."

Jase chuckled again and led the horses into the darkness at the rim of the fire where the picket line was stretched. Morgan walked toward the fire, moved a few steps beyond it, and dumped the bedrolls in the dirt. As Amber watched curiously, he spread them out side by side, then came to sit down across the fire from where she sat.

He took a plate from the stack beside the fire and filled it with the delicious smelling stew Jase had prepared. He held the plate toward Amber, but she shook her head emphatically.

"I'm not hungry, thank you," she snapped.

"Suit yourself," Morgan returned with a shrug.

He began to eat, ignoring Amber totally while she seethed with indignation. The truth was, she was starving and the stew smelled heavenly, but her battered pride would not permit her to admit it. So she sat in stony silence, watching Morgan eat while her mouth watered.

The other outlaws came to dish up their food before drifting away to eat on their blankets scattered around the fire. She noticed none of them put a blanket close to the two Morgan had spread out. She wondered why. Then it suddenly dawned on her that he meant for her to sleep with him, and the others knew it and were giving him space for a little privacy.

Her heart leapt into her mouth as her gaze flashed to him across the fire. He sat calmly finishing his meal as though she had ceased to exist. She felt faint as she put one hand to her mouth to squeeze off the whimper of panic that washed over her. It was too horrible to imagine.

What was she going to do? Her mind raced furiously trying to devise some kind of defense, but she soon realized it was hopeless.

She had learned she was no match for him physically from the episode earlier so fighting him off would be impossible. Plus, there was the chance that if she put up too much of a fight, he would give her to the others when he was finished with her himself.

A low moan bubbled up in her throat while she tried to imagine what it would be like to be ravished on the ground like some kind of animal while the others awaited their turns, snickering and watching in lewd anticipation.

She thought she was going to vomit again when the men became very quiet. She looked up to see Morgan put aside his plate and rise to his feet, extending his hand to her as he moved around the fire.

She swallowed hard, her legs trembling violently as he pulled her to her feet. Her eyes were wide as they searched his dark face, but Morgan took her arm and led her past the clearing into the bushes just beyond. Then he untied her hands and motioned toward the protecting cover of the underbrush.

"If you need to do anything, do it now. I don't mean to get up in the middle of the night and wander around out here with the snakes," he said curtly.

It took a couple of seconds for Amber to realize what he meant. Then her face colored as she turned quickly away, moving a few feet into the brush.

"And don't get any ideas," he warned her while he listened to the rustle of her clothing.

He waited patiently until she finished and ventured from the brush, her face still pink with embarrassment. He noticed the wide fearful eyes and pale face as she stood facing him, the full moon lighting the night so he could plainly read her features.

"Now what?" she asked in a shaky voice.

"Now we get some sleep."

He took her hands and retied them carefully, making sure the rope was secure but not so tight that it cut off the circulation.

"You don't mean to..force yourself on me?" she asked finally in a firmer tone.

The pause before he answered seemed like an eternity, but was in reality only a couple of seconds. Amber watched his handsome face, holding her breath while she waited for his reply.

"Rolling around in the dirt like a pair of animals is not my idea of a good time. Some things are best done without an audience."

Amber struggled to hold her gaze steady. His face was shadowed by the darkness, but she could sense his gaze flicker over her trembling body in a manner that made her knees weak with fear.

"You...you spread the blankets so close together. I..I thought you..that maybe..that you meant..." she stammered uncertainly.

"I spread the blankets together so I can keep an eye on you tonight. I don't trust you and I trust Patch even less."

His voice contained a trace of amusement that made Amber's cheeks flame with embarrassment.

"Oh, I see," she mumbled in a low tone as she dropped her head to avoid his eyes.

Morgan smiled to himself as relief flooded through her face. He took her arm and guided her back through the rough area toward the campfire. Amber glanced up at him several times, but Morgan remained silent and offered no further comment on the sleeping arrangements.

"How long before you expect to hear from my uncle?" she asked to break the uncomfortable silence.

"A couple of days."

"And then what?"

"And then either I give you back or I don't."

"And if you don't?" she persisted doggedly.

His gaze touched her momentarily in the darkness, but she felt the gaze without seeing it. When Morgan made no attempt to answer the question, she took a deep breath and halted in the path. He paused as she turned to face him, trying to see his face clearly in the gathering shadows.

"Well? You haven't answered my question."

"I don't intend to," Morgan told her impatiently as he gave a firm tug on her arm. "I don't make a practice of planning too far ahead. In my business, it pays not to be too optimistic."

"Why do you want to hurt my uncle? What could he possibly have done to make you hate him so badly that you want to kill him?"

Again Morgan chose not to answer, but continued toward the clearing where his men were bedding down for the night. Amber felt another chill come over her at his silence. She would have preferred threats and anger to that cold, ominous silence that emanated from him like a blanket of foreboding.

"Do you hate him so badly that you would kill me to hurt him?" she asked in a shaky voice.

"I don't know yet," Morgan said. Then remembering his promise to Cooter, he added, "I don't kill women as a rule. There are other things I could do that would be more effective than killing you, I suppose."

"Such as?"

Again she felt his eyes touch her as he led her around a small patch of cactus in the path. Amber stumbled over a hidden root and gasped in alarm when Morgan's strong hand caught her to prevent her from falling.

Morgan made no effort to answer her question for they had arrived back at the campfire. He dropped his hand from her arm and walked ahead of her to the blankets he had spread out, then sat down and began pulling off his boots. Amber watched, a little confused, but finally went to the other blanket and dropped wearily onto it. Morgan removed his hat and boots and lay back on the blanket, using his saddle for a pillow.

Noting that he had not removed the gunbelt, Amber asked, "Do you actually sleep with that thing on?"

Morgan ignored the question. "Lay down and go to sleep," he told her instead. "Don't get any ideas about running off in the middle of the night. I'm a very light sleeper. You wouldn't get very far in the dark, and I don't think you want to make me that angry."

Amber stared at him in frustrated silence for a moment before lying down beside him. She turned onto her side with her back to him and folded both hands beneath her cheek. The ground was hard and cold so she fidgeted for a bit trying to find a comfortable position.

A few moments later when she had become still, she was startled when Morgan suddenly moved closer, turned onto his side, and wrapped a long arm around her waist, drawing her backwards against the warmth of his body. She stiffened in apprehension, but when he made no further movement, the tension drained slowly from her tired body.

She was bone weary and regretted turning down the food he offered her, for her stomach was growling. Her cheek still ached where he had slapped her earlier. She wondered if his head hurt where she had struck him with the tree limb. She certainly hoped so for she had never been treated so badly in her life and the worst part was the man had not answered any of her questions fully. She still had no idea what was going to become of her or why he hated Uncle Owen so badly. She moved restlessly, then felt his arm tighten about her waist.

She looked down at the hand that rested so possessively on her stomach. It appeared to be a perfectly normal hand, strong and brown with long nimble fingers, but she knew it was no ordinary hand. It contained the skill of an accomplished gunfighter, adept at killing with masterful accuracy and no remorse. She shuddered involuntarily to think that hand might snuff out her uncle's life in a few days, perhaps her own, as well. No, she must not think about that, she told herself sternly as hot tears of frustration filled her eyes. She must find a way to prevent Morgan Devereaux from carrying out his twisted plan of revenge on dear, unsuspecting Uncle Owen.

She choked back a sob, biting her lip until she tasted her own blood. She would not allow that horrible man to know she was crying, she vowed angrily. He had kidnapped her, he might even kill her, but he would not break her spirit. Before this nightmare was over, Morgan Devereaux would be very sorry for what he had done to her. She would find some way to stop him before Uncle Owen walked into the trap he had set. She just had to.

***

Amber blinked, peering into the gray dawn and started to move when the arm around her slender waist tightened.

"Don't move," Morgan whispered softly in her ear.

Something was wrong. Amber sensed it immediately, but the tone of his voice was enough to convince her to do exactly what he said. She commanded her alarmed body to relax. A second later she felt his hand withdraw ever so slowly from her body.

Then suddenly, with a motion so abrupt Amber didn't have time to blink, Morgan rolled away from her, flinging the blanket aside as he lifted the pistol from the holster. A heartbeat later the deadly gun exploded, sending a bullet through Patch's brain as he crouched, his own gun drawn and aimed at the blanket where Morgan had lain sleeping a second before. Patch paused as though suspended in space for a moment, then toppled headlong into the dirt at Morgan's feet.

Before the echo of Morgan's shot died away the camp was awake. The bandits swarmed around, staring in surprise at Patch's lifeless body as Morgan reholstered his gun and rose to his feet.

"What the hell..." Jase McCally blurted as he looked from Patch to Morgan.

"That was some shot," one of the others commented. "Morgan got him before he could fire and his gun was already out."

"Get him out of my sight," Morgan growled as he turned away. He reached down to pick up his boots and put them on.

"You want us to bury him, Morgan?" Jase asked.

"Hell no," Morgan answered without looking up. "Drag him off out in the brush and leave him for the coyotes."

Amber couldn't believe what had happened. She sat up, rubbing her eyes and staring with horror first at Patch's body, then at Morgan who was calmly rolling up his blanket.

"What kind of man are you?" she cried in disbelief, her eyes wide and accusing. "You just killed that man! The very least you can do is give him a decent burial!"

Morgan sat down to pull on his boots. "That's real generous of you, Miss McCandless, considering that he meant to kill me and rape you."

Amber gulped and swallowed quickly. Two of the outlaws were dragging Patch's body away, but she caught sight of the trickle of blood that ran down his nose and dripped into the dirt. Morgan's bullet had caught him directly between the eyes. She wished fervently she hadn't looked.

"It's all your fault. If you hadn't forced me off the stage this wouldn't have happened."

"It would've happened sooner or later. Patch's kind are looking to die from the minute they're born. It's just a question of when."

The casual tone of his voice baffled Amber completely. The man had just killed another man, yet he was rolling up his bedroll as if nothing had happened. She stared at him in amazement.

"One might say the same about you," she pointed out contemptuously.

Morgan raked his hair back from his eyes and put on his hat, glancing at her again, this time with a slight grin curling his lips at the corners.

"I suppose you could," he agreed. "The difference is that I'm better with a gun than most men. It'll take somebody smarter and better than Patch to catch me off guard. You might even think about being a little grateful, Miss McCandless. If I hadn't killed him, you'd be a very unhappy young lady about now. Have you ever seen a woman after six men took a turn with her? It's not a pretty sight."

"How would I know about such terrible things? I've never been around men like you before!"

There was an expression of disbelief on Morgan's face as he

studied her.

"I suppose you're as pure as the driven snow," he grunted sarcastically.

"I am a lady, Mr. Devereaux! How dare you imply otherwise!" The amused disbelief on his face made her want to slap him. "Why do you find that so hard to believe?" she demanded indignantly, scrambling to her feet to face him.

"You're a McCandless, aren't you?"

Bewilderment flashed across her face. "What's that supposed to mean?"

Morgan didn't answer, but turned away and walked toward the picket line to begin saddling the Appaloosa. Amber hesitated, then grabbed up her saddle and hurried after him, as fast as she could drag the heavy saddle across the rocks.

"Answer me, damn you!" she cried angrily.

Morgan threw the saddle across the horse's back, pausing to shoot a mocking glance at her. With her long hair falling around her shoulders, she looked to Morgan like a schoolgirl.

Amber stood waiting for an answer, her back ramrod stiff and her eyes flashing with outrage. "What do you know about me? You only met me yesterday, how could you possibly know anything about me?" she persisted.

"I know you left Texas twelve years ago to live back east with your mother and her folks until they all died. I know that you're going to inherit Owen McCandless' empire, half when you're twenty-one and the rest when he dies. I know that you were engaged to some city slicker who cooled off real quick when he found out you had to live here in order to collect your inheritance. How am I doing?"

Amber stared in open-mouthed astonishment, her eyes widening with each detail he revealed. "How could you know so much about me?"

"I've made it my business to know as much about Owen McCandless as I could over the past twenty years. That includes you."

"Twenty years? You were only a child twenty years ago and I wasn't even born yet."

Morgan nodded grimly as he cinched the saddle tight. Her surprise gave him a sense of satisfaction.

"I was ten years old the last time I met your uncle. But I swore that someday I'd find him again and I'd kill him. In the meantime he's built an empire. The law can't touch him because he owns it, just like he owns that town of his and everybody in it. So I had to find some other way, and you, Miss McCandless, are that way.

"You see, I know that you're the most important thing in his life. He'd give everything he owns to get you back, except I've seen to it that he won't be able to raise the cash. So he'll have no choice but to come after me. It's the only way to get you back and when he does, I'll be waiting for him."

His words held the first real emotion Amber had heard from him. The words, while softly spoken, were filled with such bitterness that she flinched inwardly.

"You dare cast aspersions on my honor and my family because you hate my uncle for some...some misguided perception of something that happened when you were a child? I'll have you know, sir, that my mother was a great lady and my father was the most honorable man in the whole world. How dare you presume that I'm..I'm immoral simply because I share the McCandless name! I'll have you know I am very proud of that name!" Amber said furiously.

Morgan watched her with amusement dancing in his dark eyes. The girl reminded him of a bantam rooster.

"I never met your mother," he said after finishing tightening the saddle cinches. He leaned both arms across the saddle to meet her furious glare evenly. "I saw your father once, the night he tried to stop your beloved uncle from murdering my family. So perhaps my impressions of your parents aren't quite correct. Welch keeps telling me that I shouldn't judge all McCandless' by your uncle, but I have trouble remembering."

Amber's expression was disbelieving.

"My father and Uncle Owen killed your family?" she asked in a hollow, strained voice. She had dropped her saddle and now came between the two horses. It was difficult to endure the cold, bitter hatred that burned in his eyes.

"Not your father," Morgan corrected, keeping his voice in that soft, menacing tone. "Your father had no part in it. He tried to stop your uncle and got knocked cold for his trouble. You could even say your father saved my life."

He paused, his eyes focused on Amber, though his thoughts had gone back twenty years as he remembered the compassionate, horrified face of the younger McCandless as he held the hysterical boy who vomited wretchedly after his life had become a living nightmare.

With a visible shake, Morgan brought himself back to the present. Amber was staring at him, her face pale. Her lips trembled slightly before she clamped her mouth tightly closed to still the quivering.

"You might also say that your father saved your life, as well, Miss McCandless. His effort to help me twenty years ago is the only reason you're still alive. However, I've paid my debt to your father by not killing you, so I figure we're all square."

His words hit Amber like a cold shower. She blinked rapidly, trying to choke back the blinding fear that gripped her. "Surely you don't blame me for what you think my uncle has done?" she managed to stammer.

"Like I said, your name's McCandless, isn't it?"

"I can't believe Uncle Owen could do anything so vile," Amber told him in a stronger tone.

"I didn't think you would."

Morgan surveyed her irritably. It had been far easier to plan his revenge on Owen McCandless when the tool he planned to use to lure the rancher into his trap was a faceless stranger.

Grudgingly, he had to admit that Cooter's estimation of the girl was becoming more and more likely. He found that a disturbing thought. He preferred dealing with abstracts, rather than people or feelings. People were almost always liars, and feelings were traps that were best avoided. He found himself wishing he had never promised Cooter that he would try to make the girl see what the doting, generous uncle she loved so dearly, was truly like.

He regarded Amber's puzzled face with an impatient shrug as he turned toward the campfire Jase had started. Amber stared at his broad back as he moved away from her, then hurried after him. He had sat down by the fire and was nonchalantly eating his breakfast. She hesitated before taking a seat and accepting the plate of food Jase McCally offered her. She wanted an explanation of the accusations this man had made against her uncle, but it was obvious he didn't intend to discuss it any further.

'Well, it's not over yet, mister,' she told herself. 'You've got some tall explaining to do and I won't let you rest until you do it.'

Eating with her hands tied was awkward, but Morgan made no effort to release her, even long enough to eat. So, Amber had to do the best she could by balancing the tin plate on her knees and lifting both hands with each bite. She was amazed to find she had any appetite at all after witnessing Morgan blow Patch's brains all over the campsite, but all the previous hours without food made her empty stomach over-ride the horror. She hurriedly ate the beans and bacon before Morgan changed his mind about feeding her.

Even before she had finished eating, the outlaws began to break camp. Within minutes Amber was back in the saddle, following Morgan further into the hills. The air was cooler now, but the sun was still warm on her back as they climbed higher among the rocks while the terrain steadily became more rugged.

Amber made a few feeble attempts at conversation, but gave up when Morgan refused to do more than grunt impatiently. At one point, when the trail widened to allow two horses to walk abreast, she took advantage of the opportunity to look Morgan over again.

He didn't look like a gunslinger, she thought, as she studied him beneath the brim of the floppy hat he had given her earlier. Gunslingers were a scruffy lot generally, she'd assumed from the articles in the Boston Globe. Small, steely-eyed, and wearing big mustaches and scraggly beards, that was what she thought they looked like. The man riding beside her was certainly not like that.

Morgan Devereaux was obviously a man who was proud of his appearance and took pains to maintain it. And he had every right to be proud of the way he looked, she thought irritably.

"Devereaux...that's French, isn't it?" she asked suddenly to break the silence.

Morgan barely glanced her direction before looking away again. "Yes," he answered shortly, offering no further explanation.

"I'd guess your father was French and your mother Spanish, perhaps?" she continued doggedly, in hopes she could get him to talk.

Morgan turned his head to send her a direct gaze, but instead of answering her question asked, "Don't you ever shut up?"

Undaunted by the irritation in his voice, Amber shook her head, refusing to look away. "I don't think it's unfair to try and learn something about you, Mr. Devereaux....should I call you Mr. Devereaux, or would you prefer Morgan?"

"It makes no difference to me," he grunted after a weary sigh at her persistence.

"I prefer Morgan," she decided, eyeing him thoughtfully. "As I was saying, Morgan, I think it's only fair that I know something about you. You seem to know a great deal about me and my family. I don't think it's unreasonable to want to know a little something about the man who has kidnapped me and probably intends to murder me."

When he made no effort to reply, Amber grew impatient with his silence and tried again. "Well, am I right? Was your father French and your mother Spanish?"

"What makes you think my mother was Spanish?" he asked with a glance at her.

"Your complexion," Amber returned with forced cheerfulness. "And the color of your hair and eyes."

"Does that mean you got your blonde hair from your Scottish

father and your persistence from your Irish mother?"

In spite of herself, Amber smiled, her cheeks dimpling. Despite his irritation at her questions, Morgan admired her beauty.

"Touch," she said brightly.

Morgan allowed himself a brief grin, but looked away before Amber could see it. He shifted in the saddle in order to observe her more closely. Finally, he decided to answer her, and said, "Yes, Miss McCandless, my father was French and my mother was Spanish. Now I've answered your question, you answer one for me."

Amber nodded.

"This fancy-assed fellow you were engaged to back east...did you sleep with him?"

Amber's eyes widened and a deep scarlet blush began at her toes and surged upward until her face was flaming with embarrassment and anger. "How dare you! What possible business is that of yours?" she demanded furiously.

Morgan shrugged while he watched her with a cold, sardonic smile that made Amber even more uncomfortable than his blunt question.

"Just curious. You said you were virtuous, didn't you? I find that hard to believe. You were engaged to that fellow, weren't you? I figure a man would have to have ice water in his veins not to try his damnedest to get you between the sheets."

Amber stared at him uncertainly. She couldn't decide if he had insulted her, or in his own offhanded way, paid her a compliment. The solemn gleam in his eyes told her nothing, but the half-smile that touched his lips made her wonder if he was teasing her, or merely being crude.

"I'll have you know, Mr. Devereaux, that I am not the kind of girl who lets a man take liberties, engaged or not!" she snapped, glaring at him furiously.

"But he tried, didn't he?"

"Larkin was a perfect gentleman! He knew I was a lady and he treated me as such. I don't suppose a man like you would understand that!"

"I don't suppose," Morgan agreed mildly. His dark gaze flicked over her in a manner that made Amber blush again. "He couldn't have been much of a man if he let you get away."

Amber wondered why she felt the need to defend Larkin, when indeed, she had often thought much the same thing. "Larkin had his own life in Boston. He was quite successful. It would have been very difficult for him to start over out here."

"In other words, he was a fancy dresser and a fancy talker, but when it came right down to it, he didn't care enough about you to come back to Texas with you. He couldn't be terribly bright to give up all that McCandless money and you too."

Amber tried to think of something to say that would defend Larkin against such an attack but after thinking about it for a moment, decided it was best to drop the subject altogether.

"How much further is it?" she asked in an effort to change the subject.

Morgan grinned as he turned back to look around the area, then looked back at her. "Two hours more."

"Tell me something, if my uncle did the terrible thing you say, why is it that he doesn't know why you're persecuting him?" she asked when he became silent again.

Amber felt the chill that radiated from Morgan's cold, black eyes as he stared at her levelly. "Because he's forgotten. It meant nothing more to him than stepping on an insect. He got what he wanted from it and promptly forgot how he came by it. That's the kind of man he is."

"I don't believe you," Amber said emphatically. "Nothing you could say would make me believe Uncle Owen could do anything so evil. You're only saying such terrible things about him to make me doubt him, but it won't work. I'm not falling for anymore of your tricks!"

"I don't give a damn what you believe, Miss McCandless, but I'm afraid you're in for a rude awakening one of these days. There's a time coming, probably sooner than you think, when you're going to see a side of dear Uncle Owen you've never dreamed of. Take my word for it."

Amber was suddenly afraid. Was it possible that twenty years ago her uncle had done what this man accused him of? No! Devereaux was lying. Owen McCandless could never have done such a thing. It was a trick of some kind to try and separate her and her uncle. That's all it was. Morgan was lying— he had to be.

CHAPTER TEN

Two hours later, Amber roused from her thoughts to notice a distinctively festive air among Morgan's men. For hours they had ridden in silence broken only by an occasional brief exchange before lapsing back into bored silence. Now they straightened in their saddles, and their rugged faces became more animated, their conversation growing louder and more boisterous.

Their air of expectancy told her they must be getting close to their destination. Only moments later Morgan pulled his mount to a halt and leaning toward her, deftly tied his bandanna over her eyes.

"What's happening? What are you doing?" she asked in a frightened voice.

"Where we're going there's only one way in or out. If I let you see the way, I can't let you go. You wouldn't like that, would you?"

While she was relieved that he was being more pleasant, she was bitterly disappointed that she would be unable to see the way into Welch Mandell's hideout. Instead of dwelling on that, she decided to take heart from the fact that Morgan had insinuated she would be released eventually. For the first time since this nightmare had begun, she felt a flicker of hope.

Morgan hesitated a second before taking up the reins of Amber's horse to lead her through the secret opening in the side of the mountain that loomed before them. The girl had visibly relaxed when he hinted that she would be set free, and Morgan cursed himself at his slip. He had to be more careful, he warned himself irritably. In order to keep her under control, he had to make her believe her life depended on her absolute compliance. Another slip like that one could be disastrous.

He let his gaze slide over her slowly from head to toe and back again. Her golden hair spilled down her shoulders in radiant splendor, her bound hands rested on the saddlehorn, and her lush, full lips pressed together beneath the bandanna that covered her eyes. A sardonic smile touched his lips as his eyes rested on the swell of her breasts against the fabric of her shirt. Patch did have a point, he thought as he directed his attention to the matter of getting through the narrow, secret entrance in the mountain. He would have to free her eventually, but there was no sense in letting all that beauty go to waste. Morgan had never been a man to waste time.

Amber clutched the saddlehorn as the horse began to climb, gripping him tightly with her knees as the animal maneuvered around twists and turns in the path. She was sure the horses were walking in single file when she felt the bright sunshine fade behind her and a cool, almost damp feeling closed in around her. She wondered if they were passing through a tunnel of some kind. She racked her brain trying to remember what the terrain had looked like before Morgan had blindfolded her, but nothing significant came to mind. She was furious with herself for not paying closer attention, for now it would be impossible to find her way back here again. Then she reminded herself that she was safer not knowing. The less she knew, the less of a threat she was to Morgan Devereaux, and the better her chances of leaving this place alive.

She felt the sun warm her face. Moments later the horse came to a halt. She blinked rapidly to readjust her eyes to the glare of the sun when Morgan removed the bandanna. Without a word, he began leading her horse forward once more.

Amber looked around as the animals began to descend the steep, rocky path in single file, gasping at the sight that lay before her on the canyon floor. Welch Mandell's hideout lay three hundred feet beneath the rim of the box canyon, accessible only by a twisted, dangerously steep path that wound its way down the sides of the canyon to the floor below.

She heard a sharp whistle, followed by an obscene cat-call that made her head snap upward to find two men with rifles poised on the face of the cliff above the path, one on either side. Realizing the off color remarks were directed at her, she quickly looked away, staring straight ahead at Morgan's broad shoulders, flaming with embarrassment.

The Leopard's Lair, as it was known, was like any other small western town. From her vantage point high above it, Amber could see one main street running the length of the settlement with several smaller streets branching off on either side. She could make out a large boarding house at the far end of the main street. Beyond it was a sprawling building with a banner proclaiming it to be a saloon.

Several small buildings lined both sides of the main street. As the horses picked their way down the winding path closer to the canyon floor, Amber was able to make out signs that identified them as a general store, a blacksmith shop located at the end of the street nearest the path into the settlement, and a gun shop. Across from the smithy was a livery stable surrounded by corrals where thirty or forty horses milled about, and a cafe.

On the side streets were many smaller buildings, which Amber decided must be the homes of the members of Mandell's gang who had families. By now they had reached the smooth canyon floor and were moving into the town past the stables and corrals.

Amber noted with astonishment, the swarms of children playing in the streets. They were all ages, many of them with the dark olive skin and raven hair that proclaimed their Mexican heritage. They were, for the most part, clean and neatly dressed.

Next door to the saloon stood an impressive ranch style house, painted white and topped with red Spanish tiles. Amber was astounded to find such an elegant house in the midst of such a place and correctly assumed it was the home of the outlaw king Welch Mandell. She wondered if she would have a chance to see him for herself. The saloon girls on the stage description of Mandell intrigued her.

Her thoughts were interrupted when Morgan turned off the

main street onto one of the smaller side streets. Amber looked about in alarm, for he was leading her horse into what appeared to be a residential part of the settlement. He was looking straight ahead, paying no attention to the group of small boys who had gathered along the side of the street to watch wide eyed as he rode past. The open admiration on those young impressionable faces disturbed her. Couldn't these children find someone more respectable for a hero, she wondered bitterly.

All thoughts of the children vanished from her mind when Morgan stopped in front of a small frame house, painted white and surrounded by a matching white picket fence. He swung down from his horse and turned to lift Amber from her saddle.

She stumbled forward on legs stiff from too many hours in the saddle, wishing he would take his hand off her arm, as he propelled her down the walk toward the comfortable looking house.

Before they reached the door, it flew open and a stout little Mexican woman rushed out to greet them. Her coal black hair was braided and coiled around the back of her head. Her dark eyes were sparkling, and the welcoming smile on her round, cheerful face revealed several gold teeth.

She burst into an animated conversation in rapid fire Spanish as she walked backwards toward the house, wiping her hands on her apron and eyeing Amber speculatively.

"Speak English, Consuela," Morgan ordered with the closest thing to a genuine smile Amber had seen yet.

"Sorry, *senor* Morgan," the plump little woman said with a nod, while she reached behind herself to push open the door, then backed into the dark, cool interior of the house. "It is good to have you home," she added in heavily accented English.

Morgan released Amber's arm, removed his hat, handed it to the waiting Consuela, and then turned back to untie the ropes from her wrists. He moved to a dark, heavily polished cabinet that stood beneath the window at the opposite side of the room. Opening it to reveal a well stocked liquor cabinet, he poured himself a drink from one of the crystal decanters inside.

Having tossed back the drink with one swallow and poured another, he turned back to Amber. She was standing in the same spot he'd left her, just inside the front door with a confused, half frightened expression on her face as she examined the room. As he watched her, she lifted her wide golden eyes to meet his thoughtful gaze.

"Want one?" he asked indicating the liquor.

Amber shook her head, moving further into the room. "No thank you."

The house was cool and comfortable, immaculately clean and quite well furnished. It had a pleasant, peaceful air that surprised her. She could smell the delicious aroma of baking bread somewhere in the house, and assumed the kitchen must be just off the room they were in, since Consuela had disappeared in that direction. There were several hanging pots scattered about the room containing green, leafy house plants. On the couch were handmade tapestries of colorful Mexican design. The floor beneath her feet was covered with a soft carpet in several shades of blue.

"Is this where you live?" she asked after assessing the room.

Morgan nodded, his coal black eyes studying her while he noted with sardonic amusement the conflicting thoughts racing through her mind, each one mirrored by those amber eyes.

"Am I to assume, since you've brought me here, that you've reached some decision about me?" she asked in a clear distinct voice that was a sharp contradiction to the anxiety in her face.

"I've decided to let you choose for yourself. But before you do, there are a couple of things you ought to know."

"Like what?" Amber asked cautiously.

"You have two options, Amber," he said, noting her surprise at his use of her given name. "You can choose to accept my terms, and in return you'll have my protection. Or you can choose not to accept my terms, and I'll give you to my men."

He ignored the sharp intake of her breath and the way she had paled, and continued in the same nonchalant tone.

"I should warn you, though, that there are between forty-five and fifty men in the compound right now. Less than half of them are married. The rest are a greedy lot. They hang out at the saloon, gambling away their shares of the loot and humping the whores upstairs. If you choose that option, I'll take you down to the saloon and put you up for sale, but you ought to know that when the first buyer gets through with you, he'll make the same offer to the rest. By morning, you could easily have been with twenty or twenty- five men, maybe more."

He paused to study her white, terrified face. "It's up to you, Amber. What's it going to be; one man or twenty?"

Amber stared at him in horror. Her legs felt useless beneath her as she stumbled to a cane-backed chair nearby and sank into it. His dark eyes held hers prisoner, cool, appraising. His calmness infuriated her, but she had learned he would do exactly what he threatened.

Finally she found her voice and squeaked, "What kind of choice is that?"

"A fair one, at least as fair as you're going to get."

"What do you want me to do?" she whispered in a choked voice.

She dropped her head, unable to look at him. He didn't answer right away, but instead rose to his feet and crossed the room, coming to a halt in front of where she sat in dejected silence, fighting back tears.

She slowly looked up at his handsome, unreadable face. She flushed when his dark eyes traveled lazily up and down her trembling body before coming to rest on her face. Then he reached down to cup her chin with the index finger of his left hand, forcing her eyes to focus on his.

"You're a smart girl, Amber," he told her in a softer tone. "Smart enough to make the right decision to keep yourself alive. Now listen to me well; inside this house you're as safe as a baby in its mother's arms. Outside it, you're only safe when you're with me. That means, you are not to leave this house unless I'm with you."

Amber searched his face, unable to discern anything of his

true thoughts. "I thought the men would do what you say."

An amused smile touched his lips for a second before he replied. "Sober they do; they know what will happen if they don't. Drunk, as most of them will be tonight, is another matter. You're a very beautiful young woman, Amber. The kind of woman men would kill for. This town is filled with killers.

"Whatever you may have heard about outlaws having their own code of honor is horseshit. The only thing they understand or respect is force, somebody being faster with a gun than they are. That's why I said you're safe when you're with me, but I won't be around twenty-four hours a day to guard you. When I'm away, the only place you'll be safe is inside this house, because the men know better than to trespass on my property."

"Am I now to be considered your property, Mr. Devereaux?" she inquired coldly.

"For the time being. As long as you do what you're told, you'll be safe. Cross me just once, Amber, and I'll drag you to the saloon by the hair and make a present of you to the others. *Comprende?*"

When Amber nodded woodenly, he let go of her face and called to Consuela. The little Mexican woman came scurrying from the kitchen and looked up at him expectantly.

"*Si, senor,* Morgan?"

"Consuela, this is Amber McCandless. She's going to be my guest for awhile."

"*Su amante, senor* Morgan?" she suggested with a sly smile at Amber's pale face.

"*Mi amante y mi prisionero,* Consuela." he answered. He looked back to Amber's puzzled features. "Consuela will take care of whatever you need until I get back."

"Where are you going?" Amber cried in alarm.

Again his eyes flickered over her slim body, dwelling for a moment on the ripe swell of her breasts straining against her shirt. "Business before pleasure, Amber," he said with an amused smile that made her flame with embarrassment.

He turned back to the housekeeper and spoke to her in fluent

Spanish for a moment after which she smiled and nodded, then hurried back into the kitchen.

"I told Consuela to prepare a bath for you. I'm sure you'd like to freshen up after that hot, dusty ride. She'll have some food for you too, when you've bathed." He nodded toward the adjoining bedroom. "You'll find everything you'll need in there. I won't be long."

"I'm supposed to wait here like a willing lamb for you to return?" Amber spat.

His dark eyes danced at her indignant outburst. He ran his fingers though his thick, black hair before putting his hat on with a grin. "I'm not going to force you, Amber. We have a deal, remember?" he reminded her. "You keep me happy, and I'll keep you alive."

"And just how do I go about doing that?"

"We'll figure that out when I get back," Morgan told her softly as he moved past her toward the door.

"Do you make a habit of exacting such a deplorable bargain with women?" she asked contemptuously.

Morgan swung around to face her, his black eyes stabbing into hers with an intensity that made Amber back up a step involuntarily. "No. Usually, I just take what I want. But in your case, Amber, I wanted you to agree to my terms, and being the intelligent young woman you are, you made the only sensible choice. This way I get what I want and you have agreed to give it to me willingly.

"If you think you can change your mind at the last minute; don't. You'll find that lust has no conscience and I have less than most. We've struck a bargain, Amber, and one way or the other, you're going to hold up your end of it. How unpleasant it is depends entirely on you. For my part, I intend to enjoy every minute of it."

CHAPTER ELEVEN

Morgan rode down the main street of the town the law called the Leopard's Lair, paying little attention to the loud guffaws and occasional curses coming from the men who lounged against the porch columns and in cane-backed chairs along the shaded sidewalks. He never socialized with the men. Welch had taught him that to be the leader meant keeping yourself just a bit aloof from the ranks. You couldn't afford to take the chance of getting too close to one of these men because the day might come when that man would take advantage of your friendship and shoot you in the back for the reward on your head. He wondered sometimes if he would have to spend his entire life watching his back, always sitting facing open doorways, and sleeping with one eye open.

Jase McCally was the closest thing to a real friend, outside Welch, that Morgan had, but that too, was a relationship of cautious doubt. Jase was a likable fellow about Morgan's age, who was willing and eager for friendship, and on many occasions over the past four or five years had tried to get closer, but Morgan carefully kept the relationship as business-like as possible. It wasn't that he doubted Jase's loyalty. It was that any true friendship, with the exception of Welch, would take away from his dedication to the goal he had set for himself. He would not be deterred from that goal. When this was finished perhaps, but not now.

He drew the Appaloosa up in front of Welch's elegant home and draped the reins over the hitching post. Walking down the boardwalk to the front door, Morgan shook his head in amazement. Known even by the lawmen he taunted as a gentleman bandit, Welch certainly lived the part. Somehow, this grand house with its fancy furnishings, had always seemed just a bit out of place in Leopard's Lair. The house was like a shrine to Mandell's unlawful ways and in many respects Morgan felt that was exactly what Welch wanted; a monument to his life of crime.

He knocked on the front door with its stained glass window at the top, but did not wait for an invitation before opening the door and stepping inside. Once inside, he was met by Welch's Mexican housekeeper, who told him Welch was in the study awaiting his arrival. Morgan moved down the long hallway to the study at the back of the house, past expensive paintings and ornate statues sitting on marble stands.

The door to the study was ajar and Morgan pushed it open and stepped inside. A grin curled his lips at the sight of the only man in the world he trusted. Welch Mandell was seated behind his impressive mahogany desk littered with maps and drawings, smoking his cheroot and chewing the end like he did when he was impatient.

Welch Mandell was a striking man. Fifty years old, he was tall, broad shouldered, powerfully built with blonde hair that age was turning more silver than gold. He had sharp gray eyes, the color of the Colt.45 strapped at his waist, now hidden by the tan silk waistcoat he was wearing. He was slim, immaculately groomed with a freshly trimmed mustache that he often smoothed when in deep thought, and had a wardrobe that would have been the envy of any eastern dandy.

The hands that had earned him the nickname of The Leopard lay in peaceful repose on top of the desk, the cheroot dangling from his lips.

"Well, it's about goddamned time!" he roared upon seeing Morgan.

Morgan grinned as he moved to the liquor cabinet under the open window and poured himself a drink before coming around the desk to sink into the gold leather chair opposite Welch.

"I'm right on time and you know it," he replied, smiling fondly at the older man. "If anything, I'm ahead of schedule."

"Well, goddamnit, Morgan, have you got her? Where is she?"

Welch demanded impatiently.

Morgan nodded, took off his hat, placed it on the corner of the desk, and sipped from his drink, enjoying Welch's chafing discomfort. "Of course I've got her, Welch. Have you ever sent me out on a job I didn't complete?"

"Well, where is she? Is she all right? I hear you killed one of the men over her."

"Will you take it easy? She's fine, she's at my place, and Patch needed killing anyway."

A frown creased Welch's brow as he absently flicked away the ash from the end of his cheroot while he studied Morgan doubtfully. "Your place? What the hell is she doing there? You were supposed to bring her to me."

"I changed my mind," Morgan replied casually. "I've decided to exercise my right and keep her for myself."

Welch bolted upright in the leather armchair, his gun-metal gray eyes narrowing. "Now, wait a minute, Morgan. That wasn't the plan. You're to turn her over to me until McCandless makes his move."

"Why should you have all the fun?" Morgan challenged quietly, his dark eyes studying the discomfort on Welch's handsome face. "The first thing you taught me was, that what I took was mine, the rite of capture, remember? I captured her, Welch. I want her, and I intend to have her."

Welch settled back in his chair and cleared his throat noisily. He turned in the swivel chair to pour himself a liberal shot of brandy from the cabinet, while trying to gather his composure. It was times like this he wished he had not taught Morgan so well, times when his words came back to haunt him.

Welch sipped his brandy and gathered his thoughts, pausing to direct a disgruntled glare at his young captain across the desk. Morgan watched him relentlessly, making the hair on the back of his neck stand on end.

Jesus Christ! Why had he ever taught Morgan to look a man straight in the eye without blinking? Those coal black eyes were piercing enough to make a man think he could read your thoughts. God help us both if that's true in this case, Welch thought uneasily.

"What's the matter, Welch, getting selfish in your old age?" Morgan taunted with a grin.

"Hell, no," Welch snorted with an uneasy glance. "I don't want the girl for the reason you think. It's just that..well, her father was like a brother to me, Morgan. You know that, and I promised Cooter she wouldn't be harmed."

"She won't be," Morgan assured him mildly, grinning when Welch's heavy brows raised in surprise. "She's agreed to my terms, so there's no reason for her to be harmed. As for Cooter, he knew he was taking a risk when he told you she was coming back to Texas and we hatched up this plan."

"I don't like it, Morgan. I don't like it at all," Welch growled, flicking away the ash from his cheroot.

"Well, I do. Look, Welch, I give my word I won't hurt her. I'm just going to enjoy her company for a while...the way you taught me, remember?"

Welch nodded uneasily as he drew deeply on the cigar. "I never thought that when I took you to that Mexican whorehouse on your fourteenth birthday, that what you learned would come back to haunt me," he said unhappily. Then his smoky gray eyes narrowed as he leaned across the desk and tapped a long, manicured finger emphatically. "I'm warning you, Morgan, that girl better not have a mark on her. Do you understand me? If she does, you'll answer to me."

Morgan observed his mentor with mild amusement over the rim of the glass as he tossed back the remainder of his drink. "Are you threatening me, Welch?"

"You're goddamned right I am!" Welch affirmed vehemently as his eyes locked with Morgan's. "If I find out you've mistreated her in any way, Morgan, I'll challenge you for her."

"You think you can take me?"

Welch's silver head moved in a slight nod, his gaze never leaving Morgan's face. "I taught you everything you know, smart-ass. I taught you, and I can still beat you," he said confidently.

Morgan's lips twitched, then curled at the corners in a genuine smile. "You say that like you mean it, old man."

"Old man? I can kick your ass any day of the week, sonny," Welch responded as a grin crept into his face. "Now, tell me about her. What's she like?"

"Like the picture you showed me of her mother," Morgan answered as he got up and crossed to the liquor cabinet to refill both their glasses. "Except maybe more beautiful. She's everything Cooter said she was."

"Then I can see why your pecker's hard already. I didn't know her mama well, but she was, without a doubt, one of the two most beautiful women I've ever known,"

"Yeah? Who's the other?" Morgan asked as he sank back into the chair across the desk from Welch.

For the barest instant Welch avoided his gaze, but then met the serious, thoughtful expression on Morgan's face. "The only woman I've ever loved," he answered quietly.

"Don't let Francine hear you say that. She'll catch you asleep and cut your pecker off."

Welch smiled and sipped his brandy, but made no reply. At the moment, his mind was a million miles away from Francine Comstock, the woman who ran his saloon, and who had been his mistress for the past ten years.

"You mean the married woman you told me about? The one who wouldn't leave her husband and run away with you?" Morgan prompted curiously.

A ragged breath slipped from Welch's lungs as he nodded.

"I don't understand, Welch, why you didn't just take her?"

"She had a family, Morgan, children. I couldn't take her away from them. I loved her too much for that."

"But you lost her anyway," Morgan reminded him, touched by the pain in Welch's gun-metal eyes.

"Yes, I did," Welch agreed. "She was the only good thing in

my life and I lost her. I guess that's why I can understand how Owen must have felt when Althea fell in love with his brother, how it must have ate him up inside."

"You've never told me her name, this woman you loved so much."

Welch raised one gold eyebrow at the sarcasm in Morgan's voice. "Don't be so quick to scorn love, Morgan. If you're not careful, one of these days you'll fall for some pretty little filly. When that happens, you'll be ready to pack your gun away and want to start over too."

"Don't count on it, Welch," Morgan snorted. "There are too many women in the world to settle for one. There hasn't been one born that could make me love her. Love, hell, what is love anyway? It's a word, that's all, just a word you use to coax some proper little thing into dropping her drawers."

Welch swirled the brandy in his glass while he studied Morgan's handsome, skeptical face. "That's what I thought too, once. I thought love was for fools, then I found out I was as big a fool as the rest of them. Even bigger, because the woman I loved was already married. No, Morgan, love is very real and usually very painful. I have the feeling if you ever find that out, you'll move heaven and earth to have the woman who steals your little black heart."

"Heart? I don't have one anymore. Owen McCandless ripped it out twenty years ago, right in front of my eyes. Feelings are worthless unless they help you get what you want. Isn't that what you taught me, Welch?" At Mandell's uneasy nod, Morgan went on. "Right now, the only emotion I know is hate and until I get Owen McCandless in my gun sights, it's the only one I'll ever have."

"Just be sure you don't transfer that hatred onto an innocent girl," Welch warned him.

"You think the only reason I want her is because of the old man?"

"The thought has crossed my mind."

"Well, you're wrong. There's more to it than that, Welch. She's beautiful. She's got spirit, and she's smart in a funny kind of way. And she's got the nicest set of tits I've seen in a long time," Morgan told him with a devilish grin, his eyes dancing.

Welch stirred uncomfortably and set down his brandy glass to pull on the cigar again. This conversation was making him very uneasy. He and Morgan had often discussed the various physical attributes they found interesting in some female or other, but those same things seemed obscene, indecent when it was Price's daughter.

"You said she agreed to your terms. How did you manage that?"

Morgan grinned as he stretched his long legs out beneath Welch's desk. "Like I said, she's a smart girl. I merely pointed out that she would be smart to stay on my good side and she saw the light. Besides," he added mischievously, "she was interested enough in me before she found out who I was. I think with a little cultivation, she may turn out to be quite a prize."

"Just you remember, this is not one of Francine's girls at the saloon," Welch growled. "She's been raised to be a lady. I know because her mama was one. I doubt she's ever been with a man."

"That's what she says," Morgan agreed with a smile that made his dark eyes dance. "I guess I'll know soon enough."

Welch squirmed in the big chair. His eyes narrowed to smoky gray slits while he studied Morgan across the desk. He was the only person alive who could see beyond that black veil that covered Morgan's emotions to the true nature of the man. Sometimes what he saw wasn't pleasant. What he saw now surprised him, for Morgan seemed truly intrigued with Amber McCandless.

"Morgan, I'm asking you to remember that Price McCandless saved your life once. Don't pay him back by hurting his daughter," he advised in a soft meaningful tone that made Morgan's brows arch in scorn.

"You don't have to remind me what I owe Price McCandless. I owe him my life. In the meantime, I should get a little something for my time and trouble and I'll take it in trade with the girl. I don't think that's asking too much, do you?"

Welch stared at him, then shrugged. "What difference would it make if I said no? You've got your mind made up, nothing I can say will change it," he grunted. "But I don't like it, Morgan."

"You made the rules, Welch," Morgan pointed out. "It's too late now to change them. The girl belongs to me, unless you're serious about challenging me for her."

"And what if I did, Morgan?"

"Then I guess we'd find out if you can still outdraw me, wouldn't we?"

Morgan's voice was soft, almost casual, but Welch caught the underlying current of steely determination below the surface. They sat staring into one another's unblinking eyes for several long moments. When finally Welch looked away first, his hands had begun to shake. He gripped his brandy glass to still the tremors as he forced a smile.

"Goddamn!" he breathed slowly. "I think you mean it, Morgan." Then he pulled on the cheroot and exhaled a fine plume of smoke toward the ceiling before adding, "All right, take the girl, but remember my warning. Not one hair better be harmed on her head or, so help me, I'll call your hand."

Then he smiled again as he ground out the cigar in the silver plated ashtray on the desk. "When do I get a look at this female that you're so worked up about? I can't wait to see what it is about her that makes you so damned determined."

"All in good time, Welch," Morgan replied as he tossed back the remainder of his drink and rose to his feet. "Maybe in a couple of days when I've had time to get to know her better," he added with a devilish grin.

He picked up his hat and put it on as he crossed Welch's soft carpet to the door. Pausing in the doorway, he turned back to observe Welch's uneasy face with a grin. "Don't worry about her, Welch. She's in good hands."

With a parting grin, he walked through the doorway, closed

the door securely behind him, and moved quickly down the hallway and out into the waning sunlight. It would be dark soon and
there were things he had to do before returning home to Amber.

***

Welch Mandell refilled his brandy glass and stared moodily
out the open window. Through the sheer curtain blowing about
in the light breeze, he watched Morgan gather up the Appaloosa's
reins and lead him down the street. He was still staring into space
when the study door opened.

"You're a goddamned fool, Welch Mandell, to let Morgan bring
that girl here. It was bad enough for him to take her off the stage
and turn her over to you, but now, my God, he's going to keep
her!"

Welch turned in the swivel chair, glaring at Francine Comstock.
"How the hell did I know he'd get a hard-on for her?"

"You should have expected it. You know how Morgan is with
women, or perhaps I should say, how women are with him. He'll
have that girl wrapped around his finger. Then what are you going
to do?"

"Just exactly what we've planned to do," Welch growled as he
lit another cheroot. "He'll sleep with her a few times and that'll be
the end of it."

Francine's finely sculptured brows rose doubtfully as she glided
into the room, closing the door behind her. She moved toward the
desk and perched one slender hip on the corner nearest Welch,
studying him with concern.

"It doesn't sit well, does it, Welch, knowing that in a little
while, Morgan will be sleeping with Price's daughter?"

Welch made no comment, but his golden brows knitted in
irritation while he chewed the end of the cigar between his teeth.
Francine's expression softened as she lifted one elegantly manicured hand to gently smooth back a lock of his unruly silver-blonde

hair. Her painted lips parted in a genuine loving smile as her cat-green eyes filled with emotion.

"Welch, Welch, what have you done?" she chided gently. "Don't you know how dangerous this game is that you're playing with Owen McCandless? What are you going to do if Morgan learns the truth?"

Welch's big shoulders moved in a shrug beneath the expensive silk waistcoat as he glanced up at Francine's beautiful porcelain features so furrowed in concern. "Who's going to tell him, Owen McCandless? Morgan will never believe anything Owen might say," he grunted.

"Won't he? Owen can be very convincing when he chooses, or so you've told me. All he has to do is plant the seed in Morgan's mind and that idea will fester until Morgan confronts you. What will you say to him, Welch? How will you be able to explain keeping the truth from him all these years? How can you possibly justify teaching him hate and vengeance, when all along his parents were killed for protecting you?"

Welch's keen gray eyes narrowed contemptuously. "I didn't teach him to hate. Owen McCandless taught him that without any help from me."

"But you taught him to kill, Welch," Francine pointed out quietly. Her fragile, painted beauty reflected pain when Welch pulled away from her caress. "You took that hate inside him and nurtured it, fed it, kept it festering, and all the time teaching him to use that gun until he was just like you."

"I raised him like he was my own after Owen killed his folks," Welch growled defensively, avoiding her gaze.

"Yes, you raised him," she agreed. "Raised him, trained him, made him a killer. You raised him to kill Owen for you, Welch, because you couldn't bring yourself to do it. What do you think Morgan will do when he figures out how you've used him all his life to do something you weren't man enough to do yourself?"

"That's enough, Francine!" Welch commanded coldly. "I'll deal with Morgan when and if I have to. You're underestimating him. He knows what I've done for him. He won't forget it."

"You're a fool, Welch," Francine said bitterly. "You've raised him better than that. If he ever learns how you've lied to him, he'll kill you, Welch, and you know it as well as I."

Welch lifted the brandy glass with an unaccustomed tremor in his hand that made the liquor slosh. Francine saw it and moved from the desk top to his lap. She placed her long arms around his neck and drew him close.

"Oh, Welch, please put a stop to this before it goes any further. Take the girl back to Owen before Morgan learns too much. Please, Welch."

Welch placed the cheroot in the ashtray and put his arms around Francine's trembling body, burying his face in her hair. "I can't, Francie. I gave Cooter my word. I have to do this for Price," he told her gently, his voice muffled by the swirls of rich auburn hair.

"For God's sake, Welch, you've killed the other six men in the posse that night. One of them was a Texas Ranger. Can't you give it up? It's been twenty years!"

Welch shook his head with a long ragged breath, then kissed the nape of her neck. "Somebody has to save that girl from Owen and since I'm the only man in the world he's afraid of, it has to be me. I have no choice."

Francine leaned back in his arms until her jade eyes met his and held, though the pain he saw cut Welch like a knife. "Welch, for God's sake, be honest with me for once," she pleaded, hating herself for groveling, but unable to stop. "Welch, don't you see what you're doing? You're lying to yourself, and to me. You told me years ago that you could never love me the way I hoped, and I accepted that. I know you've never stopped loving somebody else."

"What the hell are you talking about?" Welch asked impatiently.

Francine gently smoothed the furrowed lines from his headhead with the back of her hand, her eyes filling with tears. "Isn't it enough that Morgan may learn Owen's men were searching for you that night? Do you really want to face him if he should find out that the woman you've been in love with all these years, is his mother? Do you know what that would do to him, Welch, and to you?"

CHAPTER TWELVE

Amber stood alone in the cool, dark room watching Morgan's broad shoulders disappear down the street. Then, overwhelmed with despair, she sank down onto the couch and began to cry. Finally, after several minutes passed, she rose on shaky legs, wiped her eyes resolutely, and began to confront her situation. First, she had nowhere to go and no one who would help her escape. Second, she was certain the danger outside this house was greater than inside; and third, she had made a bargain with Morgan Devereaux and he would be returning soon to exact payment.

Oh, God, what had she done, she thought frantically as she wiped at her red nose with the back of a sleeve. In a little while, that man would be back to violate her body in whatever way he chose. It made her weak with dread. Suppose he wasn't satisfied with her and gave her to his men anyway? She bit her bottom lip, trying to remember bits of conversation she had heard from friends at school; something that might help her please Morgan Devereaux, but it was a blank wall.

Mother, oh mother, why didn't you prepare me better, she cried silently. Althea's admonition to wait for marriage was sadly inadequate in this instance. Amber squared her shoulders as a light of determination came into her golden eyes. Given a choice between Morgan Devereaux and his band of outlaws, she had made the only logical decision. She would simply have to do her best to please him. Perhaps if she explained how little she knew of such things, he would find a little patience, she thought hopefully.

She rose to her feet and wandered through the archway into a cool, stone kitchen to find Consuela humming softly as she rolled out dough on a long wooden table. To the immediate right of the

table stood a porcelain bath tub on curved iron feet, steaming
with hot water. Consuela noticed her with a pleasant gold toothed
smile and dried off her hands as she came around the table.

"*Senorita* ready for her bath?" she asked with a heavy Spanish
accent.

Amber nodded, then blushed when she realized the little
woman was waiting for her to undress and step into the tub. She
turned her back, hurriedly stripped off her clothes, and sank into
the delicious water with a sigh. Consuela took her clothes to the
back door and laid them outside on the red stone steps to be laun-
dered later. Coming back inside, she handed Amber a long handled
bath brush, then went back to her chores while the girl scrubbed
herself and washed her hair.

"Consuela," Amber said as she laid back in the warm water,
hoping it would help the tension drain away. "Do you know him
well?"

Consuela's braided head nodded soberly, but she smiled as she
deftly rolled out tortilla dough. "*Si, senorita,* I have known *senor*
Morgan for many years."

"Do you just work for him or do you live here also?"

A lively cackle of amusement rippled from the woman's lips as
she shook her head. "Oh, no, *senorita,* it is not as you think. *Mi
esposo*..my husband, was killed five years ago and I had no place to
go. *Senor* Morgan gave me a job looking after his home, but I do
not live here. I have a small house down the street," she explained.

Amber was mulling this over in her mind when Consuela held
up a large towel to wrap her in as she stepped out of the tub. She
dried herself thoroughly, pausing to glance at the little Mexican
woman curiously.

"Does he often bring female prisoners to his house?"

Consuela shook her head with a serious expression. "Oh, no,
senorita, he has never brought an *amante* to his home before."

Amber's brows knitted in thought as she recognized the word
from Morgan's earlier conversation with the woman. "*Amante,* what
does that mean?"

"It means lover, *senorita. Senor* Morgan has many women like the ones at the saloon down the street, but he has never brought a woman here."

Amber's cheeks flamed as she quickly glanced away from the woman's expectant expression. "I am not his lover," she said stiffly. "He kidnapped me and he's holding me for ransom. I am his prisoner."

Consuela's dark eyes danced in her plump olive face as she nodded seriously. "Before the new dawn breaks, the beautiful *senorita* will be his lover, no?"

"Not by choice, I assure you," Amber snapped.

Consuela patted the girl's damp hair with one end of the towel, then led her toward the bedroom at the other end of the house. "*Senor* Morgan sent one of his men ahead with instructions for me to provide you with suitable clothing. I hope you will find everything to your liking."

Having said this, she opened a wardrobe door to display a filmy silk nightgown floating from a hanger. Amber's eyes widened in astonishment when Consuela took it from the wardrobe and held it up for inspection. It was gorgeous, made of ivory silk with very thin straps to tie it in place on her shoulders, so sheer it was all but transparent. Her face flooded with embarrassment and she swallowed before she was able to find her voice.

"It's very beautiful, Consuela," she squeaked at last.

"*Senorita* will be very beautiful," Consuela said reverently. "*Senor* Morgan will be pleased."

Amber prayed to God that it was so, fingering the cool silk of the exquisite gown.. She thought she would, by far, prefer to please him than be ravished by the gang of killers who rode with him.

"Is *senorita* hungry?"

Amber shook her head, trying to swallow past the lump in her throat. It would soon be dark. He would be returning, she thought worriedly, glancing out the curtained window. How could she think of food when he might be on his way at this very minute?

"I must go now," Consuela announced to Amber's surprise. "I

have prepared a meal and left it on the stove. *Bueno noches, senorita,* I will return tomorrow."

Amber watched with growing distress as the plump little woman gathered up her shawl and scooted out the back door. No doubt the woman wanted to be gone when he got back. Well, so did she!

She dropped the towel and slipped into the gown. It was a perfect fit, she noted with disgust. The man had an uncanny ability to judge her size, it seemed. She found a set of inlaid silver brushes on the vanity that stood against one wall of the room and sat down to brush the tangles from her long hair.

She brushed her long hair until it dried and hung in swirls around her shoulders. By now it was dark and the air was filled with a chill that made her shiver.

Her throat felt tight and raw, her stomach seemed queasy as she wandered aimlessly through the house touching the colorful tapestries that lay across the couch in the outer room. She ventured to the front window and pulled the curtain aside to peer out into the night. She jumped back, letting the curtain fall back into place when gunfire suddenly erupted down the street, filling the night with flashes of light followed by the report of the shot echoing against the canyon walls. Accompanying the shots were loud bellows of laughter that made Amber weak with fear. She ran back into the bedroom, threw herself across the wide double bed, and pulled the heavy Mexican blanket up over her to block out the sound of that frightening laughter.

She was so scared! A tear seeped from beneath her lashes to spill down her cheek onto the bed. She wished fervently that her mother was there to tell her what to do. A bitter laugh burned her throat as she thought how ironic it was that she had saved herself for marriage and now her honor was about to be taken by an outlaw who lived by his own rules, with no regard for anyone else's feelings. It just wasn't fair!

She didn't think she could have more tears left, but they kept boiling up inside her, spilling out in hot bitter drops that burned her eyes, until at last she drifted into a restless, anxious sleep.

***

When Amber awoke later, she sensed almost immediately that she was not alone. Her eyes fluttered open slowly, but she lay immobile, trying to remember where she was. When it came back to her, she sat up and rubbed her eyes, wondering if Consuela had lit the lamp before she left, for it was now burning brightly in the adjoining room.

She glanced toward the doorway and felt the blood freeze in her veins as Morgan's tall frame materialized in the archway. He was hatless, his raven hair falling over one eye as he lounged against the door frame, and although he appeared completely relaxed, Amber sensed the tautness, the constant state of alertness that lay just beneath the surface.

"How..how long have you been there?" she asked through lips that seemed stiff and wooden.

"A while," was his noncommittal reply. "I'm glad you're awake. I was waiting to eat until you woke up and I'm starving."

She rose hesitantly from the bed, wrapping herself in the colorful *manta* as she got to her feet.

"You won't need that," Morgan said, indicating the blanket wrapped securely around her shoulders. "Leave it."

He waited until she reluctantly put the blanket back on the bed before walking back into the other room to sit down on the couch. Amber followed silently, painfully aware of the sheerness of the nightgown and the way it hugged her curves like a second layer of skin. Although she avoided looking at him, she could feel his eyes sweep over her as she padded across the room to take a seat on the edge of a cane-backed chair.

She raised her head, her eyes widening in surprise, when she saw the lace covered table and two matching silver candlesticks that glowed with soft flickering light. On the small table were two plates of appetizing food and a large bottle of wine, complete with two wine glasses.

"I don't understand," she stammered with a gesture at the

table.

"What did you expect? For me to come bursting in here, tear your clothes off, and ravish you on the floor?" Morgan asked in a sarcastic tone that made her face flame with embarrassment.

"I certainly never expected candlelight and wine from..an..an outlaw," she flared back. "I thought pain and degradation were more your style."

"Then, you thought wrong, didn't you?" he replied coolly, his dark eyes flashing over her again, pausing at the enticing swell of her breasts above the low neckline of the gown.

Amber motioned toward the bottle of wine, chilled and inviting. "So you're going to get me drunk first, is that the idea?" she asked haughtily.

His handsome face broke into a smile so brilliant it held her spell-bound. His olive skin gleamed in the soft light, his ivory teeth a flash of splendor that transformed his appearance, making his coal black eyes dance with amusement.

"No, not exactly. You said you've never been with a man. If that's true, it'll be easier for you if you relax, that's all."

"Oh, I see," Amber sniffed. "You want it to be as painless as possible. How thoughtful of you!"

"If you'd rather be thrown down on the floor without any niceties, we can do it that way too," he offered, his eyes narrowing in contrast to the easy smile on his face.

He watched in mocking silence as Amber's false bravado wilted. A moment later, she shook her head and swallowed.

"Then come over here and sit beside me," he commanded in a deceptively soft voice.

Amber forced her trembling legs to obey as she glided soundlessly across the room and sank down onto the couch beside him. She tried to keep her head down and her eyes averted as he deftly opened the bottle of wine and poured it into both glasses.

He had bathed, shaved, and dressed in clean clothes since she had last seen him. He was wearing a pair of charcoal colored trousers and an ivory shirt that clung to the contours of his body, revealing the powerful muscles that rippled in his shoulders and upper arms. The shirt was open half way down his chest to expose a heavily muscled torso covered with dark hair. He had rolled the sleeves up to the elbows, revealing strong sinewy forearms also covered with dark hair. Amber stared at his hands as he set the wine bottle back into place, shivering involuntarily. He was, without any doubt, the most masculine male she had encountered in her life. That was not a comforting thought.

She forced her eyes away from his strong brown hands, her gaze resting on the gunbelt that lay around his waist. She was seated on his left, the gun butt only inches from where her hands lay in the lap of the silk nightgown. She licked at her lips as the thought occurred to her to grab the gun, and make him take her home.

A soft chuckle roused her from her thoughts. She lifted startled eyes to find Morgan watching her with an amused grin curling his lips. "Don't even think it, Amber. You don't want to spoil a nice evening by doing something so foolish, do you?"

She shook her head as she reached for the wine glass he held out to her. The rich red liquid swirled dangerously close to the edge as her trembling hands lifted it to her lips. It tasted sweet and refreshing when she gulped it down and held out the glass for more.

He refilled her glass and watched as she sipped it more slowly, savoring each drop. He moved one plate in front of her and began to eat from the other. Amber tried to eat, but her throat had closed up, refusing to allow anything but the wine to slide down. Finally he pushed his plate away and drained his wine glass.

"You haven't eaten anything."

"I can't..I'm not hungry," Amber murmured while her mind raced to find some way of stalling him a little longer.

"Then we're wasting time," he said as he moved the table aside and turned to face her. "Stand up."

Amber stared at him in confusion for a moment, then obeyed

silently, rising on stiff legs to stand in front of him, twisting her
fingers anxiously while his dark eyes moved lazily over her.

"Turn around."

She did so hesitantly, painfully aware of how the sheer silk
clung to each curve of her body. Her heart was pounding so hard it
filled her ears with a loud thumping that sounded like thunder. It
made her breath seemed choked, almost painful.

She could not bring herself to look into his face, but she felt
his eyes burning into her body, scorching her flesh as he studied
her. She bit her lips together to stop their trembling. Her face
colored with embarrassment when she realized her nipples had
hardened and were standing erect beneath the filmy gown.

"Take off the gown."

Amber hesitated, frozen in place, then raised her head to whisper, "I can't, please, don't make me...I can't.."

Morgan did not speak, but lifted the pearl handled pistol from
its worn holster to cradle it in the palm of his hand. As Amber
watched in horror, he calmly raised the gun, and shot off the knot
that held the gown tied in place on her right shoulder. The bullet
severed the cloth without touching her skin, slamming into the
wall behind her with a deafening roar.

"Now shall I shoot off the other one?" Morgan asked pleasantly, chuckling softly when she shook her head vigorously.

Amber swallowed tightly and raised her trembling hands to
untie the strap on her left shoulder, then slowly lowered the gown
to the tops of her breasts.

"All the way, Amber," Morgan prodded while motioning toward her feet with the pistol.

Amber looked into his face, seeking mercy, but found his features as inscrutable as before. She hesitated, swallowing again and
squeezing her eyes together tightly, then with a shuddering breath,
let the gown fall to the floor in graceful shimmering folds. She
kept her eyes closed in mortification, but she heard the sharp intake of his breath when she stood before him, at last completely
naked.

For a moment Morgan's breath ceased as he stared at her voluptuous body in the soft glow of the candlelight. From the top of her shining head down the graceful neck to her firm white breasts with nipples, dark pink and erect, down the hollow of her flat stomach to the blonde patch of fluff between her slim thighs, she was even more incredible that he'd imagined. He felt his body leap to life with desire.

He slowly got to his feet, holstered the pistol, and moved toward her. Amber heard the couch creak from his weight and opened her eyes, staring in fascination at the erection that strained the crotch of his trousers. He halted directly in front of her and reached to take her into his arms. Amber whimpered softly as his hands moved across her bare back, pulling her closer while his head lowered to allow his lips to nuzzle at the silky flesh just below her ear.

"Put your arms around me, Amber," he commanded in a voice suddenly hoarse with desire.

She obeyed silently, clenching her eyes shut as her arms hesitantly encircled his neck, feeling the heat from his body warm her skin. The buckle of his gunbelt cut into her flesh and she flinched, then pulled back. Without letting her out of his embrace, Morgan reached down to unbuckle the gunbelt and dropped it behind him onto the couch.

Gathering her to him again, his hands caressed the firm flesh of her buttocks, cupping each one to press her tightly against him. Amber felt hot and light-headed as if she couldn't breathe, her chest heaving with the effort to catch her breath. She was trembling so hard it would have been impossible to stand if not for his strong arms that surrounded her, molding her to the hard maleness of him. For a moment she thought she might faint from the overwhelming rush of feelings that flooded through her.

"Kiss me, Amber," he murmured through the silk of her long hair.

Amber hesitantly pressed her lips to his, keeping her mouth closed, then pulled away quickly.

"Again, like you mean it," he ordered savagely, his dark eyes burning into hers with an intensity that made her shudder.

"I..I can't..I..I..mean..I..don't know..how..." Amber stammered awkwardly, feeling strangely foolish and embarrassed at the same time.

"Like this," Morgan growled as his lips came down over hers, warm and demanding, his tongue forcing entrance into her mouth, seeking her own and setting off explosions of warm, puzzling sensations that left her breathless. She answered his kiss, uncertainly at first, then with more confidence as the kiss deepened. Perhaps it was the wine that made her light-headed and flushed. Or perhaps it was the touch of his hands on her bare flesh that caused her to lean into his embrace as her tongue touched his, causing a flash of fire to leap through her veins.

Then in an unexpected motion, Morgan bent to scoop her into his arms. He carried her swiftly into the bedroom and laid her down on the double bed. Amber watched wide-eyed and fascinated, as if she was standing far away watching herself, as he quickly shed his clothes, staring in mute fascination until he stood beside her, tall and lean and muscular. She heard him laugh softly and raised her head to stare into his handsome face, and shuddered from the hot intensity she could see in his eyes.

She could hear him breathing, could inhale the clean masculine scent of him, feel the heat emanating from him as he towered above her in the dim light. The raw desire that filled his eyes made Amber weak with emotions she did not understand.. She gripped the colorful Mexican *manta* that covered the bed, closing her eyes and turning her head away, trying to combat the unaccustomed surge of longing that was threatening to overwhelm her.

"Look at me, Amber. Open your eyes and look at me," Morgan commanded in that low savage tone that demanded obedience.

Her eyes flew open, her head turning on the pillow to send him a look of confused desire. "Please, just do it and get it over with. Stop torturing me," she whispered.

Morgan's brows arched in momentary surprise. "You are much

too beautiful to torture, Amber," he said while his eyes moved lazily over her naked, shivering body in a manner that made her blush profusely and sent a surge of warmth through her that made her head turn into the pillow.

She gasped in surprise when he lay down beside her and took her back into his arms. He pulled her against him, his hands moving slowly, tantalizingly over her bare flesh, caressing the hollow at the base of her spine while his warm mouth claimed hers again. The touch of his naked body against hers sent shock waves crashing along her thighs and stomach, making her nipples feel taut. She had never seen a naked man before, or touched one. How could she have imagined the astonishing effect it would have on her senses?

She could never have imagined that the touch of his hands would feel like flames leaping along her body, or that his lips would feel like bolts of lightning striking her as they moved lazily across her throat.

The sensations his touch created were delightful. She was startled to discover that she was no longer afraid, but was enjoying his touch and his kisses. She wanted it to go on and on. She wanted to know more, to explore this tantalizing new experience further.

Although it had been years since she had lived on the ranch, Amber could remember seeing the animals mate when she was very young, so she had some idea what to expect now. To her surprise, he did not go about it right away, but continued to kiss her, his warm lips moving lazily on hers, as though he was in no hurry. While his mouth claimed hers, his tongue plundered, his hands moved over her silken skin slowly, exploring every hollow and valley. She gave an involuntary moan when his lips moved down her throat. Then a gasp as his hands caressed her breasts, not roughly as she might have expected but gently, almost tenderly, and then his mouth was there, warm and wet, sucking gently at her swollen nipples.

This was not what she had expected. She had resigned herself to pain and cruelty, not this slow tantalizing exploration that filled her with unfamiliar sensations which made her feel out of control and fearful of her own emotions.

He slid his hand down her thigh between her legs, pulled them apart, and poised himself just above her. Then he was thrusting into her. She drew in her breath sharply, crying out at the unexpected pain as she raised up from the bed, burying her face against his chest while she pushed frantically trying to dislodge him.

Above her, his head snapped up, his eyes widening with the sudden knowledge that she was, indeed, a virgin. "Goddamn!" he swore softly, staring down at her incredulously. "You weren't lying." Then he groaned and thrust into her again and again as if he couldn't stop, each time deeper making the hot stinging pain between her legs sharper.

Amber gritted her teeth, determined not to cry out again, her hands now clenching in the bed clothes as he moved against her in hard smooth strokes until she knew she had taken the whole length of him and the pain began to lessen.

He bent his dark head to nip gently at her breasts, then lifted it to claim her soft parted lips in a long sensuous kiss that left her faint and dizzy. She felt strange, as though she were an observer to this act instead of a participant, for while she felt betrayed by the sudden pain, the touch of his mouth on her breasts and lips flooded her with unbelievably pleasant sensations.

"*Bruja,*" he whispered hoarsely. "*Amante...bruja..*"

As he continued the hard quick thrusts into her, Amber felt his body dampen with a light film of sweat that mixed with the clean masculine scent of him to form a heady combination that made her senses reel. A moment later she felt his shuddering release.

She felt Morgan slide off her as he rolled over to sit on the edge of the bed. She opened her eyes, staring in surprise when he stood up and walked into the living room with no attempt to cover his nakedness. She reached down to pull the spread up over her bare breasts as he returned carrying the two glasses filled with wine and sat down beside her, extending one glass to her.

Amber took the glass hesitantly, watching him warily while rapidly blinking back the hot tears that burned her eyelids. The dim light played along his body, defining the muscles that rippled in his shoulders and arms, glistening off the black hair on his chest.

She was confused. There wasn't the smug triumph she had expected, only a thoughtful gaze that made her blush deeply and pull the covers higher around her throat.

"Drink your wine before it gets too warm," Morgan suggested pleasantly.

Amber had to use both hands to steady the glass, for she was still trembling violently. She sipped at the wine and stared at him over the rim of the glass while she tried to ignore the dull ache between her legs.

"I was wrong about you." Morgan's voice was casual but it contained a trace of puzzlement. "Did I hurt you?"

"Do you really care?" she snapped back, angry and accusing.

Morgan's steady black gaze revealed nothing as he sipped the wine and studied her in the dim light. He took note of the tremor in her voice, the tears that filled those enormous golden eyes, and the quiver in her chin as she proudly held her head up to glare at him like a wounded lioness. She was exquisitely beautiful, he thought as his eyes drifted down her tense, blanket covered body, then back to her face. More beautiful than any woman he had ever known, probably too beautiful for her own good.

"Do you feel better now? Now that you've scored another point against my uncle?" she said scornfully, although her voice lacked the sting she intended. She was too bewildered, too despondent for her accusations to have the bite she would have liked.

"This had nothing to do with your uncle," Morgan corrected gruffly. "I've wanted to do this since the first time I saw you."

Amber's brows arched in surprise for a moment before her eyes narrowed and her lips formed a snarl. "Do you always just take what you want? Regardless of who it hurts or..or other people's feelings?"

"Yes," Morgan replied with a direct gaze that made hers waver, then look away. "I learned a long time ago that if you wait for somebody to give you anything, you'll be waiting forever."

"That's the kind of attitude I'd expect from a man like you!" Amber flared angrily.

Morgan's left hand instantly gripped her throat, hard enough to partially cut off her breath, but not hard enough to seriously choke her. He leaned forward, his dark eyes blazing, his lips curled back over his teeth in a snarl that made Amber weak with fear.

"Don't try my patience, Amber," he told her in a soft ominous tone. "You stay alive only as long as I choose. Remember that."

He released her throat and Amber coughed and rubbed it gingerly, staring at him in horror. "What..what is it you want from me?" she stammered a few moments later.

He didn't answer right away, but let his hand move slowly from her throat downward along her stiff body, pausing to caress her breasts before moving onward, always keeping her eyes locked with his.

"That's simple, Amber, I want you. Right here in my bed whenever I feel like it. You'd be smart to cooperate."

His voice was deceptively soft, almost gentle, as he slipped his hand beneath the spread to run it slowly over her bare flesh. Amber gasped as his warm hand touched her, but was unable to break the burning contact with those piercing black eyes. Finally she swallowed and shook her head.

"I'll try to do what you want," she said in a hushed, defeated tone.

There was no triumph in Morgan's face as he removed his hand from beneath the spread, only a mild satisfaction that she had agreed to his terms without too much of a fuss. "So tell me, my little *salvaje gato*, how is it that you kept that fancy-assed easterner out of your pants?" he asked a few moments later after Amber had taken a healthy drink from her wine glass. An amused smile lit his face at her surprised expression and the blush that stained her pale cheeks.

"He took no for an answer," she mumbled without looking at him.

"Unlike me."

Her head raised in confusion at the teasing banter in his voice, surprised to find a cheerful smile on his face that transformed his appearance so drastically it made her head whirl. "I doubt that you know the meaning of the word," she said cautiously. "You might apologize for not believing me about...about..you know."

"I said I was wrong. I should have listened to Welch."

"Welch? Welch Mandell?"

Morgan nodded. "Yes. He warned me that I was underestimating you. He was sure you are as much a lady as your mother. Seems he was right."

Amber was puzzled at the off-handed compliment he had just given her and wondered if he had meant it as such. But it was his reference to her mother that snagged her attention. "My mother? What could an outlaw like Welch Mandell possibly know about my mother?"

"A great deal it seems. Though to be perfectly honest, he knew your father much better."

Amber's eyes were wide with astonishment as she stared at him silently. A wry smile touched Morgan's lips as he studied the surprise on her beautiful face.

"I see Uncle Owen failed to tell you about his past association with Welch."

"How could Uncle Owen know a man like that?"

"Years ago your father and Owen McCandless had a partner in the ranch when they first started out...Welch Mandell," Morgan explained with an amused smile. "Welch and your father were close friends back then. They remained friends through the years until your father's death. So Welch knows a great deal about both your parents and your darling uncle."

"I don't believe you," Amber challenged with a touch of her

normal spirit. "Uncle Owen said he'd never met Welch Mandell. Why would he lie about that?"

Morgan sipped from the wine glass, laying his left hand casually on the spread covering her breasts in a possessive manner that made Amber want to pull away. She was afraid to, afraid of stirring that terrifying anger that lurked just beneath the surface of that cool exterior.

"A man like Owen McCandless doesn't want anyone to know that he was once associated with such a notorious outlaw. It might cast doubt on his spotless reputation," he replied sarcastically. "I'm afraid, Amber, there are a great many things about your uncle that he's kept hidden from you."

"Isn't your unreasonable hatred for my uncle the reason for what you've done to me?" she questioned with a weak gesture from a trembling hand.

"Maybe, in the beginning," Morgan admitted nonchalantly. "But you're very beautiful, Amber. Too much of a temptation for *a man like me* to resist. And I see no reason why the time spent waiting for your uncle's reply should be wasted, when it can be enjoyed in so many pleasant ways."

The light that began to glow in his dark eyes made Amber shudder in dismay. It was obvious what he had in mind. She licked her lips quickly and sipped from her glass, trying to think of some way to keep him talking. "If Welch Mandell was such good friends with my father, why is he allowing you to do this to me?"

"He's not thrilled with the idea, but it's my right. He can't argue with that." He set his empty glass aside and took hers from her trembling hand, as well. "You may as well stop stalling, Amber," he said with a taunting grin. "The night is still young and we have lots of time."

The sharp intake of her breath combined with the expression of panic that flooded her face made him smile grimly as he pulled the spread from her wooden, protesting fingers and slid beneath it to gather her into his arms again.

"If you thought I'd just go to sleep and forget about you, I'm afraid you have a lot to learn about me, Amber. I don't require a lot of sleep. On the other hand, there are things I do require a great deal of and you, my beautiful *princessa de oro,* are the thing I require greatly."

Before Amber could protest, his warm lips claimed hers in a deep fiery kiss, his tongue seeking hers, setting off shock waves of unsettling sensations that left her weak and helpless. His naked body warmed her belly with renewed passion as it again grew hard and erect against her. His hands moved slowly over her flesh, leaving a path of sensual pleasure that disturbed her more than her fear. As his warm mouth trailed down her throat, alternately nipping gently, then nuzzling until her breath was coming in heated gulps, Amber moaned softly and pushed against his chest.

"Oh no, please, not again, no, no," she whimpered brokenly. The prospect of giving in to those unfamiliar, heated feelings again, filled her with dismay.

Morgan lifted his dark head, his eyes locking with hers with such fierce intensity she was unable to look away. "I won't hurt you this time, Amber," he said in a hoarse voice that revealed the depth of his desire.

"Please, not again, please," she implored with wide tear-filled eyes.

"Yes, again..and again..until I've gotten my fill of you..if that's possible."

His mouth silenced any further protest she may have had while his hands moved lazily on her skin, caressing her swollen nipples, then down the velvet hollow of her belly deftly forcing her legs open to allow a firm, but surprisingly gentle exploration of the soft channel below the blonde triangle between her thighs.

When his dark head dipped to nip at her puffy pink nipples Amber found her voice at last. "Please, if you're going to do this..please..just do it and get it over with," she begged breathlessly.

"No, Amber, only animals mate like that. I intend to savor every moment, every inch of you, every delicious, tasty morsel until I know your body as well as I know my own. Until you can't stand it a moment longer...until you beg me to put an end to the torture and make love to you. Until you want it as much as I do."

"No, no," she protested weakly. "I won't do that...I'll never do that."

"Yes, you will, Amber," he promised as his ebony eyes burned into hers. "You may be naive and inexperienced, but I'm not. By the time I have to return you to the outside world, no other man will ever be able to make you feel the way I can...ever."

He cut off her muffled protest with his mouth, firm and demanding, while his hands continued their expert assault on her senses until Amber was lost in a fog of sensual delight, moaning softly beneath his lips. She felt faint, plunging deeper into the waves that washed over her, carrying her away against her will.

Then, with a muffled groan, Morgan moved quickly to cover her body with his own, thrusting into her with slow smooth strokes that lifted Amber higher into that fog of delight. There was no pain this time, only a sensual pleasure she was helpless to fight.

"Look at me, Amber," Morgan ordered in a low savage voice. "Look at me. Keep your eyes open."

Amber whimpered softly, her face pressed against his hard chest, her hands reaching, clinging to his forearms as he plunged into her deeply again and again. The command in his voice was impossible to ignore and reluctantly her eyes opened to stare with a searing gaze into his. His dark face was only inches from hers, his eyes blazing with a passion-fed fire that reached out to sear her flesh.

"You're my woman, *bruja,* only mine," he said hoarsely, his lips nipping and nuzzling at her ear, then dipping to the smooth curve of her shoulder. His voice was so low and husky Amber wasn't able to fully understand the words. "You belong to me..Jesus...you are so beautiful..so sweet...*bruja,* you have bewitched me...."

As he plunged deeper and faster, Morgan felt Amber's body shudder, felt her hands slide up his arms to move over the muscles in his back. Unable to think clearly for the rising pinnacle of passion that boiled inside him, Morgan groaned deeply and plummeted past the point of reason, releasing his pent-up passion into her.

After a moment of lying spent, he slid off her to lie beside her, taking her back into his arms. She was still trembling when he reached down to pull the spread up over them both. Her face was pressed against the damp hair on his chest, her eyes closed tightly against the satisfied expression she was certain filled his handsome face.

"Sleep now, little *bruja,*" he murmured into the warm silk of her hair.

Amber snuggled closer to his hard, warm body and drifted off to sleep almost immediately with her head cradled in the hollow of his shoulder, her warm breath drying the sweat from his skin. When her soft breathing told him she was asleep, he leaned over to plant a kiss on her slightly parted lips. His eyes traveled over her slender form as she slept in the confines of his arms and a slight smile curled his lips. She looked like a sleeping princess, a *princessa de oro,* as he had called her—a golden princess.

"Sleep well, *bruja,*" he murmured as he relaxed beside her. But he was not ready for sleep yet, for his mind was too busy trying to determine how this beautiful, spirited girl had managed so completely, in a few hours time, to bewitch him, fill him with such a fierce desire to possess her that, even now, his body stirred again from her nearness.

CHAPTER THIRTEEN

From his perch in one of Owen's deep leather chairs, Cooter Jackson watched the proceedings with carefully concealed amusement. Owen and Sheriff Riker had been going at it like this for over an hour. He couldn't decide which was the funniest, Owen's determination to bring in outside help, or the sheriff's outrage at the suggestion that he was unable to cope with the situation on his own.

Owen looked tired and haggard as if he hadn't slept in days and Cooter was sure he hadn't. Since the message had arrived at the ranch two days before, Owen had paced the study, shouting orders and changing his mind a hundred times or more. His first instinct had been to round up all the men and begin an instant manhunt, but Cooter had wisely pointed out the folly of such a plan. Firstly, the message had given explicit instructions that should Owen do anything except comply with the ransom demands, Amber would be killed immediately. Secondly, neither Owen nor the sheriff had the slightest idea where to start.

"I don't want to hear anymore about it," Owen roared, slamming one clinched fist upon the desk top for emphasis. His face was lined and grim. For the first time, Cooter saw that Owen was showing his age. "I've already wired the Texas Rangers' office in Austin. They're sending one of their best men. He's on his way."

"One man?" Steven Riker jeered. "What do you think one man can do against Devereaux and Mandell?"

"Maybe nothing. Then again, he can't possibly do any worse than you have. You read the note," Owen went on in a quieter, more resigned tone as he slumped into the chair behind the desk and paused to light a cigar from the case Quincy had filled twice since Amber's abduction. "If I send out a big search party, they'll kill Amber. Perhaps the ranger can find their trail, their hide-out, something."

"How will they know whether or not you send out a search party? Mr. McCandless, can't you see they're counting on you being too scared to send one out? You can't just sit here waiting for a miracle. We have to do something now!"

Owen stared glumly at the tense face of the young sheriff across his desk and idly flicked away the gray ash of the cigar. His blue eyes were blood-shot and his hand trembled slightly when he lifted the cigar to his lips. For a moment, Cooter almost felt sorry for him.

"Be realistic, Steven. Mandell has obviously been planning this for some time. He's got his people everywhere. We're probably being watched every minute. Any move we make against him in force, he'll know about before we have time to be effective."

"If that's true, why don't you just pay the ransom?" Riker grunted.

A wry smile briefly touched Owen's face, then he shook his head. "I can't, it's just that simple. I don't have the money."

Cooter contained a smile at the astonished expression that flashed across the sheriff's face. Steven Riker had to blink rapidly and swallow twice before he could find his voice.

"I don't understand, Mr. McCandless. How can you not have the money?"

Owen wearily gestured toward the open window. Beyond the fluttering curtains, Riker could see two dozen ranch hands milling about down by the corrals, talking in subdued tones among themselves.

"I have assets totaling well over that amount. Probably several times over but....those assets are tied up in land, cattle, mines, and the like. As for cash, my cash on hand doesn't even come close. Oh, I can come up with the money but it will take time, weeks, maybe months, and time is the one thing I have in limited supply right now."

"But if you don't pay the ransom they'll kill Amber!" Riker cried.

"Maybe not," Cooter pointed out from his perch in the deep leather chair. "Maybe he's bluffin'."

A bitter snort ripped from Owen's throat as he glanced scornfully at the old wrangler. "And I can walk on water," he sneered. "You know better than that, Cooter. Welch Mandell will do exactly what he says he will if his terms aren't met to the letter. The life of one innocent girl won't cause him a minute's worth of concern. You know that as well as I."

Confusion replaced the surprise on Steven's face as he looked from one man quickly back to the other. What was going on here? Had he missed something?

"Don't you think the fact that Miss Amber is Price's daughter might have some bearin' on that?" Cooter asked quietly. The old man's deep blue eyes pinned Owen's in a challenge that filled the air with tension, despite the softness of his voice.

"Not for one goddamned minute! If anything, it only makes his revenge sweeter. He's got to know what Amber means to me. That's why he's doing this.

"Anyway, I can't afford to take that chance, Cooter. I can't pay the ransom in the time he's given me so I've done the only thing I can. I've called in expert help from the Rangers. It's their job to deal with men like Mandell and Devereaux. As far as I can see, it's the only thing I can do to save my niece's life."

"As far as I can see you're a damned fool!" Cooter told him at the doorway where he'd paused with one gnarled hand on the brass doorknob to look back over his shoulder. "Pay the ransom, Owen, even if you have to bargain with Welch for more time. You start messin' with the Rangers, gettin' them involved in this, and you'll be sorry. Take my word for it, you'll be sorry."

Owen flicked the ash from his expensive cigar into the crystal ashtray beside him. His icy blue eyes narrowed beneath furrowed brows as he stared hard at Cooter. "I don't need your advice, old man. And, Cooter," he added. "You better get your priorities in

order. You're either with me on this or against me. You can't have
it both ways."

The old wrangler's gaze never wavered. He eyed Owen steadily
for such a long time that Riker began to wonder if Cooter would
ever reply. When he spoke finally, there was a razor edge to his
voice that caught Owen off guard, and made the sheriff's brows
raise in confusion.

"My priorities are in order, Owen, always have been. I want to
see Miss Amber returned safely no matter what it costs and no
matter how the price is met, whether it be in money or blood.

"I'm warnin' you, Owen, no matter what Welch's intentions
are toward Miss Amber, you put the Rangers on him and you'll
start somethin' you cain't finish. Maybe you should think about
your priorities, Owen. Which is more important to you, your
goddamned money or Miss Amber's life? Think about it."

Without giving Owen a chance to reply, the old wrangler
limped through the doorway, then slammed the heavy doors shut
behind him with a resounding bang.

Owen ran one hand through his graying hair, briefly resting
his head in his hands. Then he shook himself, and straightened up
to reach for the half-smoked cigar.

"What was that all about?" Riker asked with a puzzled glance
at the closed doors. His eyes came back to Owen's concerned face
as he moved to take the chair Cooter had vacated.

"None of your goddamned business!" Owen barked with a
meaningful glance in Riker's direction.

"Look, Mr. McCandless, if there's something more to this that
I ought to know..."

"I said it was none of your business!" Owen roared. Both his
hands had clenched into fists on the desk top. "Cooter is an old
fool! I don't know why I bother keeping him around. He used up
his usefulness to me years ago."

"I think he's right about bringing in the Rangers."

Owen lunged up from his chair and stalked back and forth
across the expensive Oriental rug several times. The cigar was

clinched between his teeth, raising soft smoky rings toward the ceiling as he paced. Riker watched, wondering just how much more Owen knew than he was willing to reveal.

In spite of Owen's heated denial, Riker was quite certain there had been a good deal of truth in what Cooter had said. His eyes narrowed as he recalled the almost intimate way the two men had discussed Welch Mandell. Owen McCandless knew Mandell all right, and quite well, if Riker was correct. The old liar had sworn he had never met the outlaw only a couple of days before right here in this house. He wondered what it was that Mandell wanted revenge for. He'd give his left arm to have the answer.

"Bringing in the Rangers is a chance I have to take," Owen said at length. Riker was roused from his thoughts at the abrupt sound of the rancher's voice, but Owen continued to pace, speaking more to himself than to the sheriff. "I can't pay the bloody ransom, at least not in the time they've given me. I've got no other choice. I've got to find where they've taken Amber and get her back myself. There is no other way."

"What if you can't, Mr. McCandless? The Rangers have been hunting for Mandell's hideout for years, and it's never been found. What makes you think one Ranger will be able to find it now?"

Owen swung around to face him, his face grim with determination. Through the weariness and worry, Riker still felt the chill that lay behind those icy blue pools.

"Because I have no other alternative, that's why! I'll find that cutthroat bastard if it means combing every inch of those mountains on my hands and knees. I'll get Amber back. You can count on that. And when I do, Welch Mandell and his renegade pal Devereaux will have reason to regret the day they tangled with me."

"But what about Amber? What if Mandell finds out you've brought in the Rangers? He might kill her before you can get to her."

"If one hair on her head has been harmed by either of them, they better pray the Ranger gets them before I do!" Owen vowed in a cold ominous tone that left no doubt in the sheriff's mind of his intentions.

"Now stop whining for God's sake, Steven. I don't want to hear another word about 'what if.' I want my niece back safe and sound and I'll be very grateful to the man who helps me accomplish that."

He sank back into the chair and rolled himself beneath the heavy desk. Folding his hands, he smiled craftily.

"I'm increasing the reward on Devereaux another five thousand dollars and I'll match that with another five thousand for Mandell. Put the word out. And, Steven," he added. "If you help me get Amber back safely, there's another twenty thousand for you personally. Does that inspire you to look just a bit harder for some clue?"

Sensing the rancher's vulnerability, Riker pressed his advantage.

"That's a generous offer, Mr. McCandless. However, a monetary reward isn't what I had in mind."

"Spit it out, Steven. Name your price."

"I want Amber. That's my price. If I help you get her back safely and make sure Mandell and Devereaux will never get in your way again, it should be worth a lot more than money. I want Amber for my wife. That's my price."

Owen's astonishment changed to outrage. "You're insane! I'll never agree to that arrangement!"

"Oh, I think you will, Mr. McCandless," Steven replied confidently. "You see, I may not know exactly what kind of connection you've had with Welch Mandell in the past, but I'm willing to bet you don't want it made public. I can guarantee that won't happen. I'm a lawman; what could be simpler than a lawman making certain Mandell doesn't live long enough to reveal anything you want kept quiet? All I need is your word that when it's over and the dust has settled, that Amber will become my wife."

"I won't be blackmailed!"

Riker chuckled softly, never taking his eyes from Owen's face.

"That's such an unpleasant term, Mr. McCandless. I prefer to think of it as a purely business arrangement. It's up to you. Just how important is it to you that Mandell remain a stranger?"

"Goddamn you, Riker!" Owen stormed. His face had turned pale beneath the Texas bronze. A white ring had formed around his tightly compressed lips from the rage that roared through him. It was a struggle to keep his fury from erupting into violence. The smug smile on the sheriff's face made his hands itch to reach inside the top drawer of the desk and erase that confidence with the.45 Colt that lay there, but he contained the thought with a visible effort and tried to think rationally.

After several tension filled minutes passed while he debated, Owen sighed and sagged in the chair. He reached for another cigar and cursed himself for the way his hand shook when he held the gold lighter to the tip of it.

"All right, Steven, we've got a deal. But," he added sharply to erase the victorious grin that flashed across Riker's face. "There are two conditions. First, Amber must be returned safely and second, Welch Mandell must not be taken alive. Understand?"

Riker nodded before allowing himself another smile. Then he got to his feet and moved around Owen to the liquor cabinet beneath the window. He poured two liberal shots of Owen's imported brandy into crystal glasses, placed one on the desk before the rancher and took his seat again.

Owen ignored the drink and continued to stare grimly at the smug younger man. Riker sipped his brandy until curiosity claimed him. "Just how well do you know Mandell, Mr. McCandless?" he asked with an air of anticipation.

"None of your goddamned business!" Owen snapped. "Let's get one more thing straight, Steven. Whatever connection exists between myself and that murdering outlaw is no one's business and I will not tolerate any further questions on the subject. Is that clear?"

"Crystal clear, Mr. McCandless." Riker finished his drink and rose to his feet with a smile. "Anything else?"

"Yes, get the hell out of my office!" Owen snarled. "Don't let me see your face again until you have some news."

Riker shrugged and walked toward the door. He paused to look back, but Owen had already dismissed him and was lost in his thoughts.

Riker left the house and mounted, passing in front of the office window on his way out of the ranch yard. Owen watched him ride away through narrowed eyes. "I've lived fifty-five years by my own rules," he said grimly. "No smart-assed kid is going to blackmail me at this stage of the game. Once Welch has been dealt with, my young friend, you've got quite a surprise coming. You'll have a hard time holding me to my word when you're as dead as he is."

CHAPTER FOURTEEN

Amber stirred, her brows furrowing in uneasiness at the unfamiliar arm wrapped around her body. As the morning air chilled her nostrils, she unconsciously snuggled closer to the man sleeping next to her. Slowly her sleepy mind awoke and her eyes popped open. Realizing it had not been the nightmare she had prayed she would awake from, she knew the owner of the long sinewy arm that held her so possessively was her captor.

As she came further awake, she realized she was lying on her side, her face pressed into Morgan's hard chest. Even in the gray dawn's chill, she was shocked at the tingle that spread through her blood at the feel of their bodies touching beneath the Mexican *manta*.

She lay very still, afraid to move for fear of waking him. The dull ache between her thighs and the tenderness in her breasts were sharp reminders of the consequences of arousing this man. So she lay perfectly still and listened to the thumping of her heart in the quiet that had settled upon the outlaw compound.

If she were completely honest with herself, she would admit that the past night in his arms had not been totally unpleasant. Of course, she reminded herself sternly, she had been at a considerable disadvantage for while she was a novice at making love, Morgan Devereaux was a master of the art. She could hardly blame herself for a mild physical response when he had the experience to play her body like a violin. A warm flush covered her at the memory of the unfamiliar surge of passion that had erupted deep within her. How was she to know she possessed such strong feelings? Her mother had only spoken vaguely of a wife's duty and how certain things had to be borne in exchange for the protection of a husband's name.

Amber closed her eyes briefly as the image of her mother and father suddenly flashed into her mind. She could remember waking up early and trotting down the hall of that little house at the opposite end of *Sierra Vieja* from Uncle Owen's grand mansion to find their bedroom door closed, and the muffled sounds of soft laughter coming from inside. She smiled as she realized her mother's stern admonitions were more than a bit hypocritical. She was certain now that her parents had enjoyed a very satisfactory physical life and wondered why her mother had not told her how pleasant it could be.

Shifting a bit so she was able to tilt her head upwards, Amber had to remind herself this man was an outlaw with no scruples, for he looked like a young, almost innocent boy as he slept. Locks of ebony waves fell over his forehead. Long sooty lashes shadowed his cheekbones, making it difficult to remember that he was not the innocent he appeared at this moment. She blushed again when she remembered learning that the olive hue of his skin was the same all over his body.

Again she felt the guilty stirrings of appreciation as she stared at him in the early morning light. He was incredibly handsome, like one of those Greek gods she had read about in school. He was male perfection personified, she decided with an appraising glance downward.

Though he was covered by the blanket, she now knew his powerfully muscled body as well as she knew her own. She'd certainly had ample opportunity to get acquainted with it during the past hours. From the granite biceps in his upper arms, down his furry chest with ropes of muscles that rippled when he moved, down his flat, hard stomach and beyond to the strong, muscled thighs and long sinewy legs, he was the picture she had carried in her mind for years of the perfect male; strong, handsome, virile, and sensual when he chose to be.

She wondered how she could still find this man so attractive after what he had forced her to endure in the preceding hours. She was deeply disturbed by the conflicting emotions that roared through her. She should hate Morgan Devereaux for what he had done to her and part of her did hate him fiercely. But there was another part of her that would not be silenced. A part that responded to his touch with such a fever it left her breathless.

She pressed her lips together tightly with renewed determination to keep her hatred for him uppermost in her mind. He was a terrible man, she told herself; an outlaw, a killer, a cold ruthless man who used other people for his own twisted purposes with no regard for their feelings. His treatment of her was proof of that. So why did she still sense another side of him, something warm and tender that lay buried so deep inside that bitter shell he had built around himself? There had been fleeting glimpses of a kinder side of his nature when he was making love to her.

Even as she stared at him, his eyes opened. It was a moment before Amber realized he had caught her staring. She gasped and drew back as far as the arm around her would allow. Her cheeks burning with embarrassment, she refused to meet his amused eyes, focusing instead on the ceiling.

"See something you like?" Morgan taunted softly, his dark eyes gleaming.

Amber refused to answer, twisting the blanket in her nervous hands. What if he took her curiosity as a sign that she wanted him to take her again?

"It's not like you to keep quiet for very long. What's the matter, Amber, you're not sick, are you?"

"No, Mr. Devereaux, I'm not sick! You needn't worry. I'm not going to die before you collect your ransom."

The soft chuckle that followed her heated statement made her even more furious. She finally looked him in the eye, trying to maintain that direct, piercing gaze, but lost the battle and glanced away.

"Good, I'm glad to hear it. It would be a shame to waste what time we'll be together," Morgan replied with a teasing grin.

"Don't you think about anything else?" she snorted, pulling the blanket up around her neck. She tried to pull away, but Morgan held her firmly.

"Now, how could any man think about anything else with you around?" he inquired softly as his dark head dipped to nuzzle at the hollow of her throat. The touch of his lips sent a shudder of pleasure through Amber. She fought back the gasp that burned her throat.

He rolled toward her, moving beneath the blanket to take her fully into his arms. His hands began a sensual exploration that made her tingle with anticipation as he deftly opened her legs with one knee.

Lying on top of her, kissing her lush, parted lips Morgan was surprised at her lack of resistance. She wasn't responding to his caresses as he would have liked, but neither was she fighting him. Maybe she had finally accepted the fact that she belonged to him. If that was true, it would only be a matter of time until she would look forward to making love with him. A frown crossed his face when it occurred to him that some part of him would not be satisfied until she desired him as much as he desired her.

The thought was a disturbing one. Morgan had never worried about how much pleasure a woman might find in his arms. He took his own pleasure without much concern for the woman's needs, but there had never been any shortage of willing females, so he supposed he wasn't too unsatisfactory in that department. However, until this glorious mixture of little girl and breath-taking woman stumbled across his path, he had never felt the need to completely satisfy a woman. What was there about this tantalizing little vixen that brought those feelings to the surface? Had she so totally bewitched him with her stunning body and wide, innocent amber eyes that he was falling prey to the same tricks as other men?

He shook his head, wondering about the implications of it all, then decided he was wasting time. In a few days his life's goal would be reached and he would have to return her to the outside world. There would be time enough then to sort it all out. For now his body demanded the exquisite gratification it would find between her silken thighs.

***

Later, Amber lay quietly watching him from the warmth of the bed while he rose and moved about the room locating his clothes. In a few moments he was standing in front of her wearing the charcoal trousers and ivory shirt of the previous evening. She was unaware of the tiny smile that softened her lips as she watched him.

The sun was up now, filling the room with warm light, making sunbeams dance around her head. When Morgan glanced up to give her a quick smile, she felt her heart skip a beat. Every time he smiled, she was amazed at the change in him. It was almost as though he changed from one man into another. She felt much safer with the one who smiled.

"Well, come on," he chided gently with a teasing grin. "It's time to get up, sleepy head, unless you want to spend the entire day in bed. If that's the case, I have to have breakfast to keep up my strength."

Amber realized he was teasing, but her face burned. She lifted her chin and put as much ice in her voice as she could muster when she replied briskly, "I didn't realize you had a limit, Mr. Devereaux. I thought you never ran down."

Morgan laughed softly, his dark eyes dancing with mischief, making it hard for Amber to keep up the facade of aloofness. "There are limits to everything, Amber. "

He flashed a quick glance over her body. Unconsciously, Amber pulled the blanket tighter around her throat, her wide golden eyes watching him warily now.

For an instant, irritation flared in the depths of those coal black eyes that studied her so thoughtfully. His lips compressed into a thin line at her defensive actions, but then he smiled again and stepped away from the bed.

"I don't know about you, but I'm starving."

He walked into the living room and returned in a moment with a bundle containing Amber's dress and the frilly underthings she had been wearing when he took her from the stage.

"You can put these on for now. After breakfast, I'll take you down to the store and get you some new things."

He tossed her the bundle and turned back into the living room. Amber waited a moment, then hopped out of bed and quickly slipped into the welcome warmth of the clothing. Although it was mid-June and the merciless Texas sun could fry an egg at noon on the plains, here in the box canyon it was cool.

Keeping her ears tuned to the other room, Amber fastened the last of the buttons on the high-necked dress and ran the brush through her tangled hair. In moments she was neat and tidy. She turned from the mirror with a satisfied smile. Then her eyes fell upon the stained sheets that told the grim story of her lost virginity. The smile quickly faded and became a bitter grimace.

"Has Consuela come?" she called in an effort to break the despair that had settled upon her.

"No," came Morgan's answer from the other room. "I told her not to come today."

Amber had entered the living room and was standing in the archway eyeing him coolly. Morgan glanced up from buckling the black leather gunbelt into place around his waist, wondering how women could change from one mood into another so quickly. He tied the leather thong around his thigh and straightened up to his full height, staring at her silently for a moment.

Amber choked back the shudder that had begun at her toes and was rushing upward at a dizzy pace. Whatever had made her think he was anything but a black hearted gunslinger, she wondered vaguely as her narrowed eyes swept over him, landing with a contemptuous glare at the deadly .45 strapped to his left hip. He wore the gun like most men wore a hat, easily, naturally, as though it was a normal part of him, a functioning organ.

Morgan watched the conflicting emotions tear through her eyes. "It may surprise you to find out I can cook," he told her with no outward acknowledgment of her feelings. When he turned toward the kitchen, Amber followed.

"Yes, Mr. Devereaux, it would surprise me," she said haughtily. "I had no idea you knew how to do anything but kill people and terrify helpless women."

Morgan stopped so abruptly that Amber almost stumbled into his back. He swung around to face her with all the grace of a mountain lion about to strike. His black eyes glittered dangerously, his lips now a thin line that curled back over perfect ivory teeth in a snarl that sent shivers of fear down her spine, made her instantly regret the harsh words.

"I know how to do a lot of things well, Amber," he said in a low savage tone that was more frightening than if he had shouted. "Killing and terrorizing are only two of my achievements. Another is the ability to cut out your tongue so smoothly you won't even miss it until you try to speak. One more nasty remark from you and I'll be only too happy to demonstrate. Do you understand?"

Amber nodded frantically, her eyes wide with fear, one hand at her throat. His ebony eyes held hers in a silent, ominous gaze that made her knees weak. Then Morgan reached out to touch one satiny cheek with a forefinger.

"You are so beautiful, Amber," he went on in that same terrifying tone. "I gave my word to Welch you would be returned unharmed. Don't make a liar out of me. I don't want to scar you forever; that would be such a waste, but if you fail to keep a civil tongue in your head, you'll leave me no choice. I don't take shit like that from my men and I'm sure as hell not about to take it from you."

Satisfied the panic stricken expression on her face meant she was completely convinced of his sincerity, Morgan turned away and proceeded into the kitchen. Amber followed meekly behind, her rebellious thoughts subdued for the moment by stark terror. She took a seat in the chair by the small oval table he indicated and watched as he dug into cupboards and drawers to find the utensils he needed. In moments, delectable aromas were filling the kitchen. In spite of her fear, Amber sniffed the air eagerly. It came as a surprise to realize it had been ages since she had eaten and now her stomach was gnawing in anticipation.

"I'll set the table if you'll tell me where to find everything," she offered meekly.

Morgan turned with a concealed smile at her downcast eyes. Her cheeks were beginning to recover the bloom that had been lost when he scared the defiance out of her. He motioned toward a cupboard parallel to the table, then turned back to the skillet on the wood stove.

"In there..help yourself."

Amber scurried to take plates and glasses from the cupboard and set two places at the table. She opened two drawers before locating the silverware, then finished the place settings. The glasses were hand-blown crystal, heavy and elegant; the silverware genuine sterling silver with scroll work on the handles that indicated the work of a master. She glanced from the hand painted china to the broad shoulders that filled the ivory shirt with rippling muscles.

"At the risk of losing my tongue, may I ask a question?"

Morgan turned his head and nodded. He contained the smile that tickled his lips, kept his face inscrutable. She wasn't one to remain docile very long, but somehow it was that very quality that made her so damned fascinating.

"As long as you can speak to me in a civil tone."

"Where did you get all these lovely things?" she asked with child-like curiosity.

"I didn't steal them, if that's what you're thinking."

"I wasn't insinuating anything," she retorted in a more defensive tone. "I was merely asking."

Morgan moved toward the table, silently filling the plates with something that smelled wonderful. "I bought them," he explained matter of factly without looking at her. "Most of it anyway. The glasses and china I bought in Mexico and the silverware, what's left of it, belonged to my mother."

Amber picked up her fork with curious eyes, turning it over to examine the delicate scroll effect more closely. "It's extraordinary. It must be very valuable."

"Only to me," Morgan replied bleakly as he placed a plate of hot tortillas wrapped in a cloth on the table, then took his seat. "A few pieces were all I was able to salvage. Most of them were tarnished beyond repair by the fire."

Amber's brows lifted in surprise, her fork pausing halfway to her mouth while she stared at him across the table. "Fire? What fire?"

"The one your beloved Uncle Owen started with my mother's lace curtains."

"I don't understand."

Morgan looked at her thoughtfully, his eyes veiled and inscrutable, but the strain in his voice was strong enough that Amber caught it when he spoke finally. "I don't want to talk about it."

Amber knew it was useless to try to get anymore information from him. She didn't want to risk angering him again, so she sighed and dropped the subject. Turning her attention to the food on her plate, she was surprised to find it both delicious and different. There were scrambled eggs with a mixture of onions and peppers in a tasty sauce containing Mexican spices. It was heavenly. She cleaned her plate, then reached for another hot tortilla. Munching it slowly, she watched Morgan finish his eggs and sip from the delicate china coffee cup.

"That was delicious, Mr. Devereaux. You can cook."

Morgan studied her over the rim of his coffee cup. He settled back in his chair and rested his elbows on the table, cradling the cup between both palms.

"Thank you," he said dryly, smiling slightly when her cheeks flushed with confusion. "Learning to cook is a matter of survival when you live alone. Or maybe self defense. And stop calling me

Mr. Devereaux, my name is Morgan. That's what I prefer you call me."

"I'm sure if I fail to obey, you'll cut out my tongue," Amber remarked with a spark of her former defiance.

"You'd certainly be a lot less trouble if you couldn't argue," he said agreeably.

"You prefer meek little mousy women then? Someone who does exactly what you say without challenging your male superiority?"

Surprisingly, Morgan grinned and shook his head. "I didn't say that. Although there's a lot to be said for a woman who knows her place."

The insolence in his voice rankled. How she wanted to erase that confident smirk from his handsome face! The fact that they were separated only by the small table didn't help her mood any. Even though he was across the table from her, she could feel the sensual tension between them as his dark eyes flickered over her possessively. The arrogance of the man!

"You're a very insolent man, Morgan Devereaux. Do you seriously believe the only purpose a woman has in this world is to serve your..your crude needs? I'll have you know I have a certificate to teach school. I am not one of your mindless little tarts whose sole use in life is to lay down every time you snap your fingers!"

Further enraged by his amused silence, Amber leaped to her feet. "And furthermore, I intend to see that you pay for the abominable way you have abused me! I'll see you hang if it's the last thing I ever do."

"That's been said by more capable people than you," Morgan pointed out dryly. "It hasn't happened yet."

"Oh, but it will! My uncle will see to it."

"Your uncle is a dead man, Amber," Morgan told her in a deceptively soft voice. He set the cup back into its saucer and rose to his feet, leaning forward with his palms placed on the table until his lean dark face was only inches from hers.

Faced with the growing danger she could see in his snapping

black eyes, Amber felt her legs go weak with sudden fear. Her rash anger had gotten the better of her common sense again, making her hastily regret her brave words.

"The clock is ticking off the minutes he has left. If you have any sense at all, you'll curb that reckless tongue of yours. I am not a patient man and you've just used up the last warning I intend to give you. If you wish to leave this canyon alive and healthy, sit down and shut the hell up!"

Amber sank back into her seat, clenching her fingers tightly together to still their trembling. She swallowed and finally raised her head to find him calmly sipping the last of his coffee as though nothing had happened. The sparkle of anger had left his eyes. In fact, a tiny smile played at his lips as he observed her silently.

"You are the most exasperating woman I've ever met," he said at last with no trace of anger.

Amber stared at him in astonishment. He was like a chameleon, the way his moods switched so abruptly from unspeakable danger to amusement. She bit her lip, wondering when she would learn not to anger him.

"I didn't mean to insinuate you were brainless," he went on. "I am aware of your intellect, Amber, but at times you certainly don't show it. You take every word I say and turn it into a personal insult."

"Forgive me. It's difficult to be pleasant when you've been kidnapped and know you're being used as bait in some sinister plot to murder your only living relative," Amber said. Although her voice was soft, she met Morgan's gaze defensively. "I resent what you've done to me and I want to see you pay for it. Is that so unreasonable?"

"No, I suppose not," he agreed. "In your place I'd probably feel the same way. But you'd do well to remember that you stay alive only as long as you're of some benefit to me, whether it's being a hostage for money or in my bed. When you cease to be of value to me, you cease to breathe. The faster you accept that and stop fighting me, the easier it will be for you."

"So I'm supposed to smile and be your whore and thank you for the privilege? I'll do what you demand of me, Morgan Devereaux, to stay alive, but there'll be a day when you'll be in my position. When I hold your life in my hands, believe me, you'll find me as merciless as you've been to me. I swear you'll pay for what you've done to me, if it takes the rest of my life."

0223-SLAT

CHAPTER FIFTEEN

Amber was acutely aware of Morgan's firm hand beneath her elbow as he propelled her along the dusty street toward the store. After turning onto the main street from the quiet little side street on which Morgan's house was located, Amber was instantly fascinated by the peaceful air that prevailed in the settlement.

She glanced around at the distant canyon walls, squinting into the bright sun. She could barely make out the trail that wound down the canyon into the town. Further up, toward the point where the trail burst from the steep crags, she could faintly make out the figures of two men with rifles whose barrels caught and reflected the sun.

"This is incredible!" she breathed in awe. The wonder on the girl's face lit up her enormous eyes with a sparkle that turned them topaz as she turned her head to see everything.

Morgan looked down with a grin. "It's called The Leopard's Lair."

Amber tilted her face up to watch him while he spoke, irritably noting the quiet pride in his voice. Wasn't it bad enough that he was an outlaw without being so proud of it?

"I grew up here. Of course, all this wasn't here then," he went on with a gesture toward the building they were passing.

"Why is it called that?"

"After Welch, I suppose. Years ago somebody called him The Leopard and the name stuck. Welch found this place accidentally twenty-five years ago, not long after he left your father's ranch. He brought me here after my family was killed. It's been my home ever since."

"It's just like any other small town," Amber remarked. Her

bright eyes were everywhere at once trying to take it all in. "It's got everything McCandless has."

Morgan grinned again and nodded. He seemed oblivious to the admiring glances of the women they passed. Several of his men lounged on the boardwalks. Morgan nodded when they greeted him with a wave or comment, but Amber couldn't help but shudder at the secretive glances they stole at her beneath the brims of their hats.

Morgan was instantly aware of the tensing of her arm beneath his fingers. Unconsciously Amber drew closer to him, anxiously scanning the clusters of outlaws.

"There's nothing to be afraid of," Morgan assured her quietly. "Nobody will raise a hand to you unless I tell them. They're a respectful lot when they're sober."

"How do you keep them in line?"

Morgan grinned inwardly at the way his words had calmed her fears. Despite her fear of him, she was more trusting than she realized. She instinctively knew he would protect her. That knowledge gave him a strange feeling of pride.

He suddenly realized she was staring at him curiously. "Morgan?" she was asking in a puzzled voice.

"Yes?" he replied quickly with an effort to pull his thoughts back to the moment.

"I was asking how you keep the men in line."

"They're afraid of me."

"Do you like that? Knowing that men fear you?"

Morgan shrugged. "I've never thought about it. As long as it's effective, I don't suppose I really care one way or the other."

"It seems like a terrible way to spend your life. Don't you have any friends?"

"I'm afraid not having friends is a hazard of the profession. But I've learned to live with it. Besides, I've got Welch. He's more than a friend, he's more like a father. He raised me like his own, gave me a home, taught me how to survive in the world."

"I'm not sure he's done you any favors," Amber commented

dryly. "If you can't trust anybody and spend your whole life alone, I can't see where you're any better off."

"There are more important things, Amber, than having friends. Like knowing how to make your own way...not having to depend on anybody but yourself."

"But if you don't let yourself get close to other people, how can you be happy?"

Morgan smiled at her wide-eyed innocence. She had not pulled away from his caress, but seemed content to stroll beside him down the street ignoring the admiring stares of the gang members who lolled about under the porches of the shops out of the sun. It was pleasant to walk beside her, talking about something other than Owen McCandless.

"Maybe I don't need other people to be happy."

She glanced at him incredulously. "Everyone needs people! You can't go through life without ever needing someone else."

"The only people I need is a woman once in a while. There are plenty of those right here in the saloon."

Amber stared at him open-mouthed for a moment before her indignation set in. "I see, anyone will do, is that it? Just any old body will serve your purposes?"

Morgan sighed inwardly. He wasn't sure how, but he had managed to insult her again.

"I think we'd best change the subject," he said curtly.

Amber agreed silently. She did not want to risk his anger again. It was much more pleasant when he was being nice. "Perhaps you're right. I don't want to argue."

When Morgan did not reply for a few moments, she looked around at the shops they were passing. They had already passed a gun shop, cafe, what appeared to be a two story boarding house, and were now nearing the store Morgan had mentioned. This out-law town was well kept and in remarkably good condition. Who would have thought outlaws took such pride in a hideout?

Morgan drew her toward the mercantile. The front door was standing open. As they walked into the store, Amber was struck by the similarity of this place and Floyd Roscoe's store in McCandless. Except for the location, the two could have been identical. Tables were piled high with trousers and shirts, along the walls were lower tables with a variety of handmade boots. There was even a selection of dress goods.

On the wall behind the counter hung a collection of handguns and rifles. Amber also noted shelves of ammunition behind the counter, along with an assortment of camping equipment and blankets. Everything imaginable was here, even canisters of stick candy lined the counter on one end.

Morgan suppressed a grin at the surprise on her face. She turned to drink in the store's contents. After a few moments of awed silence she turned to stare up at him.

"Is there anything you and Welch Mandell have overlooked?"

Though her tone was sarcastic, Morgan noted an underlying current of respect in her voice. He studied her beautiful face with its high cheekbones splattered with golden freckles and her pert little nose, then shifted his gaze downward to her full lips, so inviting and yet so unspoiled

While she stared up at him curiously, Morgan's gaze traveled to her eyes. Those clear amber colored eyes were a mirror into her soul. He wondered if it was those eyes that bewitched him so.

"I don't think so," he drawled. "Women's things are back this way," he added as he drew her toward the back wall of the store. "Pick out whatever you think you'll need. Take your time, there's no hurry."

"Thank you," she replied stiffly with an aloof sniff. She moved away from the disconcerting warmth of his hand and began to sort through the stacks of ladies things.

Morgan moved toward the door to give her room to make her selections, but kept a watchful eye on her. Leaning one shoulder against the open door frame, he reached into his shirt pocket to take out one of Welch's imported cheroots, and lit it. Inhaling leisurely, he glanced at Amber from time to time, smiling to himself at her furtive glances around the store in search of another exit.

As he watched her, he saw her face fill with dismay when she realized there was only one door and he was standing in it. When she suddenly glanced at him, the muscles in his jaw tightened at the determination that flared briefly in the depths of her eyes. She had not yet given up on finding an escape, he thought grimly. He would have to keep a close watch on her. She was stubborn and didn't fully realize the danger of straying from the protection of his house.

He would have to impress upon her the lack of morals among the members of this community. The looks of envy and open lust she had received from the men outside had not gone unnoticed. While she didn't understand the implications, he did. An unfamiliar stirring of protectiveness filled him. Outside the protection of his house or his presence, a beautiful woman was open prey to these lustful vultures. The thought of Amber's body being brutally violated made his chest constrict with fierce anger.

"My goodness, what a disturbing expression, Morgan. And on such a lovely day, too."

The soft female voice snapped Morgan from his thoughts. He looked around quickly, his scowl fading into a slightly embarrassed grin as he saw Francine Comstock.

"Morning, Francine," he mumbled, lifting the cheroot to his lips to cover his momentary surprise.

"What's wrong, Morgan? Didn't your evening go as well as you planned?" the woman queried with an amused smile. "Don't tell me young Miss McCandless didn't appreciate your charm."

"I've had more cooperative women," Morgan replied dryly.

"I'm sorry to hear that, dear. But I'm sure, given a little time, you'll have her eating out of your hand. You always do, don't you?"

Despite himself Morgan grinned, flicking the ash from the cheroot onto the boardwalk just outside the door. He knew Francine was teasing, but it didn't bother him. He had known Francine for nearly ten years. She had come to the Lair at Welch's request to run the saloon and its thriving business upstairs. She had become

Welch's mistress shortly afterwards, but not before she had demonstrated her expertise to Morgan on more than one occasion.

Francine shifted uncomfortably under Morgan's penetrating ebony stare. He was smiling, yet she sensed an uneasiness in him that was out of character. She shared Welch's discomfort at being the recipient of that piercing black stare that seemed to read her thoughts. Remembering Welch's precarious position, she shuddered and looked away, wishing again that Welch had not engineered the kidnapping of Owen McCandless' niece.

From the moment she had overheard Welch and Morgan discussing their plans, she had been plagued with a premonition of doom she had been unable to shake. It was never stronger than at this moment.

Turning her head, Francine looked around the store to find the girl who was the focal point of that feeling. It was impossible to miss Amber McCandless. Even if the store had been crowded with other women, there was only one who could possibly be Price McCandless' daughter. She studied the golden haired beauty poking listlessly through a stack of calico material, then glanced back at Morgan to find that he was staring at the girl with a gleam in his coal black eyes she'd never seen before.

"She's beautiful, Morgan, very beautiful. I can see why you're so taken with her," she commented quietly, feeling a keen sense of regret.

"What gives you the idea I'm taken with her?" Morgan asked with a disgruntled scowl. "She's beautiful all right but she's as bad tempered as a Missouri mule."

Francine shot him an irritated glance as she placed her hands on her hips. "Well, what the devil did you expect?" she declared. "For the poor thing to melt in your arms? Good heavens, Morgan, you should have better sense!"

"What the hell do you mean by that?" Morgan growled, coming upright in the doorway and sending the half smoked cheroot flying into the street.

"I mean, you fool, that you kidnapped that poor girl off a

stagecoach, dragged her across fifty miles of mountains, brought her here so you could hold her for ransom, and screw her whenever you feel like it. I know you, Morgan, and you feel like it a lot. Not to mention killing Patch right in front of her eyes. The poor thing is terrified and who can blame her? Can't you have a little compassion, for God's sake!"

Throughout Francine's heated tirade Morgan watched her with narrowing eyes, his jaw twitching as his irritation grew.

"It's no concern of yours, Francine."

Francine swallowed and backed up a step, blinking rapidly while she tried to recover from the coldness in his voice. "All right, Morgan, you're right. It is none of my business, but I should hope that along with the trade Welch taught you, he also taught you a little simple pity for those not as strong or ruthless as you."

"Welch taught me to take what I wanted. That's what I've done."

Francine stared at him for a moment, then slowly shook her head. "I feel sorry for both of you, Morgan, you and Amber McCandless. A woman should have a choice of sleeping with a man whether that choice is made for money or love. Money you don't need and love you don't understand. I wonder if you ever will."

"I don't need your pity or your sermon, Francine."

"That's what's so sad, Morgan," she replied softly, lifting a fingertip to gently touch his cheek. "You don't think you need anybody."

Morgan jerked his head away from her touch, his eyes flashing with slow burning anger. "I don't. If you want to feel sorry for somebody, feel sorry for yourself, Francine. Don't you know you'll always be Welch's second choice? He couldn't have the woman he wanted so he settled for you."

He felt little satisfaction at the wounded expression that filled her eyes, but he couldn't seem to stop the hateful words spilling from his mouth. "If you're waiting for Welch to marry you, you're a fool. You're a whore, Francine. You've always been a whore and I've no doubt you'll always be one."

Francine darted a quick look at Amber, who had stopped looking at clothing and was staring at them curiously. "What about her, Morgan? You've made her a whore. Is she any better than me? You're right; I am a whore, but at least I had a choice. That's more than I can say for that girl."

With that, Francine whirled and abruptly left the store, her shopping forgotten. Morgan stared after her for only an instant before striding across the store toward Amber. She looked up at his lean dark face in wide-eyed bewilderment. She hadn't been close enough to hear the conversation between him and the rather flashy looking woman, and could only wonder what had been said, but there was no mistaking the tears she had seen in the woman's eyes as she fled the store.

Morgan's face was unreadable. She sensed that cold, frightening anger building, waiting for the right spark to set it off.

"Have you found what you need?" he asked her almost casually, his tone filling her with relief. Whatever words he had exchanged with that woman, at least he wasn't taking it out on her.

"Yes, I think so," she replied, wishing she had the courage to ask him about the auburn haired woman.

"Good, then let's go."

Amber followed him meekly to the counter where a lanky, sandy-haired cowboy grinned wickedly as he looked her over, idly fingering the undergarments she had laid on the counter. His hawkish gaze touched on the swell of her breasts, but a glance at Morgan's face stopped him cold.

Hastily, the man looked away from her and dropped the garments, quickly figuring their cost. Morgan slipped his arm casually around her shoulders. She looked up at him and noticed there was a glitter in his eyes, warning the young outlaw that he was treading on dangerous ground. His left hand had moved to rest on the butt of the pistol on his hip in silent threat.

Relief flashed through Amber, but it was coupled with resentment at his possessiveness. While she waited in rising impatience, Morgan took a roll of bills from his pocket and paid for her purchases. Their business completed, he led her from the store back into the bright morning sunshine with her bundle tucked under his arm.

Outside once more, Amber's eyes darted down the street toward the saloon and the impressive white house that stood on the opposite side of the street. For an instant, she saw Francine watching them from the double French doors that opened onto the balcony. Then the woman quickly dropped the curtains back into place.

"Who was she?" Amber couldn't resist asking. Her shorter legs had to hurry to keep up with Morgan's long strides as they moved back down the street in the direction they had come.

"Who?"

"The lady in the green dress you were talking to in the store."

"That was no lady, that was Francine Comstock."

"Who is she?" Amber persisted despite the reluctance she sensed in him to discuss the matter.

"Welch's mistress."

Amber's lips formed a silent exclamation, but she decided not to press him. It was obvious Francine Comstock was a subject he would rather not talk about. She wondered why.

Finally she could contain her curiosity no longer. "I heard her mention my name, didn't I?"

Morgan didn't answer. After a moment she sighed and gave up. She was learning if he didn't want to discuss something, he wouldn't.

"How has this place escaped discovery for so long?" she asked after a few moments of silence.

"Because there's only one way in or out and that's heavily guarded. From the outside there's no sign of an entrance," he explained. "You have to know exactly what to look for, otherwise you'd never find it. The law has been all over it a thousand times and never found it."

The quiet pride in his voice rankled Amber's nerves. But at least he was talking again. "How do you get all the supplies into this canyon?"

"Pack trains from Mexico."

Before Amber could ask another question, a young woman with coal black hair and eyes and the same olive complexion as Morgan's sauntered from a porch across the street. She was quite beautiful in a sleazy kind of way, Amber decided. She was wearing a bright plum colored dress with very thin straps, cut so daringly low it revealed most of her small bosom. The sensual smile on her lips was an open invitation to Morgan as she approached.

Morgan halted as she came closer, observing her with an irritated expression. The woman halted directly in front of him and placed her hands on her hips.

"So, this is what has kept you away for so long," she said with a pout. The hostility that blazed at Amber from the depths of the other woman's eyes made her unconsciously draw closer to Morgan for protection.

"Not now, Jenna," Morgan said, but the woman pointedly ignored the warning in his manner.

"I waited for you last night, but you never came," the girl went on with a beseeching gaze. "Jase said you had another woman." Her voice had grown cold, her face darkened with anger, and the hateful glance she threw Amber made the girl's skin prickle with uneasiness.

Morgan tugged at Amber's arm and moved past the pretty Mexican girl without replying.

Suddenly the woman grabbed his arm, flinging herself in front of him again. "You can't treat me like this, Morgan!" she cried.

Morgan jerked his arm free and pushed her aside. For a moment, his eyes locked with hers, coldly glittering, but the girl clutched at his sleeve again.

"Morgan, I love you! You can't just push me aside like trash. I won't stand for it!"

Wild-eyed despair flooded the Mexican girl's face. Tears seeped beneath her dark lashes, cutting tiny rivulets through her heavy makeup.

"You're making a fool of yourself, Jenna," Morgan told her curtly. "Go back to the saloon before you make me do something I'll be sorry for."

"You're never sorry for anything you do!" the girl accused loudly, not caring that all conversation had stopped along the street as all eyes were focused on her. "You use me whenever you feel like it, but you don't care about my feelings. I love you! You know that! But the minute some..*anglo*...comes along, you forget about me!"

Jenna's hurt, angry eyes now jumped to Amber. Her lips curled back over tiny white teeth in a vicious snarl. "It's all your fault! If you hadn't come here, he'd still be mine. You *anglo* bitch!"

Jenna's claw-like nails stabbed at Amber's frightened face, but before she could attack, Morgan stepped in front of Amber. Amber gasped in horrified surprise as Morgan grabbed Jenna by both shoulders and shoved her away. She landed in a crumpled heap on the ground, flinging one arm up to protect herself from Morgan's fury.

Instead of hitting her as Amber feared, Morgan towered over the girl, his dark angry eyes boring into Jenna's. His hands clenched and unclenched while the ivory shirt strained across the rigid muscles in his back. When he spoke to Jenna in rapid fire Spanish, his voice was so calm and soft it raised the hair on the back of Amber's neck.

"If you ever try to hurt her again, I'll kill you," he told Jenna in Spanish. "Now get up and get back to the saloon where you belong. Stay away from my woman, Jenna, or you'll regret the day you were born."

Then he turned on his heel and walked back to Amber, took her by the hand and led her down the street. Jenna lay sprawled in the dust for a few moments, then staggered to her feet amid the hoots of laughter from the men watching from the boardwalk. Her dark eyes blazed with fury at Morgan and Amber as they walked away. She lifted one shaky hand to smooth several strands of raven hair that had come loose from her chignon, her lips forming a twisted sneer at the slender blonde girl on Morgan's arm.

"No man does this to me, and gets away with it, Morgan Devereaux,. And that *blanca* bitch will pay for taking you from me. You'll both pay!" she vowed to their departing backs.

CHAPTER SIXTEEN

Texas Ranger Ryan Tyrell shifted uncomfortably in the deep leather chair in from of Owen McCandless' desk. He was a big man, well over six feet tall, and powerfully built. His face was like tanned leather from years of exposure to the burning Texas sun, his hair a rare mixture of gold and brown. He could not be considered a handsome man. His ears were a bit too large and his jaw a bit too square, but his aqua-marine eyes were clear and perceptive.

He shifted again, glancing uneasily about the room once more. He had never felt comfortable in such luxurious surroundings. He felt at home on the prairie with the rabbits and coyotes, sleeping in the open with nothing but a blanket and the stars for company. A house like this, with its many expensive furnishings, did not suit his taste nor his size.

"So you've been a Ranger for awhile?" Owen McCandless asked. His intent blue gaze was fastened on Ryan in an unwavering stare while he drew on the cigar he had been holding loosely between his fingers.

"Fifteen years," replied Ryan in a rich baritone. He returned Owen's probing stare irritably. The rancher was wasting time, and time was the one thing Ryan hated to waste. He was so close this time. Welch Mandell was almost within his grasp. He couldn't sit here all day making polite conversation with a rich rancher when he had work to do.

"Tyrell," Owen mused thoughtfully while he pondered the ranger's name. "Sounds familiar, yet I can't place it. Have we met before somewhere?"

"No, Mr. McCandless, I don't think so. Maybe you've met my father. He was a Ranger, too, years ago."

Owen studied the lawman doubtfully. He couldn't remember anybody by the name of Tyrell, yet it seemed strangely familiar.

From his position in one corner of the office, Cooter Jackson studied the ranger. So Jim Tyrell's boy had grown up to become a Texas Ranger, too. It was surprising it had worked out that way. It hadn't been too many years since Cooter had heard that Ryan Tyrell was on the wrong side of the law himself. He'd had a good sized reputation back then for being fast with a gun. Now here he sat, using his expertise with a six-gun on the side of the law instead of against it.

Cooter shook his head, marveling at how ironic life was. Who would ever have guessed that a double dealing snake like Jim Tyrell would sire a son as straight as this? Since his change of heart, Ryan Tyrell's reputation as an astute, honest lawman had grown until now he was as well known for it as he had been a few years earlier as a fast gun for hire.

Cooter shifted uneasily in his seat and cast a veiled glare at Owen. Why hadn't the fool listened to him when he insisted it was a mistake to bring in the Rangers? It was bad enough that Morgan was so dangerously close to discovering Welch's secret, but now Welch had Jim Tyrell's boy on his trail, too.

No doubt Ryan Tyrell had asked for this assignment in hopes of getting Welch within his gun sights. A chill of apprehension crept down the old wrangler's spine. Ryan Tyrell had been waiting twenty years for a chance to kill Welch Mandell.

He wished they could call it off, return Amber, and forget the whole thing, but it was much too late for that. Whatever was going to happen was already set in motion. There was no recalling it. God help them all.

"Mr. McCandless, could I see the ransom note?" Ryan asked Owen.

At the question, Cooter pulled his dismal thoughts back to the present.

"Of course." Owen opened a drawer, produced the letter, and handed it across the desk to the ranger.

Ryan scanned the contents, laid the letter on top of the desk, and settled back in his chair, crossing his legs again. "I don't suppose you can raise the money?"

Owen gave a bitter snort, shaking his head while exhaling a plume of gray cigar smoke toward the ceiling. "If I could, do you think I'd have asked for help? What they're asking is insane."

"Fifty thousand dollars is a ridiculous amount. Devereaux and Mandell must know you can't raise that much," Ryan mused thoughtfully. After sitting silently for a moment, he leveled an unwavering blue-green gaze at Owen's worried face. "Welch Mandell isn't foolish, nor is Morgan Devereaux. I'm surprised they'd bother with a stunt like this. It makes me wonder if there isn't another reason for it."

"What do you mean?"

"Is there a chance Mandell or Devereaux might have a more personal interest in your niece?"

"Of course not!" Owen scoffed. "My niece has only recently arrived here from Boston. How could she possibly have any connection to those murderous outlaws?"

"Outlaws, yes, Mr. McCandless, but murderous? To my knowledge, Morgan Devereaux has never killed a man who wasn't trying to kill him," Ryan replied. "There's no denying he's Mandell's lieutenant, but I'd hesitate to call him a murderer."

"That's an interesting statement coming from a lawman," Owen said scornfully. "Do I detect a trace of admiration, Tyrell?"

The ranger nodded slightly. His sharp gaze held on the rancher's dubious face with unyielding firmness. "I expect you do. I admire any man who can stay alive in Morgan Devereaux's business. I've never met the man myself, but my colleagues say he's faster with a gun than any man alive, with the possible exception of Mandell. Having had a reputation of my own at one time, I know what pressure that puts on a man. I don't envy him."

"And Mandell?"

A coldness came into the ranger's eyes. "Mandell is another story," Ryan said curtly. "But, whatever else Mandell may be, he's not stupid. He's a careful man. He never makes a move without thinking out each step. That's what puzzles me about this kidnapping."

"I don't follow you," Owen countered.

Ryan eyed Owen shrewdly, sensing an uneasiness that aroused his curiosity. It was more than concern for his niece's safety, but Ryan couldn't put his finger on it.

"What I mean, Mr. McCandless, is that, knowing Mandell's methods as I do, there's no doubt in my mind that he's been planning this for awhile. He's bound to know you can't raise fifty thousand dollars so quick. So he must have another reason, something more personal maybe."

"What the hell are you getting at?" Owen demanded.

"Any chance you might know Mandell or Devereaux?"

"Of course not! How could I possibly know men like that?"

"You're a rich, powerful man, Mr. McCandless. Somewhere along the way, there's always the chance you may have crossed one of them."

"That's ridiculous!" Owen snapped.

"Then maybe someone who's close enough to one, or both of them, to set up an operation like this," Ryan suggested. "Powerful men always have enemies, Mr. McCandless."

"Are you suggesting that this was an inside job?"

Cooter felt a cold trickle of sweat drip down his spine.

"It has all the earmarks of one," Ryan answered. "Someone had to know your niece was taking the stage to El Paso and pass along that information to Devereaux. How else could he have known?"

"I suppose someone at the stage office could have relayed the information."

"That's one possibility," Ryan agreed. "I have a few ideas that shouldn't take too long to check out. And I want to take a look at the spot where Devereaux stopped the stage."

"If you're thinking about following his trail, you can forget it," Owen told him dejectedly. "Riker has already been over that trail.

The tracks end a few miles from the New Mexico border. Devereaux made sure someone erased all traces of his trail."

"He's smart all right. He's had a good teacher. Still, I'd like to check it out myself. There's always the outside chance the sheriff overlooked something."

"Suit yourself, Tyrell, but don't forget I'm running out of time."

"I'm aware of that, Mr. McCandless. That's what worries me. It's obvious Devereaux doesn't plan on collecting that ransom. There must be another reason why he'd demand an amount he's got to know you can't pay."

"You said that before but I don't have the slightest idea what that might be," Owen growled. "I've already told you, I don't know Devereaux or Mandell or know of any reason they would take my niece."

"Maybe not, but it's my guess one or both of them intend to destroy you. What would you have to do in order to raise the cash to pay the ransom?"

"Sell my cattle, my sulfur mines, my railroad contracts, and most of my land," Owen replied gloomily. "That would take time, perhaps weeks. Are you telling me to start liquidating my assets?"

"No, not yet. I have another idea."

"I hope it works, Tyrell. I only have a few days left. If anything happens to my niece, I'm holding you and the Rangers responsible. What's your idea?"

"I'll let you know when I've checked out a few things. In the meantime, sit tight and if you hear from Devereaux, let me know right away."

"I doubt he'll contact me again," Owen told him bitterly. "I'm supposed to run an ad in the *McCandless Tribune* when I've got the money ready. After that, I'm to wait for further instructions."

Ryan tapped the ransom note with a callused forefinger, then looked back to Owen. "Yeah, I know, but if I'm right, you're going to have to stall for more time. We've got to keep the girl alive until I get things worked out."

"Are you thinking of laying a trap for Devereaux?"

A brief smile touched the ranger's lips as he nodded. "Yes, Mr. McCandless, that's exactly what I'm thinking. And I've got a good idea how to go about it, but we have to move slowly and carefully. We can't afford to spook him. He might harm your niece. If there's one thing I know about Devereaux and Mandell, it's that they always keep their word. If I make a wrong move, they'll kill her. That's a chance I don't want to take."

"Why do I get the feeling that your interest in Devereaux and Mandell is more than strictly a part of your job?"

Ryan returned the first steady gaze Owen had directed at him since the beginning of their conversation. He was certain the rancher was hiding something. Maybe when he knew what it was, he'd have the key to this kidnapping.

"I've been on Mandell's trail for a long time, but he's always managed to elude me. This time it'll be different."

The chill in his voice made Cooter flinch. Whatever the ranger had in mind, he had to find out and warn Welch. Soon. Another man with a motive for revenge was one too damned many.

Ryan stood and reached for his hat lying on one corner of Owen's desk. "I'll be in touch, Mr. McCandless," he said. Without waiting for a response, he left the room. Owen slumped behind the desk and crushed out the remainder of his cigar with a vengeance. He turned to the liquor cabinet beneath the window, poured two liberal glasses of whiskey, then motioned for Cooter to join him at the desk.

The wrangler limped across the room to take the chair the ranger had vacated. He took the glass from Owen and sipped from it slowly. The whiskey burned, but left a mellow feeling that helped ease his tension.

"That is one dangerous man," Owen remarked with a glance out the open window at the disappearing form of the ranger.

Silently, Cooter agreed. He took another sip of the whiskey and forced himself to relax. It wouldn't do for Owen to notice his uneasiness in view of the ranger's suspicions about an inside man.

"I think Welch has met his match," Owen went on gleefully. "I just hope I'm there when the son-of-a-bitch gets it. I can't think of anything I'd like better than seeing him spill that sanctimonious blood all over the ground."

"Do you really want that, Owen?"

"Why the hell shouldn't I?" Owen snapped. "That bastard has been a thorn in my flesh for twenty-five years. I want him out once and for all."

" I know you've had your differences over the years, but the two of you used to be close."

"That was years ago, Cooter. You saw how the ungrateful bastard repaid my generosity. And now look what he's done to me," Owen growled. He tossed back his drink and quickly poured another. He offered the bottle to Cooter, but the old wrangler declined with a wave.

"But it's all just about over with. This ranger knows his business. I'm convinced of that. He'll take care of Welch and Devereaux."

Cooter was afraid Owen might be right, but kept his thoughts to himself as he sipped at his drink.

Owen leaned back in the chair and swirled the whiskey around in his glass. After a moment he looked at Cooter again.

"Does the name Tyrell sound familiar to you? I could swear I've heard that name before."

Cooter nodded. "Didn't you have a lawman named Tyrell on your payroll about twenty years ago?"

Owen thought for a moment, but the blank expression on his face told Cooter he couldn't remember.

"Did I? I don't remember. What became of him?" Owen inquired in a bored tone.

"Welch killed him."

CHAPTER SEVENTEEN

"You're bleeding. Take off your shirt and I'll put it in some water to soak before the stains set."

Amber did not wait to see if Morgan obeyed, but took the bundle of newly purchased clothing and tossed it onto the sofa on her way to the kitchen to heat some water. She put a few sticks of wood into the stove and pumped vigorously on the iron pump handle, filling a kettle with fresh water when it finally rushed into the enamel sink, then set it on the stove to heat.

She turned to find Morgan leaning against the archway. He handed her the ivory shirt, watching while she pumped cold water over it and rubbed the bloody sleeve to remove the stains.

Satisfied that she had done her best to salvage the shirt, Amber rummaged in the cabinet drawers until she found a neat stack of clean white towels. She wet one thoroughly and turned back to clean the long bloody scratches on Morgan's right forearm.

"This really should have some antiseptic," she said briskly. "Fingernail scratches are easily infected."

Morgan did not speak, but stood quietly, leaning his left shoulder against the archway while she rinsed out the towel. She wet the towel from the kettle of lukewarm water, and patted it along the nasty nail marks. She wished he would say something. His silence made her uncomfortable, increased the anxiety building in the pit of her stomach.

It was not his wound that plagued her. Unable to resist a darting glance upward through her thick lashes, she felt herself tremble, felt her knees weaken at the sight of his bare chest and muscular shoulders. The warmth of his body seemed to surround her, made her keenly aware of the clean, pleasant scent of his skin and subtle, but potent, masculinity.

She bit her lip, determined to ignore the unsettling effect being so close to him had on her senses. Resolving to keep those wicked, disturbing thoughts at bay, she looked up into his lean, dark face. It came as no surprise to find him watching her thoughtfully. "I suppose that girl was your..your girlfriend," she said in an obvious attempt to make conversation.

"You suppose wrong."

Relief flooded through her. If she could get him to talk, perhaps this disquieting tension in her body would ease. "She said she loved you."

"Jenna says that to a lot of men," Morgan returned dryly. "It's part of her job."

"She sounded sincere to me." She put the towel away and stood watching the muscles in his back surge when he moved away briefly to open a cabinet in search of the ointment he wanted.

Amber took the small jar from him and opened it. She stuck one finger into the jar, then began to gently apply the ointment to the scratches. Morgan leaned against the archway again as he held his arm out toward her.

"You don't know her like I do. Sincerity is not one of Jenna's strongest traits."

Amber decided not to ask what strong traits the girl did possess. From her mode of dress, it was all too obvious. She did not really care to hear it expressed in Morgan's frank terms.

"What did you say to her in Spanish?" she asked instead.

"I told her to stay away from you."

Morgan replaced the lid on the ointment jar, put it away, then moved through the house to the bedroom to get another shirt from his wardrobe. Amber followed along behind him. She took the clothing from the bundle on the sofa and put it away in the wardrobe obviously reserved for her.

"Don't you know any nice girls?"

His soft chuckle made her flesh tingle. She turned to find him tucking the tail of a dark blue, long sleeved shirt into his trousers. His dark eyes held hers in a mesmerizing gaze that Amber was helpless to break, while he deftly buttoned the shirt.

"I do now," he told her in a low, husky voice that made her eyes widen warily. He had that look again, the one she was learning to know so well. It was more than a facial expression, although there was a noticeable tensing around his mouth and his ebony eyes had taken on a hot gleam. It was an aura that was almost physical. It reached out to Amber, enfolded her in its sensual web, rendering her helpless to escape; indeed, leaving her weak with anticipation.

Strange, how the only two emotions she could interpret in this mysterious, fascinating man were anger and desire. She didn't know which of the two scared her more.

Involuntarily, Amber moved a step backwards, forcing a weak smile. "Am I to assume from that, that you consider me a nice girl?" she asked in as haughty a tone as she could summon from her stiff lips.

Morgan's dark head moved in a slight nod, although he looked a bit puzzled. "Why shouldn't I?"

"There was a time you certainly didn't."

"I was wrong. I assumed because you're related to Owen McCandless that you were as immoral and tainted by wealth and power as he is," Morgan replied with a shrug.

"Okay, beside me, do you know any nice girls?" She began to fidget with the lace at the cuffs of her dress. Even though he was talking, he still had that expression of intent that made her breath labored and her chest feel tight.

"No, I guess not. A man with my reputation doesn't get a chance to meet many nice girls. They tend to run for cover when I come around. I can't say I blame them."

He observed her nervousness with an amused smile.

She touched the tip of her tongue to her dry lips and moved another step backward. "If you don't meet any nice girls, how do you expect to ever get married? Surely you don't intend to marry someone like that girl in the street. She's quite lovely, I suppose, but hardly the kind of girl a man would want to settle down with and raise a family."

"Maybe I don't want to get married," Morgan suggested with an amused sparkle lighting up his eyes. "Why should I settle down with one woman?"

The irritation on Amber's face brought another soft chuckle from his throat. Then the expression changed rapidly to fleeting panic when he closed the distance between them and gripped her chin in one hand, titling her face upward until she was forced to look into his eyes.

"Is that all you ever think about?" she hissed in a voice that vacillated between haughtiness and fear. The half-smile on his handsome face did little to relieve her anxiety. He studied her with an amused, thoughtful expression that sent daggers of excitement plunging into her chest, making her breath become short and gasping.

"Lately, it seems to be," Morgan replied, his dark face only inches above hers, his warm breath tickling her cheek, sending shivers down her spine.

Unconsciously, she closed her eyes, lifting her lips to him, expecting to feel the delightful plundering that only his commanding, sensual mouth could make her feel. When nothing happened, she opened her eyes and blinked in bewilderment. Slowly, embarrassment flooded her face with color.

"Sorry, Amber. Business before pleasure. But hold that thought, I'll be back soon."

By the time Amber's mouth had snapped shut, he had picked up his hat and left the house. She ran to the bedroom window to fling back the curtains. Morgan moved through the front gate and closed it behind him as Jase McCally rode up leading the Appaloosa. She watched him swing up onto the horse with the grace of an Indian warrior, then pause to glance toward the house.

Catching sight of her, he grinned devilishly, and tipped his hat to her in a silent salute.

Amber flung the curtains back into place and jumped back from the window. A moment later she heard the hoofbeats of the two horses moving down the street. She threw herself face down on the bed and began to cry miserably.

All her resolve not to allow herself any emotion when he touched her had melted at his first touch. She hated herself for being weak. He was toying with her, manipulating her, and she was letting him. How could she allow herself to fall under the spell of those ebony eyes until she felt like she was drowning and the only thing that could save her was the strength of his arms around her, and the raw power of his body?

What must he think of her? She really was no different than that sleazy saloon girl that had attacked her.

She tossed and turned for a time while thoughts of self-loathing and despair ran wildly through her mind. She had to get away from him. Soon, before she was lost forever. She realized with painful clarity that given time, Morgan Devereaux could assuredly bend her will to his own. The most frightening thing, however, was that she was rapidly losing what little resistance she had left.

***

"I don't like it! I don't like it one damned bit!"

Welch Mandell emphasized the words by striking the top of the mahogany desk. He rose to pace back and forth, finally returning to drop into the heavy leather chair behind the desk and light a thin brown cheroot.

"Owen is stalling. I feel it in my gut."

"What reason could he have for that? Unless he's not as crazy about the girl as you and Cooter seem to think."

"No, I'm not wrong about that."

The effects of two nights without sleep were beginning to tell on Welch. There were tiny lines of fatigue around his mouth that

Morgan hadn't noticed before. The gun-metal eyes were tired and red.

"It's the money, it has to be. Owen can't raise it and he's trying to find a way out without having to sell anything. The cheap son-of-a-bitch!"

"I thought that was what we wanted."

"It is, but it's still infuriating," Welch growled, after exhaling a plume of aromatic smoke into the air. "And we should have heard from Cooter by now. I'm getting worried about him."

"Maybe he wants us to sweat," Morgan suggested.

"Or maybe Owen's getting suspicious of him. He's in one hell of a bad spot if Owen finds out he's our inside man. Owen will kill him. He wouldn't bother to think about it twice."

"Cooter knew that going in."

"Yeah, I know," Welch grunted sourly. "But I promised him my protection. If anything happens to that old man....."

"If it will make you feel better, why don't I take a ride into McCandless and see what's going on?"

"No! It's too dangerous, Morgan. Hell, the whole state of Texas may be out looking for you. It would be suicide to stick your head out of here until it's time."

"So what's new?" Morgan inquired with a nonchalant shrug. "It's best to know what McCandless is up to and right now Cooter is the only one who knows for sure. I'm going."

He rose to his feet and picked up his hat from the corner of Welch's desk where he had tossed it. He moved toward the door, his mind made up.

"Goddamnit! I said no!" Welch roared behind him.

Morgan turned in surprise at the urgency in Welch's raw voice. Welch vaulted from the chair, crossed the room, and caught Morgan's arm.

"What the hell is wrong with you?" Morgan demanded. "You're as nervous as a cat. Will you relax and let me handle this?"

Welch let his hand drop slowly from Morgan's arm as an embarrassed grin spread over his face. The searching intensity in

Morgan's eyes made him even more uneasy. He turned away, walking slowly back to his chair while he tried to get his raw nerves under control. He had to get a grip on himself before Morgan got any more suspicious.

"I'm sorry, Morgan," he mumbled. "We've waited so long for this. I just don't want anything to go wrong. Cooter is an old man. He's no match for Owen, he never was."

"I'd say he's done one hell of a job so far," Morgan said, studying Welch. It wasn't like Welch to avoid looking him straight in the eye as he was doing now. That, combined with Welch's uneasy manner, made the hair rise on the back of his neck.

"What's really bothering you, Welch? I know you, remember? Better than any man alive. Whatever's eating at you, it's more than worrying about an old man who probably has more nerve than either of us."

Welch swallowed, hating himself for the way his hands had begun to sweat. Now was the time to tell Morgan the truth, the whole story, but his throat constricted, clamped off his breath, made his mouth as dry as cotton. Staring into those piercing black eyes, Welch realized he couldn't. He loved Morgan as his own son. How could he possibly hope to make him understand now?

"It's the girl, isn't it?" Morgan asked.

Welch mentally shook himself and grasped at Morgan's question as a way out of answering the first question truthfully, cursing himself for evading the issue. There might be a day when he was forced to face Morgan for lying all these years, but there was also a chance he would never know. It was a chance Welch decided to take.

"Yes, I suppose it is."

"Does the fact that I'm sleeping with her really bother you that much?"

"Hell, yes, it bothers me. It bothers the hell out of me."

Morgan made no further comment until he had helped himself to a tumbler of Welch's finest whiskey and made himself comfortable again. He sipped the whiskey in a leisurely fashion while he studied Welch across the desk.

"Why? I gave you my word I wouldn't hurt her and I haven't."

Welch snorted, flicking away the ash from his cigar in a thoroughly irritated manner. "If I know you, Morgan, she's lucky if she can walk by now," he muttered.

Morgan's soft laughter made Welch grimace with annoyance. "What's the matter, old man, jealous because you can't get it up but once a week if you're lucky?"

"Hell no! I can get it up whenever I want," Welch retorted. He gave the younger man a dark scowl that made Morgan laugh again. "Goddamnit, Morgan, you may be younger than me, but I can still do anything you can and probably a hell of a lot better. Especially when it comes to women."

"It may surprise you, Welch, but the lady isn't all that unappreciative of my...talents," he said with a grin.

"No, Morgan, it wouldn't surprise me in the least. That's what worries me."

"What the hell does that mean?"

Welch crushed out the stub of his cheroot and poured himself a drink from the whiskey bottle Morgan had left on top of the cabinet. "Goddamn, Morgan, I don't want that girl falling in love with you. She's not like Jenna or Francine. If she falls in love with you, you could destroy her, and I'm warning you right now that I won't stand for it. If you hurt that girl, you'll answer to me."

"I don't see the problem," Morgan replied casually while twirling the whiskey around in his glass. "When this is over she'll go home and tell everybody I raped her. Who's going to blame her for anything? It'll just be another charge they can hang me for, if they can catch me. She'll be so busy spending all the money McCandless is leaving her, she won't have time to give me a second thought."

Welch shook his head slowly. "For a smart man, Morgan, you don't know shit about women, especially well bred ones like Amber. If she falls in love with you, it could scar her for the rest of her life.

"It may mean nothing to you, but it's different for her. I know how persuasive you can be. That girl hasn't got a prayer against your experience or your black-hearted charm."

"You're borrowing trouble, Welch," Morgan told him cheerfully. "The only thing she feels for me is purely physical, and she's fighting that every step of the way. Hell, she wants to see me hang as bad as everybody else in Texas."

"We haven't settled this yet. A lot can happen in a few days," Welch pointed out sourly. Hell, it would serve Morgan right if he was the one to fall in love and get his guts kicked out. He hadn't realized he was grinning until Morgan's voice drew him from his thoughts.

"What's funny?"

"I was just thinking how I'd love to see you on the receiving end of being dumped. Maybe Amber McCandless is just the woman to show you how it feels."

"Don't hold your breath, Welch," Morgan replied confidently. He finished his drink and got to his feet. "I'm taking a ride into McCandless tonight. Have Jase watch the house until I get back."

He settled the black Stetson on the back of his head as he walked toward the door. Welch knew it was useless to argue. He picked up his nearly empty glass and stared at Morgan's departing back.

"All right, goddamnit, go on, but be careful."

Morgan turned to send him a cheerful glance over his shoulder. "Stop worrying, for Christ's sake. Nobody will be expecting to see me anywhere near Owen McCandless' town. See you tomorrow."

The door closed softly behind him and his footsteps receded down the hallway with his silver spurs jingling merrily. Welch gulped down the remainder of his drink and poured another.

Cocky little bastard, he thought irritably, when Morgan passed beneath the window on his way up the street. Welch watched until Morgan disappeared from sight. Then he chuckled aloud, a dry, grim sound.

"Whatever he is, you've got yourself to thank, Welch," he said aloud. "That's what you wanted, wasn't it? A younger version of yourself? I doubt Elena would be very proud of the way you've raised him. He's what you've made him and, by God, you're going to have to live with it...or die because of it."

CHAPTER EIGHTEEN

Morgan rode swiftly toward *Rancho Devereaux*. Upon reaching McCandless shortly before dark and nosing around a bit, he had taken time to make a purchase at Roscoe's Mercantile before resuming his journey. He smiled as the Appaloosa covered the miles rapidly.

Welch would have apoplexy if he knew how Morgan had walked into the mercantile just before Floyd Roscoe was ready to close for the night. It had been a dangerous thing to do, but it had felt good to stroll right into Owen McCandless' town and look the situation over. Welch had warned him many times that he was too damned arrogant for his own good. He was probably right.

He had learned that the news of Amber's kidnapping was the talk of the town. What Owen intended to do about the ransom demands, however, was the cause of speculation, but everyone was betting McCandless wouldn't sit still for it.

He slowed the horse to cross a small stream trickling cheerfully through the prairie, paused to breathe in the familiar scent of home. This was *Rancho Devereaux*. From the boundary of the stream to a long forgotten marker miles to the east, lay five hundred acres of land that had belonged to his father until Owen McCandless needed a trail to the railhead in Fort Worth.

Another hour passed before he reined the Appaloosa to a halt. A blackened chimney, now almost completely overgrown with weeds, loomed up before him, bathed in the moonlight. Four huge cottonwoods stood at what had once been the four corners of his mother's yard. His eyes narrowed sharply as they focused on one; the cottonwood where they'd hung his father.

He swung down from the saddle and dropped the reins. The

horse dropped his muzzle to munch contentedly while Morgan walked through the grass covered remains of his home. The wood had long since rotted, the well shed fallen, the rocks his parents had labored so hard to dig up and lay into place to form the curb for the well were tumbled and scattered. A rotten plank crunched beneath his boots as he moved through the yard to a spot not far beyond.

Taking off his hat, he stood staring silently down at the three graves he had helped Welch scratch in the hard Texas earth. The wooden markers were faded, almost erased by the rain and the sun and the relentless Texas wind. He ran one finger gently over the faded names of the family he had buried here twenty years ago. Welch had carved those names with a pocket knife.

Morgan knelt beside the middle grave to brush away the dead leaves. He pulled a handful of prairie grass from the marker post from which hung the lopsided faded name. His face softened when he realized the wild rose he had planted on his mother's grave was still alive, its pink blooms reaching above the carpet of grass to wind up the marker.

The sound of hoofbeats coming rapidly from the northwest suddenly intruded upon his thoughts. He rose to his feet, hooked his thumbs in his gunbelt, and waited for his visitor to dismount.

Long shadows hid the man's face as he swung down from his horse and limped the couple of yards to where Morgan waited. Cooter Jackson pushed his worn Stetson to the back of his head, then scratched absently at the side of his neck.

"Hoped I'd find you here."

"Welch is getting worried. He thought maybe McCandless had gotten suspicious of you," Morgan said.

Cooter shook his head. "Not yet. But he's stickin' to the house like glue. I ain't been able to get away."

"What's the situation, Cooter?"

Something about the old wrangler's manner made Morgan wary. Cooter was fidgeting uneasily. It made Morgan cautious. He quickly scanned the moonlit plains for some sign Cooter had been followed, but the horizon was empty and peaceful.

"Owen's called in help, Morgan. He sent for the Rangers and one showed up today. And not just any ranger either; it's Ryan Tyrell." Cooter's voice was raspy with strain. He plucked nervously at the bandanna around his throat and kept looking over his shoulder as though expecting to find someone there.

"Who the devil is Ryan Tyrell?"

Cooter stepped past Morgan to stand solemnly before the trio of graves. After a moment he turned back to face Morgan, making a brief gesture toward the graves.

"Jim Tyrell's boy. Warn Welch. Jim Tyrell is the ranger who led the lynch party for Owen the night...well, you know what night I mean. Welch hunted him down a few months later and killed him." His eyes narrowed as disgust filled his face. "Now his boy's growed up to be a lawman. Just what this kettle needs; another fish to throw into the pot."

"Why all this concern over one crooked ranger? It's not as though we didn't expect McCandless to pull something like this. He can call in the whole damned army of Texas Rangers, but it doesn't change anything. We've got him right where we want him, Cooter. Sooner or later he'll have to make his move."

"He'll make it all right," Cooter predicted worriedly. "He ain't plannin' on payin' the ransom, not if he can find some other way."

Morgan nodded in agreement as they moved back toward their horses. "Welch is worried about you, Cooter. Are you in danger?"

Cooter shook his head as he picked up his horse's reins. "Not yet. But this ranger already thinks there may be an inside man. I doubt it'll be long before Owen gets around to thinkin' about me."

"Maybe you better pull out now, Cooter. Come back to the Lair with me."

Cooter shook his shaggy head stubbornly. "No sir! You need me right where I am and that's where I'm stayin' till we see this thing through."

Morgan studied the old man with admiration. After a moment of silence he nodded with a brief smile. "All right, but be careful. If you need to contact us, leave a message in the stump, but do it at night and make sure no one is following you. I'll be checking the stump everyday in case you need us. Keep in touch."

Cooter agreed with a curt nod, then caught Morgan's sleeve as the gunfighter turned to pick up the Appaloosa's reins. "Morgan, this ranger's big trouble. He ain't like his old man. No sir! This Ryan's as straight as an arrow. Nothin' crooked about him."

"What makes you so sure of that?"

Cooter paused, tugging at his bandanna before lifting concerned eyes to Morgan's curious face. "The same way I knew his old man was no good the first time he rode into *Sierra Vieja*; a real strong hunch right here," he said, patting his belly. "Course I don't reckon he knows anythin' about his old man's dirty dealin's. This man's smart and he's tough. And from what I hear, he's damned fast with a gun. He wants Welch bad. It's written all over him."

Morgan considered the old man's warning thoughtfully for a few seconds. Then he laid a soothing hand on Cooter's shoulder with a smile. "Then we'll have to keep a close eye on this ranger, won't we? At any rate, we'll deal with that problem when we have to. Right now what we have to worry about is being sure what McCandless is planning."

"That's what I'm here for."

"Just watch yourself," Morgan cautioned.

"Don't worry about me," Cooter told him stoutly. "I'll take care of my end. You and Welch just take care of yours."

Cooter mounted, then paused to look down at Morgan in the darkness. The pale moonlight bathed the gunfighter's face with soft light, mellowing the tight lines around his mouth, giving his lean face a more youthful appearance.

"Is Miss Amber all right?"

"Of course, she is," Morgan assured him with a brief smile. "She's not thrilled to be in our company, but she's fine. Naturally she can't wait to see me hang," he added with a wider grin.

"Naturally," Cooter replied dryly. "Before this is over she'll be thankin' you."

The memory of Amber's beautiful face flashed into Morgan's mind, those luminous golden eyes blazing with scorn for him and his kind.

"Somehow, I doubt that, Cooter. Even if she accepts the truth about darling Uncle Owen, I doubt she's going to be grateful to any of us for pointing it out to her. I think its more likely that she'll do everything in her power to forget she ever knew me."

Cooter missed the dry sarcasm in Morgan's voice. He had faith in Price's daughter. He knew she would eventually forgive them all for what they were doing. She had to. It was for her welfare. She'd see that sooner or later.

Morgan lingered a few minutes after Cooter rode away. Dropping the Appaloosa's reins, he walked back to stand before the three graves for a moment. He took off his hat, ran his fingers through his thick black hair and bowed his head. He couldn't pray, he didn't remember how. He doubted if God would listen to anything he had to say anyway. So he silently reaffirmed his vow to his family that someday soon, Owen McCandless would pay for what he had done here. Maybe then they would find peace. Maybe he would, too.

***

Hidden behind a clump of cottonwoods a quarter of a mile away, Ryan Tyrell watched as Cooter Jackson made his mysterious midnight rendezvous. Though the moonlight shed considerable light, he was too far away to see the second man clearly. However, this clump of trees provided the only cover nearby, so he decided to stay where he was. Trying to get closer would be too dangerous.

The meeting lasted only a few minutes before Cooter rode past him in the direction of the McCandless ranch. The second man hesitated a bit longer while Ryan watched curiously, trying to get a glimpse of his face.

The man seemed about to leave when he suddenly left his horse and walked a few feet into the darkness where he halted, took off his hat and bowed his head. After a few moments the man strode back to his horse, mounted, then rode northward at a fast pace.

Ryan couldn't see his face. The only thing he could tell at this distance was that the man was tall and wore a hat with silver conchos around the crown that reflected the pale moonlight. He managed to catch a good look at the horse as the man rode away. It was an Appaloosa.

Ryan moved his own horse from the shelter of cottonwoods and rode to the spot where Cooter Jackson had met the second man. He reined his horse to a halt, turning in the saddle to take a good look around. This had obviously been someone's home at one time.

Ryan walked his horse through what must have been a yard. Then he saw the grave markers rising from the prairie on lop-sided crosses. He swung down to walk closer.

With the moon behind them, it was impossible to read the names on the worn rotted wood, so he took out a match and struck it, peering into the shadows. The lettering was very old, hardly legible, but Ryan went from grave to grave until he had read three names: Franco, Elena, and Paloma.

He stood back and ground out the match into the dirt. Scratching his head in thought, he looked from the graves into the distance several times. Who could Cooter Jackson have ridden so many miles in the middle of the night to meet, and why? Why here in this deserted cemetery? More importantly, what, if anything, did it have to do with the kidnapping of Amber McCandless?

When he spotted Owen's wrangler riding away from the ranch at such a late hour, Ryan had followed him. He felt certain the old cowhand knew a great deal more about this situation than he wanted known.

The question was, how much did Cooter know and whose side was he working for? The three graves reaffirmed Ryan's opinion that this kidnapping had more to do with revenge than money. The man Cooter Jackson had met was the key. That man knew the three people buried beneath those worn, dilapidated markers.

A gut feeling told him Owen McCandless was a dangerous and ruthless man. If he had anything to do with the deaths of those three people buried in the prairie, it might explain this whole confusing puzzle. At the moment, only two people knew the answer he was seeking; the man who had ridden away toward the north, and Cooter Jackson.

CHAPTER NINETEEN

Amber awoke at dawn, feeling strangely disoriented. Wondering vaguely what was different about this morning, she reached behind her to search the warm sheets.

Her eyes flew open as she realized Morgan was not beside her. He had not returned! She sat straight up in bed, looking for the slippers she had placed beside the bed before retiring. It had been very late before she had finally drifted off to sleep. Even then she had slept fitfully, getting up several times to look out the window, hoping to see Morgan riding up the street.

All she had seen, however, was the lone figure of Jase McCally watching the house as he had been instructed. It had been shortly after noon when Jase knocked politely on the front door to inform her of Morgan's sudden departure. Jase had only told her Morgan had business elsewhere.

After reminding her that he would be close by, Jase had tipped his hat to her respectfully and taken up his post across the street. There he had stayed since noon the day before.

Rising, she moved toward the living room, her nose wrinkling as she smelled tobacco. The hair at the back of her neck stood on end at the realization that she wasn't alone. Quietly, she moved into the living room.

The room was dark and silent with gray shadows filling the corners as the sun began its ascent into the sky. She jumped in fright as one of those shadows moved.

An instant later relief flooded through her veins as Morgan materialized from the shadows. Amber's legs went weak with relief. She sank down quickly on one end of the couch and put a shaky hand to her throat.

"Morgan! I didn't hear you come in."

Morgan rose from the opposite end of the couch and moved into the light beyond the shadows at the front of the house. He was smoking a thin brown cheroot and holding a glass of whisky in one hand.

There was something different about him. She had never seen him except well-groomed and neat, but the man who stood before her now was neither of those things. A day's growth of beard shadowed his strong jaw. His black hair was rumpled, hanging over his forehead in silky waves. His shirt was open to his waist.

A shudder of uneasiness ran through Amber as she stared up at his lean, veiled features. His coal black eyes surveyed her with a steady, speculative gaze that sent shivers of alarm down her spine. The scent of horse sweat and tobacco combined with the vague odors of bay rum and whiskey assailed her and she realized with a start that he was drunk.

His silence was so ominous, Amber felt an icy thread of fear slice through her. Her eyes were drawn to the black, hand-tooled leather gunbelt that rested low on his left hip. God, did he never take that terrifying thing off except when he was forcing her to submit to his crude physical demands! The rising sun reflecting off the numerous notches in the ivory pistol grips made Amber fight back a shudder of revulsion.

"What's the matter, Miss McCandless? The sight of me disgust you?"

Amber rose and gave him a scornful glare. "You're drunk! I'm going back to bed!" she snapped.

With surprising speed, Morgan moved to cut off her retreat with a strange, frightening smile on his face that sent a surge of real fear through her veins. She found herself flattened against the wall staring up into his glittering black eyes, caged in by the hands he'd placed against the wall on either side of her.

"What's your hurry?" Morgan drawled lazily, his glance taking in the sheer, silk gown she wore before returning to rest on her pale face. "Have a drink with me."

Amber's nose turned up in disgust. " I don't think so!"

Morgan shrugged and moved away, refilling his glass from the liquor cabinet. Amber could not suppress a shudder of relief as he moved away. She edged another step toward the bedroom, but froze at his harsh command.

"Sit down, Amber!"

Her stiff legs refused to budge. She stared at his ominous, glowering face through a haze of alarm, cowering slightly when he moved to stand in front of her again.

"You'll go to bed when I tell you," he growled in a low, husky voice. He turned to set the glass on the arm of the couch, then again placed a hand on either side of Amber's body to prevent her from moving away. Letting his gaze flick over her tremulous form again, he smiled wickedly. "What's the matter, Amber? Are you afraid of me?"

With an effort, Amber glared at him. "You'd like that, wouldn't you?" she hissed. "No, Mr. Devereaux, I am not afraid of you!"

His smile was a flash of ivory against the deep bronze of his skin as he studied her face, seeing the fear she was trying desperately to keep from showing.

"No? Liar!" he taunted, with a mocking smile that sent shivers down Amber's spine. He raised one hand and trailed a finger down her satin cheek, noting the anxiety that leaped to her face. "I suppose you prefer men like Larkin Prentiss, smooth talkers and fancy dressers. Right?"

When Amber made no effort to answer Morgan shrugged and went on. "I've known a few women like you, Miss McCandless. You have this proper, prissy exterior, all genteel and delicate. You sit around sipping tea out of elegant little cups on those dainty little lace doilies, making polite small talk about the weather and clothes and parties.

"And all the time you're thinking about some cowboy with dusty boots and long hair, wondering what he'd be like in the sack. Your kind may marry the Larkin Prentiss' of this world, men with money and good manners who take their clothes off in a closet so as not to embarrass you, but when you want to feel like a woman, you look for a man wearing chaps and worn boots instead of a fancy dressed gentleman."

"I assume you're coming to some point," Amber challenged through stiff lips. She glared back into his mocking black eyes, unable to break the mesmerizing gaze that held her prisoner. Her throat felt tight, her mouth as dry as cotton, her breath constricted in her chest while he continued in that same low, deceptively soft voice that made her nerves tingle.

"My point, Miss McCandless, is that it's because of what I am that you're attracted to me," he told her with such perception it made her wince.

He cut off her heated denial with a finger laid across her lips. His breath was warm on her cheek, the scent of whiskey strangely not unpleasant when it reached her senses. She was painfully aware that he had moved closer and now his hard muscular thighs were pressing against hers. The cold metal of the gunbelt buckle chilled her stomach through the thin nightgown in contrast to the heat that emanated from his tall powerful body.

"I may not have your fancy eastern upbringing, Miss McCandless, but I'm not stupid. I know that somewhere in that proper, Bostonian ladylike heart of yours," he said with the jab of a brown finger into her chest, "Is a real woman who keeps her feelings all locked up tight, waiting for the right man to come along with the key."

"And I suppose you think you're that man!"

Another lazy grin drifted across his lips. "Yes ma'am, I do believe so."

Fury leaped through her face. She stretched to her full height, a full foot shorter than Morgan, and jabbed a finger into the soft black hair covering his chest.

"You are the most conceited, arrogant, selfish, disgusting creature that God ever created!" she cried. "I'll admit that you're handsome, in a rather primitive sort of way, but I'll have you understand that I am not attracted to you in the least!"

A soft chuckle rippled from him, his dancing gaze drifting over her again in a possessive manner that made her grind her teeth.

"But you know what, Miss McCandless? It's those very 'primitive' qualities that make you smile in your sleep and reach for me."

Furious denials sprang to Amber's lips, but for some reason she couldn't spit them out. The sardonic smile on his lips told her he was expecting her to deny it. She would not give him the satisfaction.

She stared at him with as much aloofness as she could muster, her lips curling back in a sneer. "I'm afraid you have grossly overestimated your charm, Mr. Devereaux. You may have forced yourself on me, but I can't wait to get away from you!.."

"You should never issue a challenge like that to a man who thrives on challenge," Morgan told her in a low husky voice as he bent his dark head to nuzzle his warm mouth against her neck.

Whether it was the arrogant confidence in his voice or her own inner fears Amber was not certain, but blind panic made her abruptly shove both hands against his chest, pushing him backwards far enough to free herself.

She made a frantic dash for the bedroom, intent on putting as much distance between herself and Morgan as possible. With surprising speed, Morgan recovered his balance and grabbed her arm. Amber spun around, her nails stabbing for his face, her bare feet kicking futility at his legs. His strong hands clasped her wrists and flung her backwards into the wall, knocking the breath from her lungs momentarily and sending a red haze flickering before her eyes.

Morgan's dark eyes narrowed dangerously. His hard body pressed her against the wall painfully. His mouth ground into her lips, his teeth bruising the tender flesh until Amber tasted blood and wondered vaguely if it was hers or his.

His hands pinned her to the wall, the weight of his body forced her breath to come in labored gasps. Amber tried to bring up one knee into his groin, but it was impossible with his body pressed so tightly against her own.

With a soft, sinister chuckle Morgan released her mouth long enough to whisper against her lips. "You don't want to do that, *mi princessa de oro*. How could I make love to you?"

His voice was a low, savage whisper that jangled Amber's raw nerves. Already she felt the hardness of his erection against her belly. She struggled to free her hands from his grip, feeling helpless, at his mercy as he continued to hold her in a vise-like grip that made her arms ache.

"Let go of me, you vile, murdering outlaw!" she spat in a voice that was more a whimper than a command.

Morgan's response was a kiss so deep it made her toes tingle. His mouth forced her lips apart to grant his tongue entrance, revolving inside her mouth, igniting tiny explosions of excitement that made her mind reel. Abruptly, he released her arms, cupping her breasts through the sheer material and teasing both nipples roughly until they stood in rosy peaks.

Despite the unaccustomed roughness, Amber felt her knees go weak at the touch of his hands. Her body seemed to burst into flames when he clutched the shoulders of the gown and pulled it down to reveal her breasts. She went limp when he dipped his dark head to suck first one rosy tip, then the other. The roughness of his beard only seemed to enhance the sensual pleasure his hot mouth provoked from her flesh.

Amber fought her way from the blossoming cloud of passion that roared within her. Realizing both his hands were occupied with her breasts, she grabbed for the Colt in the holster on his hip. The safety loop over the hammer defied her attempt to remove the weapon. It gave Morgan time to realize what she was doing.

A growl of fury rippled from his throat. He seized her wrist and pried her fingers from the butt of the gun. Amber cried out in pain, but made one last desperate grab for the pistol. Morgan's left hand held the gun in place while the right caught Amber's shoulder and flung her away.

She landed with a thud on the bedroom floor. Sparks erupted behind her eyes when her head hit the hard floor. She shook her head to clear away the dense fog that filled it, then struggled to her knees. She crept backwards, her eyes wide with terror as Morgan advanced menacingly.

A sob bubbled up in her throat at the dangerous glitter in his eyes. She knew he was going to kill her this time. His jaw was set in a hard line as he towered above her cringing figure.

Her lips formed a silent plea that could not get past her frozen lips. Suddenly he reached down and removed the pistol. Amber closed her eyes tightly and waited for the explosion she was certain was coming, but they flew open again in shock when he pressed the cold metal into her hand.

"Go on, Amber, shoot," he told her with a taunting smile that did not diminish the glitter in his black eyes. "You want to kill me, so go ahead. You've got the gun. Use it. Shoot me."

Amber stared up into his mocking face. The challenge in his eyes was so blatant, it was an open dare. She shook her head shook violently and let the gun drop onto the bed.

"No," she whimpered.

"Why not? Don't you have the guts to kill me?" he taunted with a sinister grin that chilled her blood. "You wanted to badly enough a moment ago. So what's stopping you now?"

Amber stared at him without answering, caught by the strange tremor in his voice.

"Don't you think it's loaded?"

Morgan reached down to pick up the gun. Pointing it toward the ceiling, he pulled back the hammer and fired. The bullet slammed into the ceiling with a roar that made Amber's ears ring. Then he pressed the gun into her hands again.

"There are five rounds left, Amber. You should be able to kill me with that many shots. Go ahead. What's stopping you?"

"Stop it! Stop it!" she screamed. She threw the gun down on the bed and covered her ears to block out his taunting voice. When he didn't move or make another sound for a few moments, she lifted her tear streaked face to find him regarding her with a pensive gleam that contained a hint of humor.

"I'm not like you!" she cried. "I can't kill another human being so easily!"

"Then why did you grab for my gun?"

"Because you're terrifying me! I gave you my promise that I'd do what you wanted, but you were hurting me. I wanted to make you stop," she whispered in a choked voice.

Morgan said nothing, staring down at her with that piercing gaze that made her feel helpless. She preferred his sarcastic taunts to this ominous silence. She swallowed in an effort to steady her voice. She stood on shaky legs and slowly pushed the gown from her hips, letting it fall to the floor. Then she moved forward, hesitantly put her hands on his chest and made herself look into those glittering black eyes.

"I'll do whatever you want, Morgan. Please don't hurt me."

Morgan's arms went around her, pulling her naked body tightly against him. His erection burned through his clothes into Amber's skin. Her slim arms slipped around his neck, her fingers entwining in his thick black hair as his mouth claimed hers in a deep sensual kiss that set her body tingling.

Her passive submission fed the burning need in him. The desire that had made him ride like a madman through the night to reach her took control of his senses. He knew he was being too rough, bruising her soft flesh with his hands and lips, but the urgency within him demanded satisfaction. He quickly shed his clothes and pushed her back onto the bed, opened her legs with one knee and entered her with a force that made her gasp.

Amber's body accepted his swollen manhood painlessly. She lay beneath him, gritting her teeth against the bone crunching thrusts while he rode her ruthlessly, his breath coming in short, labored gasps, his eyes closed and his dark head thrown back. His body was quickly covered with a light mist of perspiration as he came closer and closer to release from the demons ripping at his insides.

"I'm sorry, *princessa*," he whispered in a low husky tone that sent shivers through Amber's veins. "I can't help myself. Forgive me for hurting you."

Moments later, he groaned deep in his throat and shuddered, driving himself deeply into the warm moist depths of her unresisting body as he spent himself with such force, it made sparks of light ignite behind his closed eyes.

Almost immediately he rolled off her. He sat up on the edge of the bed, putting one hand over his eyes while his breathing returned to normal. After a moment, he looked at Amber's pale face among the tumbled covers, his lips tightening at the way her fingers had clinched in the sheets.

Amber was stunned at the raw exposed emotion she saw in his handsome face. Whatever was driving him had lifted the black veil he kept over his eyes momentarily to allow her a brief glimpse into his haunted soul.

He looked quickly away as though aware he had revealed too much, then snatched his clothes up from the floor. He dressed rapidly without looking at her except when he reached over her to retrieve the Colt wadded in the bed clothes. Slipping it into the holster on his hip, he finally drew a long breath as he turned those dark, disturbed eyes to her.

"I'm sorry, Amber," he mumbled in a voice so low Amber wasn't sure if she heard him correctly. Before she could speak, he strode rapidly from the room. A second later she heard the front door close behind him.

She lay stunned, unable to think, her body throbbing. After a time, she sat up, trying to piece the puzzle together. Then the bright rays of the morning sun reflected off an object on the dresser. Slowly she crossed the room to pick it up. A gasp of surprise escaped her lips at closer examination.

It was a music box, lined in rich red velvet, elegantly adorned with sterling silver trim and inlaid pearl in the delicate lid. She opened it gently to hear the soft familiar strains of "Shenandoah." It was exquisite.

She hugged it to her breast, tears filling her eyes. Morgan had obviously brought it as a gift for her. But why had he brought her a beautiful gift and then treated her so cruelly? What was driving him? Why did he guard the tenderness she felt was hidden somewhere deep within? Where had he been and what had made him return a dark forbidding stranger?

0223-SLAT

CHAPTER TWENTY

After storming into Welch's office to report his meeting with Cooter, Morgan retreated to the saloon at the end of the street. There he proceeded to drink himself into a pleasant alcoholic fog that blotted out wide amber colored eyes filled with fear.

It was nearing midnight when he finally stumbled down the street toward home. He glanced up toward Welch's bedroom window and smiled drunkenly at Welch's figure outlined by the lamp's glow behind him.

"What in the world is wrong with him?" Francine asked, peering around Welch into the street below. "It's not like Morgan to drink so much. I don't think I've ever seen him so drunk he can't walk straight."

"Then you've never seen him after a visit to that place. It happens when he goes there. He's drinking to escape the ghosts," Welch said thoughtfully.

"But those ghosts can't be escaped, can they, Welch?"

Welch's lips twisted in a sardonic smile. "No, not yet anyway. But soon, Francie, very soon."

"I pray you're right, Welch," Francine murmured against his back.

"So do I," he said quietly.

***

Amber stiffened in alarm when Morgan slid into bed beside her. She lay frozen, expecting any second to feel his body demand her attention, then let out a sigh of relief when his steady breathing told her he was asleep.

She relaxed again, breathing in the scent of his skin. He had bathed, shaved, and changed into clean clothes during his absence. As sleep drifted across her mind, she wondered which man she would wake up with the following morning; the dark, sinister stranger of today or the handsome gunfighter who had taken her from the stage and turned her blood to liquid flame with a touch.

***

The distinct odor of smoke filled Morgan's senses. His eyes flew open, widening at the sight of bright orange flames licking from the lace curtains. Fire! He had to do something!

He saw his father's body hanging grotesquely from the cottonwood in the corner of the yard. Voices...lots of voices...laughing obscenely...screams..pleas for mercy...smoke rising..a half dozen horses riding out of the yard..voices still laughing as they disappeared into the darkness...silence, except for the fire crackling..still, deathly silence..then shrill, high pitched screams of terror..Paloma! I'm coming, Paloma!

Somehow his frozen legs moved, brought him to his feet running toward the house, tripping over his shoe laces, stumbling, his heart pounding so hard his ears roared.

Papa! Do something! Papa! he screamed. Another shrill scream of terror snapped his head back toward the house. The door was open. He ran toward it, but flames and thick black smoke choked him, made him cough and his eyes water. He could see Paloma standing up in her crib, her tiny arms outstretched, her chubby pink baby face screwed up in terror, her mouth open and wailing. Norgie! he could hear her calling him...Norgie!

The heat..the flames..everywhere! He ran around the house to the kitchen window, but his hands were seared by the intense heat when he touched the window pane. Hot! Too hot! Then his terrified eyes fell on his mother's body sprawled on the floor near Paloma's crib. Her long black hair was spread out like a fan around her face, her pretty blue dress bunched up around her thighs, her skin smudged with red...blood!

Mama! Get up! Mama! Don't you hear Paloma screaming? Mama! Why was she so still? Mama! Mama!

"Mama!" he shouted as he jerked upright in bed, his chest heaving with exertion and his body drenched with cold sweat.

He was shaking so hard his teeth were chattering. He groaned deeply, swung his legs from the sheets and moved to the edge of the bed. One hand covered his eyes while the other raked through his tumbled hair to brush it from his face. With an effort he got to his feet, slipped into his trousers, and walked into the living room on trembling legs.

He was pouring himself a glass of whiskey and trying to calm his pounding heart when he realized Amber was standing in the archway, staring at him with wide, concerned eyes.

"Sorry I woke you," he mumbled with an embarrassed glance in her direction.

"You were having a nightmare," Amber said. She padded across the cool floor to stand nervously behind him. "Are you all right?"

He nodded and took a deep breath, filling his lungs with air that was free of smoke. His powerful body was still covered with cold sweat, his chest was heaving with exertion. He gulped down the burning whiskey and took another long breath before looking at Amber.

"Yes, I'm all right. Go on back to bed."

"Do you have nightmares often?"

"Too often," he replied bitterly over the rim of the glass.

"Is it always the same dream?"

Morgan nodded with a bitter smile touching his lips. "Yes, always. It's come once or twice a week since I was ten years old. You'd think I would've outgrown it by now, wouldn't you?"

"Why don't you tell me about it?" Amber invited with a soft smile. She sat down on the couch and patted a spot beside her. "Maybe telling someone else will help make it go away."

"Not in this case," he replied dryly. He refilled the glass with whiskey and came to sit beside her, leaning his elbows on his knees as he stared straight ahead. "The only thing that will erase this nightmare is putting a bullet through Owen McCandless' black heart."

Amber's breath caught in her throat, but she swallowed as she laid a warm hand on the knee nearest her. He wasn't wearing the gunbelt. That made him less formidable, more human, more vulnerable.

"Don't you think it's time you told me about it?"

He turned to look at her at last, studying her face silently for a moment, then he nodded curtly and took another sip from the glass.

"Maybe you're right. Maybe it's time you heard the truth about your uncle."

It was several moments, however, before Morgan could begin to talk. The pain had been locked inside him for so long he didn't know how to begin.

"It started the year I was nine. We had this ranch, five hundred acres, not all that much really, but it was good land. We had a few cattle and a couple dozen pure-blooded Arabian horses."

Amber's brows arched in surprise, but she kept silent.

"The land was my mother's dowry. My grandfather was a Spanish land baron before the war with Mexico. He managed to hold onto that piece and gave it to my mother when she married.

"It was just the four of us; my parents, my baby sister, Paloma, and myself. We never had a lot of money, just enough to get by, but we were happy. Until Owen McCandless decided he could save time and money by driving his herds to the railhead in Fort Worth. The only problem was that my father's ranch lay smack in the middle of the route.

"He came first to make my father an offer for the ranch, but my father refused to sell. McCandless came again, a couple of times, each time raising his offer, but my father always turned it down. The last time he came, he told my father if he didn't sell, he'd find some other way to get us off the land."

A faint smile came to Morgan's lips. "McCandless obviously didn't know shit about my father. He was a good man, he hated violence, but there wasn't a man ever born that he was afraid of. He stood up to McCandless, told him to get off his land. He wasn't interested in selling and he wasn't going to be driven off what belonged to him.

"Things were pretty quiet after that for a while. Then the summer I was ten, things began to happen. At first it wasn't much, just fence torn down, little things like that. Then it got worse. Rocks thrown through our windows in the middle of the night, threats, livestock stolen, equipment destroyed, our barn burned.

"That's about the time Welch came into our lives. He'd been shot, was nearly dead when my folks found him, took care of him and when he was better, he hired on as a cowhand. But when it turned out that he was fast with a gun, McCandless got nervous. Maybe he thought my father had hired Welch's gun. Anyway, not long after that, Welch and my father were returning from town with supplies one day when a group of McCandless' riders fired on them.

"Welch shot back and killed a couple of them. My father insisted he leave the ranch before McCandless could come back with the law. I remember Welch didn't want to leave, but my father told him it was the only way, so in the end Welch left."

His voice stalled and he took a deep breath while gathering his thoughts. "That night just about dusk, I was at the well drawing water for my mother when Owen McCandless rode into the yard with five other men. One of them was a Texas Ranger. The ranger told my father Welch was a wanted man and they knew we were hiding him. My father said Welch wasn't there, but McCandless looked at the ranger and said, 'String him up. He's hiding an outlaw and you know what the law says about that.' Then they lynched him."

Morgan's voice had become harsh and cold, his chest was heaving with the effort to get it out of his memory and into words. "They tied his hands behind his back, tied a rope to one of their saddles and threw the other end over a limb of the cottonwood in the corner of the yard. Then they hauled him off the ground, dangling like a side of beef until he choked to death."

Amber's gasp of horror tightened her grip on Morgan's knee. He was staring straight ahead, his body beginning to perspire heavily. She noticed his hands were trembling until he interlaced his fingers to keep them still.

"One of the men jerked out his knife and went to cut the rope. I remember he was white as a ghost and shaking so hard he could hardly hold the knife steady. He told McCandless to stop it, that what he was doing was murder, but McCandless only laughed and called him a coward, said if he didn't have the guts to be a McCandless to go back to the ranch and wait.

"This man reached out to cut the rope when McCandless hit him in the head with the barrel of his pistol. Then they saw my mother in the doorway. She was in shock, I guess, like me, because she couldn't seem to move. The ranger and the others got off their horses and started toward her. She started screaming and McCandless slapped her, knocked her down. Then he grabbed her by the hair and dragged her into the house and slammed the door.

"I could hear her screaming, over and over, then she stopped. In a few minutes, McCandless came out and the ranger went in. I ran to help her, but Owen McCandless kicked me in the face. When I came to, I was behind the wood pile. The man who had tried to stop McCandless was holding me. I remember he was all bloody and he was shaking. He tied his bandanna around my head and told me to be quiet or his brother would kill me too."

Morgan turned bleak ebony eyes to Amber with a weak smile. "That man was your father, Amber. Price McCandless. He tried to save my father, but couldn't...but he did save my life, by hiding me.

"A long time went by while the others took turns with my mother. When they finished with her, Owen McCandless went in a second time and I heard a shot. Then he set fire to the curtains. They rode off laughing."

"My father?"

"He passed out behind the wood pile with me. They left without him. I tried to move, but my legs were frozen. I couldn't move. I could see the fire spreading, smelled the smoke, and then I heard Paloma screaming. Finally, I made myself get up and I ran to the house.

"I could see Paloma standing up in her crib, could hear her screaming my name, crying for me to come get her." A strong shudder passed through him as his voice broke. "Oh God, I can still hear her screaming my name. She was just a baby...eighteen months old...but I couldn't get into the house. Flames were everywhere, the smoke was so thick I couldn't breathe.

"I ran to the kitchen window to see if I could get in there. That's when I saw my mother lying on the floor. I knew she was dead. There was blood everywhere, in her hair, on her legs."

He shuddered again as Amber choked back a sob.

"I must have passed out then. When I came to it was late, the house was burned to the ground. So I sat in the grass and threw up until I couldn't anymore and then I went to the shed to find a hay scythe and cut my father's body down.

"Your father was gone. He must have come to while I was unconscious and left, because I was all alone. I remember trying to dig the graves and having to stop every few minutes to vomit. I was still digging the next morning when Welch found me. He helped me bury my family and took care of me."

Morgan turned his head at last to look at Amber with such raw emotion in his eyes, it almost took her breath. "When I stood over my family's graves, I swore I would see Owen McCandless in hell for what he'd done and I will..if it takes my last breath to do it."

He rose to his feet and walked a few steps away, standing with his back to Amber while he stared out the window into the sleepy streets of the Lair.

"Oh, Morgan, I'm so sorry," Amber said behind him.

Her voice was barely a whisper and when Morgan swung around

to face her, she was pale and trembling. Her golden eyes seemed enormous in her white face as she blinked back tears of horror and sorrow.

"I don't need your sympathy, Amber. I only need you here to make Owen McCandless come after me."

She got to her feet to pad across the floor and place a hesitant hand on his arm. He stared at her with a puzzled expression while she gathered her courage. "Morgan, what happened to your family was a horrible thing, but there's something I must ask."

"You don't believe me, do you? You just can't imagine darling Uncle Owen could do anything like that." Morgan's voice was cold, filled with sarcasm as his eyes mocked the doubt he saw in her face.

Tears filled Amber's eyes. She reached to brush them away while she searched Morgan's dark face for a hint of the vulnerability he had shown earlier. But it was gone, hidden behind veiled eyes that viewed her contemptuously.

"He's my uncle, Morgan. Surely you can understand why I don't want to believe he could do something so vile. Isn't there some chance that you were mistaken? You were a terrified child, perhaps you were wrong. It could have been bandits or.."

"It wasn't," Morgan cut in sharply. "I know what I saw, Amber. It was Owen McCandless. Your dear uncle wasn't satisfied with owning half the state of Texas. He wanted five hundred lousy acres that lay between him and what he wanted. He was smart; he knew when the railroad came into McCandless it would come through my family's land. He was protecting an investment that undoubtedly made him a fortune when the railroad was built.

"I'm sorry that you had to learn this, Amber. I'm sure you'd rather go right on believing what a wonderful man your uncle is, but he isn't. He's a murdering, thieving, low-life and one day very soon, it's going to catch up with him."

"And what about you, Morgan? You can't get away with this. You've got to know that. The law will hunt you down and kill you."

Morgan nodded as a grim smile formed on his lips. "Maybe. Even so it will have been worth it."

"Will it? Morgan, you have lived your entire life plotting revenge. Look at you! You could be anything you choose to be. You're handsome, intelligent, you have leadership qualities most men only dream of, but what have you become? A gunfighter with a price on your head. There's only one way this will end, Morgan, if you don't stop it now.

"Listen to me," she pleaded, her eyes searching his face for a sign of understanding. "It's not too late, Morgan. Take me back and forget this madness you're planning. If my uncle is guilty of the horrible things you say, I will personally see that he's punished."

"Punished!" Morgan snapped scornfully. "Owen McCandless owns this state, don't you realize that yet? He owns the courts and the judges and the law. He could commit cold blooded murder on the main street of McCandless with a hundred people watching and not even be questioned. My family wasn't the only one he destroyed to get what he wanted, Amber. There have been many others. He's always taken what he wants and if anyone got in his way, he either ran them out or if they refused to run, he killed them. How do you think he's built such an empire? It wasn't with brotherly love; it was with bullets and blood."

"Morgan, you must be mistaken. Uncle Owen isn't like that. He's kind and generous and caring. He's rich and powerful, yes, I won't deny that, but he's a good man, Morgan."

"You think so? You cross him once, Amber, just once, and he'll turn on you like a lobo and he'll tear you to pieces just as he would anybody else who got in his way."

"I don't want to hear anymore," Amber cried. She whirled to leave, but Morgan caught her arm and swung her back to face him. Amber flinched at the bitterness in his eyes. He looked cold and dangerous again, making her heart pound with anxiety.

"There's more and you're going to hear it all," he growled. He gave her a slight push toward the couch. She sank down weakly and stared at him with growing apprehension.

"I suppose you think your father's death was an accident, don't you? Well, it wasn't. Owen McCandless made it look like an accident, but it was murder, Amber. Your Uncle Owen killed his own brother twelve years ago."

"I don't believe you. It's not true," Amber wailed.

"It is true. Your father was an honest man, Amber, a decent man. He couldn't go along with the things Owen was doing and he threatened to expose him. So Owen killed him and made it look like an accident."

"Why are you doing this to me?" Amber whimpered. She stared at him disbelievingly, tears filling her eyes and sliding down her cheeks.

"You don't have to take my word for it, Amber," Morgan added in a gentler tone. "Ask Welch or Cooter Jackson. They both knew your father and they know Owen. Owen doesn't like having people around who knows what he did in the old days. He's very carefully created an image he shows to the world and very few people, alive at any rate, know what he's really like. He guards that part of his past very carefully. That's why he had to kill your father, Amber. To keep that image intact.

"It's also why Welch left the ranch years ago, why Owen tried so hard to kill him, too. They were all partners in the beginning. Did he tell you that? Owen, Price, Welch, and Cooter. Now there's only Owen. Welch is an outlaw, Price is dead, and Cooter is an old man who has stayed alive the best way he could. That means keeping his mouth shut and selling his share of the ranch to Owen at a fraction of what it was worth."

Amber stared up at his lean face for a moment longer, then jumped to her feet and ran into the bedroom, threw herself face down on the bed and sobbed into the covers.

Morgan finished the drink in his hand and poured another. He sat down on the couch, lit a cheroot and smoked it in morose silence while Amber cried bitterly in the next room. His chest felt tight. His throat ached from holding in scalding tears of his own. He angrily brushed his eyes with the back of one hand, then swallowed another mouthful of the burning whiskey.

He had cried all the tears inside him when he was ten years old so why did he suddenly find his eyes burning now with the urge to cry like a baby? It must be the whiskey, he reasoned irritably. God knew he had consumed enough of it in the past day and night to make even the strongest man melancholy.

Or maybe Amber was right. Maybe finally putting his nightmare into words and telling someone else relieved some of the burden he'd carried inside for so long.

At any rate, she had to be told. Even if she didn't believe one word of it, she had to hear the truth. It was time she knew what kind of man her uncle was.

Still, the sound of her sobs made his chest hurt with a peculiar ache that was unfamiliar to him. He wished he hadn't had to hurt her. She didn't deserve it. She was not responsible for her uncle's wrongdoing. Morgan wondered, for the first time, if using her to achieve his goal was a wise thing to do.

CHAPTER TWENTY-ONE

Morgan rose with the intention of going into the bedroom and trying to comfort Amber. While a woman's tears had never bothered him much in the past, the sight of Amber's golden eyes filled with suffering created the urge in him to do something to relieve her torment.

A loud knock on the front door made him change directions. Irritably, he turned to open it. Jase McCally's grinning face greeted him.

"Sorry if I'm interrupting anything, Morgan, but the boss wants to see you right away."

"Any particular reason?"

"Yeah," McCally drawled. "Seems he's heard from the girl's old man. Looks like McCandless wants to talk."

***

There was a full moon the night Morgan and Welch rode to meet with Owen McCandless. Ten men rode behind them through scrub timber and rocks as they made their way down the mountain to the Texas plain. As the land evened out, the great hulking shadows of cottonwoods loomed from the plains.

A half mile from the appointed meeting place, Welch reined to a halt and looked over his shoulder. The men had been instructed to wait just beyond rifle range while Welch and Morgan went forward to speak with the rancher. At a nod from Welch, Jase McCally led the men to a clump of nearby cottonwoods.

The two horses moved forward at a trot. Birds fluttered overhead as a jackrabbit family scurried to get out of the way.

"I don't like this," Welch grunted to Morgan. "It's too damned quiet."

"We both know there's a chance we're walking into a trap," Morgan reminded him. "But even if McCandless is a fool, the ranger isn't. He won't try anything now. He'll wait and make his move when he's ready, on his own terms."

"You know a hell of a lot about lawmen for a man who's on the other side of the fence," Welch remarked dryly.

"I like to think I know more about them than they know about me."

The clink of bridle bits made Welch's grin fade instantly. In the clearing ahead, he saw three men waiting. It was easy to pick Owen from the trio. The arrogant way he sat a horse had been burned into Welch's memory.

"Remember, Morgan," he murmured without turning his head. "Let me do the talking. You keep a lid on your temper. Our time is coming soon enough."

Morgan made no reply, but cast a glance at Welch as they approached the clearing. They reined their mounts to a halt. For a moment, no one spoke.

Owen McCandless resisted the urge to squirm when he looked into that pair of gun-metal eyes directly in front of him. God, how he had always hated the way Welch could stare a man down. It was goddamned unnerving.

"Mandell, I'm Ryan Tyrell, Texas Rangers," Ryan said coldly.

"I know who you are," Welch told him without taking his eyes from Owen's face. "And I know why you're here, but we didn't come alone. My men are waiting out of sight. If for some reason we don't return by dawn, Mr. McCandless here will be short one very lovely niece. I'd think about that before you signal to the posse you've got waiting behind you."

Ryan's lips twitched with admiration. Welch Mandell was a professional, if nothing else.

"Now that we've got that out of the way, let's get down to business," Welch growled. "I assume you don't have the money.

Why else would you ask for a meeting? What's the matter, McCandless, having trouble coming up with the cash?"

Owen's face flooded with fury. "You son-of-a-bitch! You know goddamned well I don't have that kind of cash lying around!" he snarled.

"That's no way to speak to the man who has your niece, McCandless," Welch couldn't resist taunting. He knew he was walking on eggshells, but the open contempt in Owen's face could not be ignored. "She's beautiful. Looks a lot like her mother."

Owen's face went pale in the moonlight. He swallowed his rage and tried to think rationally. The man who sat staring at him now with such contempt, bore little resemblance to the man who had ridden out of the ranch yard thirty years earlier. That man had been young and unpredictable, but this man was so confident, it made the hair on the back of Owen's neck stand on end.

Time had been good to Welch, Owen saw irritably. His once blonde hair was now streaked with silver, which only enhanced his looks. His powerful body was still muscular. The gray eyes were even sharper than Owen remembered.

The quiet, understated manner that had invoked Owen's hatred of this man so many years before still emanated from him. It never seemed to matter whether Welch was covered with dust and wearing sweaty clothes or all dressed up in his Sunday best, he'd always had a way about him that exuded confidence and virility. It was that, as much as anything, that had made Owen grow to hate him.

"I think we'd all be better off to cut the gab and get this over with," Cooter Jackson suggested nervously. He was mounted between Owen and the ranger with his gnarled hands clinched around the saddlehorn so their trembling would not betray his anxiety. Goddamn Owen and Welch both for putting him right in the middle of this meeting. He was too damned old for all these games. He was sorely tempted to pull out his pistol and blow that arrogant smirk off Owen's face and be done with it. Had it not been for the ranger....

"Cooter's right," Ryan was agreeing. "Let's keep this as business-like as possible. We all want the same thing."

For the first time, Welch's eyes left Owen to move to the ranger. The hate blazing from those aqua-marine colored eyes was so intense a lesser man might have felt uneasy, but Welch met the ranger's cold stare evenly as he sized him up. "So you're Jim Tyrell's boy," he drawled. "How appropriate that you be here."

"I thought so too," Ryan returned with an effort to keep his voice steady. "I'm happy to know that you remember my father."

"I remember him well. I hope that you're a better lawman than he was. He had a fondness for whiskey and cards. It eventually led him to treachery and murder. I hope you'll be more careful."

"I'm a very careful man, Mandell," Ryan said coldly. "Someday you and I have to have a personal talk about my father."

"Any time, ranger," Welch replied meaningfully, then brought his attention back to Owen. "You've got one day left, McCandless. If you don't have the money by midnight tomorrow, I'm afraid your niece will be a very sorry young lady."

"That's why we called this meetin'," Cooter explained in a rapid effort to defuse the tension. He could see that Owen was quickly reaching his breaking point and might do something foolish.

Welch's brows arched in amusement at the fury he observed in Owen's face. "Really? I'm not in the mood to make a deal, McCandless. I want fifty thousand dollars, not a penny less, and I want it tomorrow."

"I don't have it!" Owen barked. "I can get it, and I will," he hastened to add. "But it'll take time. That's all I'm asking for, just a little more time."

"Time for what?"

"Time to sell off enough assets to raise the cash."

Welch smiled at the plea in Owen's voice. God, how sweet it was to see him squirm. "How much time?"

"A month, that's all I need."

"That's out of the question," Welch returned sharply.

"Welch, for God's sake, give me more time!" Owen pleaded, his bravado gone in the face of Welch's unrelenting position.

Ryan's eyes snapped to Owen's imploring face. He had used Mandell's first name like an old acquaintance. Ryan shifted his attention to the outlaw. There was a satisfied smile on Mandell's face that told Ryan he was taking great pleasure in seeing McCandless beg. Whatever was going on here between these two men had nothing to do with money. It was personal. So personal, Mandell was willing to sacrifice an innocent girl to get his revenge.

"You'll have to convince my companion, I'm afraid," Welch drawled. He made a slight motion of his head toward Morgan. "It's up to him. The girl is his prisoner."

"So you're Morgan Devereaux," Ryan mused aloud before Owen could speak. At Morgan's nod, he added, "I've heard a great deal about you. They say you're as fast with a gun as they come."

Morgan did not speak, but sat in a deceptively relaxed manner on his horse as he returned the ranger's thoughtful stare. The coldness in those dark eyes astonished Ryan. He had never seen a man with eyes like that. He had already noticed the icy stare the gunman had been directing at McCandless. It made him wonder how Morgan fit into Mandell's scheme.

"But then you've had an excellent teacher," Ryan added grudgingly.

Again Morgan nodded, but did not speak. After a moment, he turned his attention toward McCandless once more. Hatred burned his throat, made his fingers itch to reach for the pistol lying only inches from where his left hand rested on his thigh. One bullet now and it would be over, but that was too fast, too easy. McCandless hadn't been that merciful. He must die slowly, painfully until he begged for death to relieve his torment. That was the only way. He forced his fingers to relax and swallowed his bitterness.

Ryan saw the instinctive, almost over-powering desire to kill flash into Morgan's eyes. Saw, too, the supreme effort it took for

the gunfighter to get control of his emotions. So it wasn't just
Mandell that wanted McCandless, it was Devereaux too, perhaps
even more so. God, what he would give to know what was behind
all this.

"A month is all I'm asking for," Owen was saying. He seemed
oblivious to the raw hatred gleaming in the gunfighter's eyes. "You
can wait a month for that much money."

"I've waited long enough," Morgan grated in a strangely soft
voice. "I'll not wait another month."

Owen studied Morgan's dark face. There was something almost familiar about this man, something that tugged at his memory,
but he couldn't put a finger on it. Something told him he had seen
Morgan Devereaux before, or had he?

"I'll give you two weeks," Morgan said suddenly. His response
shocked himself as much as it did Welch, whose head jerked around
in astonishment. The surprise in Morgan's eyes told Welch he did
not know what had made him say it.

Morgan made a slight shrugging movement, then returned
his attention to the rancher. Then it suddenly occurred to him
why he had given McCandless more time. He wasn't ready to let
go of Amber yet.

"All right, two weeks, but I can't promise anything," Owen
said belligerently.

"Then I'll make you a promise," Welch said contemptuously.
He maneuvered his horse alongside Owen's until they were separated by a couple of inches. "In two weeks, if you don't come up
with the money, Owen, you can expect a very unpleasant package
to be delivered to your door."

The outlaw's voice was soft and calm, so low Ryan could not
make out all the words, but the way Owen's face blanched told
him all he needed to know.

Owen reached out a shaky hand and clutched Welch's forearm. "Welch, for God's sake! Have mercy! She's done nothing to
you."

A cold sardonic smile curled Welch's lips. "Mercy? The word

mercy coming from your mouth amounts to sacrilege!" he snorted scornfully. "You don't know the meaning of the word! You're so goddamned sanctimonious, Owen, you make me sick!

"You better go home and pray, Owen. Pray that you can come up with the money in the time Morgan's given you. Because if you don't, I'll show you mercy. Remember, I learned it from you!"

Welch whirled the Palomino stallion, then he turned back briefly to say to Ryan, "Stay out of this, ranger. It's none of your business. Stick your nose in it and I'll kill you, just like I killed your old man."

He dug his heels into the stallion's sides to send him streaking across the plains. Morgan hesitated a moment longer, pausing to shoot Owen one last contemptuous glance. As he turned the Appaloosa to follow Welch, Ryan caught hold of the bridle.

Instantly, Morgan's hand went to the butt of his gun. Ryan carefully kept his gun hand in sight as he moved his horse closer in order to look into the gunfighter's face at close range.

"I don't know exactly what is going on here, Devereaux, but I will find out, and you won't get away with it. I'll stop you. You've got my word on it."

"You heard what Welch said, ranger. It goes for me, too. Get in my way and I'll kill you," Morgan replied softly.

The two men studied each other for a long second before Ryan nodded. "All right, Devereaux, I've warned you. Give up the girl now. Turn yourself in and I'll see to it you get a fair shake. If you go through with this, I'll hunt you down like a lobo wolf and I'll see you hang."

"Fair shake?" Morgan snorted. "There's not a court in this state that would give me a fair trial." He jerked his head toward Owen, with a cold sneer curling his lips. "He owns every one of them. Just like he owns you."

"No man owns me," Ryan contradicted with glittering eyes. "I work for the state of Texas, not Owen McCandless. Give yourself up, Devereaux, and I give you my word, you'll get a square deal."

Morgan studied the ranger's calm green eyes in silence for a moment before a tiny smile curled his lips. "You say that like you mean it, ranger. Too bad I don't believe you." His eyes became cold, his voice hard. "You see, I learned a long time ago that the law is bought and sold by men like him. I learned it from your old man. It's a lesson I'll never forget."

Without another glance at Ryan's puzzled face, Morgan whirled his horse and urged it into a gallop. Ryan stared after him in surprise, watching the way the moon reflected off Morgan's silver hatband as the man rode away. A slight grin tugged at the ranger's lips as he watched the outlaw disappear into the darkness. Devereaux was riding an Appaloosa!

He looked at Cooter Jackson as the three men turned to make their way back to the ranch. The old wrangler's face was carefully expressionless, but Ryan caught the tremor in Cooter's hands when he lifted the reins.

It was about time he and Cooter had a long, private conversation.

CHAPTER TWENTY-TWO

It was midafternoon the following day when Morgan and Welch returned to the Lair. They had backtracked for hours to be certain they had not been followed. It had been a silent journey for Morgan was preoccupied on the way back.

"It's the girl, isn't it?" Welch asked abruptly, breaking the silence.

"What?"

"The reason you gave McCandless more time than we'd agreed. The girl..Amber. You're not ready to turn her loose."

Morgan scowled at Welch's perception, then shrugged. "It's only one week more than we planned to give him anyway. What's the difference?"

"You're not getting sweet on her, are you?"

The look Morgan shot him made Welch uneasy. His hands had begun to sweat so he wiped them on the thighs of the tailored black trousers. Morgan's refusal to confirm or deny his question brought a sick feeling to the pit of his stomach.

"Stop worrying. She's a challenge, that's all. In two weeks I'll be bored with her and be glad to give her back."

"Is she that good in the sack?"

Morgan shook his head as he pushed the black Stetson to the back of his head, grinning at Welch's obvious discomfort. "Not yet, but she has potential."

"Oh, for God's sake!"

Morgan's dark eyes danced. "You want me to tell you about it, Welch?"

"Jesus Christ, Morgan! Shut up about it, will you? I really don't want to know!"

Morgan laughed softly at the way Welch's face had flooded with color. "Sure you do, Welch. Don't you remember how you used to always want to know about it?"

"Not this time! Goddamnit, Morgan, it's bad enough that I know it without giving me details!"

"Are you going to tell me that if you got the chance, you wouldn't take her to bed?" Morgan asked with a wicked grin.

"Hell, no, I wouldn't!" Welch answered emphatically. "She's young enough to be my daughter, for God's sake."

"That's never stopped you before," Morgan pointed out. "I remember that little Mexican filly down in Juarez a couple of years ago. She was every bit of fourteen. Hell, Welch, you humped her till she could hardly walk."

"She was sixteen and it's not the same thing," Welch growled.

"The hell it isn't."

Welch shifted in the saddle, facing Morgan with an embarrassed flush in his face. "She's Price's kid, goddamnit. It'd be like humping my own daughter. Damnit, Morgan, try to think of it from my position. It would be the same as if I humped your little sister. How would you like that?"

Morgan studied him thoughtfully for a moment, then nodded. "I see your point. Sorry, Welch, I guess in your position I might not be as calm as you. If it was me and you were humping some of my kin, say my mother or my sister, I'd probably kill you so damned fast you'd be dizzy."

Welch's face went white at Morgan's casual statement. He cursed himself for the way his hands began to sweat and shake. He wet his dry lips with his tongue and tried to recover his composure before Morgan noticed.

"All right, you understand how I feel. So let's not talk about it anymore," he croaked in a tight voice.

Morgan nodded, already lost in his own thoughts. A smile tugged at his lips as he thought about how to make up for the rough way he had treated Amber the last time they made love. It would be different now, he vowed to himself.

***

Amber heard the shouts of welcome far down the street. She jumped to her feet, dusted off her clothes, and smoothed her hair. She had spent the greater part of the morning in the front yard on her knees planting marigolds and petunias along the inside of the white picket fence and down both sides of the walk.

It had taken a bit of persuasion to convince Consuela to purchase flower seed, but once the woman came home with them, Amber had been hard at work.

The uneasiness she felt earlier came back as the gritty sound of a horse's hooves caught her attention. She looked up to find the sandy haired outlaw from the mercantile drawing his horse to a halt just outside the fence. He tipped his sweat stained hat and smiled.

"Them flowers shore will be pretty," he said pleasantly with a nod at Amber's freshly dug flower beds.

Amber nodded briefly, then turned to go into the house. The young outlaw was polite enough, and he couldn't help the long jagged scar that ran from the corner of his right eye down his cheek. However, the scar gave his face a sinister quality that even his friendly smile could not erase.

"Sounds like the boss is back," he said with a glance toward the canyon trail. "Guess that means Morgan will be here soon. My name's Luther, ma'am. Luther Simmons. I just wanted to let you know, if you ever need anythin', you just let me know."

Amber nodded again, then Luther rode down the street. She forgot all about Luther Simmons as Morgan's Appaloosa cantered into sight.

She did not bother to deny the pounding of her heart when he pulled the animal to a halt and swung down from the saddle. He draped the reins over a picket in the fence, then pushed the gate open.

Amber suddenly felt embarrassed. She was painfully aware of the grass stains on her skirt and her dirty hands. Pushing back loose strands of hair with the back of one hand, she found it hard to look him squarely in the face.

He certainly did not look as though he had gone more than twenty-four hours without sleep. Except for a day's growth of beard that shadowed his lean face, and a layer of dust that covered his chocolate brown trousers and black boots, he looked surprisingly refreshed.

There was a sparkle in the depths of his dark eyes that mystified her. She gave her rumpled skirt a nervous shake, blushing when he looked around the yard to survey her handiwork.

"What's this?" he asked pleasantly. "Looks like you've been busy while I was away."

Amber's tongue felt thick with unaccustomed nervousness. She watched his face for a hint of what he was thinking, but could tell nothing.

"Flowers...I mean they will be flowers soon," she stammered. "I was so bored with nothing to do and I thought it would help pass the time. Consuela went to the store for the seed. You don't mind, do you?"

"No, why would I mind? I've thought of it myself, but just never found the time."

Amber's eyes widened apprehensively when he reached out to rub gently at her cheek. "Looks like you really got into your work," he said dryly as he removed a smudge of dirt from her face.

His finger trailed slowly down her cheek before Morgan let his hand drop back to his side. When she looked up at last, she was surprised to find him studying her thoughtfully.

"So tell me, what have you planted, *princessa?*"

Amber jumped at the chance to break the awkward silence. She began pointing to the various flower beds, explaining which variety of flower she had put in each one.

Morgan was only half listening. He was more interested in the sound of her voice. Her hair looked like spun gold in the sunlight. Her cheeks were flushed, but Morgan's glance was drawn to the firm swell of her breasts against the snug bodice of the print dress.

The simplicity of the garment made her beauty even more en-
chanting, accenting her tiny waist and slender hips in a manner
that made Morgan's groin tighten with that familiar ache.

When she finished her explanation, Amber turned to find him
staring and blushed to the roots of her hair. "You haven't heard a
word I've said," she accused softly.

"Of course I did," he denied with a mischievous grin. "I'll
admit my mind was wandering a bit, but I heard you." Then his
face sobered. "Come on in the house, Amber. I need to talk to
you."

Alarm leaped into Amber's face, making it rapidly lose the
color in her cheeks. She leaned against his hard body as he wrapped
one long arm around her shoulders and began walking toward the
house. The tightness in her chest made breathing difficult, made
it necessary for her to swallow several times in rapid succession
before she could find her voice.

"You've seen Uncle Owen, haven't you? You've spoken to him
about paying the ransom."

Her anxiety did not lessen as Morgan opened the door and
waited for her to enter. Once inside the cool house, Morgan indicated that he wanted her to sit down on the sofa which Amber
did, mainly because her legs had gone weak and refused to hold
her up any longer. Morgan pitched the black Stetson onto the
liquor cabinet, then poured himself a liberal glass of whiskey before turning to answer her question.

"He is going to pay the ransom, isn't he?"

"That's what he wants me to believe."

"You don't believe him?"

"Not for a minute."

"But why not? Didn't you tell him you would kill me if he
didn't?"

"Yes, and I'm sure he believes me. But, in order to raise the
money, he'll have to sell off part of his empire and he isn't about to
do that, Amber, not even for you."

"I don't believe you!" she cried with a flash of her old defiance.

"He will pay! I know he will! Uncle Owen loves me, he won't let anything happen to me!"

Sympathy flickered in Morgan's dark eyes at the alarm in her voice. "You still don't understand, do you? Owen McCandless has buried too many people to get what he has; he's not going to part with it."

"What are you saying, Morgan?" she demanded.

"He's stalling for time. He's trying to devise some way of getting you back without it costing him a dime."

"I don't understand."

"He asked for a delay," Morgan explained patiently. "He says he can't raise the money by the deadline we set and needs more time. So I gave it to him. Two more weeks. That means you'll be my guest for a while longer."

Amber's heart leaped into her throat, as much from the unexpected pleasure that swept through her as from the faintly amused expression that came to Morgan's face. She swallowed and wet her lips, trying to sort out her confused emotions.

"If..if you know he's stalling, why did you agree to give him more time?" she asked hesitantly.

Morgan's expression revealed nothing, but he felt the urge to smile. He had seen the pleasure that flashed across her face. The satisfaction he felt at that moment was difficult to contain.

"Because first, it makes him think he's gained the upper hand for the moment. And second, because it gives me that much more time with you."

Amber's face filled with color. "What do you hope to accomplish, Morgan?" she asked. It took an effort to hold his gaze. She wished she could read his thoughts. "Do you think two more weeks will change my mind about Uncle Owen? Do you think you can make me believe that he murdered my father or that he's given you the right to kill him? Or do you think that with a little more time I'll come to enjoy what you take from me so casually?"

Morgan frowned at the sarcasm in her last comment, but in a

moment a tiny smile curled his lips at her belligerence. "Yes, Amber. To both questions."

"Well, you're quite mistaken," she snapped, her eyes flashing defiantly. "I will never believe Uncle Owen could do anything to harm anyone. It was a long time ago and it was dark and..and you were only a child. You were mistaken, that's all.

"And..and Uncle Owen loved my father. He would never have done anything to hurt him. I'll never believe he had a part in my father's death!" she added before she lost her courage.

"Liar!" Morgan told her softly. "You're trying to convince yourself, not me."

"I do not wish to discuss it any further!" Amber cried, flouncing off the sofa with her head erect and her shoulders stiff with indignation.

Morgan watched her leave the room in a huff. He drained the glass and set it aside. Then he went to the kitchen to ask Consuela to prepare him a bath, whistling a cheerful tune that made Amber's teeth grate with annoyance.

From the front windows, she saw Consuela cross the yard and go out the gate. Amber went to the window and looked out. The Appaloosa was still tied to the picket fence, which meant Morgan was still in the house

He had to be in the kitchen. Probably stuffing food into his face, she sniffed. After a few moments, she padded toward the open archway of the kitchen. and peeked inside the room.

Her eyes widened. Morgan sat in a tub near the hearth, his head thrown back. Gray smoke rings floated upward from the cheroot that dangled from his lips.

"You may as well come in and join me."

Amber jumped, coloring with embarrassment when she realized her approach had not been as silent as she had thought.

"Do you have eyes in the back of your head?" she asked irritably, moving into the room and coming to a halt beside the tub, hating herself for letting her eyes sweep over his lean body.

Morgan opened one eye and nodded. "You could say that.

One of the tricks of the trade."

Removing his clothes from the chair where he'd left them, Amber placed them on the table and plopped down. She propped her chin in one hand and stared moodily at him. "Have you always been this smug?" she asked sarcastically.

Morgan chuckled. Leaning his head further back to see her clearly, he noted the annoyance on her face and the pink flush that stained her cheeks as she tried to keep her eyes from wandering over him.

"Confidence," he corrected cheerfully. "Not smugness, Amber."

"Then you have an over abundance of confidence."

"Maybe," Morgan agreed with a grin. "But my confidence has often kept some fool kid with a yen for a reputation from calling me out. I learned a long time ago that the more confident I appear, the more disturbing it is to someone who's thinking about trying me."

"Then it's all an act?"

Morgan's dark head moved in a slight negative motion. "No, I'm probably the best there is."

"Isn't there anybody who can outdraw you?"

He considered her question for a moment. Then he shrugged and replied, "Maybe, but no one I've found yet."

"Not even Welch Mandell?"

Morgan shrugged again, still studying her thoughtfully. "Maybe, who knows? It's never been put to the test and there's no reason it ever will be."

"Morgan," Amber said earnestly, suddenly struck with an idea. "Will you teach me to shoot?"

"Why?"

"So I'll know how to defend myself in case something goes wrong and you don't come back from one of your visits to the outside," she explained cautiously.

Morgan studied her thoughtfully, admitting to himself that

what she said made sense. If he failed to return someday, she'd need to know all she could about protecting herself.

"I don't mean how to kill somebody, just teach me how to use a gun for my own protection," she added when he didn't answer right away.

"Amber, you can't learn to use a gun that way," Morgan answered patiently. "You never pull a gun unless you intend to use it and you never use it unless you shoot to kill."

"Why is that?"

"Because, *princessa,* it's the only way you can be certain that whoever you're shooting at doesn't get a second chance."

"I suppose Welch Mandell taught you that too," Amber said scornfully.

"That's lesson number one on how to stay alive."

"But I don't want to kill anyone. I only want to know how to defend myself. Can't that be done without killing?"

"Not as far as I'm concerned," Morgan grunted. "You either mean business or you keep the gun in your holster. It's that simple."

"But you use a gun professionally. I don't wish to become as skilled as you."

"Good. I don't have that much time," he replied dryly.

"Does that mean you'll teach me?"

Morgan nodded, a grin playing at the corners of his mouth. He drew on the cheroot and straightened up in the tub, leaning over the edge to crush out the stub in an ashtray on the floor.

"I'll teach you how to hit what you're aiming at," he agreed. "There's no point in teaching you to draw. I haven't seen too many women wearing a gun lately."

"Can we start right away?"

He sighed, smiling at the eagerness in her face. "Can I finish my bath first?"

Amber jumped to her feet. "Of course. I'll wait in the other room."

She hurried into the living room, blushing as his soft laughter followed her. She stood uncertainly for a few moments, until it occurred to her that she was still a mess. With that thought in mind, she scampered into the bedroom to change into a clean dress. She was finishing with the long row of tiny buttons that secured the bodice when she felt Morgan's presence and turned to find him leaning against the archway.

The transformation in his appearance was, as always, startling. Freshly bathed, black hair gleaming from a brisk washing, and clean shaven again, Morgan's masculinity momentarily took Amber's breath. The chocolate brown trousers formed to his slender hips and long legs like a second layer of skin, accenting the hard muscles in his thighs. A dark brown, long sleeved shirt and black leather vest completed his attire, along with the black gunbelt now strapped into place around his waist and tied down to his left thigh. Amber felt her face burn when she realized she was staring at him with open admiration. The slight, knowing smile on his face did nothing to relieve her embarrassment.

"Am I dressed all right?" she asked quickly, averting her eyes to avoid any further contact with his, and brushing past him into the living room.

"I suppose so," Morgan replied as he straightened up and settled the black Stetson onto the back of his head. "I have no idea what the well dressed lady wears while learning to handle a six-gun."

Amber ignored the teasing in his voice. As they left the house, Morgan took her arm, and led her along the walk to the gate, opened it, and paused to let her precede him. Then he lifted her onto the Appaloosa and swung up behind her, putting one arm securely around her waist as he shook the reins free of the fence with the other.

Amber fixed her skirt around her legs and rested both hands on the saddle horn as the strong little horse cantered down the main street. Morgan took a back trail to bypass the saloon, heading instead into the open patch of land that lay between the town and the canyon wall beyond.

Morgan did not speak, but the silence was not uncomfortable.

Amber relaxed against him, aware of the arm resting around her waist and the warmth of his body pressing against her back.

His clean masculine scent made her nerves tingle. It occurred to her that there was something different about him today, something calmer, more relaxed. Yet, beneath that, she sensed an expectancy, as though this strange mood was only a prelude to something more important.

She wondered if he was pleased about having her around longer. Grudgingly, she admitted to herself that she was. She bit her lip in vexation at that thought. She was slowly, but steadily, losing her perspective about this handsome, dangerous man. That knowledge both terrified and fascinated her.

The Appaloosa halted, breaking into her thoughts. Morgan threw one leg over the horse's back and slipped to the ground, then lifted her down. The horse dropped his muzzle to the ground to graze as Morgan took Amber's arm to lead her over the rock ledges to an abrupt drop in the land.

In the shallow sink, the Lair was hidden from view. Straight ahead, rising sharply above her, the high canyon wall loomed into the sky, blotting out the direct rays of the sun. Ahead and directly against the rock wall, sat a low bench with several bales of hay behind it. Scattered all around were dozens of tin cans, rusted by the elements and punctured by bullet holes.

Morgan walked to the bench, set six of the cans in a straight row, then walked back to Amber. Taking her arm, he led her to a spot a few yards away from the targets and lifted the Colt from his holster.

"The first thing you have to learn, Amber, is to know your weapon. Know it like the palm of your hand. Know what it will and won't do," he said. He pressed the gun into her hands, then took both her hands in his as he turned the gun over.

"This is a '73 Colt.45, Amber, nicknamed the Peacemaker by someone with a macabre sense of humor. It's like any other Colt with two exceptions; one, the barrel is only five inches long, most are seven and a half, which makes it come from the holster faster than a pistol with a longer barrel, and two, the trigger guard has been cut away."

"More tricks of the trade?"

He nodded. "That one-tenth of a second can mean the difference between staying alive or ending up in the street face down. It's a double action pistol, meaning that squeezing the trigger also draws back the hammer and then releases it.

"It's reliable at twenty to thirty yards depending on the ability of the person using it. At thirty yards or so it begins to lose some of its power and accuracy so always remember the limitations and adjust the distance to your advantage."

"How far can you shoot accurately?"

"Forty to forty five yards. But I'm an expert. With a rifle, of course, your range is greater. I can hit most anything I aim at with a rifle at two hundred and fifty yards. The six-gun is for use mainly at close range."

"You mean like drawing against someone in a gunfight?"

"Yes. For anything else the rifle is more reliable."

He stepped behind her and lifted her hands to point the gun at the row of cans. "Use the sight, look down the barrel, and line up the can with the center of the sight at the end of the gun barrel. When you've got it lined up, squeeze the trigger. Don't jerk it. You'll throw your aim off and never hit anything. Always squeeze it firmly, but not too hard."

Amber closed one eye and lifted the gun. She squinted along the gun barrel until she was sure the can on the end of the row was in the sight, then pulled the trigger. The gun's roar made her ears ring as the barrel bucked upward, sending the bullet into the hay at least twelve inches above the can.

"Try it again," Morgan advised patiently. He stepped away, grinning as she brought the gun up chest high with both hands on the butt to steady it, keeping her arms straight and stiff. She aimed again and pulled the trigger, but missed the can altogether.

"Relax, Amber. You're holding the gun like it's a snake that's trying to bite you. Loosen up a little. Hold it firmly, but not too tight."

Amber tried to follow his instructions, but at the end of six rounds the can remained untouched. She was getting frustrated. Morgan took the gun and replaced the spent cartridges with six fresh ones from his gunbelt.

"Why don't you show me what you're talking about," she suggested dryly.

Morgan nodded as he dropped the pistol back into the holster. He stood in a relaxed pose, feet apart, his left arm hanging loosely by his side. Then, so quickly his movements were only a blur, he lifted the gun from the holster and fired six times, so rapidly the echoes came on top of each other, sending all six cans dancing into the air.

Smiling at the astonishment on Amber's face, he emptied the spent cartridges and loaded six more bullets into the revolver's chambers. He handed the gun to her once more. "Remember to hold it comfortably, Amber. You're squeezing it so tight your knuckles are turning white."

"I'll never learn to shoot that well," she said in a disgusted tone.

"You don't have to. Just learn to hit what you're aiming at from a reasonable distance. That's all you need."

"Can you do that every time?"

"Yes, I've spent years learning, and I still practice regularly. It takes time to learn to the point where you're really good with a gun."

"I can't see why you'd need to practice," she said in an incredulous voice while she stared at him.

Morgan gave her an indulgent smile as he pushed his hat to the back of his head. "Practice is just as important now as it was when I was learning. It's a skill that requires constant practice, Amber. A man with my reputation can't afford to get rusty. Now, try again."

After an hour, Amber's aim had improved, but her arms ached

and her eyes hurt from squinting into the bright sunlight. Her ears rang from the gun's roar, but the faintly pleased expression that flickered across Morgan's face, surprisingly, made it all seem worthwhile.

Morgan reloaded the gun, then dropped it into his holster and slipped the safety loop into place around the hammer. At his whistle, the Appaloosa trotted up with an affectionate whinny. He helped Amber into the saddle and swung up behind her.

"I was pretty bad, wasn't I?"

"Yes," he replied cheerfully. "But you'll get better with practice."

"Didn't you get tired when you were learning?"

"Sure, there were times I thought my arms would break."

"How much did you practice?" she asked in an effort to keep him talking. The strange way her body tingled from his nearness made her very uneasy. She was quite certain what this night would bring, but the flurry of excitement in her stomach warned her that she was dangerously close to losing control over the confusing emotions that made her heart race and the blood pound in her ears.

"Hours a day, every day. In the rain, in the snow, in the wind...every kind of weather you can imagine. Drawing and firing until my hands were raw and my head hurt so bad I could hardly see."

"All that work so you could kill my uncle," she mused quietly. "Why, Morgan? Why all that work to kill a man who cannot possibly compare to your ability with a gun?"

"Your uncle is no gun hand," Morgan agreed. "But he employs men who are. Like Steven Riker and that ranger...Tyrell. With men like that on his payroll, he doesn't need to know how to handle a gun. Men like that are the reason I learned, Amber, because I have to walk through them to get to him."

"Can you outdraw Sheriff Riker?"

"Yes."

"And the ranger?"

"Yes, though I suspect he'll be more of a challenge than Riker. Tyrell has the look of a man who knows what he's doing. He's not your uncle's typical gun hand. I'd say he's better than most, but that's a long way from being good enough."

The quiet confidence in his voice no longer struck a nerve with Amber. After witnessing his ability firsthand, first when he killed Patch with such ease, and now with the target practice with the cans, she was convinced he was as good as he said. Knowing the deadly way he lived his life, she could not help being relieved that his ability lived up to his reputation.

"What happens, Morgan, when you get older, when age dulls the edge you have now?" she inquired cautiously.

"Hopefully by that time I won't be in this business any longer."

"What do you mean?"

"After I square my debt with your uncle, I plan to leave this part of the country, maybe buy a small spread somewhere where my reputation won't catch up with me."

"That's not likely, is it?" she asked doubtfully. "I mean, you're a wanted man, Morgan. If you succeed in killing Uncle Owen, every lawman in the nation will be after you. How can you hope to escape that?"

"Maybe I can't," Morgan admitted, shrugging. "Chances are that I'll end up with a bullet in the back in some dingy little border town like most men in my trade do. Either age or some young punk with more luck than skill will walk off with my reputation someday."

"Why not give up now, Morgan? Before it goes any further?" Amber asked urgently, turning in the saddle to look up into his face. "It's not too late yet. You can stop while there's still time. Send me back to Uncle Owen and I promise I won't let the ranger come after you."

Morgan's faint smile sent a pang of unfamiliar distress through her chest when he shook his head. "I can't do that, Amber. I made a vow twenty years ago to see this through. I won't stop until Owen McCandless is rotting in hell...or until I am."

Amber shivered at the picture her mind had formed of his body lying face down in a pool of blood, a bullet in his back from a coward's gun.

CHAPTER
TWENTY-THREE

Cooter Jackson stuck his gnarled hands deep into his pockets as he hurried from the barn to the stables, dodging the rain drops that came pelting down from a gray sky. Once inside, he closed the heavy double doors behind him securely and moved deeper into the dim coolness.

Picking up a currycomb, he approached Sheik's stall and let himself in with the Arabian. The horse watched him warily for a moment before dropping his head back to pick daintily at a bundle of fresh hay in his feed trough. Cooter crooned to the horse while moving the comb over his powerful body.

He had always been more comfortable with horses than with people. His arthritis was acting up again, making his knees and hands ache. The damned rain only made it worse, he thought disgustedly. If things weren't bad enough already.

"That's a beautiful horse."

Cooter's shaggy head snapped up. The thunder booming had drowned the sound of the stable doors opening. He mentally kicked himself as he found himself face to face with the Texas Ranger, who had propped his leather clad arms on top of the stall, and was watching him speculatively.

When the old wrangler made no attempt to reply, Ryan Tyrell stared at him for a moment, then continued. "Arabian, isn't he?"

"Yep", Cooter replied curtly without looking up. Avoiding the man's perceptive eyes, Cooter returned his attention to grooming the horse.

"He belong to Miss McCandless?"

"Yep."

"He must have a cost a fortune," Ryan persisted.

Cooter took a deep breath and straightened up, folded his arms on top of Sheik's gleaming back, and finally met the ranger's determined gaze.

"You got somethin' on your mind, ranger, or are you just killin' time till the storm passes?" he grunted.

"You don't mince words, do you, Cooter?" Ryan drawled, grinning. "I like that, it makes my job a lot easier. Yeah, I've got something on my mind."

"Then spit it out. I ain't got all day," Cooter replied gruffly.

Ryan removed his tan Stetson and tapped it lightly against the stall, keeping his gaze locked with Cooter's belligerent blue stare. "You, Cooter, that's what's on my mind. You and your relationship to Morgan Devereaux and Welch Mandell."

"I don't know what the hell you're talkin' about."

"The hell you don't. Three nights ago you met Devereaux several miles from here at a place with three graves. I want to know why."

"Maybe it's none of your goddamned business."

"I think it is," Ryan returned in that same soft tone that rang with authority. "I think you know a hell of a lot more about this kidnapping than you let on."

"Think what you want."

"The only problem I'm having is figuring out just which side you're on."

"I'm on Miss Amber's side," Cooter replied. "She's a fine young woman. I aim to make sure she gets home safe and sound."

"In spite of Owen McCandless?"

Cooter's shaggy head moved in a curt nod. "In spite of everybody."

"I believe you, Cooter." Ryan acknowledged the surprise in the old man's eyes with a slight grin. "I've been asking around. Seems like you've been around here a long time. You probably know more about Owen McCandless than just about anybody."

"So?"

"So, you know who those graves belong to and what McCandless has done to Devereaux and Mandell to put them to so much trouble."

"What makes you think that?" Cooter demanded irritably.

"First, because you met with Devereaux. Second, because we all know that this kidnapping had little or nothing to do with a ransom, and third, because McCandless and Mandell are not strangers like McCandless wants me to think. Let's stop playing games, Cooter. Tell me what the hell's going on. What's the connection between McCandless and Mandell?"

"You've got all the answers, ranger. You tell me."

"All right. At some point, probably years ago, McCandless crossed Mandell and Devereaux. Bad enough that they're out to get him, and I think it's got something to do with those three graves in the prairie. Whatever way he was connected with Mandell in the past, he doesn't want anybody to know about it. Even if it means not getting the girl back safely."

"I'm not sure yet if you're working for McCandless as a go between with Devereaux and Mandell or if you're in on their scheme to get him."

"Let me know when you figure it out," Cooter said dryly.

Ryan tapped the Stetson against the stall again while he studied the old man. Cooter Jackson was a cool one all right. He could read a man pretty well and he knew instinctively that Cooter was not afraid of him nor was he going to reveal any information.

"You'll be the first to know, Cooter. I wonder if I were to speak to McCandless about your involvement in this, what his reaction would be?"

Cooter's shoulders moved in a nonchalant shrug. "Ask him and see."

"I don't think he'd be very pleased, do you?"

"We all do what we have to in this life, ranger," Cooter replied evenly. "Sometimes it ain't too pleasant and sometimes innocent people get hurt. So, you do whatever you have to...and so will I."

"I hope you're on my side, Cooter," Ryan told him in a soft, almost admiring tone. "You'd sure as hell make a bad enemy."

"That's right, ranger. Don't forget it," Cooter replied coldly. "I may be old, but I've got a long memory."

Ryan nodded, then he straightened up. "I'm sure you do, Cooter. Just as sure that McCandless' memory isn't nearly long enough. I've got a few more questions to ask, Cooter, and when I've got the answers I'm looking for, I'll be back to continue this conversation."

Cooter accepted the ranger's unspoken challenge without blinking. He nodded, meeting Ryan's gaze steadily. "I'll be here, ranger. I'm not goin' nowhere."

Ryan smoothed back his gold streaked hair and replaced his hat "I'm counting on that, Cooter. I've got a feeling you're looking forward to seeing McCandless on his knees. Something tells me that sight would make you a happy man," he remarked, then walked across the stable, opened the doors and melted into the gray rain as silently as he had come.

Behind him, Cooter let out a sigh of relief, then cursed savagely under his breath. The ranger's shrewd assessment had unnerved him in spite of his false bravado. Ever since that damned meeting with Welch, he'd been expecting a visit from Tyrell. At least it was over with, for the moment.

But he also knew the ranger would be back. He wiped his sweaty palms on the thighs of his rough work jeans and cursed again. The best he could hope for was that Welch would have made his move by then.

***

They had finished dinner sometime ago. Amber had washed and put away the dishes, and now stood before the front windows peering aimlessly into the falling rain. The abrupt storm had given way to a soft, steady rain that beat on the tiled roof with a gentle sound that somehow made Amber more nervous than the tension she had grown accustomed to.

"Why are you doing that?" she asked to break the silence, indicating the oiled cloth Morgan was rubbing into the worn holster.

"Keeping the leather oiled helps the gun slide out faster."

"Oh," she replied. "Another trick of the trade?"

"Yep," Morgan answered without looking up.

Abruptly, he put the gun back into the holster and hung it over the hat rack just inside the door. Amber turned when the squeak of the couch indicated his movements. She watched warily while he put the gunbelt away, then turned to her.

"Feeling restless?"

She nodded, as he leaned against the window frame only a few inches from her, with his thumbs hooked in his wide leather belt. He had removed the vest before dinner and his shirt was open at the throat, allowing a glimpse of the silky mat of dark hair covering his chest.

There was something inherently sensual about him, she admitted grudgingly. Something about the confident way he moved and the piercing black eyes that rested on her face now, filling her with the feeling that he could read her thoughts merely by looking into her eyes, while she could see nothing behind the veil he kept over his own.

"You must forgive me for letting you get so bored. I'm still not used to having someone else in the house. I forget sometimes that I'm not alone. Anyway, we've got a rainy evening and a full bottle of wine to enjoy. It would be a shame to let all that go to waste."

Amber's face colored as she looked away, pretending an interest in the rain. She stiffened when Morgan moved behind her, slipped his arms around her, and moved his lips slowly up her neck.

"I suppose that means you want to go to bed," she said tightly, trying to remain detached from the tantalizing exploration of his lips upon her flesh.

"All in good time," Morgan murmured. His hands cupped each of her breasts, his thumbs rubbing gently through the thin material to bring her nipples to instant erectness.

Amber's breath quickened. She leaned back against him shamelessly as though she suddenly had no will of her own. Her flesh felt hot and strained like she was burning from the inside out. She closed her eyes as he deftly unbuttoned the bodice of her dress, then slipped one hand inside to caress one taut, swollen breast.

"I'll..I'll get undressed," she stammered. She stepped away from him, then hurried into the bedroom to change into the silk nightgown. Funny, how her hands were shaking as she tried to pull the garment into place on her shoulders.

When she reentered the living room, Morgan had closed the curtains and blown out all the candles but one. Its glow softly reflected off the crystal wine glasses he had filled and set on the table beside the couch.

She glided into the room to perch on the couch beside him, taking her glass from him nervously. She sipped the sweet red wine, then licked her lips. Putting the glass aside, she turned toward him.

"I'm ready now," she said hesitantly, keeping her head down to avoid his eyes.

"You say that like you're being led to a firing squad," Morgan remarked dryly. "You might be surprised to know that some women actually enjoy making love."

He lifted one brown finger to stroke gently across her satiny cheek, frowning when she deliberately pulled away from his touch. She stared at him with wide eyes full of distrust.

"I think there must be a world of difference between what you've done to me and making love."

"You're probably right," Morgan agreed. "But I intend to remedy that tonight."

"I think I can manage it," he replied with a steady gaze that quickened her pulse. "You be the judge."

He took her into his arms, pressed her body against him, and kissed her with such lazy thoroughness it left Amber breathless. His tongue explored the recesses of her mouth, searching out every crevice in slow deliberate inquiry that ignited into sparks of delight that sent shivers up her spine. His hands caressed the hollow at the base of her spine, then cupped her slender buttocks and pulled her closer.

Amber's blood raced like liquid fire that devoured her resistance until she was helpless to combat the titillating waves of excitement that roared through her veins, blotting out any other thought. Her arms slipped around his neck, her fingers weaved into his thick black hair while her mouth answered his kiss with a mind of its own.

Morgan rose to his feet. He pulled her up into his arms and carried her into the darkened bedroom. He put her down on the bed, then paused long enough to strip out of his clothes before lying down beside her and taking her back into his arms.

Amber looped her arms around his neck, running her hands over the muscles in his back and shoulders. She luxuriated in the hard masculine feel of his body. Her senses were filled with the scent, the feel of him and though her mind struggled to regain control, she was lost to the touch of his lips and his hands moving slowly, enticingly over her flesh, engulfing her in flames of desire previously unknown to her.

Struggling to maintain control of her senses, she felt Morgan kiss her mouth, then her eyelids, whispering huskily into her ear, "It's all right, *princessa,* stop fighting it. Let me make love to you like you deserve."

As his lips silenced any chance of protest, Amber realized dimly that she was lifting her hips to allow him to slip the gown from her without resistance. It was too late to protest. Her body was gnawing at her, demanding satisfaction from the flames of desire blazing inside her.

She felt dizzy from the intensity of the emotions swirling around her. She felt as though she was in a heavy fog, lost and helpless, clinging to Morgan as a drowning man would cling to a branch. Bright lights exploded behind her eyes when his lips trailed lazily down her body from the swollen peaks of her breasts, past her belly button, to the blonde patch of fluff between her thighs.

A low, half-frightened moan burst from her lips as Morgan moved down the bed, lowered his head, and parted her thighs to allow his skilled mouth access to the rosy pink flesh, expertly teasing each sensitive, quivering crevice. Amber thought her body would explode into multicolored fragments. Her nails dug into the hard muscles of his shoulders as moan after moan rushed from her parted lips. Her head rolled from side to side on the pillow, fanning her hair into a tangled mass of damp curls.

Never would she have dreamed that her flesh could experience such rapture, such all absorbing sweet torment. Her back arched, bringing her hips against his mouth as her body began to tremble violently. Then, suddenly, she felt Morgan move back up her body to claim her lips again in a fiery kiss that turned her blood into liquid fire.

She felt his lips rain soft hot kisses across her face, down her neck and back up again, alternately kissing then nipping gently. When his hands cupped both swollen, aching breasts, teasing the hard coral tips, Amber clenched her fists into the sheets to prevent wild cries of pleasure.

Her body burned, screaming for release from the exquisite torture that liquefied her bones and turned her mind into a blazing inferno. Her nails stabbed into his back with a hunger she did not understand, begging for an end to the sizzling desire flaming inside her.

"Say you want me, *princessa*," Morgan commanded hoarsely against her ear. "Tell me you want me and I will end your torment."

Amber's eyes opened, blazing at him with liquid golden fire. Her parted lips quivered with the effort to speak, but for a moment she could only nod weakly. "Yes, Morgan," she whispered hoarsely at last. "Yes, please..."

Trance-like, Amber watched him cover her body with his own. He entered her with a gentleness she would not have believed him capable of. For a long moment, Morgan lay motionless, staring down into her eyes, savoring the desire gleaming there. Then Amber moved beneath him, urging him to release her from this exquisite torture. He began to move in slow deliberate thrusts, each one deeper and stronger until Amber began to tremble violently.

Amber raked his back with her nails. Lifting her legs, she ensnared his hips, raining hot, damp kisses across his neck and shoulders. She felt suspended in time and space as though nothing else mattered except his arms around her and his body giving hers such pleasure, she was certain she was going to explode into tiny fragments at any moment. She had never known such wild, wanton pleasure. She gave herself over to it completely, arching her back against Morgan's powerful body, receiving each savage thrust eagerly as she climbed closer and closer to that pinnacle of release that she sought so desperately.

Morgan forced himself to take long breaths to steady himself before he lost control. This was the hardest thing he had ever done, make love so slowly, to put a woman's pleasure before his own, yet it was also the most exciting, erotic experience of his life. A film of perspiration covered his body. His lungs ached with the effort to remain in control of his emotions. His chest hurt from forcing himself to take deep breaths while his body screamed for relief.

Morgan's thrusts increased in tempo, moving against her with hard smooth strokes until she suddenly arched against him, crying out in rapture while her body jerked uncontrollably in her final spasms.

Amber's arms went around him to draw him close as he moved to lay beside her, cradling her head in the hollow of his shoulder while she slowly regained her senses. When she opened her eyes at last, she was staring into his face. She expected to find a smug, satisfied smile, but instead found a steady ebony gleam that mystified her. There was no arrogant reminder that he had predicted she would eventually give herself to him this freely.

Amber snuggled deeper into his arms. She felt happy, satisfied, totally content. This experience had changed her forever from a girl into a woman, had bound her in some unexplainable fashion to this man. For the moment, she felt no guilt or shame. Only the glow of a woman whose body had been completely satisfied.

Morgan said nothing, for he suddenly had no words. This experience had touched him more deeply than he cared to admit. He had bedded many women, most of them professional whores who knew all the tricks to excite and satisfy a man. Yet, this girl with her wide eyed innocence had managed to reach some virgin depth he could not explain.

"Morgan, why did you bring me the music box?" she asked after a period of comfortable silence.

Morgan's shoulders moved in a slight shrug to cover the momentary embarrassment of her question. "I thought you'd like it. I was in McCandless in the mercantile and I saw it...and I thought it fit you somehow."

A smile curled Amber's mouth. She adjusted her position so she could look directly into his face. "How do you mean?"

"I don't know..it just fit you. It was beautiful and delicate and the song it played made me think of you."

"Because it was sad?"

"No. I guess because it's soft...sort of peaceful."

"Do you think I'm beautiful and delicate?"

"Beautiful, yes..delicate, sometimes," Morgan answered with a grin. He bent his head to lightly kiss her forehead, then lay back and closed his eyes.

"Morgan, why haven't you always been as gentle as you were just now?" she asked softly.

Morgan opened his eyes to return her curious gaze with a steady, veiled one. He glanced down at her finger trailing light circles in the hair on his chest and lifted one hand to brush the tumbled golden waves from her face.

"I was too busy trying to show you who was boss. And punishing you for being Owen McCandless' kin," he said after a moment. "I've never known many women who thought that gentleness was important. The women I've known were more concerned with getting it over with so they could bring in the next customer."

"Can it be like this until you let me go?" she asked, suddenly certain that she had nothing to fear from him. She knew instinctively that his previous threats had been nothing more than that; threats in order to keep her under control. She had never been safer in her life than now in his arms.

A grin curled Morgan's lips, making him appear younger, more care-free while he nodded. "I think I can manage that. No guilt, Amber? No shame at making love with me...and enjoying it?"

"No," she replied honestly. "I'll feel guilty later. When this is over and I'm home again, I'll probably hate you for the way you've made me feel tonight. But no, Morgan, no guilt, not now. This is a chapter of my life I hope no one will ever know existed but you and I. What I feel now is private and I hope I'll be able to forget it when I'm home again, pretend it never happened. But for now, while I'm with you here, I will not feel guilty."

"You belong to me, *princessa*. You know that now, don't you?" Morgan murmured against her silky neck.

Amber's head moved in an affirmative nod. "Yes, Morgan. For now I belong to you."

In moments, she was sleeping soundly in his arms. Her warm breath stirred the hair on his chest and dried the last beads of perspiration from his skin. In the gathering darkness with the soothing rain falling outside, Morgan watched her sleep.

"Sleep, *princessa de oro*. But never forget you belong to me. Not just now or for a few days, but always. No other man will ever make you feel what you've felt with me tonight."

He reached down to pull the blanket up over them, then settled down to sleep. She was his for two more weeks, then he must send her back to her own life, a life he could never share. It was that simple. But Morgan knew he would not forget her, just as he knew she would not forget him. If he were the kind of man who believed in fate, he would almost think this tiny slip of bewitching female was his destiny.

But he had never believed in anything except his ability with a gun and a vow he'd made twenty years ago.

CHAPTER
TWENTY-FOUR

Two mornings following Mandell's meeting with McCandless, Steven Riker came down the stairs in the Longhorn Saloon to discover a visitor.

Dressed in a fashionable gray broadcloth suit with a matching silk vest, starched white shirt, and a black string tie, Steven Riker made an impressive picture as he came leisurely down the stairs at six o'clock in the morning. It was his custom to make an early inspection of the town before settling down in the hotel's restaurant for a lengthy breakfast.

"You got a visitor, boss," the mustached bartender informed him as he passed the long mahogany bar on his way to the batwing doors.

Steven grimaced in irritation. He paused to look at his reflection in the long mirror above the bar and smooth his lapels into perfection. Shining the silver badge on the silk vest with the heel of one hand, he scowled at the bartender.

"At this ungodly hour? What the hell could be that damned important?"

The bartender shrugged and went on wiping glasses, ignoring Steven's foul mood. "She didn't say, boss. Just said she had information for you. Been here most of the night."

Steven squared his shoulders and gave himself another glance in the mirror before turning to look around the saloon. The large room was dim and full of shadows. His gaze eventually fell on a small figure at a back table. He stalked up to the table, slapping his gray Stetson down on it to attract the attention of his unwelcome visitor.

"You've been waiting for me?" he growled.

The girl's raven hair fell softly about her face when she looked up from the half empty whiskey glass in front of her. Her black eyes flashed with impatience at the arrogant expression on the sheriff's handsome face.

"Yes, Sheriff Riker, I've been waiting all night," Jenna Ruiz informed him scornfully.

"If you're looking for a job, I'm full up right now. Check with me in a couple of days."

Steven dismissed the girl and turned away.

"I can lead you to the *gringa senorita,*" Jenna said loudly behind him, smiling with satisfaction when Steven froze in his tracks, then spun around to come stalking back.

"Why the hell didn't you say that in the first place!" He dropped into a chair opposite her and leaned his elbows on the table top. "What can you tell me about Amber McCandless?"

"Not so fast, Sheriff," Jenna told him in a heavy Spanish accent. "We make a deal first."

"What kind of deal?" Steven asked suspiciously.

"You give me something and I give you something. You want the *blanca* witch, do you not?" At Steven's impatient nod, she went on smoothly, "I want a job here, in your saloon."

Steven's brows arched in surprise. "That's all you want? A job?"

Jenna leaned forward until her black eyes were only inches from his. Her lips curled back from her teeth in a feral snarl. "No, Sheriff, I also want to see Morgan Devereaux lying dead at my feet! For that I will tell you how to find the Leopard's Lair."

Excitement flared in Steven's face at the prospect of bringing Amber home safely, along with accomplishing his own hidden agenda. "You know the way into the Lair?"

Jenna nodded with grim satisfaction. "*Si,* I have lived in the Lair for almost a year, Sheriff. I do not see the way in. Welch Mandell guards the secret passage closely. Only a few men know the way, all others are blindfolded before reaching the entrance."

"So how do you know where it is?"

"Look at me, Sheriff. Do I not look like a man?"

Steven's sharp blue eyes flashed over her, examining her at more length. She was almost beautiful, he thought. There was a subtle beauty in the round black eyes and pouting mouth, something sensual that stirred his blood. Her long black hair was loose, spilling around her face and shoulders in raven cascades, but her attire was anything but feminine.

Jenna was dressed in men's clothing. A loose fitting cotton shirt hid the pert mounds of her breasts in loose folds tucked into trousers held up by a belt cinched tightly around her slim waist.

"I dressed like this three nights ago and left the Lair with a pack train. No one noticed me in the darkness. Outside the canyon I left the others and drew a map to find the way back."

She drew a scrap of brown paper from inside a trouser pocket, then held it enticingly in front of Steven's eager face. He reached for it but Jenna jerked it away with a taunting smile.

"Not yet, Sheriff. Do I have the job here?"

Steven's glance raked her again, dwelling on the outline of her breasts as a lazy smile came to his lips. "Maybe. However, before I agree to give you a job, I'll have to know more about your qualifications."

Jenna smiled enticingly, rising to her feet. She tossed a lock of raven hair over one shoulder as she moved around the table to twirl a finger around the outline of the badge on his chest.

"I will show you, Sheriff. Then I will give you the map," she whispered in a low, husky voice.

"Then by all means, let's get down to business."

***

An hour later Steven arose from the tumbled bed to dress again. He looked into the gilt framed mirror at the reflection of Jenna's olive body among the sheets, smiling briefly at the sloe-eyed pleased smirk on her face.

"Do I pass your test, Sheriff?"

"Easily," Steven replied with a smug grin while he finished tying his tie. "Tell me something, why did you refer to Miss McCandless as a *blanca* witch?"

A flash of hatred lit up Jenna's eyes, narrowing them to mere slits. "She has bewitched him, taken him from me!"

Steven turned from the mirror, leaning his hands behind him on the edge of the dresser while he stared at her suspiciously. "What the hell do you mean? Has Devereaux harmed her?"

"Harmed her?" Jenna spat contemptuously. "She is living with him in his house, sharing his bed, touring the streets of the Lair on his arm smiling like a *gordo, callejon gato!* Harmed her, no! She finds *mucho* pleasure in his bed."

Steven's handsome face twisted with fury. His hands clinched into fists behind him. "You're lying! Goddamn you! You're lying!"

Jenna smiled in triumphant glee at his misery. "You are in love with her, no? Too bad, *senor* Riker. The *blanca* witch has found another more to her liking."

Steven could not speak for the fury that choked him. Jenna sighed and lay back among the damp sheets with a smile. "So you see, Sheriff, you and I have much in common. Morgan has taken your woman and she has taken my man. Revenge will be sweet, will it not?"

Steven recovered at last. He strode around the bed to rummage through her clothes until he located the map. Studying it at length, he saw that Jenna had done a remarkable job of drawing in landmarks. At the bottom were detailed directions written in Spanish, but that was no problem. He was fluent in the language. It was impossible to live in Texas without learning it.

Glancing back to the girl in his bed, his eyes narrowed sharply, filling with disgust and contempt. Laying the map aside, he reached up to pull the string tie from his collar. Then, smiling grimly at the girl's terrified expression, he moved quickly, wrapped the tie around her throat, placed one knee in her stomach for leverage, and pulled sharply until her thrashing ceased and she lay still in the rumpled bedding.

Satisfied that she was dead, Steven calmly replaced the tie around his neck and stood up. He flipped the sheets to cover Jenna's naked, lifeless body, then picked up the map.

"Whore!" he snorted. "Lucky for me you did such a good job of drawing this map. I don't need you. Good thing too, I've always hated Mexicans."

He chuckled softly as he left the room. He descended the stairs two at a time and paused at the bar with a pleased smirk. "There's a bundle of Mexican garbage in my room, Harry. Get rid of it for me, will you?" he said pleasantly to the bartender.

The heavy set man behind the bar nodded and went on wiping glasses. "Sure thing, boss. I'll see to it right away."

"Put it anywhere, Harry, it makes no difference to me as long as it's out of sight," Steven returned over his shoulder as he moved through the saloon toward the front door.

Two hours later he arrived at *Sierra Vieja* and strode into Owen McCandless' study with a pleased expression on his face. Owen sat behind the desk smoking morosely, but when he looked up at Steven's intrusion, he knew at once his visitor brought good news.

Ryan Tyrell was with the rancher, drinking coffee from a delicate china cup and feeling uncomfortable amid such luxury. His aqua-marine eyes narrowed at the sight of Steven's self satisfied smirk. He'd had an instant, intense dislike for the man. Instinctively, he knew Riker was not what he appeared, much as Owen McCandless.

Steven placed both hands on top of Owen's desk as he leaned forward with a smile. "Gentlemen, I know the way into the Leopard's Lair!"

CHAPTER TWENTY-FIVE

Amber studied Morgan's thoughtful features from across the room. He was standing before the front windows, all but oblivious to her presence. He was scowling, a sharp contrast to the more frequent smiles he had worn during the past several days.

"Morgan, what's on your mind?" she asked when she could no longer stand his silence.

Morgan glanced over his shoulder, but returned to his steady gaze out the window. "Jenna's gone. Jase told me about it last night. No one knows how long she's been gone or how she got out of the canyon without being seen."

Amber felt a pang of resentment that made her voice sharp when she spoke. "Is she that important to you, Morgan?"

"No," he answered without turning around. "It's her disappearance that bothers me."

He could not shake the disturbing memory of Jenna's angry threats that day in the street. When he learned of her disappearance, the hair at the back of his neck had stood on end. He had learned years past to listen to that warning. The sensation had often saved his life.

"I've doubled the guards at the entrance just in case," he said, more to himself than Amber. "I don't like it. Whatever Jenna is up to means trouble. I can feel it."

Amber felt a knot of uneasiness form in the pit of her stomach. She doubted that Jenna Ruiz had the capability of causing Morgan any serious trouble, but his concern made her nervous. Swallowing her anxiety, she poured him another cup of coffee from the silver pot on the table beside the couch and forced a smile to her lips.

"Come, Morgan, have some coffee with me and take that unpleasant scowl off your face."

His silver spurs jingled as Morgan walked across the room with a half-smile on his lips. He dropped onto the couch beside her with a sigh and took the cup and saucer she offered, sipping slowly at the steaming coffee as he watched her over the edge of the cup.

"Did you love her, Morgan?" Amber asked suddenly. Despite the instant displeasure that flashed into his face, she held his steady, ebony gaze, waiting for him to answer.

"Don't be ridiculous!"

Amber bristled at his tone of voice. Her own confused emotions erupted into anger at his abrupt dismissal of any possibility of emotion, even though a part of her was relieved to hear he did not have tender feelings for the Mexican girl. She set down her cup with a clatter.

"I'm not surprised," she snapped. "You don't love anyone, do you? I doubt that you even understand the meaning of the word!" Ignoring the warning in his grim features, she plunged ahead impulsively. "You take what you want from everyone. You use them and then you merely discard them when they begin to bore you!"

"Jesus Christ! Is that the only thought that ever enters a woman's head? Love?" Morgan put down his cup and rose to his feet, then crossed the room to snatch his hat from the rack inside the door.

"That's right, Morgan! Run away!" Amber cried, leaping to her feet to pursue him to the front door. "You can't have an honest discussion about your feelings because you don't have any! The only thing you understand is hatred and violence!"

Morgan's black eyes narrowed to flashing slits. He stared down at her ramrod stiff pose with her hands on her hips, her eyes filling with indignant tears, and her face coloring rapidly.

"Don't push me, Amber," he warned in a low, deceptively soft voice. "The past few days have been very pleasant. Don't spoil it now."

"Things have been pleasant because I've submitted to your vile demands!" Amber retorted furiously. She grabbed his arm when he attempted to move past her, blinded by anger to the dangerous glint in his eyes when he again turned to face her. "You only care about your crude, primitive needs, not about the defenseless woman you force your attentions upon! Jenna loved you and you treated her like dirt!"

"Jenna is a whore."

"That makes me a whore too, doesn't it? Jenna gave herself to you out of love, and I because of some momentary weakness that made me addle-brained, but it's all the same. Just a convenient receptacle for your lust!"

"There is a world of difference between you and Jenna Ruiz!"

"Indeed? I hardly think so, at least in your eyes. You view all women as whores, don't you, Morgan? What is the difference, pray tell. Did we not both lie down and spread our legs for you? Did we not both moan like wild animals in a fit of passion, begging you to favor us with your manly presence?"

"Shut the hell up, Amber!"

"What will you do if I refuse? Shoot me? Kill me like you plan to kill my uncle? You're so full of hate and revenge, Morgan, you wouldn't know love if it bit you. You don't care about anything except getting even, making Uncle Owen hurt the way you've been hurt.

"What then, Morgan? What happens when you've satisfied that murderous urge inside you? I'll tell you what happens then— nothing, that's what. You've spent your entire life for one glorious moment of revenge and when it's over you'll have nothing. You'll be a cold, empty man with no friends, no home, and worst of all, no emotion left inside you.

"Hate is the only true emotion you know. You keep your emotions under such tight control, until one day when you're ready to take them out and use them, there will be nothing. Nothing! Because revenge is all that's important to you. You're a hateful, evil man and I hope that when you finally get your revenge that you find it has a bitter taste. Maybe then you'll realize how much you've thrown away, how useless and wasted your life has been!"

Morgan stared at her in furious silence, watching her golden eyes fill with tears that she blinked away. The pain that flooded her pale face made him feel strangely guilty.

"What do you want me to say, Amber? That I've changed my mind? That I'll let Owen McCandless get away with murder? I can't do that," he said wearily.

He made another attempt to move past her, but again Amber caught his arm, clinging to him fiercely not in anger this time, but desperation.

"Morgan, if I agreed to stay with you, for as long as you want, would that change your mind?" she pleaded in a choked voice.

"No, Amber, I'm sorry, but it wouldn't."

"Do the past few days mean nothing to you?" she asked urgently as her eyes searched his dark inscrutable features for a hint of emotion. "Don't you realize yet that there can be more to your life than killing and hating?"

Morgan studied her in silence thoughtfully. The plea in her sparkling eyes touched him in a way he did not comprehend. She was so beautiful with her head uplifted in a defiant pose that contrasted sharply with the quiver in her chin.

"The past few days have been among the most pleasant in my life, Amber, but that changes nothing. What do you want to hear, Amber, that I'm madly in love with you? That I can't live without you?" His voice was soft, almost kind, the words spoken in a low tone. "I could tell you that. I could tell you all kinds of outrageous lies to soothe your feelings, make it seem less ugly to you, but I'm not going to. I want you, Amber, in a way I've never wanted any other woman, but love? Maybe you're right. Maybe I don't know the meaning of the word. Maybe I never will."

That hurt, more than she would ever have thought possible. "So you'll use me, in your bed and as bait to kill my uncle. Then you'll go on your merry way without ever giving me a second thought. Is that it? You've ruined my life, forced feelings from me you had no right to, and it means nothing to you.

"I feel sorry for you, Morgan. You're a pitiful excuse for a man!"

Morgan slapped her before he realized it, slamming her to the floor at his feet where she lay in a crumpled heap, tears streaming down her cheeks. Yet, her expression was one of compassion.

"Violence is the only way you know to deal with any situation. I can't wait to be free of you!"

Morgan stared down at her for an instant. An apology died on his lips before he could utter the words. Instead, he turned on his heel and jerked open the front door, closing it behind him with a bang. He yanked the Appaloosa's reins free of the picket and vaulted into the saddle. Swinging the wiry animal around with unaccustomed roughness, he applied his spurs to the horse's flanks to speed away down the street in a cloud of dust, cursing himself for losing his temper and striking Amber in a moment of rage, and Amber herself, for goading him past his limit of endurance.

***

Amber climbed to her feet and ran out the door. It was too late. Morgan was gone. She gradually became aware of the curious stares of Morgan's neighbors. Spanish women on both sides of her had been working in their gardens when Morgan slammed out of the house. She whirled about to re-enter the house, but suddenly changed her mind.

Morgan would cool off soon and return, expecting her to be here waiting in contrite acceptance. Well, not this time, she vowed grimly. This time when he decided to come back to force his will upon her, he'd have quite a surprise coming.

She smoothed her skirts and brushed back a tendril of hair that had fallen from the loose braid down her back and marched toward the stables. Her cheek still stung from the impact of his hand but her pride and feelings were far more battered than her body.

The large rambling stables stood on both sides of the main street. The part that occupied the same side of the street as Morgan's house was a two story structure with weathered, unpainted lumber beneath a rusty tin roof. She paused briefly in front of the building, noting that both doors were open and the upper level was stuffed full of sweet smelling hay.

She squared her shoulders, then walked resolutely inside to look for a hiding place. Let him look for her, she thought contemptuously, while her eyes adjusted to the dim light. The soft nicker of horses caught her attention so she moved in the direction of the sound. Along both sides of the building were box stalls containing about ten horses.

In spite of her sour mood, Amber responded to the welcoming neighs. Moving along one side of the stable, she rubbed each silky muzzle and crooned a few words of solace. One animal in particular caught her attention. He was a grand palomino with a gleaming golden body and long flowing white mane and tail. The big horse reached his long neck over the stall to place his pink muzzle against her cheek.

Amber chuckled with delight. He was an extraordinary horse with long legs and powerful shoulders, and an intelligence in his face that made Amber think immediately of Sheik.

"Hi there, big fellow," she crooned softly. She gently stroked his neck, then scratched behind his long ears, smiling at the soft friendly nickers that came from his throat. "You're a beauty. And well cared for, too. Somebody obviously loves you as much as I love my Sheik."

While she rubbed the horse's glossy neck, her eyes searched the loft overhead for a suitable hiding place. The stable was filled with hay so surely there was a nook somewhere, where she could curl up and wait for Morgan to miss her.

"Do you think I was too hard on him, big fellow?" she asked the palomino. "I guess he can't help the way he is, but it's such a waste. He has good qualities too. He can be gentle, even tender and really quite fun when he allows himself to be. If only he would let go of the past...."

Her voice drifted off into silence. The tightness in her chest made it difficult to breathe. Suddenly the tears began again. They streamed down her cheeks in silver rivers, falling onto the bodice of the blue and white gingham dress, making tiny splotches. It hurt so much to realize he felt nothing for her except a momentary thrill of sexual desire.

He had aroused such deep, intense feelings in her. Made her wilt into a lump of molten lava at the touch of his hands, his lips. He possessed the ability to lay bare the very essence of her soul, making her toss aside all her principals and give him everything she had with wanton abandonment, but he remained untouched by it.

She despised him for that. Despised him as intensely as she desired him. She was so confused. The impact he had made on her life changed all her thoughts and plans, made her wonder what kind of woman she was. Had she always had this dark, sensual side that had waited for Morgan Devereaux to bring it to life, or was that something he had created? Would that passionate Amber be squelched forever when Morgan was gone from her life?

As much as she wanted to be free of him, she could not help wondering how empty her life would be when she was safely back at home. But if he succeeded she would have no one. Uncle Owen would be dead. But what if Morgan was right? What if Uncle Owen was guilty of the hideous things Morgan accused him of? What if he had arranged her father's death? She resolutely wiped the tears away with the back of her hand. How would she ever know for sure?

A footstep behind her tore her thoughts away from those tormented doubts. She whirled about, suddenly remembering Morgan's warning about leaving the house alone.

"Didn't mean to startle you," Luther Simmons told her with a smile. The ugly scar down his right cheek crinkled into a sinister smirk when he smiled. Although he appeared harmless enough,

Amber moved a step away. "Nice horse, ain't he?" Luther went on, indicating the palomino. "That's Welch Mandell's horse."

In spite of the man's friendly appearance, Amber saw his eyes flicker over her, felt the hair rise on the back of her neck. Luther hooked his thumbs in his gunbelt as he leaned against the end of the stall.

"You shouldn't be wanderin' around by yourself, pretty lady. Makes a man think you're lookin' for somethin'."

Color flooded Amber's face. She drew herself up and squared her shoulders, sending him a flash of contempt as she moved toward the open door. "The only thing I'm looking for, sir, is some privacy!"

A lazy grin snaked across Luther's lips as he moved to block her path. "Morgan stormed into the saloon like a thundercloud. What's the matter, the two of you have a fight? Morgan not givin' you enough to keep you happy?" he quizzed with a soft chuckle that sounded false and hollow in the eerie quiet. "Is that why you're down here lookin' at the horses? You tryin' to figure some way of gettin' outa here?"

"Where I am and what I'm doing is none of your business!" Amber snapped. "Get out of my way. Let me pass!"

"Oh, I will, pretty lady, just as soon as you give me a little sample of what Morgan's been gettin'."

Amber's face paled. Her tongue felt thick. Her lips were as dry as sand, but she flicked her tongue across them and found her voice. "I'll give you nothing! Get out of my way and I won't mention this to Morgan. If you don't, I'll tell him what you've said. You know what he'll do then, don't you?"

Her bluff did not work. Luther continued to approach, slowly circling her in ever decreasing circles, that slick, wicked smile remaining on his face while his eyes raked her up and down suggestively.

"Who do you think he'll believe?" he challenged. "Some snotty little skirt that's tryin' to run off, or me? Hell, pretty thing, I've rode with Morgan for three years. He'll believe what I tell him."

Amber was desperately afraid Luther was right. In the mood Morgan was in, he'd believe anyone before he'd believe her. Amber looked about frantically for a weapon or a place to escape, but the stable seemed suddenly tiny and dark, offering no sanctuary.

Luther lunged at her, grabbing her skirt as he flung her backwards into a pile of loose hay. He was upon her before she could react, tearing at her clothes. Grabbing at her breasts with hot, sweaty hands, he covered her mouth with his, plunging his tongue into her mouth, suffocating her, making her gag. His body pressed hers into the hay. The hardness of his arousal bruised her thighs.

Amber struggled, shoving her hands into his chest, ripping at his face with her nails. She drew blood and Luther slapped her, making her ears ring and filling her head with bright lights. She felt dizzy, as though she was going to vomit. His rough hands yanked her skirt up around her waist as he clawed at her underclothes. She screamed, then felt darkness invade her when Luther struck her again.

Through a foggy haze, Amber heard the distant sound of cloth ripping as Luther tore her under garments off her limp, almost unconscious body. He was panting, drooling on her while he fumbled with his trousers, but Amber's mind was pleasantly fuzzy, drifting above her body.

"Luther!"

The young outlaw froze at the sound of his name. He slid off Amber, then rose hastily to his feet, sticking his shirt tail back into his trousers, and adjusted his fly. "She was tryin' to get away, boss," he whined. "I was just keepin' her from escapin'."

"By raping her?" came the hard cold voice. The owner came closer, his eyes narrowed to slits of gun-metal fury. Luther's whine died in his throat when the man pulled open his elegant black waistcoat, then dropped his hand to the butt of the .45 on his hip.

"Wasn't hurtin' her none," Luther whimpered. His eyes were huge in his thin face. His color was gone. He glanced from the hand on the pistol back to the man's face several times anxiously.

"The lady might have something to say about that."

"It ain't fair, boss. Morgan always gets what he wants. I don't ever get nothin'."

"Morgan has earned his privileges, Luther. You're just excess baggage to me. You've got thirty seconds, Luther. Draw or I'll shoot you down where you stand," came the cold, clear voice.

"Boss, I can't draw on you. I ain't got no chance," Luther pleaded.

"You should've thought of that before you tried to take something that didn't belong to you. Draw on me, Luther, or die where you stand."

"Either way I'm dead!" Luther cried.

"That's your problem."

Consciousness was slowly returning to Amber's disoriented mind. Gray shapes slowly became men. One crouching in terror, his back toward her, another facing her a few feet away. He was a big man, but the sun was directly in her eyes, blocking out any perception of his face.

As she watched, Luther made a desperate grab for the gun on his hip. An instant later one gun roared. Luther's weapon dropped from his fingers as he clutched his chest, trying to cover the rapidly spreading blotch of crimson that stained his shirt. A moment later he toppled to the floor, stone dead.

Amber whimpered in fright as the large gray shape came closer to kneel beside her and look anxiously into her white, bewildered face.

"It's all right, sugar. Nothing to be afraid of now. I won't let anything hurt you," the deep voice said to her. The man's big hand gently brushed the loose strands of golden hair from her eyes, then pulled her skirt down to cover her legs.

He helped her up, putting one arm around her waist to steady her. Amber blinked several times to clear her vision, staring into the face of her rescuer. "I don't know you. Who are you?" she asked in a faint voice.

"Nobody for you to be afraid of, Amber."

Her brow wrinkled in surprise. She scanned the man's handsome face anxiously. He seemed almost familiar, as though she had seen him somewhere, but she knew that was impossible.

"How do you know my name?"

"I know all about you, Amber," the deep voice said gently while the man gathered her into his arms like a child and turned toward the door. "I've known you since before you were born. Your daddy meant more to me than any man alive, except maybe Morgan."

"Then you must be…"

" I'm Welch Mandell."

CHAPTER TWENTY-SIX

Welch carried Amber down the street toward his house. He shouted for Francine as he kicked the front door open and proceeded to carry the unconscious girl into his study. Laying Amber down on the royal blue sofa that occupied one end of the room, he sat down beside her, gazing fondly into her beautiful face.

So this was Price's daughter, he mused. She had promptly fainted after his announcement and was only now beginning to show signs of stirring. His gray gaze ran over her slender body in mute appreciation. She was exquisite. It was no wonder Morgan was in such a state. Brilliant golden hair spread like a fan on the arm of the sofa, tiny and delicate like a fragile china doll she was. So beautiful it almost took his breath.

"She's beautiful, isn't she, Welch?" Francine asked as she knelt beside Amber to begin bathing her face with a damp cloth.

"The resemblance to her mother is uncanny," Welch said in an awed voice. "She's almost identical to Althea when I saw her the first time. Even more beautiful if anything." He sat silently staring into Amber's still face for a moment longer, then turned to Francine. "Have someone go to the saloon and get Morgan."

Alarm flared in Francine's cat green eyes. "Welch, I don't think...."

"Get Morgan, damn it. Do what I say, Francie."

"Welch, suppose he notices the....."

"If he does, he does. It's too damned late to worry about that. Just get him, Francie."

Francine got to her feet and hurried from the room. Welch picked up the cloth, slowly bathing Amber's face until her eyes fluttered open a few moments later. By the time Morgan arrived,

Amber was sitting up, sipping from a glass of sherry. Morgan dashed into the room, his eyes first landing on Welch's thoughtful face behind his desk, then to Amber's pale anxious one on the sofa.

"What the hell happened?" he demanded as he halted in the center of the room.

"It's all over, Morgan. Calm yourself," Welch advised quietly behind a cloud of cheroot smoke. "I think she's all right. No serious injuries. Just had the shit scared out of her."

"What happened?" Morgan asked again in a tight voice. He took off his hat and sat down on the edge of the sofa beside her, forcing her to look at him through sheer will.

"Luther tried to rape her," Welch said. He kept his voice steady with a supreme effort, but his hand was still shaking when he lifted the cigar from his lips. "He said she was trying to escape, she says she wasn't. She says she just went for a walk and ended up in the stables when Luther followed her in."

"Where the hell is he?" Morgan snapped. His gaze left Amber's face to lock on Welch's in an unblinking stare that demanded an immediate answer.

"He's dead, Morgan. I killed the son-of-a-bitch."

Morgan's gaze flashed back to Amber, scanning her in one quick glance. His jaw tightened in fury at the purplish bruise forming on her cheek. "Are you all right, Amber?"

She nodded silently, trying to decide if the anger that flooded his features was directed at her or at what had happened to her.

"What were you doing in the stables?"

"I told you, Morgan, she was..." Welch began.

"I want to hear it from her," Morgan cut in sharply. Now that he was convinced she was safe, the anger from their last encounter came flooding back. The glare he sent Welch was ice cold, but Welch met his brief glance with calm determination.

"I..I..was angry with you," Amber said quickly. The tension between the two men was so strong it frightened her, made her want to defuse it as quickly as possible. "I went for a walk to clear

my head. I just wandered into the stable. I was petting the palomino when he came in. I wasn't trying to run away."

"I'll bet!" Morgan snapped. He got to his feet, holding out his
hand for her.

"Amber is staying here, Morgan."

Francine's heart leapt into her throat. She was standing just
inside the doorway, wringing her hands nervously, praying that
Welch would back down, yet knowing he wouldn't. Not this time,
the girl was too important.

"I don't think you're taking very good care of her so I'm going
to. She'll stay here until we make the exchange with McCandless."

Morgan's head snapped up, his body tensing as he turned to
face Welch, his black eyes narrowing to slits of cold fury. "You're
challenging me for her?" he asked in a quiet tone that was more
audible than if he had shouted.

Welch nodded. "If I have to. I hope you have better sense than
to push me that far." He kept both hands palm down in open
sight on the desk as he rose to his feet. He watched Morgan's face
warily. Once the shock of his challenge died, fury replaced it.

Morgan's body stiffened momentarily. He walked forward a
couple of steps and halted, automatically dropping his left hand
to his side. The motion froze Welch's blood.

"All these years," he said softly, his gaze still locked with
Morgan's. "And you look at me now as though you want to kill
me."

"That's up to you, Welch," Morgan grated through clenched
teeth. "I won't let her go without a fight. Think about it before
you challenge me."

"I've already thought about it. I don't like the way she's been
treated and I don't like the possessive way you act. She's not one of
Francine's whores, Morgan. She's a lady, and it's damned well time
she was treated like one. If protecting her from fools like Luther
means I have to blow you to hell, then I guess I'll have to do that
too."

They stood glaring at one another in furious silence for what seemed an eternity, neither man giving an inch, their eyes locked together in grim determination. It took all Welch's strength to keep his hands from shaking. The cold determination he saw in Morgan's face was enough to chill a normal man's blood. But Welch Mandell was no ordinary man. He had taught Morgan everything he knew and he could tell when Morgan was going to draw. He could only pray that was enough of an edge.

A muscle twitched in Morgan's jaw. He knew Welch would not back down, but could he bring himself to draw against the man who had been like a father to him? He did not know.

Suddenly shots and shouts broke the stillness. What had been one shot now became dozens, one after another echoing against the canyon walls until the windows in the room began to rattle. Instantly, Morgan whirled and dashed out the door into the street.

The Lair had become a death trap. Dozens of men were riding up the street shooting at everything that moved. The mid-afternoon sun reflected off the silver badge on the chest of the big, leather-clad man riding in the vanguard of the posse. Grabbing Francine's arm, he half drug her back into the house. Welch met him in the narrow hallway, his gun drawn, shock making his face gray.

"What the bloody hell is going on?"

"Posse," Morgan replied curtly. He grabbed Welch's arm and turned him back down the hall toward the study. Flashing a glance at Amber, he commanded, "Get down, Amber. Those fools are shooting at everything that moves. Get down on the floor. Keep your head down."

"What are our chances?" Welch asked.

"None. There must be fifty or sixty men. That damned ranger is leading them. But on the brighter side, I saw Owen McCandless too. Get moving, Welch, there isn't much time. They'll be here before you can blink. Take Amber and Francine and get out."

"What about you?"

A slight grin touched Morgan's lips for an instant as he took the Colt from his holster. "I'll buy you enough time. Maybe I'll even get McCandless too." He gave the older man a gentle push. "Move, Welch."

Stray bullets shattered the windows of the study, sprinkling Amber with fragments where she lay huddled on the floor. Welch swallowed and nodded. There was so much he wanted to say to Morgan, but before he could speak, Morgan had run back down the hallway.

Welch ducked, bending low as he ran to his desk and yanked open a drawer. "Francie, Amber, get up and follow me. Keep low! Hurry! There isn't much time! Morgan's going to buy us all he can, but it may not be enough!"

Bullets slammed into the walls, splintering the expensive statues and art work into worthless shreds. Amber could not move. Her body was frozen in place. Terror choked her, blinding her to anything except the dozens of shots pouring into the building.

Welch pulled a book from his desk, stuck it under his coat as he holstered his gun. Reaching down, he yanked Amber to her feet.

"What about Morgan?" she shouted. "You can't just leave him here!"

"There's no time to explain, girl! Hurry!"

He hustled her down the hall in front of him with Francine scurrying along behind. At the foot of the staircase Welch abruptly turned to fling open the basement door. Amber looked around wildly. From the front windows she could see the posse bearing down on the house. It looked like a hundred men all yelling and shooting. Already the streets were littered with bodies of the dead outlaws taken so completely so surprise.

She looked toward the front door, directly in her line of vision. Her heart leaped into her mouth when she saw Morgan kneeling just inside the door, calmly reloading his gun. Bullets slammed into the wall all around him, splintering the door frames, sending glass from the windows on each side of the doorway showering the entryway. Amber screamed when he leaned back inside, giving her a glimpse of the blood that stained the right leg of his dark gray trousers. Her scream broke his concentration. He looked around for barely an instant, but it was long enough for a second bullet to slam into his chest.

"Amber! Come on!" Welch shouted, trying to pull her to safety. She pulled free of his grasp and ran screaming down the hall. Welch cursed vehemently, but had no choice but to close the basement door and take Francine through the secret passageway in the mountain to safety.

Amber flung herself across Morgan's body. Anguished tears flooded her eyes, making it almost impossible to see. The right side of his chest was rapidly turning crimson. His face was pale and filled with pain.

For a brief instant his eyes opened to stare into her face with surprise. "Amber..Amber.." he said, then his eyes closed as his head fell back into her arms.

Owen McCandless lifted his carbine and took aim at Morgan's body. Cold, blind fury covered him at the sight of his niece cradling that murdering outlaw's head, crying like a baby. He began to squeeze the trigger.

Amber recognized him through her tears. Her face froze in horror at the expression on his face. "Uncle Owen! No!" she screamed.

At that second Ryan Tyrell hit Owen's rifle barrel with his own, knocking it upward so it exploded harmlessly into the air.

"The man's already down, McCandless. There's no need to shoot him again," Ryan said contemptuously.

Owen slowly dropped his rifle into his saddle boot, scowling at Amber's anguished face. Ryan leapt down from his mount and raced up the steps. He knelt to place one hand against Morgan's throat, smiling faintly when he felt the pulse beneath his fingers. Assured the gunman was alive, he looked at Amber intently.

"You all right, Miss McCandless?"

Amber nodded as she wiped at her streaming eyes. "Morgan..is he dead?"

"No, ma'am, but he's pretty shot up." He took his bandanna

from around his neck, then opened Morgan's blood soaked shirt to peer at the wound. "The bullet was deflected by a rib from the looks of things. It's deep and he's losing a lot of blood." He pressed the bandanna over the wound and looked back at Amber's white, frightened face. "He'll live, ma'am. Providing I can get him to a doctor fast enough."

"At least long enough to hang," Steven Riker said from the edge of the porch. His blue eyes dwelled on Amber's face, narrowing in thought. It appeared the Mexican whore had been right about Amber's involvement with the gunfighter. Her tears were proof of that.

"Where's Mandell?" he asked abruptly.

Amber lifted a trembling hand in the direction of the hallway. Steven rushed past her, his gun drawn, to search for Welch. Almost immediately another ranger rode up and spoke to Ryan from his horse.

"Looks like we got most of 'em, Ryan. Like shooting fish in a barrel," he remarked with a dry chuckle. "Now if we've got Mandell too, we can close the book on this gang of cut-throats."

Amber lifted red, swollen eyes to look around in horror. Bodies lay everywhere, crumpled in grotesque positions on the street, on the balcony of the saloon. Some of them were dressed only in their underwear. Apparently, they had still been asleep when the posse entered the canyon. The guards at the canyon's entrance had obviously been taken by the same stealthy tactics that allowed the posse to enter the Lair unobserved until they were ready to begin their attack.

Flames leaped high into the sky as the exuberant posse members set fire to everything that would burn, sending terrified women and children screaming into the streets. Amber was surprised to see many of the men from McCandless among the posse.

She felt a chill of disgust as they displayed a sadistic nature she would never have believed existed in such God fearing family men. Their faces were filled with triumph as they raced about madly starting fires and howling with fiendish glee at the terrified children and sorrowful women bent over husbands and fathers lying dead in the street.

"What about the women and children, Ryan?" the ranger was asking.

"Round them up. We'll take them back to town to sort them all out. Start loading these bodies onto horses, Mike, and send one of the men to tell the wagons we'll be bringing up bodies in a bit."

"He's not here!" Steven Riker exclaimed loudly as he stomped out onto the porch. "Somehow the son-of-a-bitch got away clean!"

Ryan's head snapped up in surprise. "How could he? This is a box canyon. He must be around here somewhere. Keep looking."

Steven dispatched three men to go over the house again, then he reached down to pull Amber to her feet. She swayed against him, leaning on him heavily for support until her head cleared. Steven touched the ugly bruise on her face.

"Devereaux do this?" he demanded.

Amber shook her head mutely. She was numb with shock and fear, unable to speak or move. Her stunned gaze followed Tyrell when he bent down and lifted Morgan to his shoulders. Steven picked up Morgan's pistol from the porch and tucked it inside his belt.

"I'm keeping this for a souvenir," he said with a meaningful glance at Amber. "It's mine by rights. It's my bullet in his chest."

Amber stared at him dully, unable to say anything, only staring at him with wide eyes full of shock and dismay. She watched the ranger put Morgan on the horse in front of him, supporting Morgan's limp body with one strong arm around his waist. Steven pulled the reins of Morgan's Appaloosa from the hitching rail a few feet away, then lifted Amber into the saddle and handed the reins to Owen.

Owen turned toward the canyon trail. The Appaloosa followed along, rolling his frightened eyes and snorting his concern, but Amber was too dazed to be of any comfort to the wiry little animal. She saw Jase McCally face up in the street, dead from a bullet through the back. Further down the street her heart lurched and bile rose in her throat. Consuela's plump body lay sprawled in the front yard of her tiny little house. She had been killed while working in her garden. Hot tears stung Amber's eyes.

"She never hurt anyone," she whispered brokenly, looking back until she could not see for the heavy smoke pouring from the buildings at the end of the street.

Morgan groaned, drawing her attention from Consuela. Alarm leaped into her eyes, filling her face with the first sign of animation Owen had seen since she had pleaded for Morgan's life. She attempted to move the Appaloosa alongside the ranger when Owen grabbed her shoulder. She looked at him in surprise, recoiling from the icy blue fury that filled his eyes and contorted his face.

"Never, ever make any attempt to contact that man again," Owen ground out through clenched teeth. "He's trash, not fit to lick your shoes. He kidnapped you, put me through living hell, and now you're afraid he's going to die?" he said in a low savage voice that only Amber could hear. "If he lives long enough to reach the doc in McCandless, I'll see to it personally that he hangs. And I'll not have you making a fool of me over him. Do you understand me, Amber?"

Amber stared at him as though she was looking at a stranger. Indeed, she was. Her kind, loving Uncle Owen would never have spoken to her in that manner. This gruff, cold man was a stranger. One she did not care to know.

"Steven tried to warn me," Owen went on coldly. "But I wouldn't believe him. He told me you were sleeping with that black-hearted son-of-a-bitch, but I didn't want to believe him. You want people to think it was because he forced you to, raped you, but I know better! You're cheap, Amber, immoral...just like your mother. Ready to spread your legs for the first man that comes along with a pretty smile and a hard-on. But you won't have a chance to make a laughingstock of me the way your mother did. I'll see to that!"

"Uncle Owen, please!" Amber whimpered in fear. "You don't understand! Please let me explain!"

"Keep your lies to yourself!" Owen snapped furiously. "I don't want to hear them. It's done, Amber, over, finished! That man is going to die, by God! Whether from the bullet in him or at the end of a rope. Either way you'll never see him again, never speak to him again, never utter his name in my house! Or, by God, I'll..."

"What, Uncle Owen? What will you do? Kill me too?"

Owen's bravado wilted into a contrite mask of sorrow. Tears filled his eyes, flowing down his cheeks as sobs racked his body. "I'm sorry, princess," he said brokenly. "I've been so worried about you, not knowing what that bastard was doing to you, not knowing if you were dead or alive. Please, princess, forgive me. I don't know what I'm doing or saying. I'm not myself right now."

Amber stared at him dully, watching the tears run down his cheeks. His eyes begged for her forgiveness as his hands reached out to her in a helpless gesture. She was confused, frightened. His manner had changed so abruptly it made her doubt her own sanity for a moment. Staring at the suffering on his face now, she wondered if what she had just witnessed had been the real Owen McCandless. Was the kind, gentle uncle only a masquerade? Was he really the cold-blooded monster Morgan had described?

"Uncle Owen, tell me how you know Welch Mandell."

CHAPTER TWENTY-SEVEN

Ryan Tyrell glanced up and grimaced in irritation at the noise from the crowd gathered in front of the sheriff's office in McCandless. It had been dark for two hours already, but still the crowd hung around outside, talking loudly and making threats to take the law into their own hands.

Ryan settled back in the cane-backed chair and stared into the flickering yellow light from the lamp on the scarred desk in front of him. Riker's jail was a grim place. The outer portion contained the desk, a cluttered bookcase and file cabinet, a pot-bellied stove for heat in the winter, and a space at the west end where dozens of wanted posters hung in hap-hazard fashion. Behind the desk was a waist high railing that separated the office from the row of cells behind it. McCandless was a small town. Likewise the jail was small and for the past while, severely overcrowded.

The noise of the crowd outside again drew his brows together in disgust. It had been like this every day and half the night for two months now. Ryan was sick of it. He pushed the chair back and walked across the room to pour himself a cup of coffee from the blackened pot atop the stove, then stood at the window in the door, staring into the crowd.

His aqua-marine eyes narrowed contemptuously when Sheriff Riker strolled from the hotel restaurant, paused to light a cigarette, then eased into the crowd. A wide grin brightened the sheriff's face as he moved among the gathering, speaking to first one man then another and clapping them on the back in a friendly fashion.

Ryan stared at the sheriff's departing back, then shook his

head while he walked back to the desk to sift through the pile of papers that awaited his attention. The only difference between Riker and the gunslinger in the cell behind him, Ryan thought scornfully, was the badge Riker wore. Or hid behind.

The past two months had been bone weary for the ranger. Of Welch Mandell's fifty man gang, twenty-five had been killed in the assault on the Lair, ten more had died from their wounds, and then came the job of deciding who had jurisdiction over the crimes. For weeks now McCandless had seen a constant flow of lawmen from all parts of the nation coming to collect their prisoners for return to the scene of their various crimes to stand trial.

McCandless had seen its share of trials also. There had been five hangings already and the crowd outside was gearing up for the biggest event yet due to start the following day.

Ryan got up and walked through the swinging gate. Coming to a halt in front of the second cell, he studied the broad shouldered man who stood with his back to the office, staring out into the dimly lit streets with his elbows propped on the window ledge.

"You didn't eat much," Ryan commented, nodding at the untouched tray on the narrow cot that sat against one wall of the cell. "Can't say I blame you. I can cook better than the stuff they send over here, but that's not saying much."

Morgan turned from the window to pick up the tray. Limping from the healing wound in his leg, he crossed the cell and slid the tray beneath the door. He straightened, gripping the bars in the door and putting his weight on the uninjured leg.

He returned the ranger's steady gaze without speaking. In the two months of his captivity, he had grudgingly grown to respect the big lawman. Tyrell was a no-nonsense kind of man, straight as an arrow, and as fearless as he was honest. At first Morgan was skeptical of Tyrell's efforts to keep him alive. Now, after two months of almost constant companionship, he had to admit Tyrell was exactly what he appeared. That was surprising for a lawman.

"You want some coffee?" Ryan asked to break the silence.

"Sure, why not? It can't be any worse than the food," Morgan replied dryly.

Ryan turned away with a grin, crossing to the stove to fill a cup with the strong brew. He handed it through the bars and sat down on the wide railing that separated the office from the jail to watch while Morgan sipped from the cup.

He had made a good recovery, Ryan thought. The doc had not given Morgan much chance when Ryan brought him down from the mountains. The leg wound was more bloody than serious, for the bullet had gone straight through the thigh without hitting any bones. The chest wound was much more serious, but once the bullet was removed and the danger of infection passed, the gunfighter had steadily regained his strength.

He was still a bit pale, weak from the heavy loss of blood, but the limp was getting better each day. Ryan noted he had been spending more time on his feet the past few days.

"The doc says you're to eat, Devereaux. Can't get your strength back without food."

A sardonic smile briefly touched Morgan's mouth. He stood leaning against the barred door, studying the ranger's open face thoughtfully while sipping the coffee. "Don't worry, Tyrell. I'll be strong enough to walk into court tomorrow," he said dryly.

Ryan turned away with a scowl. He slumped back into his chair at the rough desk and stared moodily into the lamp. The pile of papers stared up at him. His gaze settled on the face of Welch Mandell glaring up from a wanted poster. It still galled Ryan that the outlaw king had managed somehow to escape the Lair. No trace of him had been found and no amount of questioning had shed any light on how he had done it. He had simply disappeared.

Ryan glanced at Morgan thoughtfully. The gunfighter was looking out the window again, paying no visible attention to the crowd, but staring into the distance as though his mind was a million miles away.

Devereaux knew how Mandell had gotten away. Ryan was also positive the gunfighter knew where Mandell was now, but he wasn't telling. Ryan had spent several frustrated hours questioning Morgan, but all he got was that sardonic, mocking gaze that revealed nothing.

The door of the office rattled, bringing Ryan instantly alert. He dropped a hand to the butt of his gun, waiting until his visitor was inside with the door closed securely behind him before drawing a relieved breath.

"Evening, Tyrell," Travis Bennett, the newspaper man, said with a friendly smile. He walked to the desk and handed Ryan a telegram, watching curiously while the ranger ripped it open, read it quickly, then wadded it into a ball and threw it into the waste basket beside the desk.

"I met Ronny from the telegraph office on my way in and he asked if I'd give that to you. Bad news, I take it."

Ryan nodded as he ran a big paw through his gold streaked brown hair. "That was from the governor. I wired him two weeks ago asking for a change of venue in Devereaux's trial. I figured what the hell, every other politician in Texas has turned down my request. Nothing to lose, right?"

Travis studied the ranger, his brown eyes shrewd. The newspaper man was small in comparison to Ryan. Bennett was in his early forties, red haired and freckle faced, certainly not a handsome man by most standards. He possessed, however, a shrewd, analytical mind that viewed those he met with the capacity to read between the lines. It was this uncanny ability that made him such a successful newspaper man, which in turn resulted in Owen McCandless' wrath.

He had discovered large scale pay-off between the railroad officials and Owen McCandless that put thousands of dollars in McCandless' pockets. Having been foolish enough to print some of it in his weekly paper, he had suffered threats and vandalism to his business. It eventually led to his being accosted when leaving the paper one night. He'd received a severe beating at the hands of some men McCandless had hired to keep him in line.

That had been five years ago. Since then Bennett had played the rancher's game, printing the local news about weddings, babies, deaths, and the like, keeping McCandless' name from appearing in his paper. Except, of course, when the rancher donated money to rebuild the school when it burned, and loaned money to the small ranchers when a drought all but wiped them out one year. But all the while Travis waited, searched, and kept careful records that were safely hidden away, waiting for the moment when he could use the information he had gleaned to topple McCandless' rotten empire.

"He turned down the request."

Travis' words were a statement, not a question for it was obvious from the ranger's manner what the answer had been.

Ryan nodded again with a sigh. He leaned back in the chair and crossed his long leather-clad legs on top of the desk. "So that's it," he said bleakly. "Devereaux goes on trial tomorrow right here. And to think I promised the man a fair shake."

"There's nothing more you could have done, Tyrell," Travis reminded him. "You've kept that mob of fair minded citizens out there from stringing him up by staying on here to keep a lid on things after Riker and McCandless did everything possible to get you recalled to Austin."

"I hate to admit it, Bennett, but I'm just about convinced Devereaux's right. He told me he could never get a fair trial because McCandless owns too many people, but I didn't believe him. Now I'm not so certain."

Bennett nodded in agreement. "McCandless owns the judges, the courts, the politicians, and most of the lawmen in this state. He wants a conviction tomorrow and a hanging..and he'll get it."

Ryan did not reply. He cupped his chin in one brawny hand and scowled into the flames of the lamp. After a few seconds the newspaper man rapped his knuckles on the desk while he looked at the big ranger curiously.

"Tell me something, Tyrell, just for my own curiosity. Why have you gone to so much trouble to get a notorious, wanted man a fair trial? What's it to you whether Devereaux even gets a trial or not?"

A thin smile pushed back the gloom in Ryan's face when he looked up at Travis. "Every man has the right to a fair trial." He glanced over his shoulder at Morgan lying stretched out on his cot, hands folded beneath his head, and smiled again. "If a lawman hadn't made sure I got a fair shake a few years ago, I'd be in the same position as Devereaux. That one man made a difference, turned my whole life around, because he believed every man has a right to a square deal. That's all, Bennett."

Travis silently reflected on the ranger's words for a moment, then motioned toward Morgan's cell. "Mind if I talk to him for a spell?"

Ryan shook his head and leaned down to take the cell keys from a nail beneath the desk. "It's all right with me if he don't mind. You trying to get a story out of him? If you are, I wish you luck. I've never seen a man who says less than that one."

Travis grinned as he followed Ryan through the swinging gate to halt in front of the cell.

"Devereaux, you want to talk to the newspaper man?"

Morgan swung his feet to the floor and sat up. "Why not? I've got nothing better to do with my time."

Ryan unlocked the cell to let Travis enter, then locked the door behind him and shook it to make sure it was secure. Then he strode back to the front of the jail to start making a fresh pot of coffee. It was going to be another long night.

Travis waited until Ryan was across the room before turning to Morgan with a mischievous grin. "Mr. Devereaux, may I have a few minutes of your time?" he asked in a professional tone. When Morgan nodded and indicated he should take a seat on the cot beside him, Travis took out his notepad and sat down.

"Morgan, how are you?" he asked in a softer voice, keeping one eye on the ranger to make sure he wasn't listening.

"I'm fine, Travis."

"How's the chest?"

"Better. What the hell are you doing, Travis? You shouldn't be here talking to me. If McCandless finds out, you could have another visit from his goons," Morgan returned in a guarded tone.

A grin splashed across the smaller man's freckled face, making him appear mischievous and daring like a young boy. "I'll take my chances. I wanted to tell you something and since Tyrell checks everybody that comes in or out of here, I figured the best way was to pretend I wanted a story for the paper."

"What is it you want to tell me? Has something happened to Amber?"

Travis shook his head emphatically. "No, as far I've been able to find out, Amber is fine. McCandless keeps her at the ranch so nobody has a chance to talk to her but Cooter came by this afternoon. He said she seems to be all right. He told me something else, too. That's why I'm here."

While Morgan waited impatiently, Travis glanced anxiously at Ryan's back. The ranger sat with his chair leaned back on two legs, his long legs crossed on the ankles, resting atop the desk. He was flipping idly through the stack of wanted posters and sipping coffee, outwardly at least, paying no attention to them.

"It's about the trial, Morgan," Travis explained quietly, a sober expression replacing the previous mischief. He looked Morgan in the eyes, putting one hand on Morgan's arm for emphasis. "In spite of the ranger's attempts to get your trial changed to another county, McCandless has paid off enough politicians to make sure it will be held right here."

"I already knew that."

"Okay, then. At the trial tomorrow Amber will be the star witness for the prosecution, Morgan. McCandless intends to put her on the stand to tell the court in vivid detail how you raped her."

"What the hell for?" Morgan snapped. His eyes flashed with anger as his jaw tightened into a hard wall of muscle. "What's he trying to do to her? With the case they've got against me they could hang a dozen men. Putting Amber through that is unnecessary!"

Travis smiled grimly and bent his head closer. "Owen McCandless is taking no chances with your fate, my friend. He wants to see you at the end of a hemp necktie. What better way to stack the deck in his favor than by putting Amber on the stand to tell half the state of Texas what perverted, sadistic things you forced her to endure?

"Hell, Morgan, by the time that slick lawyer gets through with her, it'll be a miracle if the God fearing, law abiding citizens of this sweet little hamlet don't string you up on the spot."

"I've tried to plead guilty to the goddamned charges, but the court wouldn't accept my plea. What the hell more do they want?" Morgan grated through clenched teeth.

Travis clucked his tongue in mock disbelief. "Come on, Morgan. If you really thought pleading guilty would keep Amber from having to testify at a trial, then you don't know as much about Owen McCandless as you think.

"He wants you dead, my friend, but he wants it all nice and legal, and tied with a red ribbon. He wants you tried, but he's made sure you'll be tried in his town, in his court, before his judge, and a jury of men that owe him plenty. He gets what he wants and has everybody feeling sorry for him in the bargain."

"And what about Amber?"

"You know the answer to that, my friend," Travis answered quietly. "He's making certain everybody understands she is an innocent victim in all this. You took her by force, did God knows what to her, so how can she be blamed for anything? And if testifying in open court is hard on her, then so much the better for Owen. All her pain and suffering in court tomorrow can only help his case to get you hung."

Morgan got to his feet to pace the narrow cell, seething with frustration. He ran one hand absently through his hair several times before finally coming back to drop onto the cot and rub gingerly at his injured leg. "Is there anyway you can get a message to her tonight?"

Travis shook his head with a tight smile. "He brought her into town a couple of hours ago. She's at the hotel, but he's got guards all around her. I doubt even Cooter could get to her before the trial."

Morgan did not reply. He sat staring morosely at a roach crawling across the rough wood floor, his hands clenching and unclenching in frustration.

"What are you afraid she'll say, Morgan?" Travis inquired curiously. "Do you think she might implicate herself in some way?"

The black scowl Morgan threw him brought an immediate end to the tiny smile at the corners of his mouth. He laid a comforting hand on Morgan's arm as he got to his feet. "I'm sorry, Morgan. Sorry I can't do more to help. But whatever Amber says on that witness stand tomorrow will be said and there isn't a damned thing you can do about it. Maybe Welch will...."

"No," Morgan cut in curtly. "Welch is in Mexico and if he has any sense at all, he'll stay there. Tyrell has every road and cow trail leading into this town guarded in case he tries to get me out."

"I wish you luck, my friend," Travis said. He tucked the notepad back inside his coat, then called to the ranger. Ryan let him out of the cell and locked the door. Travis was almost to the door when it opened and Steven Riker swept into the office.

Riker's eyes narrowed, his lips curling with contempt. "Isn't it a little late for you to be out, Bennett? You should be home in bed with your teddy bear by this time."

Travis' face flooded with anger. He squared his shoulders and glared up at Steven scornfully. "As long as scum like you is roaming the streets, every honest man has an obligation to be out, Riker. Trying to keep your contamination from spreading."

He shouldered his way past the arrogant sheriff to melt into the night. Steven chuckled as he strode into the office and took a sweeping look around. For a long moment he let his gaze dwell on Morgan, then directed his attention to the ranger.

"Thought I'd drop by for a final check tonight, Tyrell. Everything quiet here?"

"Quiet as a church."

Steven walked past him to the cell, halting a short distance from it to observe Morgan with sadistic pleasure. "Won't be long now, Devereaux. Tomorrow's the big day. Tried tomorrow and hung the day after. Of course, you might make things easier on yourself if you told me where I could find Mandell," he suggested with a smirk.

Morgan regarded him with a veiled black gaze that spoke volumes, but said nothing.

"Okay, if that's the way you want it. I just want you to know that when they walk you up that gallows, I'll be the man who slips the rope around your neck." Steven moved closer and lowered his voice so Ryan could not hear the next statement. "You don't have to worry about Amber though, Devereaux. I'm going to take real good care of her when you're dead. A few days with me and she'll not even remember your name.

"You see, Devereaux, I know all about you and the lady. I know she was cozying up to you, strolling around the Lair on your arm smiling up at you like a smitten school girl. Why, you should have seen the tears she cried over you! But..none of that matters now because before you stop twitching at the end of that rope, I'm going to marry her."

Morgan's jaw tensed. His whole body went rigid. His eyes gleamed with ebony fire, but he managed to keep his voice calm. "Go to hell, Riker!"

The cold arrogance in his voice sent a flush of anger through Riker's face. His hand dropped to his gun as a sneer curled his lips. "It's too bad you don't have a gun, Devereaux. I'd enjoy putting another bullet in you."

"If I had a gun, Riker, you'd be dead before you could blink."

"You talk big for a man who's about to hang," Riker jeered.

"I'm not dead yet, Riker," Morgan reminded him softly. "Until I am, don't count me out."

Steven swallowed quickly before he whirled to stride across the office. He slammed the door behind him so hard the window glass rattled. Morgan turned back to the barred window, clenched his fist in frustration and slammed it into the bars several times in rapid succession, cursing under his breath.

"He's a cocky little son-of-a-bitch, isn't he?"

Morgan glanced over his shoulder, not surprised to find the ranger perched against the railing, studying him with thoughtful eyes. Morgan did not answer. He lay down on his back on the narrow cot and folded his hands beneath his head, staring up at the ceiling in pointed silence.

"That cock-sure way of his makes you wish you had him on the inside of the cell with you for five minutes, doesn't it?" Ryan suggested with a knowing expression. "An interesting man, Sheriff Riker."

When Morgan did not speak, Ryan went on. "He has a way of getting information that makes me very curious. Like the way he came by the map that showed the way into the Lair. He said it was delivered to his room, just slid under the door, but I doubt that.

"And just now, his suggestion that the girl's relationship with you is more than meets the eye."

Morgan's body stiffened slightly, but his eyes remained focused on the leak stained ceiling of the cell.

"Course, it's possible he's drawing his conclusion from the way she reacted when you got shot. She did throw herself over you to keep the old man from pumping any more lead into you, and she was pretty scared you were going to die before I could get you down from the mountain, but still...it sounds like he knows something more.

"But then, everybody involved in this kidnapping business knows something I don't. McCandless, Riker, Cooter Jackson, the girl herself, though she refused to discuss it with me. Maybe that's partly because McCandless wouldn't leave us alone together long enough for her to have the chance. Even the newspaper man, Bennett, knows what's going on."

Morgan turned his head to level a cold, disgusted glance at the lawman. "You must have good ears, ranger," he said dryly.

Ryan grinned slightly and shrugged. "It's my business to hear things, Devereaux. What I'd like to hear from you is the truth. Why don't you tell me just what the hell this is all about?"

"The truth is very simple," Morgan said with a deliberate calmness that contrasted sharply with the flash in his dark eyes. "Money, ranger. A fifty thousand dollar ransom."

"Bullshit!" Ryan contradicted scornfully. "I was there the night you and Mandell met with McCandless, remember? What passed between the three of you that night had nothing to do with money. McCandless is scared of you, Devereaux, and maybe even more scared of Mandell. Funny thing, he told me he'd never met either one of you. He was lying through his teeth, just like you're lying now. I just can't figure out why. I know the motive behind kidnapping the girl was revenge, but revenge for what? That's the one piece that's still missing."

"You have an over-active imagination, ranger," Morgan grunted, returning his gaze to the top of the cell.

"Maybe. Then maybe I'm right. Maybe the reason you kidnapped the girl is the same reason McCandless is so determined to see you hang. What's he afraid of, Devereaux? What's he afraid you might reveal if he doesn't shut you up for good?"

"I don't have the slightest idea what you're talking about," Morgan said curtly.

"I saw him, Devereaux. Saw him deliberately try to empty a rifle into you when you were already unconscious. He had the look of a crazy man. He wanted you dead some kind of bad and I think it goes a lot deeper than wounded pride because you snatched his niece. I don't like being the only player in a game who doesn't know the rules, Devereaux."

"Then maybe you should deal yourself out of the game."

"I don't have to worry too much about that, do I? This hand is being played out in court tomorrow. The way McCandless has stacked the deck, you'll be tried, convicted, and executed before the sun sets."

"That's what happens when a man is guilty, isn't it?"

"I don't give a damn if you're guilty or not!" Ryan countered with a snap in his voice. "It won't be a fair trial and that's what galls me. Even Mandell deserves a fair hearing."

"That's very generous, Tyrell, considering he killed your old man," Morgan pointed out with a jeer in his voice that brought a flash of anger into the ranger's face.

"I know what you're thinking, Devereaux, but you can forget it. Should Mandell attempt to break you out of jail, and I sincerely hope he does, he will be gunned down. I have every road, every pig trail, every street into this town covered. He might get in, but he'll never get back out alive. I promise you that. I want him, Devereaux. I want him worse than I've ever wanted anything in my life and sooner or later I'll get him."

Morgan swung his long legs to the floor, and walked to the bars. He gripped them with both hands, leaning close to stare coldly at the ranger on the other side.

"The only reason Welch killed your old man, Tyrell, was because I didn't have the opportunity," he grated with a cold ebony glare. "Your old man was as rotten as McCandless. If he was alive today, I'd kill him all over again."

Ryan came upright and clenched his massive hands into fists, returning the gunman's steady glare.

"What the hell did my father ever do to you or Mandell to deserve being shot down in cold blood?" he demanded.

"He had his chance to draw. He just wasn't fast enough."

"Mandell shot my father down like a mangy coyote. I want to know why!"

"Ask Welch, he'll be happy to tell you," Morgan grated. Then turning on his heel, he strode to the window to stare out into the darkness in furious silence.

Ryan's eyes narrowed to slits as he stared at Morgan's back. "I intend to ask him. The very first chance I get," he ground out through clenched teeth.

Realizing he would get no more information from his prisoner, he gulped down a few lungfuls of fresh air to calm himself, then stalked away to fling himself back into the chair behind the desk.

A shadow in a second story window of the hotel across and slightly up the street from the jail caught Morgan's eye. While he stared, the shade was raised and his pulse quickened as Amber's beautiful face was illuminated by the glow of lamplight in the hotel suite behind her.

She was staring toward the jail with a sad, wistful expression that reached out to Morgan through the darkness and grabbed him like a powerful fist in the gut.

He could see her quite clearly, standing at the window in her robe and nightgown, her long golden hair shimmering like a jeweled cape around her shoulders. As he watched, she saw him at the window of the cell and raised a hand in silent greeting. Morgan acknowledged it with an uplifted hand. For a very long moment they stood staring at one another in mute silence, unaware of the traffic in the road or the loud bang of a piano in the saloon at the end of the street.

Then Morgan caught the glimpse of another shadow a second before Amber yanked the shade down and disappeared from the window into the interior of the room to be lost from his vision.

Morgan released the bars and lay back down on the cot, staring moodily at the ceiling while his thoughts churned. The next time he saw Amber would be in court tomorrow morning, surrounded by her uncle and his attorneys, and a gallery of curious spectators who waited to see how she would react to being face to face with him again.

The knot in the pit of his stomach twisted and churned, gnawing at him with silent barbs of alarm that refused to let him rest. He could only pray she would testify against him in whatever way necessary to save herself. If those clear golden eyes revealed to anyone else what they revealed to him, she would be branded a whore. Worse, Owen McCandless would learn the extent of her relationship with him. Only Morgan knew how disastrous that would be for her.

CHAPTER TWENTY-EIGHT

An endless night dragged into an equally endless morning. Amber fell asleep only moments before she was rudely shaken awake by Owen's persistent fingers on her shoulder. "It's time to wake up, princess. We don't want to be late for court," Owen said with a cheerful smile.

Amber sat up rubbing her eyes sleepily, but her mind was instantly awake. Dismay assailed her at the pleased expression on her uncle's face as he rose from the edge of her bed and moved across the room to pour her a cup of tea from the tray he had ordered sent up.

Owen had been his usual kind, generous self during the two months that had passed since his outraged behavior in the Lair. He seemed to have put that entire episode out of his mind as though it never happened, but Amber could not forget his cruel words nor the savage, wild expression on his face that day.

For weeks now, she had been a virtual prisoner in the house at *Sierra Vieja*. There were no bars on the door or windows like those Morgan was locked behind, but Owen's relentless eye resulted in the same trapped, frustrated feeling she was sure Morgan must feel.

Had it not been for the Texas Ranger's visit to the ranch a few days after her return, she might have gone on indefinitely worrying about Morgan's fate. Tyrell's brief visit assured her that Morgan had survived, but left her with the crushing dread that he would now face a trial, most likely followed by an execution.

Even Cooter was not allowed to speak with her privately. No matter what the circumstances, Owen seemed to appear each time she had a visitor. The result was a nagging despair that filled her heart and soul with dread. After Owen's vicious warning not to mention Morgan's name, she had not dared ask any questions about his welfare.

Although Owen had shown no further evidence of that maniacal stranger that froze her blood with terror, Amber was acutely aware of the subtle warning in his face whenever the subject of her kidnapping surfaced.

Owen brought a dainty china cup of tea to the bed and extended it to her with a warm smile. While she sipped it slowly, he went to the wardrobe to take out the dress he had instructed her to wear for the trial. Laying it carefully over the back of an overstuffed armchair, he smoothed imaginary wrinkles from it and said, "When the lawyer asks you about the way Devereaux treated you, Amber, how will you answer?"

Amber stared at his calm face over the rim of the cup, then set it back into the saucer with a shaky hand. "I will answer truthfully, Uncle Owen."

Owen turned toward her, but did not approach. Rather, he stood where he was, surveying her with slightly narrowed blue eyes that contained an element of warning that increased the tremor in her hands.

"And the truth is, princess, that Devereaux threatened you, beat you when you resisted his advances, and raped you. Isn't that right, princess?"

"Yes, Uncle Owen," she replied softly with downcast eyes. How she wished he would stop calling her princess! The mention of the word recalled memories of Morgan's husky voice whispering love words in her ear while they made passionate love. *Princessa de oro,* Morgan called her. Never again would she hear the word without thinking of him.

"I know it will be painful to relate those things to the court,

Amber," her uncle was saying. "But once it's all out you'll feel better."

Would she, she thought bitterly, or would *he*?

"The jury has to hear it, princess. They have to know what that bastard did to you so they can make a rational verdict."

The panic that flooded her face brought a cluck of sympathy from Owen. He quickly crossed the room to sit down on the bed beside her and draw her into a protective embrace. "There, there, sweetheart," he crooned softly, stroking her hair. "Nobody will blame you for anything. That's why its so important you tell them everything. So they'll know what a cold blooded son-of-a-bitch Devereaux is."

"He's not a son-of-a-bitch, Uncle Owen," Amber murmured against his chest. "His parents were decent, hard working ranchers. He came from a good family."

"Lies, princess, just lies!" Owen snorted. "The truth is that he's a thieving, murdering, low-down killer, but today he'll get what his kind deserves."

The harshness in his voice contrasted with the gentle way he smoothed her hair as he cradled her in his arms. Amber trembled and blinked back tears that suddenly pricked her eyelids and burned her throat. She was so confused, so torn between what to believe! If only she knew the truth!

"Now you get dressed, princess. Courts starts in an hour. Don't worry. I'll be right there beside you through it all. And when this trial is over, you'll be able to put the whole nasty business behind you and make a fresh start."

Amber did not reply. Her troubled thoughts kept going to Morgan's handsome face and strong, virile body. She wondered if she could ever be the same again. Last night, for that brief moment before Uncle Owen had entered the room and broke the spell, she had gazed across the street into Morgan's eyes, feeling the pounding of her heart fill her ears and her legs go weak. Today she would testify against him, condemn him to death with her words, all the while knowing she was helpless to change the way she felt about him.

He was an outlaw, a thief, and maybe he did deserve to die, but certainly not for any crime against her. Memories of those last few days with him in the Lair blazed painfully clear in her mind, reminding her that she had given herself to him freely, totally, without guilt or shame. She felt no guilt even now, for that dreadful moment when he lay bleeding in her arms, one thing had become blatantly obvious...she loved him.

Shortly, she would tell a courtroom full of people that he was everything his reputation proclaimed. But the most painful thing of all was that he might go to the gallows without ever knowing she loved him.

Owen's gentle tug broke into her thoughts. She climbed from the bed, brushed her hair, and washed her face. Owen left to finish his breakfast and give her time to dress. She went about preparing herself for the ordeal that lay ahead, doing things automatically, without thinking. Thinking was too painful. It was better to keep her mind blank and steel herself to the moment when she had to look across the courtroom and point the finger of guilt at the man she loved.

CHAPTER
TWENTY-NINE

The streets of McCandless were crowded with curious, gaping on-lookers as Morgan walked from the jail to the courthouse. It was nine o'clock Monday morning, September 1, 1880, he thought wryly to himself, a day these people would long remember. The day Morgan Devereaux faced the bar of justice and paid for fifteen years on the wrong side of the law..with his life.

The handcuffs cut into his wrists as he walked the three blocks with Ryan Tyrell at his side and flanked by six other Texas Rangers, three in front and three behind. The crowd around the entrance of the courthouse parted to let the lawmen escort him inside. He heard the mutters of scorn and curses of contempt, but he kept his gaze turned straight ahead, looking neither to the right or left as Ryan led him into the building.

"Blood thirsty ghouls," he heard the ranger mutter under his breath as they climbed the steps, then stepped into the shade of the courthouse porch.

His hands were handcuffed in front of him with the ranger's hand resting lightly at the elbow of his right arm. It took great concentration not to limp for the recent wound in his thigh had begun to throb painfully due to the long walk. The tightness in his chest was better. He could breathe normally now without constant pain, and his strength was returning daily. He almost grinned at the irony of it. Tyrell had saved his life, then guarded him zealously for two months so Owen McCandless could hang him. It was almost funny.

A hush fell over the gallery of spectators when he stepped into the courtroom. It was packed. Every bench was filled and still more were standing in every nook and cranny of the large room. For days now people had streamed into town for his trial, hoping for a look at the state's most notorious outlaw.

From the anticipative air among the spectators, Morgan knew they were expecting a short trial and then a quick hanging. Nobody wanted to miss seeing Morgan Devereaux hang, he thought grimly as they entered the courtroom.

From the corner of his eye, Morgan saw Cooter sitting at the end of the last bench with his gnarled hands clenched into fists. He looked straight at the old man for an instant, but kept his expression veiled in spite of the sorrowful, apologetic gaze Cooter flashed him. The raid had not been Cooter's fault. He had no knowledge of what Tyrell was planning until it was much too late to warn them. Still he looked wretched.

His eyes fell on the Catholic priest beside Cooter on the bench. A big man with a white beard and a long flowing mustache above which rested a pair of steel gray eyes.

There was a barely discernible nod of the priest's slightly bowed head, but it was enough to make Morgan's heart pound with alarm. What the holy hell was *he* doing here?

Ryan noted the grim mood of the crowd as he maneuvered the gunman down the aisle toward the defense table across a thigh-high railing from the rows of spectator seats. He knew it took all Morgan's strength not to limp. He cast a glance at the man in handcuffs, feeling a strange sense of admiration.

Even the handcuffs around his wrists seemed to enhance the confident masculinity of the man. His face was calm, the dark eyes veiled as Ryan had long since learned he could do, and his shoulders straight with perhaps a bit of arrogance in his stride made the blood lust of this assembly take notice.

If they had come hoping to see Devereaux crumble and plead for his life, they were going to be sadly disappointed, Ryan thought with an inward smile.

Dead silence held the room as Morgan approached the front

row of seats and waited for Tyrell to push open the hinged gate that allowed access to the front of the courtroom. On that first bench sat Owen McCandless. Next to him sat Amber. For the briefest of instants Morgan let his gaze meet the rancher's. Stifling the wave of hatred that flooded through him, Morgan kept his face unexpressive. Only a slight twitch in his jaw revealed any emotion.

Owen rose to his feet. A satisfied smile touched his lips. "You're not so tough without Mandell, are you, killer?" he asked softly, but in the absolute quiet of the room the words rang out like a church bell.

Morgan met the rancher's cold mocking eyes with a steady black gaze that caused Owen to twitch in spite of the handcuffs and the scores of lawmen to protect him. The chill in those inscrutable black pools froze the smile on Owen's face momentarily.

The flash of puzzlement in his face sent a surge of satisfaction through Morgan as Ryan tugged at his arm. McCandless was trying to remember where they had met before, but as yet could not put it together. Morgan hoped vehemently he would still be around when he did.

Morgan deliberately did not look straight at Amber. From the corner of his eye, he saw her sitting rigidly with her back stiff, facing the front of the room while her hands twisted the lace hanky in her lap. Then, he turned away to sit down at the table where his court appointed lawyer waited.

"Devereaux, are you sure you don't want to take the stand in your own defense?" James Collins asked, leaning toward Morgan.

"No."

"I feel, as your council, that I must advise you that not to testify in your own behalf would be a grievous error. You must realize, Devereaux, that the only hanging offense you're charged with is rape. The robbery and kidnapping charges will draw a lengthy prison sentence, perhaps even life, but Tyrell's testimony will refute the murder charges, and if I can manage to throw any doubt into the court's mind about Miss McCandless' actions toward you, it's possible you can be found innocent of the rape charge and so escape the gallows," Collins argued softly, drumming a pencil on the table top.

"No," Morgan repeated. "You leave her alone. Do you understand me?"

"But, Devereaux," the lawyer persisted doggedly. "Her testimony will send you to the gallows if unrefuted. Don't you realize that your very life is at stake here?"

"I realize a lot more than that," Morgan answered curtly. "She has to go on living here with these people. If you attack her honor by trying to make it sound like she was a willing participant in what I did to her, it will destroy her. My life isn't worth that."

Before Collins could argue, the judge rapped his gavel and called the court to order. For the next hour Morgan watched in silent amusement as the state paraded its witnesses through the court. The stage driver, the two saloon girls, the drummer, the gambler, and Mrs. Appleton each testified that Morgan had been the leader of the band of outlaws that took Amber from the stage. With each renewed accusation, the throng of spectators murmured and growled among themselves despite Collins' cross examination.

After the witnesses pointed out Morgan in the courtroom, Collins rose to his feet to ask one simple question: Did they personally see Morgan strike Amber or abuse her in any way? The answer each time was the same: No.

The state's attorney called Owen McCandless to the stand to testify about the warning message he had received written at the bottom of a wanted poster with Morgan's picture on it. The attorney then submitted the ransom note and compared the handwriting on it to the previous note, making the point that the handwriting on each was the same.

Sheriff Riker testified next, relating to the court the series of incidents against Owen McCandless that he and the rancher believed Morgan Devereaux was responsible for. Then Ryan Tyrell took the stand to tell of the meeting between McCandless,

Mandell, and Morgan. He kept his statements short and to the point, offering no additional comments of his own.

Then James Collins rose to cross examine Ryan. "Mr. Tyrell, please tell the court what you know about Morgan Devereaux."

"He's probably faster with a gun than anybody I've ever seen."

"To your knowledge, is he wanted for murder in the state of Texas?"

"No."

"Is he wanted for murder in any other state?"

"No," Ryan replied. "There's no doubt that Devereaux has killed, but he's never killed a man in cold blood or one that wasn't trying to kill him."

With that, Collins excused Ryan from the witness box. Then a hush fell over the crowd when the state's attorney called Amber to the stand. She rose on shaky legs and walked unsteadily to the bench to be sworn in. She sat down and twisted her hands nervously in her lap, carefully keeping her eyes averted from the defense table.

She was dressed in a demure gray dress with a high collar pinned with a cameo broach, and long sleeves. Her hair was arranged in an elegant French braid secured with pearl hair pins, but while she looked very proper, there was a subtle innocence emanating from her pale face and downcast eyes that grabbed the spectators, outraging them at her suffering at the hands of such an evil man.

"Miss McCandless, I will make this as painless and quick as possible. I am going to ask you four questions. Please answer each of them yes or no. Do you understand?" Basil Webster, the state's attorney told her in a kind, indulgent tone.

Amber nodded her head slowly, keeping her eyes downcast while her hands twisted the lace handkerchief into tangled ribbons.

"Miss McCandless, is the defendant, Morgan Devereaux, the man who forced you from the stage?" Webster asked.

"Yes," Amber answered in a soft voice that everyone strained to hear.

"Did he threaten to kill you if Owen McCandless failed to pay the ransom he and his cohort Welch Mandell demanded?"

"Yes," Amber answered again.

"Miss McCandless, did he physically abuse you by striking you when you resisted his advances?"

Amber's affirmative reply was slower in coming this time. She felt dizzy, sick at her stomach and her hands now gripped the arms of the chair to avoid fleeing from the next question.

"Miss McCandless, did this man force you, repeatedly and against your will, to have sex with him?"

The urge to vomit rose within her, making it necessary for her to swallow several times. There was a long, drawn out pause while her eyes for the first time flashed across the room to land for an instant on Morgan's face. His black eyes met hers in a pensive, almost mild expression with only a slight tic in his jaw revealing any emotion.

"Yes," she finally managed to whisper.

Webster whirled to face the court with a satisfied smile. Amid the loud demands for justice from the incensed on-lookers, he called in a loud confident voice. "Your honor, the prosecution rests. We ask that the jury find this man guilty of the charges of armed robbery, kidnapping, felonious assault, resisting arrest, and rape. Furthermore, we ask that he be punished to the fullest extent of the law by paying for his hideous crimes against this innocent, helpless young woman by hanging."

The judge rapped his gavel several times to restore order to the wild pandemonium that broke out in the courtroom. While the cries for Morgan's blood echoed throughout the room, Amber looked at her uncle, feeling sick from the satisfied, complacent smirk on his face.

When at last the outcries for justice and an immediate hanging died down enough to be heard, the judge looked to James Collins over the rim of his glasses. "Mr. Collins, due to the delicate nature of the charges, I'm sure you will forgo any cross examination of this witness."

"No, your honor," James Collins said from his chair. "Mr. Devereaux's life is at stake here. It is my right to cross examine Miss McCandless and I respectfully ask permission from the bench to do so."

Morgan's gaze snapped to the young, bald lawyer's face in surprise, but Collins was already on his feet approaching Amber with an expression of steely determination.

"Miss McCandless, I sympathize with your position, but you must also realize that a man's life will be decided on the basis of your testimony. I will be as delicate as possible, but I must ask you a few more questions."

"What the hell is he up to?" Owen leaned across the railing to ask Basil Webster. "I want him stopped. Now!"

"I can't do that, Owen," the lawyer replied apologetically. "It's the law. He has every right to question her. But don't worry, the second he gets out of line I'll object."

"Miss McCandless, what did you think the first time you saw Morgan Devereaux in the general store?" Collins was asking.

Amber looked at him in confusion, baffled by the question. "I don't know what you mean," she murmured.

"Morgan Devereaux is a very handsome man, isn't he, Miss McCandless?"

Amber's face colored. Her hands twitched in her lap but she remained silent.

"Please look at him, Miss McCandless," Collins requested. "Look at him and answer my question. Do you think Morgan Devereaux is a handsome man?"

Morgan read the panic in her eyes when she flashed him a swift glance. "Yes," she said very softly.

"Will you please speak up, Miss McCandless? I'm afraid the court can't hear you."

"Yes," Amber repeated in a louder tone.

"Isn't it true, Miss McCandless, that you were strongly attracted to this man from the moment you first saw him?"

Amber's bewildered eyes widened, her lips parted, but before she could answer, Morgan was on his feet. "Stop it, Collins! You've gone too far!"

Collins ignored Morgan's interference by pointedly moving closer to Amber and staring into her pale, confused face with a determined gleam. He could feel her weakening, see the doubt in her eyes, and pressed his advantage. He could already see the newspaper headlines, could feel the Texas Attorney General's office draw closer with each question.

"Isn't it also true, Miss McCandless, that Morgan Devereaux did not beat you or rape you? Isn't it true that you shared his bed willingly, indeed, gladly?"

"Goddamn it, leave her alone!" Morgan shouted above the pandemonium in the room. He was dimly aware that Ryan had risen to his feet and was yanking on his arm, but he shrugged away. The panic in Amber's frightened, bewildered face told him she was about to blurt out a confession that would destroy her. The only thought in his mind at the moment was to prevent it.

"She didn't do anything!" he shouted above the roar of the enraged crowd and the bellows of Owen McCandless' attorneys objecting to Collins' line of questioning. The judge beat his gavel, his face reddening from exertion and stress.

Finally after several minutes of chaos, order was restored to the courtroom. The judge leaned forward and adjusted his glasses from the tip of his nose where they had slipped during his heavy pounding of the gavel, staring at Morgan severely.

"Mr. Devereaux, do you have something you would like to say? If so, please do it in a manner than can be heard by the bench," he directed in an icy tone.

Morgan felt Ryan's hand fell away from his arm as Ryan sank back into his chair. Through the sudden deathly quiet that took over the courtroom, Morgan squared his shoulders and stared unblinkingly at the judge. He felt Amber's frightened eyes focus on his face. It took all his strength not to look at her.

"She did nothing to encourage me. She resisted and I hit her until she submitted. I raped her. I'm guilty, goddamn it. Leave her alone."

The words were crisp, falling like rifle shots in the silence. For an instant before the crowd roared again, he heard Amber's small horrified gasp, but kept his eyes directed at the judge.

When order was restored again, the judge leveled a somewhat surprised, but smug gaze at him in silence for a moment. Then he said, "Mr. Devereaux, I see no purpose in continuing this trial. Therefore I am prepared to pass sentence on you at this time. Having confessed the crime of rape, I sentence you to be hanged one week from today. I'm only sorry that you can be executed only once. If there was a stiffer penalty than death for what you've done, I would gladly see it carried out. Court is adjourned!"

"You're a damned fool, Devereaux," Ryan said in a low voice as he rose to take Morgan back to jail. "She was weakening. In another minute she would've told the truth and saved your hide."

Morgan met his eyes with a steady mocking expression. "Sometimes the price of the truth is too high," he said evenly.

The courtroom was again filled with demands for immediate justice, shouts of outrage, and offers to help carry out the sentence, but Morgan did not hear them. For a moment as Amber left the witness stand and he turned to leave the building, their eyes met and locked.

The pain in her chest made Amber weak, made her breathing shallow, and her stomach churn. She stared at him in shock and dismay. His gaze was steady, calm, and strangely satisfied. She wanted to go to him, throw her arms around him and tell him....

Then a wave of dizziness flooded over her. The last thing she saw before crumbling to the floor in a dead faint was the flicker of something in the depths of his coal black eyes that said more than any words could have.

He had sacrificed whatever chance he had of escaping the death penalty to save her reputation, and perhaps her uncle's everlasting wrath. He'd saved her...at the cost of his own life.

CHAPTER THIRTY

Amber climbed to the top rail of the corral to rub the silky muzzle of Morgan's Appaloosa. It was dusk. The ranch yard was empty for the cowhands were all inside at supper. She had skipped dining with Owen, preferring to spend a few minutes of quiet with the wiry little horse.

The long ride from town had been spent in silence. Owen had not spoken one word to her since the trial. When she regained consciousness after fainting in the courtroom, she was in the carriage on the way back to the ranch. Though she sensed displeasure in her uncle's manner because of her behavior at the trial, he had said nothing. She could not decide if that was good or bad.

"His name's Diablo."

Amber's head snapped around, her tawny eyes widening at the realization that Cooter Jackson knew the name of Morgan's horse. The old wrangler limped to where she sat and folded his arms on the top rail of the corral, nodding his head at the Appaloosa.

"How do you know that?"

"I know a lot of things."

"Cooter, is it true that my father and Welch Mandell were friends?"

"Yep."

"Then Uncle Owen knows him too." Following Cooter's affirmative nod she asked, "Why would he lie about it, Cooter? Why does he insist he never met Welch Mandell?"

"That ain't for me to say, Missy," Cooter grunted uncomfortably.

The creaking of a door made him look toward the house. A

scowl darkened his face at the sight of Owen striding toward them.

"Missy, come to my room tonight, at midnight," he said urgently.

"Why, Cooter? What can you tell me then that you can't tell me now?" she protested in surprise.

"There's no time to explain, Missy," the old man insisted with an anxious glance at Owen. "Just promise me you'll come..and don't tell nobody. Not a soul. Understand?"

Amber barely had time to agree with a nod before Owen arrived. He lifted her down from the fence with a beaming smile. Tucking her small hand in his, he led her to the house to join him for an after dinner glass of sherry.

"It's all behind you now, princess," he said confidently. "From now on it's the two of us, just the way it's supposed to be. Starting first thing in the morning, you learn the business of running this spread. From the ground up."

He rattled on, his good mood scattering away the dark doubts she had, until she looked back over her shoulder. Cooter stood at the corral still petting the Appaloosa with such sadness in his face she was startled.

Then, Diablo raised his head to whinny after her and tears suddenly burned her throat. She looked back at Owen with a feeling of despair. He was cheerful because Morgan was going to die. The very thought made her ill.

With a visible effort, she shook herself from the painful, haunted thoughts and forced herself to listen to Owen's cheerful chatter. Tonight when she was alone she would cry, but now in his company she put on a smiling face. Midnight, tonight. She would be there.

***

The wind whipped Amber's long flowing robe around her ankles, making it difficult to hurry across the ranch yard. She looked anxiously overhead at the moonless sky with banks of clouds hanging low and menacing. A streak of lightning tore a brilliant, jagged pattern through the clouds, illuminating the yard with an eerie, glowering chill that matched Amber's mood to perfection.

Ever since Cooter's urgent request, she had been apprehensive. The uneasy way he had avoided her questions and the almost frightened look he had given her uncle at the corral made her throat tighten with dread.

She knew, even without Cooter's confirmation, that the secret meeting in his quarters adjoining the private stables was going to reveal the answers to a lot of unanswered questions. There were things he could tell her, and seemed inclined now to do so, that she felt compelled to hear. Things she needed to know, but the sick feeling of dread in the pit of her stomach warned her that she might also learn things she would not want to believe.

She cast another glance over her shoulder at the massive house and forced a mouthful of fresh air into her lungs. The house was dark, silent. She hurried toward her destination.

There was only a thin layer of light from the window in Cooter's room when she stealthily approached the door. The very fact that he had covered the window made her uneasy for Cooter rarely sealed his room from outside view. In answer to her light knock, the door swung open with a protesting creak and a gnarled hand pulled her inside.

Cooter stuck his head outside to take a swift look around to be certain she had not been observed.

The dim glow from one lamp turned very low illuminated the small comfortable room as Amber moved further inside and lifted a hand to pull wind blown tendrils of hair from her face.

"Cooter, what's this all about? Why all the secrecy?"

"Just bein' careful, Missy," the old man grunted. He pulled a cane-backed chair up to the card table in the center of the room, indicating that she should sit. "Cain't be too careful these days."

"Careful of what?"

"Everythin'...everybody. You want some coffee, Missy?"

Amber shook her head, her gaze following him to the pot bellied stove. Though it was September and still warm at night, there was a fire in the stove and Cooter's ever present pot of coffee warming on top. He poured himself a cup and turned back to her with the grimmest expression on his weathered face she had ever seen.

"Things sometimes ain't what they seem, Missy. People either."

"I assume you're referring to Uncle Owen," Amber said with an ever increasing feeling of doom.

"Yep, that's part of it," Cooter agreed. "But like I told you this afternoon, Missy, it ain't my place to say."

"Then, why in heaven's name did you insist I come out here in the middle of the night?" This mysterious, secretive stuff was becoming less amusing all the time.

"I said it ain't my place to say," Cooter replied. "But there's someone who can. That's what this is all about, Missy."

Before the words had left his mouth, a shape materialized from the shadows in the deeper recesses of the room. Amber's face paled. Her eyes widened with alarm, and one hand jumped to her throat as the big gray shape took on human form as it moved into the light.

"Oh, my God!" Amber whispered. "W-what are you doing here? How..? D-Don't you know half the state is looking for you?"

Welch Mandell smiled as he slid into a chair across the room. "Don't be alarmed, Amber. There's nothing to be afraid of. I wanted to talk to you and with the mood of the lawmen in the area, Cooter thought this would be the safest way."

Amber stared into his handsome face partially hidden in the shadows. His silver blonde hair shimmered in the pale light, enhancing the bronze of his skin. He was a big man, filling the room with his presence, but Amber instinctively knew she could trust him. She had known that from the first moment she met him back in the stables in the Lair and now, with those dark gray eyes filled with a strange wistfullness, those feelings of security were even stronger.

"How did you escape? I mean..they searched everywhere but

you had disappeared. How did you do that? Morgan told me there was only one entrance," Amber blurted out in amazement.

"Amber, a man in my position should never build a town in a box canyon without having an escape route. My house was built over an old mining tunnel that goes all the way through the mountain," Welch explained with a smile. "There was a trap door hidden in the basement. It was disguised so well even Tyrell couldn't find it. And if you hadn't been so headstrong, young lady, you'd have gotten out the same way."

The color was slowly returning to Amber's cheeks. She could not seem to tear her eyes from Welch's face. Something told her again he seemed familiar, but try as she might, she couldn't put a finger on what it was about him that gave her this impression.

"Morgan's going to hang, did you know that?" she demanded. The shock of his appearance was fading, leaving her with a surge of anger and contempt. "He was shot and captured. And now he's going to hang."

"That's why I'm here, Amber," Welch told her in a kind, almost gentle tone. "You didn't seriously think I'd let Morgan go to the gallows, did you?"

The slight reproving element in his voice grated on Amber's nerves. "If you're so concerned about him, why haven't you done something?"

To her immense bewilderment, Welch laughed softly and in a moment Cooter joined in. Amber look from one to the other in total confusion.

"What did I tell you?" Cooter asked Welch with a smug grin. "I told you she was Price's kid all right, didn't I?"

"That you did, Cooter," Welch agreed with a nod. Then his eyes grew somber as he leaned forward in his chair, placing his elbows on his knees to look directly into Amber's baffled face. "Amber, Morgan is like a son to me. I would never let him hang. However, getting him out of jail will not be easy. We need your help."

"My help?" Amber echoed in astonishment. She looked from

one man to the other, before settling on Welch's intent face. "What can I do? There are so many lawmen around all the time it would take an army to get to him."

"Amber, do you love Morgan?"

Her face colored as she glanced away. "What difference would it make?"

"Maybe the difference between him going to the gallows or walking away a free man." Welch smiled at the startled expression on the girl's face. "I have a plan, Amber, but it will take all three of us to pull it off."

Amber's glance jumped to Cooter. "Cooter too?" she asked doubtfully.

An indignant expression quickly filled the old man's face. "Why the hell not? I can ride, Missy, and I can shoot if I have to."

"Amber, if my plan works there won't be any shooting. We supply the means and Morgan will do the rest by himself."

"You mean get a gun to him in jail?" she asked. When Welch nodded she felt a cold stab of fear slice through her heart. "But the guards, there's so many of them. He could be killed."

"That's why I have to reduce the odds a little, even them up some. Are you willing to take the chance?" Welch asked softly. The confusion in her eyes told him more than she could have imagined. There was hope, fear, desperation, and a great deal of love in those golden eyes. It made Welch both happy and sad.

"Amber, I know you love Morgan. No woman runs through a hail of bullets for a man unless she loves him. And after what I saw today, I'm willing to bet the feeling is mutual, although he may not know it yet."

Surprise widened her eyes. "What do you mean?"

"I mean, that he stood up in court and threw away whatever chance he had of escaping the gallows so you won't be shamed or have to face Owen's wrath. That was a noble thing to do and since Morgan is not a terribly noble man, love is the only explanation."

"I don't understand," Amber stammered. The loud pounding

of her heart filled her ears, made it difficult to hear anything else. "How could you possibly know that unless you were there?"

"Oh, I was there," Welch said with an amused smile. "In the middle of the courthouse, not ten feet from Owen, right under his nose. Don't underestimate me, young lady. I haven't stayed alive fifty years by being stupid. Sometimes it's more beneficial to take the discreet approach."

"You mean a disguise?"

Welch nodded affirmatively. "The law is looking for Welch Mandell, the gunfighter, the outlaw. But with the town full of people from all over the state hoping to get a look at Morgan Devereaux, they certainly weren't going to notice a humble priest."

The humor that twinkled in his eyes brought a smile to Amber's lips and heightened the color that had begun to bloom in her cheeks.

"Do you really think Morgan cares for me?" she asked in a hesitant voice that was hopeful, but afraid.

Welch nodded soberly, his face now serious again. "Not a doubt in my mind, Amber. However, he's never let himself love anybody before. It won't be an easy matter now to break through those barriers."

He grinned in a sad kind of way that peaked the girl's curiosity. "But..you're a beautiful young woman, Amber, and there's a lot of your daddy in you. If you want something badly enough you go after it, so if you want Morgan you'll have to fight for him. And that won't be a simple task. You'll have to fight his past, his reputation, the law, and hardest of all, probably Morgan himself."

"What he did today was the most unselfish thing I've ever seen," Amber said softly. The light in her eyes was enhanced by the warm glow of the lamp as it cast a golden halo around her shoulders.

She looked up directly into Welch's gun-metal eyes and gave a firm nod of determination. "Yes, Mr. Mandell, I'll do whatever it takes to help Morgan escape. But you've overlooked something."

"What's that?" Welch asked curiously.

"Cooter promised me some answers tonight. I'd like to hear them."

Welch stared at her for a long moment as though in deep thought. Then he rose and walked into the shadows behind him. He returned carrying a long, thin ledger which he held against his chest for a moment while his gaze met Cooter's across the tiny table. As though with some secret message passing between them, he silently laid it on the table before Amber, then stood back and hooked his thumbs in the worn brown leather gunbelt that rested on his hip. Even without the customary elegant clothes, dressed now in dark trousers and a plain dark gray shirt tucked beneath the gunbelt, he had an air of authority and animal grace that made Amber wonder what he might have been had he chosen a different path in life.

"What is this?" she asked staring up at him.

"That book contains all the answers you're seeking, Amber."

"I don't understand," she fretted with a downward glance at the worn, dog-eared book. "Whose is it? Where did it come from?"

"It's yours," Welch explained with a sad smile. "It's been in my hands for safe keeping since your daddy died. He wrote it, Amber, it's his journal. By rights it belongs to you now. Take it, read it, keep it if you want or destroy it when you've finished, but if you really want answers to all your questions, you'll find them in there."

Sudden tears stung her eyes. She lifted the worn cloth cover to read the inscription inside the hard backing. "Property of Price McCandless." She looked back to Welch's face and swallowed. "Is this the diary my mother mentioned before she died?" she managed to ask. "The one Uncle Owen said didn't exist?"

A tic twitched in Welch's jaw. From the corner of her eye Amber saw Cooter's hand shake when he lifted the coffee cup from his lips. The tension that suddenly filled the room made her heart pound with anxiety.

"Yes," Welch answered. "Your mother gave me the journal after your daddy's funeral, Amber. You see, Price gave it to Cooter the night he was killed, for safe keeping with instructions not to read it except in the event of his death. Four hours later Price was dead. Cooter read the journal, then gave it to your mother, but she insisted I take it to keep it out of Owen's hands."

Alarm flared in the depths of her eyes as a pain shot through her chest. "Why was it so important that Uncle Owen not see it?" she forced herself to ask.

Welch's gray eyes held hers in a gaze of subdued anger, but when he spoke his voice was soft and calm. "Your daddy also made Cooter promise him that if anything happened to him, Cooter would see to it that you and your mother left *Sierra Vieja* and went back east. After Althea read the journal, she understood why. When she told Owen she was taking you away, he refused to let her go. He made crazy threats, wild promises. It wasn't until I showed him the journal that he agreed to let the two of you leave Texas. It's this journal that's protected you all these years, Amber. And this journal that Owen would kill for."

"Do you believe Uncle Owen killed my father"? she demanded through stiff lips.

"Yes."

"Why?" she demanded fearfully.

"The night your daddy was killed, Missy, somebody fired a shot that spooked the herd into a stampede," Cooter told her slowly as the painful memories choked his voice. "After it was over..and your daddy was dead..I checked his saddle. The cinches had been cut almost in two, sometime after he saddled his horse to go on night herd. There was no way those cinches could've held up under the kind of chase we had that night. It had to be Owen. He was the only one who had anythin' to gain by your daddy's death."

"I don't believe that!" she protested wildly. She hurled herself from the chair to stand glaring up at him, her eyes flashing with defiance and fear. "Uncle Owen loved my father. He would never have harmed him!"

"Owen loved your mother, Amber. He always loved your mother. They were engaged to be married, but your mother took one look at Price and it was all over with Owen. He hated Price for taking Althea away from him and he never forgave Price for it," Welch corrected.

"How do you know that?" Amber challenged. "Were you there? Did you see it? You're only guessing! How could you possibly know Uncle Owen well enough to think him capable of murder?"

"I know Owen McCandless probably better than any man alive," Welch replied quietly. "I know how he thinks, how he reacts to danger, what limits he'll go to in order to protect himself."

"How could you possibly know all that?" she cried. "Were you friends?"

"Owen and I have never been friends."

"Were you neighbors then?"

Again Welch shook his head. "No, Amber, we were never neighbors."

"Then how can you possibly say that you know Uncle Owen well enough to make such accusations?" she demanded haughtily with flashing eyes.

"Because he's my brother."

The color drained from Amber's flushed cheeks. Her knees suddenly went weak and she stumbled back into the empty chair. Staring blankly up into his steady compassionate eyes, Amber knew instinctively he was telling the truth. Everything about him screamed it at her.

"Y-You're my father's brother? My u-uncle?" she whispered through wooden lips.

"Yes, Amber."

Her head moved slightly to bring Cooter's grizzled face into focus. "You knew this all along and you've never told me? Why, Cooter?" she squeaked.

The old man shrugged uneasily as he glanced at Welch as though searching for guidance. He found it in the depths of the steel gray eyes, then looked back to the girl with an embarrassed flush rising in his face.

"It was the only way I knew to protect you, Missy," he said

gruffly.

"Protect me? Protect me from what, Cooter? I don't understand any of this."

She reached across the table to grasp both his gnarled, callused hands, hands that had helped her up when she fell from her first pony. Gentle, patient hands that had clumsily dried her tears when she skinned her knees.

"From Owen, Missy." Cooter coughed, then cleared his throat nervously and tapped the journal in front of her with a brown finger, bent and warped from the crippling arthritis that racked his body. "It's all in there, Missy. Your papa says it better than I could."

"Oh, God, it's true, isn't it?" Amber whimpered in sudden fear. Her pleading eyes flashed to Welch's face above her in the lamp light. "Uncle Owen killed Morgan's family, didn't he? Just like Morgan said."

"Like Cooter said, Amber, Price explains it better than we can. Read the journal, sweetheart. Listen to your daddy's words. Then you'll understand everything," Welch suggested gently.

"Why did you change your name?" she questioned suddenly. Her fingers slid from Cooter's hand to grip the journal, holding on so tightly her knuckles whitened.

Welch grinned, a warm splash of ivory against the bronze of his face. "I thought I would save Price a lot of embarrassment. Mandell was our mother's maiden name. I took it when I left the ranch. Owen told folks I was dead."

A bitter smile twisted his features as if recalling the past was so distasteful it required supreme effort to call it forth. "You see, Amber, our folks died when Price was very small. He was my shadow, tagging behind every step I took, trying to do everything I did." That memory was a pleasant one, for his lips curled into a genuine smile.

"When we were older, Owen staked this place. Of course it was nothing like the ranch you see now. Just a couple hundred acres of sagebrush and cottonwoods, but it was going to be our empire. We fought the Comanches, the Mexicans, rustlers, wild animals, the wind and floods, and the droughts for it. But mostly Owen and I fought each other.

"Price used to say that me and Owen were extremes and he was a combination of both. I guess that's a pretty accurate description. Owen and I were always like grease and water, we never saw eye to eye on anything. I don't even know why..it just worked out that way.

"Owen had a dream of this empire with thousands of cattle and horses, lots of money in the bank, fancy clothes...gold jewelry. Price and I lived that dream with him. The only problem was, that Owen, in the beginning at least, was willing to work and starve to make it happen. I wasn't.

"I was young and impatient, about your age now, Amber, and I wanted everything fast and easy. Owen and Price were willing to spend every day, seven days a week in the saddle rounding up strays and branding calves. But not me. Come Saturday evening I went to town. I was a whole lot better with a gun and drinking and playing cards than I ever was at being a cowboy. Finally Owen and I fought about it one time too many and I rode out. And I never looked back.

"The next thing I knew, I'd killed a man in a gunfight. Pretty soon the word got out that I was fast with a gun and ranchers up north started hiring me to keep out the squatters. That's when I changed my name.

"By that time *Sierra Vieja* was starting to turn a profit and Owen was finally getting some of the respect he wanted so badly. So, in the best interests of all concerned, I changed my name and Wendall McCandless became Welch Mandell. You know the rest."

"So that's why Uncle Owen denies knowing you? To protect his standing in the community?" Amber asked with wide, confused eyes. This was so unbelievable, so incredible her mind could hardly comprehend it.

Welch's head moved in affirmation. "A man in his position

can't afford to have people find out his brother is an outlaw. The embarrassment would ruin him."

"Then Morgan and Cooter are the only ones who know?"

A shadow leaped into Welch's eyes. He looked away for a moment. When he faced her curious eyes again, she saw a deep sadness in him, something that filled his face with a haunted, almost desperate expression that brought instant alarm to her heart.

"Not Morgan, Amber. Cooter knows and Francine, and now you. But Morgan has no idea Owen McCandless is my brother," he answered heavily.

"And you can bet there'll be hell to pay when he finds out," Cooter added sourly.

Welch shrugged. "Probably so, Cooter, but that's a bridge I'll cross when I come to it. Right now the important thing is breaking Morgan out of jail before Owen's cronies string him up."

"Mr. Mandell,..I mean..should I call you Uncle Welch or Uncle Wendall or.." Amber stammered.

"I think Welch will do fine," he returned with a grin.

"Welch, in the house that day, before the posse came, would you and Morgan really have fought each other?"

"I don't honestly know, Amber."

Amber studied his handsome, troubled face and found it difficult to believe that the famed gunman even the eastern newspapers wrote about was her uncle. She let her eyes drop to the brown gunbelt that hung around his middle, feeling the same chill that she always experienced when she allowed her eyes to dwell on Morgan's gun. The Leopard. Welch Mandell. Wendall McCandless. It was too much to comprehend at one time.

"I read about you in Boston. The papers said you were the fastest gun alive, Welch. They say the same about Morgan. Even that Texas Ranger said it in court today."

"Are you asking which of us is the fastest?" Following her curious nod, his face became grim again. "I don't know the answer to that question either, Amber. I'm not even sure if that's the issue.

The real question is whether or not I could draw against Morgan at all, not whether I can beat him."

"When you come up against anybody as good as he is, you better not take time to think about it," Cooter grunted.

"It's time for you to get back to the house, young lady," Welch told her in an attempt to shake off the gloomy mood that had settled upon them. "Take the journal, Amber. Read it. Then meet me here at the same time tomorrow night if you still want to help break Morgan out of jail."

She nodded in agreement and rose to her feet, holding the ledger close to her chest as she neared the door. Pausing before reaching for the knob, she turned to send them both a shaky smile.

"Don't worry, no one will know about the journal," she assured them, then slipped through the creaking door into the night.

***

When she finished reading the journal, Amber, for the first time, understood the raw, bitter desire for revenge that drove Morgan. It could easily become the driving force in a person's life.

She knew now that Owen McCandless was the monster Morgan had told her he was. She also knew he had to be stopped. He had lived by his own rules for far too long. It was time he had to account for all the lives he'd ruined. Her father's journal would provide the means to bring him to justice.

She tried to imagine Morgan's reaction when he learned Welch's true identity. That Welch had been able to keep it from him was a miracle in itself, but that alone might not be enough to push Morgan into killing him. But the revelation that Welch and his mother had been lovers would be more than Morgan could bear.

Someday, if they were successful in breaking him out of Owen's jail, Morgan would learn of Welch's deception. There was no doubt in her mind about his plan of action then. She dried her tears with renewed determination. The immediate task was to get him out of jail.

When she crept to Cooter's room the following night and slipped inside, a grim resolve blazed from her eyes. The first words she said to her uncle were, "What can I do to help Morgan?"

CHAPTER THIRTY-ONE

The door of the jail opened and closed with the creak of protesting hinges, but Morgan did not look up. Assuming it was the porter from the hotel restaurant coming to retrieve his supper tray, he continued to stand at the barred window with his back to the office.

He was jarred from his pensive thoughts by the sound of a determined female voice.

"I want to see him!"

"But, Miss McCandless,....." the startled deputy stammered.

Morgan jerked around, his dark eyes widening at the sight of Amber.

"I'm not in the mood to argue, Deputy...?"

"Deputy Rogers, ma'am," the pot-bellied, red faced man answered quickly as he whipped off his hat in a show of respect.

"Deputy Rogers," Amber amended coldly. "I wish to speak to that man in private!"

Bewilderment covered the wheezing deputy's face. "But, Miss McCandless, after what that feller's done, I wouldn't think you'd have anythin' to say to him."

Amber's eyes blazed with anger at the man's stubbornness. "Can you think of anyone who has more to say to him, deputy?" she snapped. "I have plenty to say to that vile, disgusting creature and because I'm a lady, I want to say it in private. So, if you will please leave me alone with him for five minutes, I would greatly appreciate it."

"But, Miss McCandless," Rogers repeated. "I can't let you in the cell with him. Sheriff Riker will have my hide."

"Will this make you feel better about disobeying the sheriff's orders?"

Morgan caught the flash of gold as the girl handed the deputy a twenty dollar gold piece. Rogers took it, but glanced around at Morgan doubtfully, then back to the girl.

"I don't know, Miss McCandless. I don't like the idea of you being alone with him."

Irritation made Amber's eyes sparkle. She stamped her foot in vexation and glared at the man's persistence. "Oh, for heaven's sake! What can he do? You'll be right here the whole time. All I want is the opportunity to scratch his eyes out before they hang him. I don't think that's asking too much, do you? After what he's done to me?"

Rogers considered it, then grinned slowly at the picture she had painted and reached down to take the cell keys from beneath the desk.

"Well, all right. But five minutes, no more. The sheriff will be back before long and if he finds you here, he'll have a fit."

Amber nodded stiffly as he handed her the keys. "Pitch 'em out here till you're done. I'll be right over here. Give a holler when you're ready," Rogers said as she walked toward the cell. She unlocked it, went inside, and slammed it behind her with a clang, making herself jump at the loud noise. She pitched the keys outside, watching Rogers to make sure he kept his word, her gaze following him as he picked up the keys, then lumbered across the room where he pointedly made himself busy.

Then, she looked up at Morgan at last. He stood in front of the window watching her through narrowed black eyes, his hands clenched into fists. Amber squared her shoulders beneath the cloak as she marched across the narrow space separating them with such determination in her face that Morgan's brows rose.

Halting directly before him, Amber had to gather her strength. His nearness was over-powering, the subtle man smell of him filled her senses with a sensuality that made her nostrils quiver.

"Amber, what the hell do you think you're doing?" he growled in the seconds it took her to pull herself together.

Amber gritted her teeth, then slapped his face. The blow stung her hand more than it did his cheek and knocked the hood from her hair. Immediately there was an apologetic expression in her eyes while a lazy half-grin came to his lips. He rubbed his cheek as he stared back into her determined features.

"That's what I'm doing here, you scoundrel!" she hissed. "I wanted to see you just once before they string you up. To tell you just what a despicable, thoroughly disgusting creature you are!"

Tears of pain wet her eyes, contrasting sharply to the angry, indignant inflection in her voice. When he did not respond, her voice dropped to add urgently, "Morgan, please, play along with me."

One brow raised quizzically, then his lips twisted into angry, thin lines as his body tensed. "Have you lost your mind? Get the hell out of here before somebody sees you!"

"And furthermore, you miserable cad!" Amber went on in an enraged voice that she made certain would carry to the deputy. "I will be at the foot of the gallows when they walk you up the steps Monday morning. I want the last thing you see before they drop you through it to eternity to be my face. I want you to see me and know what you've done!"

"Amber, for God's sake, don't do this," Morgan said harshly in a low whisper. "Let it be."

She shook her head. It took all her strength just to return his puzzled, angry glare and not fling herself into his arms. "I can't do that. This is much too important."

Then she leaped forward, springing on him, pushing him back against the wall. While one small hand pounded furiously at his chest and shoulders, the other whipped inside the cloak and pressed the cold steel of a Colt into his hand. Realizing there was no stopping her, he took the weapon with a sigh of resignation. Keeping her body between himself and the jailer's line of vision, he slipped it under the mattress of the cot.

Amid cries of outrage and indignation, Amber rained blow after blow with tiny clenched fists upon him. Morgan stood still, making no attempt to defend himself. A slight amused smile alternated with irritation and concern while she played out her role.

"Did Welch put you up to this?" he asked softly.

She bobbed her head affirmatively between howls of contempt.

"Tell him I said he's a damned fool, and so are you," he grated, then caught her wrists to hold her away from him.

"Just do your part," she panted. "At ten o'clock, not a minute before."

"All right, Miss McCandless," Morgan stated in a firm, clear voice. "I think that's enough. You've called me nasty names and pounded on me long enough. A condemned man has some rights."

Deputy Rogers lumbered toward the cell with a highly amused grin. While he fumbled with the keys, Morgan suddenly jerked Amber into his arms. The impact with his long, hard body took her breath. She glanced up into his dark, amused eyes to stare at him curiously.

Morgan's head bent, then his lips claimed hers in a long sensuous kiss that made her legs tremble. As he moved his mouth to touch her silky neck, he whispered, "Why are you doing this?"

She looked into his eyes as his head lifted. "Don't you know, Morgan?"

He shook his head, his gaze boring into hers.

"Because I love you," she whispered softly, then flung herself away from him as Rogers opened the cell door.

Knowing the deputy was lounging at the open cell door, Amber drew herself up and slapped Morgan's face once more for effect and whirled about, flouncing from the cell with a satisfied smile the deputy mistook for revenge. Halfway to the door she halted, turning back when Morgan's lazy drawl reached her quivering senses.

"Miss McCandless, I regret our association has to end like this. But if I have to hang for something, I can only say that it has been well worth it."

Amber's already flushed face turned scarlet, not so much from his carefully controlled tone of voice as from the hot caress she read behind the dancing ebony eyes. She stood open-mouthed staring at him for a moment before snapping her lips together. It took a supreme effort to put a haughty sneer on her face and make her eyes cold.

That one brief moment in his arms had totally unnerved her, made her acutely aware of how badly her body ached to feel the strength and power in those iron hard muscles released in the slow, blinding passion that left her weak and completely at his mercy. Looking at his handsome, guarded face behind the iron bars, she knew it was the last time she would ever see him and those past fleeting moments would be the last time her body would melt at his touch.

She could not control the violent trembling in her knees, or the tears that burned her eyes. Morgan leaned against the bars, gripping them slightly above his head with both hands, watching silently as her emotions changed so rapidly no one else would see. Her eyes ran over him quickly, devouring each detail to store in her mind for future reference. From the top of his black hair that drooped over one eye rakishly, down the wide shoulders and flat stomach to the slender hips and long legs that filled the snug trousers to sensual perfection, he was manhood consummate. Amber shuddered, trying to remember why she was here.

"Good-bye, Mr. Devereaux," she said with a tremor the jailer interpreted as relief, but was in reality the voice of a woman who knew she was losing the man she loved. "I trust you will not forget what I've said."

"No, ma'am," Morgan replied with a wicked grin that transformed his face into impish mischief. "May I say it's been a pleasure, Miss McCandless?"

"No, you may not!" she snapped.

A slight shrug strained the shoulders of his dark blue shirt while he lounged against the bars, observing her with casual amusement. "Well then, may I say that you're beautiful when you're angry?"

She sent him a warm gaze that touched him across the dingy

room like a caress. Then with an effort, she whirled around and slammed out the door. Once outside, she ran down the street blindly, stumbling over her long skirts, wiping her streaming eyes with the back of a clenched fist.

She hurled herself into the buggy Cooter had waiting in the alley behind the sheriff's office and flung herself into the old man's arms. Cooter wrapped a protective arm around her shoulders and drew her face against his shoulder as the team moved quickly through the dark, quiet streets.

"Don't cry, Missy," he crooned sympathetically. "He'll be all right. You'll see."

"But I'll never see him again, Cooter," Amber sniffed, her voice muffled by his protective arm. "He'll escape and I'll never know where he is or if he's all right."

Cooter did not know what to say to comfort her. The buggy sped through the night on its way back to *Sierra Vieja* while the girl cried miserably and the old man wished he knew how to ease her pain.

"Men like Morgan stay alive by their wits, Missy," he said at last. "He has to keep movin'. If he stays in one place too long, people recognize him, then some fool decides he can outdraw him and calls him out. Next thing somebody's dead. You don't want that, do you, Missy?"

"No, Cooter, of course not," she whimpered. "But a man can change, can't he? Is there some rule that says he can't change?"

Cooter did not answer. Silently he thought it best for everyone if Morgan Devereaux got on his horse and left Texas as fast as possible. Better for himself, but more importantly, better for the weeping girl on the buggy seat whose sobs gradually slowed to hiccups as the ranch loomed up in the distance.

***

"You're a cool son-of-a-bitch," Deputy Rogers remarked after the door slammed behind Amber's fleeing figure. He rattled the cell door as a precaution, then rested his ample rear on the railing. "For a man who's gonna hang for humpin' old man McCandless' niece, you act like it was damn near worth it."

Morgan's unexpressive face lifted for a moment. "Maybe it was," he said dryly.

Rogers walked away, scratching his head and slumped into the chair behind the desk in the outer office, muttering to himself. Morgan turned to the window, his expression tightening as the buggy sped past carrying Amber back to safety. His fingers clenched around the bars as he silently cursed her foolishness.

And what about Welch? That damned fool was supposed to be safely in Mexico and what does he do? Slip into town in an outlandish disguise to attend the trial right under Owen McCandless' nose! And now he'd convinced Amber to participate in a jail break!

His gaze moved slowly to the edge of the cot. As the door opened, he sat down on the slight lump the pistol made in the mattress.

Steven Riker and another deputy had returned from supper and now sat around the office making small talk. When an hour passed without Rogers mentioning Amber's visit, Morgan began to breathe easier.

Morgan stretched out on the cot with the pistol under the mattress beneath his head and waited. Amber had said ten o'clock which meant Welch was out there somewhere waiting to create a diversion of some kind to draw part of the guards from the jail.

While he waited, Morgan's mind went over and over Amber's whispered confession of love. He irritably rubbed his forehead. Jesus Christ, why did she have to say that? Having heard it put into words made it all too real. It never occurred to him to doubt her sincerity. In the time he had known Amber, he had quickly realized the girl did not possess an insincere thought.

Funny, he thought bitterly, he had heard those words before but never had they been uttered with such conviction or never had he instinctively believed them. His hands clenched into fists on the cot as his brow puckered into a scowl. What the hell did he care anyway, he argued with himself? Nobody asked her to love him. He didn't need it.

He turned his head to observe Steven Riker strolling toward him with that familiar arrogant stride and smirk that made him grit his teeth with the effort to keep his face expressionless.

Riker pushed aside the swinging gate to lean against the bars of Morgan's cell. "Well, Devereaux, it's Wednesday night. You've got four more days."

Morgan did not reply. He stared up at the ceiling, ignoring the sheriff in a way that infuriated Riker.

"What's the matter, gunslinger? Cat got your tongue?" Riker asked sarcastically.

"I've got nothing to say to you, Riker."

"That's too bad cause there's something I want to discuss with you." When Morgan refused to rise to the bait, Steven tried again. "I just had me a talk with Owen McCandless. Looks like me and that fetching niece of his will be tying the knot before long."

"Somehow I doubt that."

"Oh yeah? Why is that?"

"Has anybody bothered to discuss the matter with the lady?" Morgan countered with a question of his own.

"That makes no difference. She'll do what the old man tells her," Steven replied confidently.

"Then both of you have a lot to learn."

"I suppose you do know more about her than I do, at this point anyway," Steven conceded with a smirk. "I've been meaning to tell you, Devereaux, that little stunt you pulled in court was real touching— the way you stood up and confessed to keep that lawyer from asking some very embarrassing questions. It was almost noble the way you jumped to her defense."

"I'm glad you were pleased."

"So tell me, gunslinger, was crawling between her thighs worth dying for? I can't help wondering if all that proper Boston upbringing hasn't put ice water in her veins."

A muscle twitched in Morgan's jaw. The movement was slight,

but was enough for Riker to know this conversation was not pleasing to his captive audience.

"Any little tricks you'd care to share with me? Anything in particular that makes her moan and pant when you stick it in her?"

Morgan's boot heels hit the floor with a thud as he came off the cot. In one long stride he was across the cell with Steven's collar in both hands, slamming his face into the heavy iron bars with an impact that brought a squirt of blood from his nose. A strangled croak burst from Riker's mouth that brought the other two deputies to their feet running to his defense.

Before Steven realized what was happening, Morgan had jerked him head first into the bars several times. Blood streamed from Steven's nose while he fought wildly to break Morgan's grip on the lapels of his vest. Deputy Rogers had the presence of mind to think of his gun finally. He yanked it clumsily from his holster and stuck it in Morgan's face through the bars.

Through a blinding haze of fury, Morgan became aware of the gun and slowly let the sheriff's vest slide from his fingers. He stepped back with a long shuddering breath.

Steven shook himself, put one hand to his battered face, and stared stupidly at the blood on it when it came away from his face. Fury flooding through him, he jerked a thumb over his shoulder toward the key ring beneath the desk.

"Get the keys, Rogers," he commanded loudly. "It's time we taught this son-of-a-bitch a lesson."

Rogers hurried to the desk to snatch up the keys and returned to the cell. Steven inserted the cell key in the door while the other two stood back, grinning with delight.

"Riker, what the hell is going on here?" came a cold, harsh voice from the doorway.

Steven whirled with the keys still in his hand to see Ryan Tyrell stalk across the room and shove the swinging gate open. Ryan yanked the ring of keys from Steven's hand and rattled the door to make sure it was still locked. With a sweeping glance at the sheriff's bloody face, then another at Morgan's unblemished one, he regarded Riker contemptuously.

"This is none of your business, Tyrell," Riker snapped.

"Any time you attempt to beat the hell out of my prisoner, it's my business," Ryan returned in a quiet voice, but one that rang with authority. He looked at the other two with a sneer while they slunk away. "Since when does it require three men to take one man behind bars?"

"Look at what he did to me!" Steven snarled, gesturing to his bleeding face.

Ryan couldn't resist a grin. "You're lucky he didn't do worse than that. Now what's this all about?"

Steven refused to answer, standing stiffly and glaring from Ryan to Morgan and back again. Ryan looked at Morgan but saw nothing.

Their attention was drawn by a shout outside. Soon the street was filled with shouting, cursing people. Ryan ran to the door and yanked it open just as a deputy stuck his head inside to yell, "Fire! Fire, Sheriff, down at the livery and it's spreadin' fast!"

Riker growled a curse as he elbowed Ryan aside to run out into the crowded street. The other two deputies started out. Ryan caught Rogers' collar and hauled him back inside.

"Stay with the prisoner," he ordered, slamming the door behind him.

Rogers cursed, but slunk back to the desk, intending to sit down when he heard the distinct sound of a gun hammer cocking behind him. The hair at the base of his scalp stood on end as he turned to look into the bore of the Colt in Morgan's left hand.

"Bring the keys, Rogers, and open this door. Move, and I'll think about not killing you," Morgan said in a tone that made the hefty deputy's face pale. "Now throw your gun across the room."

Rogers wasted no time in obeying. He hurried to retrieve the keys and had the door open in a moment, then stood back with bulging eyeballs while Morgan stepped out and nudged him with the barrel of the pistol.

"Inside," he commanded. Rogers leaped to obey. Morgan slammed the door closed, locked it, then jumped the railing on his way to the door to check the street. Just as he reached it, the knob turned and it began to open. He stepped behind the door and stuck the gun barrel in Ryan Tyrell's rib cage as he walked into the office.

"Get your hands up, ranger."

Ryan obeyed slowly, mentally kicking himself for the moment of carelessness. Morgan kicked the door shut with his heel, nudging Ryan toward the cell.

"Drop your gun and put yourself in the cell."

"You can't get away, Devereaux," Ryan warned while he unlocked the door and walked inside. "You'll never get out of this town alive."

"Maybe not, but it beats the hell out of sitting here like a Christmas goose waiting for the ax," Morgan said curtly. "Throw those keys out here."

Ryan obeyed, then placed his brawny hands around the bars, watching helplessly while Morgan rummaged through the sheriff's desk, smiling at the discovery of his own weapon among the litter. He placed the gun Amber brought him in the back of his belt and went to the peg where the weapons were kept to take down his own gunbelt. Strapping it into place and tying it down, he glanced up with a satisfied gleam in his eyes at Ryan, then headed once more for the door.

Opening it, he stuck his head cautiously outside to view the activity in the street. People were shouting and yelling, horses whinnied in alarm, and the roar of distant flames created a frenzy of noise that was all but deafening. Then, he ducked back inside with a grim smile. A moment later, Steven Riker charged inside with his gun drawn.

The look of anxiety on his swelling, bruised face changed to bewilderment at the sight of his deputy and the big ranger inside the cell. "What the hell happened?" he roared. "Where the hell is Devereaux?"

"Right behind you, Sheriff," Morgan told him as he kicked the door shut and slid the bolt into place. "Now, put the gun back in your holster and turn around."

Steven's heart froze in his chest as he slowly obeyed, turning to find that Morgan had moved across the room and was dropping his gun into the worn black holster with a thin smile of ridicule that made Steven's legs go weak.

"W-W-What are you doing?" he stammered.

"Giving you your wish, Sheriff. For two months now I've listened to your bragging about how fast you are, Riker. Now's your chance to prove it. Draw on me," Morgan said in a deceptively soft voice.

Steven's face went white with alarm. His hands twitched nervously while his ferret-like tongue went to his lips.

"What's wrong, Riker? Finding out it's not so easy when the man you're facing has a gun, too?" Morgan taunted softly. "You talk big, Riker. I promised you I'd kill you if I had the chance. Remember?"

Steven's mouth was dry, his tongue felt wooden, and for the first time in his life he knew the meaning of fear. Knowing he would find no mercy from the gunfighter he had taunted, he went for his gun.

A cry of pain burst through his lips as his pistol went spinning from his hand, sailing across the desk to land with a clatter on the floor. He grabbed his wrist, stared stupidly at the blood oozing from the wound where Morgan's bullet went completely through his hand, then raised terrified eyes to Morgan's cold, amused face.

A taunting smile touched the gunman's mouth as he reached behind him to take out the pistol Amber had delivered. He kicked it across the floor where it bumped into Riker's feet.

"Pick it up, Riker, with your other hand. I'll give you another chance."

Raw, stark terror filled Steven's face now. All this time he had wanted to see emotion in the gunman's carefully veiled face, but now that he did, what he saw made him blind with fear. Instead of reaching for the gun, he turned to run for the door.

Morgan's second bullet caught him in the right leg, knocking him down and turning him into a blabbering fool. He crawled on the floor, clutching at furniture and begging for mercy while Morgan thumbed the hammer of the Colt, pumping bullets into his left leg and right shoulder. The dashing, handsome sheriff was reduced to a slobbering, whining imbecile.

When Morgan's fifth bullet ripped through him, he clutched his left shoulder, screaming in pain and writhing on the floor as his blood splashed over the rough boards.

Morgan stood over him with one bullet left in the chamber, staring down at him contemptuously. He ejected the spent cartridges and reloaded. Leveling a straight gaze at the ranger he said, "I'm not going to kill him, Tyrell."

Ryan nodded. "I'm glad to hear it."

"I'll let you do that," Morgan explained. "When he stops slobbering, ask him about Jenna Ruiz. I'm betting she gave him the map to the Lair. If you ask the right questions, I think he'll tell you that he killed her for it. You told me about the law, Tyrell, now prove it. See that this miserable son-of-a-bitch hangs and I might believe you."

He moved to the door and slid the bolt back.

"Devereaux, I'll be coming after you," Ryan said meaningfully from the cell.

Morgan paused with his hand on the door knob to look back at the big man.

"I expect you will."

Without another word, he slipped into the darkness, staying in the shadows until he spotted a horse tied at a hitch rail, grinning as Diablo lifted his sleek head to whinny a welcome. Amber had taken care of everything, it seemed. He vaulted into the saddle and dug his heels into the powerful animal's flanks to send him flying down the street in the opposite direction from the chaos at the end of the street.

CHAPTER THIRTY-TWO

The big house was quiet and dark when Amber left the buggy and slipped through the kitchen door. The faint aroma of the roast they'd had for dinner left a pleasant homey smell that wafted to her nostrils as she tiptoed through the kitchen to reach the stairs, but this great house was no longer home.

In place of the serene feeling of homecoming she had known when first arriving from Boston, now Amber could only feel bitterness. She paused at the foot of the long curving staircase, gathering her strength. She only wanted to be free of this place with its sadness and bitter memories. The plan that had begun forming in her mind on the trip home from McCandless gained momentum as she climbed the staircase.

She would leave this place as quickly as plans could be made. She would speak to Cooter tomorrow to enlist his aid. To leave without her uncle's knowledge would be virtually impossible.

She slipped along the dark hallway lit only by two candles in crystal sconces that threw eerie shadows, making Amber wonder why she had never noticed the gloom before. She knew the reason. She had been so happy to be back in Texas with her uncle that she had not seen the unpleasant things. She had not wanted to see anything but the peaceful picture she had painted for herself.

Removing her shoes, she hurried past her uncle's rooms on bare feet. The light beneath his door made her wary so she held her breath, tiptoeing down the hall to her room at the end of the hallway.

Her hand paused on the ornate door knob, her brows lifting in concern at the soft glow of light sifting beneath the door. Had she lit a lamp before sneaking out the back way to meet Cooter after dinner? She could not remember, but at the time her mind had been so filled with doubts and fear for Morgan's safety, she might have lit a dozen lamps without noticing what she was doing.

The door swung open soundlessly and she slid inside, removed the dark cloak and set her shoes down all at the same time. The lamp on the tiny desk in which lay the treasured journal was lit. Her rooms, consisting of a sitting room and private bath that adjoined the sleeping quarters, were large and elegantly furnished so the lone lamp made only a dent in the darkness beyond it, leaving great hulking shadows that made her uneasy.

She pitched the cloak onto her bed as she let out a long sigh of relief. With a glance at the mantle clock above the white stone fireplace that dwarfed one end of the room, she saw it was almost ten o'clock. Within a few minutes Morgan would either be free and on his way to Mexico, or dead, killed trying to escape. She rubbed absently at the ache in her chest as though it might relive the pain of uncertainty.

Then, as she turned to go to the wardrobe in one corner of the bedroom to take out her night clothes, she gave a shocked gasp when a large shape evolved from the shadows. A moment later her alarm became real terror when Owen's face became visible in the lamp's glow. Amber's hand went to her throat. Her lips worked soundlessly, trying to recover both her voice and her composure. It would not do to let him know how frightened of him she was now.

Her gaze flashed to the desk where the journal was hidden. The drawer was closed, but she could not tell if Owen had discovered its presence. Fear choked her, made her weak, sick at her stomach. If Owen had discovered the journal, her life, as well as Cooter's, was in grave danger. Owen had killed before, he would surely kill again to cover up his crimes. If he had killed his own brother, he would have no qualms about killing a niece.

"I've been waiting, Amber," his deep voice growled as he came closer. "Where have you been?"

"I-I-I went for a ride, Uncle Owen," she stammered frantically. "I-I couldn't sleep and..and I thought a nice long ride might help me relax."

His dark brows lifted as a cynical smile twisted his lips. "Really? Are you accustomed to Cooter accompanying you on such rides?" he jeered in a voice that made the girl's heart pound in her ears.

She could not reply. Her lips seemed to be made of wood, her tongue thick and frozen. She involuntarily backed up, seeing Owen's anger mounting at the movement, but unable to help herself.

"You're lying, Amber," Owen continued in that cold, derisive tone that turned her blood to ice water. The panic in the girl's eyes fed his suspicions, making his rage mount to uncontrollable proportions. "I saw you return in the buggy with Cooter. You see, I was concerned about you, Amber. You haven't been out of your room for two days now, had all your meals sent up on a tray, but when I came to check on you a couple of hours ago, I found only an empty room.

"You've lied to me, Amber. You haven't been ill at all. You've been avoiding me, hiding in your room, while you plotted to sneak away into town to see that murdering outlaw. That's where you've been, isn't it?"

Amber's voice was frozen. Her limbs seemed to be made of granite for she was unable to move. She knew her face was white, her eyes filled with fear, but she was helpless to prevent it.

"You slipped into town to see that man after everything he's done. After the shame and embarrassment he's caused me. You deliberately disobeyed me, Amber. You sneaked away like a common street whore to see a man who violated you, who used you to hurt me. A man who isn't fit to live."

Amber's lips moved noiselessly in an effort to deny his accusations, but no words came out. Owen watched her through narrowed eyes that flashed coldly while he smiled at the terror in her face.

"I'm accustomed to having my orders obeyed, Amber. My men obey me. Should I expect less from my own kin? I see that I've been much too lax with you. I've tried to be understanding, tried to be patient about your moping and depression, hoping it was only your guilt and shame that made you so unhappy.

"I see now that I was wrong. You obviously still have a soft spot for that murderous man. He's tainted you, Amber, made you unclean and addled."

He paused as though waiting for her to speak, but the best she could do was shake her head, her lips parted and her eyes wide with fear. Owen clenched his fists at her silence. Even a denial would have been preferable to her muteness.

"What evil power does this man have over you, Amber?" he demanded in a tone that made the girl move another step back. "What has he done to you that prevents you from forgetting him?"

"He's done nothing, Uncle Owen, except make me love him," Amber choked out at last. The rage that flooded his face made her instantly regret the words, but it was much too late to take them back.

"Love him!" Owen thundered. "Love him! He's not fit to tie your shoe laces! He's common, vulgar...he's filth!"

"Then I'm filth also!" Amber cried in Morgan's defense. "I love him and if it were in my power I would set him free!"

A vicious smack from Owen's meaty hand knocked her backwards against the wall, making her head spin. Her knees buckled, letting her slide down the wall to the floor, but Owen yanked her upright, slapping her again and again while he screamed accusations.

Amber's head roared. She tasted blood from her split lips and knew she was going to faint. She heard someone scream in fear and pain when Owen caught her shoulders and began to shake her until she thought her head would snap off. Another vicious blow silenced her screams while he continued to shake her furiously.

A heavy blanket of fog descended upon her, blacking out the pain as Owen vented his rage upon her. Tears blinded her, her throat ached with screams that could not get past the malicious pounding of his big hands. He let her slide to the floor, but her torture was not over for Owen began to kick her in the stomach and thighs. Oddly, she did not feel the pain from his heavy boots.

He was going to kill her if he did not stop soon, she thought dimly. She began to pray that God would relieve this unbearable torment as Owen dropped to the floor beside her to continue slapping and punching her. Then, as if God finally heard her, she lapsed into unconsciousness. The last thing she heard as the black cloud of relief dropped over her was Owen's curses. It was with a last trickle of sanity that she heard him ranting her mother's name in a high pitched tone that bordered on madness.

***

When she awoke, it was hours later, she realized dimly with a glance at the mantel clock as she struggled to sit up. Whimpers of pain and terror escaped her throat in cracked gasps as the memory of Owen's savage attack roared back into her mind.

She lurched off the bed, wondering how she'd gotten there, and stumbled to the door, leaning heavily against it while her numb fingers slid the bolt into place. Pushing her tumbled hair from her face, she limped to the wash stand and filled the hand-painted basin with water to begin trying to wash away the effects of Owen's violation.

She shuddered as the torn riding dress fell to the floor at her feet, not having enough strength to step out of it. Ugly bruises had formed on her shoulders and rib cage from his heavy blows. She forced her eyes downward, gasping in dismay at more nasty bruises on her thighs and stomach. She used soap and water to scrub herself until her skin was raw, but still she did not feel clean. She doubted she would ever feel clean again.

She limped to the wardrobe then, to dress in her gown and robe, then padded to the door. There was no sound in the hallway as she slipped into it to begin her stealthy journey down the stairs to Owen's study. Once inside, she padded silently to the cherrywood gun cabinet and examined her choices.

She picked up and discarded four pistols before choosing a Colt.45. She remembered Morgan's advice on choosing a weapon that fit your hands. The Colt's barrel was two and a half inches longer than the one Morgan used with such skill, but for her purposes it would do well enough.

She checked the chambers to insure the weapon was loaded, then closed the glass cabinet doors. Hiding the gun in the folds of rose colored silk that fanned out behind her, she climbed back up the stairs. Hatred blazed in her eyes as she paused briefly at Owen's door to listen to the contented snores from within.

It took a concentrated effort to walk past that room on down the hall to her own. She slipped inside, locked the door securely, and then proceeded to the desk. She opened the drawer and smiled in cold satisfaction at the sight of the worn journal.

Tomorrow she and that journal were going to Ryan Tyrell. She would see that her father's last desire was fulfilled. Owen McCandless was going to pay at last for all the lives he had destroyed. Amber fervently hoped he would hang on the same gallows he had planned for Morgan.

CHAPTER
THIRTY-THREE

The mantel clock struck two a.m. Amber stirred from a foggy state of half sleep, half exhausted awareness. She rubbed her eyes, her brows drawing together in a puzzled frown. Shuddering with revulsion, unable to put that evening's events from her thoughts, she turned to observe the clock. It was too dark to read its face, but realizing it must have been the clock striking two o'clock that had roused her, she felt under her pillow for the cold, comforting touch of the Colt.

Morgan was safe by now, she told herself. Free and on his way to Mexico. At least she had that to feel good about tonight. Even if she would never see him again, she could bask in the knowledge that Owen McCandless' evil scheme had been thwarted.

She gradually became aware that she was not alone. The hair rose at the base of her scalp as a gasp bubbled from her throat. She tore at the pillow to grab the gun, bringing it up to her chest with both hands. Terror made her weak when a shadow moved from the foot of the bed to take human form in the dim moonlight through the distant window.

"Amber?" a soft male voice called to her from the darkness.

Amber's finger hesitated on the trigger as indecision flooded over her. The shadow moved a step closer, making her eyes widen as she peered into the shadows.

"Amber? Put the gun down. I won't hurt you," the faceless voice said softly.

A second later she dropped it into the folds of the bedding as she jerked upright. Flinging the sheets off, she hurled herself from the bed into the arms of her phantom visitor.

"Oh God, Oh God," she repeated over and over against Morgan's hard chest. Relieved sobs ripped from her throat as she released the pent-up emotions she had held in careful check since Owen's attack.

Morgan held her tightly, letting his cheek smooth the tumbled golden hair while he breathed in the fragrance of her freshly scrubbed skin. She molded herself to his tall, lean frame. Her fingers clutched frantically at his shirt, holding onto him so fiercely she made it difficult for him to breathe.

When her sobs continued, Morgan's eyes narrowed above her head. He had expected a certain amount of relief to learn her plan had been successful but this wild, almost hysterical display filled him with alarm.

He took her arms to hold her away from him. Then he set her down on the edge of the bed and moved to light the lamp on the desk. Turning back, he took her trembling hands, sitting down beside her at an angle so he could clearly see her clearly. What he saw made his jaw tense and his eyes narrow to icy slits.

"Amber, what the hell happened?" he demanded in a raspy voice that made her stare up at him in sudden fear.

Realizing what he had seen, Amber jerked her hand from his to pull the gown back over the bruise.

The waves of shame that flooded her pale face hardened his features into a mask of fury as he reached out to yank the gown down, exposing not only the disfiguring bruises on both shoulders, but also twin mounds of coral tipped perfection that, at any other time, would have made his blood surge with desire. Amber whimpered, turning away from him while trying to cover herself from his probing gaze.

Morgan's strong hands held her firmly, pushing her back into the folds of bedding while he worked the filmy gown off her struggling body. He closed his ears to her whimpered protests, looming above her on the bed. When her quivering flesh was naked before him, he straddled her, forcing her hands to her sides to prevent her turning away to escape his eyes.

Amber heard the sharp intake of his breath when his eyes had traveled the length of her, seeing the hideous bruises that marked her rib cage and stomach and turned her thighs to black and blue blotches.

"Who did this to you?" he demanded in a voice so raw and hoarse Amber hardly recognized it. He moved off her, letting her roll into his arms and bury her face in his chest. "Answer me, Amber, who did this?"

She could not answer for the lump of shame that choked off her voice. Fresh sobs poured forth, wetting his shirt with tears and tiny spots of blood from her cracked lips.

"Did McCandless do this?" he demanded with sudden insight.

The terrified expression in her eyes when she lifted her head briefly told him more than any words could have. With a strangled curse, he flung himself from the bed. Amber heard his boot heels click across the hardwood floor as he bounded for the door.

She hurled herself after him, clutching his arm and throwing her naked body between him and the door. "No, Morgan!" she cried. "No! Stop it! Listen to me!"

Slowly her pleas reached him through the red hot rage that sizzled in his veins. He let go of the door knob and swallowed, staring at her with eyes so full of fury it took all Amber's courage to look into his face.

"Does he know you helped me escape?"

Amber shook her head. Her hands tightened on his arm. His chest heaved with the effort to regain control of himself. It suddenly occurred to Amber that he was trembling, his whole body shaking with the emotions roaring through him.

"He did this to you and still you want me to spare his miserable life?"

It was a statement that made Amber tighten her grip on his arm anxiously.

"Morgan, I know you were right. He did all those horrible things you told me about and many others. He killed my father because he wanted my mother for himself and because he knew my father was planning to expose him."

"I'll kill him! Right now! I'll cut his goddamned throat!"

Amber shook her head, her eyes pleading with him to listen. "No, Morgan. That's your way, but it's not my father's, nor mine. I will see him destroyed, hanged from the gallows he arranged for you, but I'll do it my own way. The right way."

He regarded her skeptically, a cynical smile twisting his lips in a mirthless expression of humor. "You mean the law? Haven't you learned anything, Amber? He owns the law. It won't touch him."

"That may have been true once, Morgan, but no longer. I have proof. I can prove he killed your family and my father. And I think Ryan Tyrell is an honest lawman. I trust him."

"One honest lawman can't do anything. The only way to stop McCandless is with a bullet."

"I don't believe that," she replied confidently. "I can prove it, Morgan. In a way even Owen McCandless can't deny."

"What way?" Morgan asked, his eyes narrowing suspiciously. "What kind of proof?"

A chill of warning flashed through Amber's body as she remembered Cooter's prediction. She had already lost both her parents. She was not willing to risk Welch's life by revealing the journal. She looked away briefly, trying to devise an answer that would satisfy Morgan.

"Cooter for one thing. He knows everything. He'll help me. And there's my word, Morgan. I'll testify in court what Owen has done," she told him anxiously.

"It won't be enough," Morgan said through clenched teeth. "Now move out of my way."

"No," she replied firmly. "If you kill him, Morgan, you'll be as bad as he is. He destroyed your family. He's caused you to live your whole life for revenge, but if you kill him now you'll be letting him win."

"I don't give a goddamn thing about winning. I want that bastard dead and I'm going to kill him, right now!"

"Then you'll have to kill me too."

Morgan stared at her in surprise. Her face was pale but determined and the warm golden gaze that touched him was filled with longing.

"Morgan, do I mean anything at all to you?" she asked softly.

"I'm here, aren't I?" he countered stiffly. "I could be halfway to Mexico by now."

"Why aren't you? Why did you come here and climb through my window instead?"

Morgan shifted uneasily under her insistent golden gaze, his outrage momentarily softening at the plea in her face. "I was worried somebody would find out you helped me escape. I came here to make sure you were all right before I go on to Mexico."

"Knowing that a posse will be right on your heels?" A tiny smile touched Amber's bruised lips. Her hand on his arm relaxed to a caress. Morgan did not reply, but stood staring down at her as though puzzled by her question. "Worry? That's all it is?"

Irritation flashed into his face, making his dark eyes gleam as the muscles in both strong jaws twitched. "What the hell are you trying to get me to say?"

"I want you to tell me how you feel, Morgan. About me."

"I've already told you," he countered warily. "I was worried about you."

"I find that very strange. I wouldn't be at all surprised to discover that I'm the only woman you've ever worried about. I know I'm the only one you've risked your life for twice. Once when you made that ridiculous, noble, wonderful confession in court so I wouldn't tell everybody how much I loved you, and now by coming here when you should be miles away."

"You think I'm in love with you?" he asked with such surprise in his voice it made Amber want to giggle.

"Aren't you? Isn't that really why you're here? Why you're ready to kill Owen in his sleep because he hurt me?" When he suddenly turned away, uncharacteristically avoiding her eyes, she smiled softly and added, "It's not a sin to care for someone, Morgan. It doesn't mean that you're weak or less of a man. In fact, it makes you stronger."

"How do you figure that?"

"Sharing yourself with another person only deepens your emotions. Only by opening yourself to another person can you truly know yourself. When you share your feelings with someone, Morgan, two separate people can become one person; sharing, loving, giving to one another."

The softness in her voice combined with the warm glow of love in her eyes made Morgan's stiff resistance slowly melt. His breathing slowed, his chest stopped heaving, and the pulse in his wrist beneath Amber's fingers normalized. For the first time, Amber saw frustration and indecision in his face, sensed the struggle going on inside him and remembered Welch's warning that he would fight any feelings for her.

"It's easy for you to say that, Amber," he said at last. "Love comes easy for a woman. They look for it at every turn, always expecting to find it."

"Is that why it's so difficult for you, Morgan? Because you didn't expect it to ever happen to you?" she prodded gently.

"Jesus Christ, woman!" he said curtly. He turned away, striding across the darkened room to stand staring out the window in uneasy silence. Amber moved to the bed and slipped back into her gown. She smiled at his broad shoulders filling the blue shirt to rippling perfection and his raven hair curling around the collar. Hatless, his thumbs hooked in the black gunbelt that rested around his slim waist, Amber was at peace for the first time since he had been wounded.

She padded across the room to lean against his back, lacing her fingers in front of his chest, breathing in the masculine scent that was his alone.

"I love you, Morgan," she said softly, but firmly enough for him to hear.

"I know that. That's what makes it so damned hard," he said with a heavy sigh. "You don't seem to realize that loving me will only hurt you. It will ruin your life if you let it, and God as my witness, Amber, I don't want to ever hurt you more than I have already."

"You've never hurt me, Morgan. You scared me silly a few times, but you've never harmed me. I owe you a great deal."

At the surprised tensing of his body, she squeezed him lightly and explained. "If you hadn't taken me off the stage, I'd never have found out what an evil man my uncle really is. And I'd have never known that I can love someone so much that I can't think of anything else."

"You'll get over it."

"Love isn't something you turn off like blowing out a candle, my darling."

"You know what I am, Amber. I'm not proud of it, but I won't make excuses for it either. There's no changing it, no going back and undoing it."

"It doesn't matter."

A bitter snort ripped from his throat. He stared out the window, resting his weight on his left leg to ease the tenderness that lingered in the other, and pulled the frilly curtains back with a strong, brown hand.

"Think before you say that, Amber. You don't realize how foolish it is. Don't you realize that I'm a wanted man? Hell, Tyrell is on my trail right now, and if I've learned one thing in the past couple of months, it's that Tyrell is a determined son-of-a-bitch. He'll hunt me for the rest of my life until he either catches me or kills me. And since I don't enjoy the thought of hanging, it'll be the latter."

"It doesn't have to be that way, Morgan," Amber argued. "You can stop, give yourself up to Tyrell and explain. With the evidence I've gathered on my uncle, all the charges against you will be dropped. You can be a free man."

"Even if that were possible, Amber, it doesn't erase my reputation. You've got to accept the fact that no matter where I go, I can never escape it. It'll follow me to my grave. There'll always be someone who thinks he's fast with a gun and willing to die to prove it. Everyone wants to beat Morgan Devereaux, to prove he's a big man."

"But...."

"I know what I'm talking about, Amber," he interjected. "I've lived with it every day of my life since I was sixteen years old. I've spent the past fifteen years always looking over my shoulder, avoiding open doors and lighted windows. Looking at every man I see wearing a gun, wondering if he's going to call me out.

"That's no kind of life for you, Amber. I could never ask you to share it. Always on the move, afraid to stay in one place long enough to put down roots because somebody always recognizes me eventually."

Her head moved in an understanding motion against his back. The raw pain in his voice revealed so much of the feelings he'd always kept so tightly locked inside him.

"I understand, Morgan," she whispered. "But it doesn't change how I feel. I love you. I would go anywhere, do anything, to be with you if I thought there was some slim chance that you cared for me."

He did not reply. If he said anything it would only strengthen her determination and someday that would hurt her worse than cutting it off right now. Still, the words he formed to send her scurrying away from him would not come out. Suddenly the thought of leaving her behind filled him with such pain, it made the pain from Riker's bullet in his chest seem like nothing

While he stood silently pondering this new found revelation, Amber sensed his indecision, the conflict raging inside him and pulled him around to stare up into his troubled face.

"Morgan, I love you. I don't care what you are or what you've done. I only care about from this moment on. But if you can tell me you don't care about me, that I mean nothing to you, I will accept your decision and let you walk out of my life without another word. Can you say that to me, Morgan, and mean it?"

He stared at her blankly for a moment while she felt his body begin to tremble again ever so slightly. Then he exhaled over her head and swallowed. "I could if I had any sense," he growled wearily. "I must be as insane as you."

Instant hope surged into her eyes. Her fingers clutched his hand while her heart began to pound so hard she could hardly hear above the roar in her ears.

"Does that mean that you do love me?" she asked softly.

The distress that was so obvious in his dark face filled her with the urge to giggle. Those few simple words that came so readily to her lips tore at his insides like fingers with claw-like nails, pulling him in two directions at once.

"Goddamn it, Amber, you're not going to be satisfied until I say it, are you?" he said accusingly. He lifted one hand to run through his hair, wishing she would move away. How could a man think rationally when she was this close?

"It's not that easy for me. Everything logical inside me says I should get the hell out of here. Common sense tells me that letting you get too close is a big mistake. I've been telling myself that for months, but somehow part of me just isn't listening.

"I've never cared about anyone before. How the hell do I know what I feel? I don't know how to love anybody. I've had precious little experience. If thinking about you every minute I'm awake and then dreaming of you when I'm asleep, if just thinking about you makes me hurt to touch you, to hold you, if just wanting to have you with me...if that means that I love you, then yes, goddamnit, Amber, I love you."

The pleased expression on her face spoke volumes when he finally looked down at her. "There, I said it, but it doesn't change anything."

"Oh, but it does, my darling," Amber said, rising on her tiptoes and reaching behind his head to pull his face down to kiss him softly.

His arms went around her instantly, pressing her against the hard length of his body. He remembered her bruised lips and answered her kiss gently with a tenderness that until now had been foreign to him. After a few endless moments, he caught a handful of her hair, gently pulling her head back so he could look into her eyes.

"I'm still leaving tomorrow morning. I'm leaving.....you'll get over this," he warned.

"Of course, Morgan," she murmured. "But that's tomorrow morning. We still have tonight."

The sultry suggestion in her voice raised his brows in surprise, then concern. "Amber, I don't think that's a good idea. I mean, I could hurt you after what McCandless has done. I don't think...."

Amber's persistent lips cut off his protest, lifting only long enough to whisper against his mouth, "Don't think, Morgan, just love me."

The warm persistent crush of her body against his, combined with the softness of her mouth moving over his face, down his neck made his breath quicken with desire. She unbuttoned his shirt, slipped her hands inside to run lightly over the cords of muscle that covered his rib cage and upper arms, then dropped her head to plant warm, wet kisses over his chest while her fingers worked to loosen the buckle of the gunbelt.

Finally, unable to resist any longer, Morgan reached down to unbuckle the belt, then untied the holster from his thigh and with a swift movement, swept her up into his arms and carried her to the bed.

For the first time, Amber helped him out of his clothes, then lifted her arms to allow him to remove the rose colored gown and pitch it to the floor atop his clothes.

"I love you, Morgan," she whispered as his lips and gentle hands quickly brought her to blazing readiness.

Morgan poised above her just before lowering himself into her gently. His dark eyes gleamed with a light she had never seen before. She had seen those carbon black pools signal his anger and his desire, but this was the first time she saw love in them.

"I love you," he whispered hoarsely as he slipped into the warm, wet depths of her silky body.

Amber closed her eyes and gave herself to the swirl of passion that engulfed her. Tomorrow he might keep his word and leave her, but now he belonged totally to her. For now it was enough.

***

Morgan carefully arose from the bed and dressed in the darkness. His lips curled into a smile at the sight of the sleeping girl. Tonight had forced him to face a difficult fact. He loved this beautiful, passionate girl and if she was willing to follow him to the ends of the earth as she said, he would move heaven and hell to have her with him.

Buckling the gunbelt into place once more, he moved to the window and thought for a moment. Tyrell was out there somewhere hunting for him. He must not allow the ranger to trail him to *Sierra Vieja*. He must keep Amber's role in his escape a secret at all costs.

He opened the desk drawer in search of a piece of paper to write Amber a note explaining his intention to leave a false trail for the lawman that would lead him away from her. He rummaged in the drawer, lifting the heavy, worn ledger to look beneath it for a piece of paper, and finally located what he wanted. He sat down at the desk, turned the lamp up a bit and quickly wrote the message to Amber.

As he got up, he remembered the ledger and picked it up to put it back in the drawer. A piece of paper fell out of it, falling open to scream up at his startled eyes.

It was a page from a Bible, faded with age, but still legible enough for him to read:

Name: Wendall Welch McCandless
Born: October 2, 1830

As he scanned the page, his eyes narrowed, became cold, filling with a fury that made him shake violently. He looked at the ledger, then opened it, reading the inscription in amazement.

So this was Amber's evidence, he realized quickly. She'd lied to him about this, keeping the fact that she had written evidence against Owen McCandless a secret. Glancing back at the page from the Bible, it was easy to see why.

He sat down again and moved the lamp closer as his dark, furious eyes devoured the words of the journal. By the time he had gotten half way through it, he was filled with a rage that blinded him to reason, making his chest hurt and the blood pound in his ears.

He read on, turning up the lamp occasionally to see it all. He closed the book just as the first gray streaks of dawn touched the sky. Then he arose and slipped from the house.

For the first time in his life there was a man he wanted to kill more than Owen McCandless, and he knew exactly where to find him.

CHAPTER THIRTY-FOUR

The Appaloosa flew across the prairie as though on wings. After so many weeks of inactivity it was a pleasure to stretch his muscles and the urgency he sensed in the man on his back made him skim the ground at amazing speed to take Morgan to his destination. By the time the early morning sun was beginning to turn the gray dawn into the rosy streaks of daylight, they were arriving at their goal an hour's hard ride from *Sierra Vieja*.

Morgan reined the horse to a halt atop the slight rise in the prairie to let the wiry animal catch his breath. After riding like a madman through the gray morning light, his anger had cooled from blinding unreason to the cold deadliness that set him apart from other men. In the time it took to reach his destination, his limbs had stopped trembling and the roar in his ears had lessened so that now as he cantered down the slope, he was in complete control again.

His lips thinned into flat lines of contempt as he drew within sight of the four great cottonwoods and saw the lone horse that waited sleepily beneath the outstretched limbs. Though it was only now becoming daylight, the heat from the September sun covered the land in a blanket of discomfort, but Morgan had not noticed for the fury in his blood blotted out all else as he slipped from the saddle and strode toward the man who awaited him.

Welch Mandell turned from his reverent vigil above the three graves in the Texas earth. One glance at Morgan's pale, tight face told him what he had feared for so long had become reality. The years of deception had finally caught up with him, and now he was face to face with the one man who had the ability to kill him. Ironic that he was the one who taught Morgan how.

"I knew I'd find you here," Morgan ground out.

"I see you've been to *Sierra Vieja.*"

Morgan came closer, his black eyes gleaming with contempt, and halted close enough for Welch to touch. "Too bad I didn't get there sooner. I could have caught McCandless in the act of beating the hell out of his niece."

Welch's gray eyes widened in shock. "W-w-what? What did you say?"

"You heard me. McCandless beat the hell out of Amber last night. But don't worry, she'll be all right and I'm going back to settle up with him as soon as I've dealt with you."

The hair at the base of Welch's neck rose slightly. In the years he had known Morgan, he had seen him angry enough to kill many times, but never had he seen such coldness, such deliberation as he saw in the depths of those inky black eyes at this moment. Still, he was remarkably calm while he returned Morgan's flat, cold stare.

"I see Amber told you."

"Amber told me nothing. This did," Morgan contradicted sharply, whipping the faded sheet from the old family Bible from his shirt pocket and shoving it under Welch's face. "This and Price McCandless' journal. Oh yes, Welch, I know everything. I found the journal by accident, but I can't tell you how glad I am that I did. Otherwise, I might never have known what a fool you've played me for all my life."

Welch glanced at the sheet of paper in Morgan's hand, knowing what it said, then looked back into Morgan's scorn-filled features with a calmness he was certain must have come from the relief at finally having it all out in the open.

"Are you going to deny it?" Morgan demanded.

Welch shook his silver blonde head. "Why should I? You've read the journal. What can I say that will make any difference now?"

"Why didn't you tell me, Welch? Years ago. Why did you let me grow up believing you really cared what happened to me? Why did you let me believe that my mother was a decent woman when all the time she was a...."

"Just a minute!" Welch cut in furiously. He walked closer, his gun-metal eyes blazing with anger. "Before you say something you'll be sorry for, listen to me for a few minutes. Let me explain."

"Explain?" Morgan snorted. "Explain how you screwed my mother behind my father's back after he saved your life, after he gave you a chance to start over? Explain how you raised me to kill Owen McCandless for you because he's your brother and you couldn't do it yourself? The only thing I want to hear from you is why. Why you lied to me!"

"You keep a decent tongue in your mouth about your mother!" Welch ordered in a voice that would have made most men cringe. Morgan only stared at him, those cold black eyes relentlessly following every motion of Welch's face, piercing, probing, demanding an explanation he could believe.

"Your mother was the kindest, gentlest, most loving woman I've ever known. I loved her, Morgan, more than anything in this world. Enough to put my guns away and try to live like a normal human being instead of a hunted animal.

"And whether you want to hear it or not, she loved me too. The trouble was, she loved you and your sister more. That's why she wouldn't leave your father and run away with me like I begged her to. Maybe deep down she still loved your father more than me, I don't know. I only know that she was an honorable woman. She put her children above everything, even herself."

"The baby she was carrying when McCandless killed her? Was it yours?"

"Yes," Welch answered simply, trying to stave off the chill that swept over him as rage roared through Morgan's face.

"I'm going to kill you for that," Morgan grated in a low, soft tone that vibrated the morning silence.

Welch met his cold contemptuous stare without blinking. "Kill me if you want, Morgan, because I lied to you about who I really am. Maybe you've got a right. But I loved your mother and I will not apologize for that. I didn't apologize to your father for it and I'm not about to apologize to you.

"You, of all men, should know what loving a woman can do, Morgan," he added in a more restrained tone. "You're not the same man you were when Amber came into your life. Three months ago you would have high-tailed it for the border without a thought of what helping you escape might do to her. Look at you now. The first thing you do when you escape the noose is head for *Sierra Vieja* to make sure she's all right.

"So don't stand there and play righteous with me. In my place twenty years ago you'd have done the same thing. I only hope you're smarter than I was at your age, Morgan. Cooter and Amber both tell me that Tyrell is a man you can trust. So trust him, Morgan. Take the chance on having a decent life and give him the journal. That, with what Travis knows, is enough to put Owen on the gallows where he belongs. And enough to exonerate you from Owen's trumped up charges. You could marry Amber, stay right here, maybe even be happy for the first time in your life. Don't throw that chance away without thinking it out."

"I trusted one man, Welch, and he made a fool of me," Morgan sneered coldly. "You were the one person in this miserable world that I thought I could trust. The only man who ever played it straight with me. You've played me for a fool since the day you found me here in the ashes and helped me bury my folks."

"That's not true, Morgan," Welch interjected.

"No? Then why didn't you tell me your name was McCandless then?"

A rueful smile touched Welch's lips. He took off the tan Stetson to run one hand through his hair, then replaced the hat at the back of his head.

"I've done a lot of things in my life, Morgan, that I've been sorry for, but not telling you the truth is at the head of the list. There hasn't a day gone by that I haven't thought about telling you.

"You see, I always meant to tell you everything about my relationship with your mother, and my true identify. When I first took you in after Owen killed your folks, I told myself you were too upset, too young to understand. Then, as you got older, it was easy to keep putting it off. You were learning to use a gun, you needed to concentrate on that. By the time you were old enough to understand, it was too late. You were so fast with that gun that even I began to wonder if you could beat me. So..I decided to keep quiet, take the chance that you'd never find out."

"So everybody knew but me!"

"No," Welch contradicted. "No one else ever knew but Cooter. God knows how many times he's warned me what would happen if you found out. Then, a few years ago, Francine found the journal accidentally, but she loves me and she was afraid you'd kill me if you knew so she kept quiet too."

"She was right."

Morgan's words were flat, accented by the hard glitter in his eyes as he started backing away. He halted twenty feet from Welch and reached down to take the safety loop from the hammer of the Colt. Welch watched him with a sinking heart. Funny, that now the moment had arrived, he wasn't afraid anymore. His palms were dry, his hands were steady, even his mouth wasn't as dry as cotton like he'd always imagined.

"Do you mind if I take off this coat first?" Welch asked. At Morgan's nod of agreement, he walked toward his horse, shook out of the warm jacket and draped it over the saddle. He removed his pistol from the worn holster and checked the cylinders before dropping it back into place. Then, he walked back to his original position twenty feet from Morgan. Glancing around at the three lonely graves in the prairie, he looked back to Morgan with a sad smile.

"If it has to end this way, it's fitting that this is the place we do it," he remarked calmly. "Twenty years on this spot I found a lost, scared little boy who had just been robbed of his family and his heritage. I helped him bury his folks and then I took him away from here and tried my best to bring him up as if he were my own, partly because I wanted him to grow up and kill my brother for what he had done here, and partly because I loved his mother and that made him seem like my own.

"I made a lot of mistakes along the way. That scared little boy grew up to become the fastest gun in this country and with my help he's gained a reputation as a killer and an outlaw. I don't think Elena would be very pleased at the job I did raising her son, and that, more than anything else, is what I'm sorry for."

When he finished speaking, Welch squared his big shoulders under the crisp white shirt tucked into expensive tan trousers and waited. Twenty feet away Morgan's left hand dropped to his side while his coal black eyes watched Welch's relentlessly. In the few seconds that passed while they stood there, each waiting for the other to draw, a thousand pictures flashed through Morgan's mind.

Pictures of a small terrified boy scratching out graves in the hard Texas prairie and a tall blonde man silently carving markers with a pocket knife while tears streamed down his face to make tiny puddles at his feet. Pictures of that same boy a few years later, laughing at the funny lop-sided cake that the tall blonde man baked for his thirteenth birthday. Pictures of a million different kinds went through his mind of that big kind, demanding man who had brought him up to be a self reliant, confident man who could deal with whatever life threw at him.

Then, as the muscles in Morgan's face worked with the conflict raging inside him, Welch went for his gun. Morgan reacted automatically, the years of training taking over now, taking control of the moment. His weapon cleared leather a split second before Welch's.

There was an instant paling of the older man's face when he realized Morgan had beaten him, then the expression changed to quiet acceptance while he waited for the bullet from the ugly Colt in Morgan's hand.

Morgan stood with the gun in his hand pointed at Welch's chest, but his finger could not pull the trigger. It was one thing to draw on his mentor, but quite another to kill him, Morgan learned in those few endless seconds. With a heavy sigh of resignation, he released the hammer and dropped the Colt back into the worn black holster.

Welch exhaled slowly. Only now did his heart begin to pound as suddenly his whole body was drenched with sweat. His hand relaxed, the pistol fell back into place, and he was finally able to force his weak legs to move toward his horse. As he gathered up the reins, a pleased smile briefly touched his lips while he watched the confused, frustrated face of the man who had almost killed him.

"Then again, Elena, maybe I didn't do so bad after all," he said softly while he swung into the saddle.

"Welch, what will you do?" Morgan asked in a raw, strained voice. His gaze had followed Welch's every step and now he turned to look up into the rising sun at Welch's face.

"There's a little spread down by Sonora I've been thinking about," Welch replied with a slight smile. "Nice, quiet little place where a man could change his name and run a few cows, and sit back and watch the sun come up in the same place two days in a row. Francine's waiting for me in El Paso. She's a good woman, you know, Morgan. She's been in love with me for ten years knowing there was another woman in my life, but she never asked any questions. She deserves a lot more than I've given her and it's about time I made up for it."

The bay moved forward a few steps, then Welch turned in the saddle to regard Morgan thoughtfully. "Think about what I said, Morgan. This may be the only chance you'll have to turn things around. Don't make the same mistake I did. Don't end up at fifty and realize all the things you've missed out on in your life could have been avoided. If you want Amber and a chance for a half way normal life, you've got to fight for it. Don't throw it away, Morgan. If you do, you'll be sorry for the rest of your life."

Welch nudged the bay into a canter and turned his head toward the Mexican border. When he was safely out of sight, he reached down to take the Colt from his holster and filled the six empty chambers. Then, with a smile of satisfaction, he urged the horse into a gallop and thought ahead to Francine.

CHAPTER THIRTY-FIVE

Amber awoke early, searched the darkness for Morgan, and sat up quickly when she realized the bed was empty. She flung herself from the covers stiffly, grimacing in pain at the sore, aching muscles resulting from Owen's brutality. In spite of her disgust and horror at what her uncle had done, there was a feeling of contentment at Morgan's reluctant admission of love.

He was gone, she realized with a sinking heart. Had he left her forever after having promised faithfully just before she fell asleep in his arms that he would find some way for them to be together? No, he would not do that, she told herself firmly. He would not just ride away without even saying good-bye.

Her gaze fell on the sheet of paper on the desk by the window. She snatched it up with a sigh of relief at his scrawled message promising to return shortly and work out something about their future. Then, her relief turned to panic when she realized the journal lay on top of the desk instead of in the drawer where she'd left it. It could only mean that Morgan had discovered it, read enough of it to learn Welch's true identity and was at this moment probably on his way to settle the score.

She hurried to check that the bedroom door was securely locked, then dressed quickly in a riding skirt and a cotton shirt and her old scuffed boots. Then, tucking the ledger under one arm and snatching up the heavy pistol from her bed, she silently let herself out the bedroom door and slipped from the house.

A few minutes later, a disgruntled Cooter sat rubbing his eyes while the frantic girl told him of the previous night's activity. After calming the old man down from his rage at learning of Owen's savage attack and informing him of her plan to see Owen pay for his crimes, she told him that Morgan had discovered the journal and her fears that he would go after Welch.

"What will we do, Cooter?" she wailed. "We've got to stop him from doing something he'll always regret."

Cooter scratched his grizzled gray head and regarded her with serious blue eyes. "There ain't nothin' we can do about it, Missy. Welch and Morgan have got to play this hand out all by themselves. All we can do is wait."

Despite the girl's frantic protests, Cooter's cooler head won out. So they waited in the quiet little room just off the stables. Amber could not think of going to the ranger now, without knowing if Morgan was going to return safely or not at all. So Cooter made another pot of coffee, took down his rifle from above the door in case Owen McCandless came looking for the girl, and sat down to wait.

***

Owen rose with a guilty feeling creeping into his bones, but shook it off with a scornful grunt. By the time he had bathed, shaved, and dressed in an elegant tan broadcloth suit with a matching silk vest and crisp white shirt, the guilt that plagued him had vanished. He slipped into gleaming knee high calf skin boots and went down the stairs to enjoy a leisurely breakfast while the ranch slowly came to life.

Amber would see reason, he assured himself over a second cup of coffee. In a few days she would accept the fact that this was the way it had been meant to be and get over her anger. He could give her everything her heart desired; clothes, jewels, prestige, wealth beyond even her wildest dreams. In a few days when she'd cooled off, after Morgan Devereaux was swinging at the end of a rope, she'd see things his way.

Quincy, Owen's butler, gave him a curious side-ways glance at the sly chuckle that slipped out unconsciously. He only wished Price, his sanctimonious baby brother, knew the way he had worked things out. Price thought he'd won all those years ago when he took Althea and moved from the big house into that hovel a few miles away, but he'd shown Price that he always got what he wanted, one way or the other. He'd lost Althea, but what he had now was a prize even more rare. Amber was even more beautiful than her mother and when that gunfighter was out of her system, she'd see the excellence of this situation and be grateful.

He finished his coffee and paused to light a cigar as he went down the hall to his office. The wide smile vanished from his face as the office doors swung closed behind him. The color drained from his face when he saw the Colt's gaping mouth staring at him from behind his desk.

"Good morning, McCandless. I trust you slept well," Morgan drawled with a cold smile.

"What the hell are you doing here? How did you get into my house?" Owen roared when he recovered his voice.

The cold, flat glitter in the gunman's eyes made Owen wary, but at the moment his outrage got the better of him.

"I decided to pay you a visit before I continue on my way. What's the matter, McCandless? You don't look happy to see me," Morgan taunted softly.

"How the hell did you get out of jail?"

"I walked out, with a little help from my friends."

"Steven Riker will hunt you down like the snake you are!" Owen bellowed.

"I wouldn't count on that if I were you. You see, the last time I saw the sheriff, he was flopping around on the floor of his office with five of my bullets in him. But don't concern yourself, McCandless, he won't die. He'll live long enough to hang for killing Jenna Ruiz if I know Tyrell."

The quietly spoken words sent a chill through Owen. It took a moment for him to recover his bluster. "What the hell do you want, Devereaux?"

Morgan shook his head with a cold steely smile. "Your problem, McCandless, is that you think everything has a price attached to it. Open the door and tell your butler to tell Cooter Jackson you want to see him. Do it slow and easy, McCandless. If you so much as blink wrong, I'll kill you on the spot."

Owen wet his lips and moved to obey with stiff legs. He stuck his head through the heavy double doors to tell Quincy to rouse Cooter and have him come to the house at once. Then he shut the doors again and turned to face Morgan.

"Now what?"

"Now we wait."

Within five minutes both Cooter and Amber burst into the room. Morgan had to smile at the ferocious determination that filled the old wrangler's grizzled face when he stepped into the room in front of the girl with a squirrel gun leveled at Owen.

Morgan's eyes flashed to Amber's pale face and for a moment his expression softened. "You all right, Amber?"

She nodded numbly while her confused brain tried to figure out what was going on. "Welch?" she managed to squeak.

"On his way to Mexico," Morgan answered with a smile at the relief that flooded her beautiful features.

Morgan's eyes hardened as his gaze came back to Owen. He stood up, pushed the chair back from the desk, and moved around it, motioning that he wanted the rancher to take the seat. Owen moved across the room to sink into the leather chair with a glower.

"I might have known you had something to do with this, Cooter," Owen sneered with a withering glance at the old man. "Had I known I was harboring a rattlesnake in my pocket all these years, I'd have stepped on it years ago."

A grim smile of satisfaction lit Cooter's face as he hefted the squirrel gun. "I've waited thirty years to see you squirm, Owen," he said gruffly. "I let you steal my fourth of the ranch. I let you make a killer of one brother and I let you kill the other, but I thought I could save the missy from you. Even I had no idea you were rotten enough to hurt her like you did last night."

Amber's shaky hand on Cooter's arm stopped him from tight-ening his grip on the trigger of the heavy caliber gun. It took a supreme amount of will for Cooter to restrain himself, but the girl's gentle insistence finally won out.

"Try and prove anything," Owen smirked confidently as he leaned back in the chair and flicked away the ash from the expensive cigar into the crystal ashtray on the desk. "It's the word of an old fool and a trashy girl who spread her legs for a killer against mine. Who do you think a jury will believe?"

"A couple of days ago you might have been right," Morgan said in a flat voice. He turned to glance at Amber. "Did you bring it?"

Amber nodded as she stepped around Cooter to hand Morgan the journal. The florid outrage drained from Owen's face as Morgan held up the book.

"I see you recognize this, McCandless. It seems Welch kept this for years as a way of protecting Amber and her mother from you. It's an interesting book. I spent most of the night reading it."

With a cold, glittering smile at the rancher's ashen face, he continued. "I would have killed you while you slept, but Amber convinced me her way was better. That's a tough decision for me to make, McCandless, considering how many years I've waited to kill you. Then, last night when I learned what you'd done to Amber, it was almost more than I could stand. You should be grateful that she wants to see you hang because if she didn't, you'd be dead now and I wouldn't be as kind to you as I was to Riker."

Amber's finely arched brows raised in question. Morgan glanced at her to explain. "I gave Riker the chance to draw on me before I left his company last night. I don't think he'll be so eager to challenge anybody else for awhile."

"What is it you want from me?" Owen bellowed. "Who the hell are you?"

"I was hoping you'd ask me that," Morgan replied insolently as he moved to place the journal on the desk in front of the rancher. "Turn to page ninety-one, McCandless. You'll find your answer there."

Owen's numb fingers sifted through the pages of the ledger to find the page Morgan mentioned, then dropped his gaze to read. When he'd finished, he lifted his head to stare at Morgan with a disbelieving expression. The flat, bitter gleam that blazed from the gunman's eyes sent the first real shudder of terror through Owen that he'd ever known.

"Remember now, McCandless?" Morgan asked in that soft, deadly tone. "I was there that night. I saw you murder my father, rape and murder my mother, and then burn my little sister to death. If your brother Price hadn't hid me, you'd have killed me too.

"But that's where you made your mistake, McCandless. You forgot about me. You let me live. And now I'm here to make sure you die for it."

Owen's frozen lips worked soundlessly as his mind flashed back twenty years to reproduce the terrified black eyes of a little boy trying to protect his mother. At last he knew why Morgan had seemed so familiar all this time.

"Amber...Amber..princess...y-you can't let him do this," Owen stammered with his hands outstretched toward her.

"There was a time in my life, Uncle Owen, when I thought you were the most kind, loving man on earth. But you murdered my father, you branded my Uncle Welch a killer, and last night you beat me upstairs in my own room. I trusted you. I loved you, but now I only want to see you pay for the horrible things you've done and with the help of my father's journal, I will," Amber hissed with such coldness in her voice it made Owen flinch.

"I'll be going now, McCandless," Morgan said with cheerful conviction. "For reasons that should be obvious, I can't stay around to see the fun, but I'll make you one promise before I go. If for some reason the law doesn't hang you, I'll be back, and I'll kill you."

"And as soon as I see you hang, I'm going to be with him," Amber snarled to rub salt in Owen's wounds. "I'm going to sell off everything except Cooter's portion and what belonged to my father and then I'm going to set fire to this huge mausoleum of horrors and burn it to the ground as a tribute to the people you murdered to build it."

"My God!" Owen croaked, half rising from the chair, his eyes beseeching her cold, determined face. "Amber, princess, you can't mean that! Don't you realize that I did it all for you? Everything was for you! I did none of it for myself. It was all for you and your mother! Surely you can understand that."

The scorn in Amber's golden eyes pierced his soul worse than the pain of a thousand daggers. Her bruised lips snarled back in contempt as she moved forward a step.

"I don't want it!" she shouted. "I hate you and everything you've done! You're a monster! You've contaminated everything you've ever touched! I pray that I can live down the shame you've cast upon my father's name by trying to amend some of the damage you've done with your greed!"

Owen stared at her in speechless bewilderment as she turned to Morgan and flung herself into his arms. Sobs ripped from her throat while she held onto him fiercely.

"Amber, pull yourself together and go for Tyrell. I've got to go, but I'll send for you as soon as it's safe. Now come on, smile for me," Morgan prompted gently with a smile.

She sniffed and lifted a weak, trembling smile. Then with a firm push at his arm, she told him, "You better get going. Tyrell could be only a few minutes behind you."

Looking to be sure that Cooter's rifle was still trained on Owen, Morgan nodded as he dropped the Colt back into his holster. He kissed her gently, then held her away from him. His dark eyes devoured her slender beauty, storing each curve and valley in his mind to warm him through the lonely days ahead.

Perhaps it was the sight of Amber's absolute devotion to the gunfighter that drove Owen over the edge of reason. With a strangled curse, he yanked open the top desk drawer to haul out a Colt, bringing it up chest level to fire at Morgan's back as he began to turn for the door.

Amber's terrified scream mingled with the roar of gunfire as

Owen hung suspended in space for a moment, staring stupidly down at the blood spurting from his body to stain the frilly white shirt. The pistol dropped from his numb fingers to the desk with a clatter and then he toppled headfirst to the floor.

Morgan had whirled at Amber's scream, his hand streaking for the Colt, but Owen was dead before he could fire. His eyes jumped to Cooter, who still held the rifle tightly, but the expression on the old man's face was just as confused as Morgan's.

"Don't move, Devereaux," came an authoritative voice from the doorway behind them. Morgan's hand froze at the sound of Ryan Tyrell's command and a second later the big ranger moved into the room to take Morgan's pistol.

Morgan's gaze flashed to one still smoking barrel of the double barrel shotgun the ranger carried, pointed at the middle of his chest. He glanced back to Owen, cut almost in half by the blast of that short range, murderous weapon, and then back to the ranger in stunned amazement.

"That's twice I've saved your bacon from McCandless," Ryan announced with a tight smile. "At least this time I know what the blue blazes is going on."

He smiled slightly at the shock on Morgan's face.

Amber flung herself into Morgan's arms, burying her face in his chest to block out the grizzly sight of Owen's body sprawled on the carpet. Ryan motioned to Cooter with the shotgun.

"Put that squirrel gun down, Cooter. You won't be needing it now," he advised, amused at the apologetic glance the old man threw at Morgan.

"It took me a long time to put together all the pieces," Ryan went on as he moved to nudge Owen with the toe of his boot. Satisfied the rancher was beyond help, he returned his attention to the trio in front of him. "I'll admit you had me pretty confused, Devereaux. Then, last night this pair sneaked you a gun into jail and Mandell provided enough confusion to make getting out of town easy enough.

"Oh, by the way, you were right about Riker. He was more

than happy to confess killing the girl for the map," he added as though it was an after-thought. "You might be interested to know that a full detachment of Rangers is in town now cleaning up Riker's assorted businesses.

"The thing I couldn't figure out was why you wanted McCandless so bad," Ryan mused aloud. "Then, last night after you made Swiss cheese of Riker, I had a visit from Travis Bennett. It's amazing how much information one little newspaper man can have, isn't it? He provided me with enough proof to not only hang McCandless and Riker, but clean out the rat pack of state politicians that were involved with McCandless' crooked schemes. By now I'm sure the big shots at the railroad that paid McCandless all that money are high-tailing it for greener pastures."

"How did you know where to find me?" Morgan asked.

"I asked myself whether or not Miss McCandless was important enough for you to take the time to say good-bye before heading for the border and in view of her performance last night, decided she was.

"You see, Devereaux, you underestimated me by judging me by the same standards you judge all lawmen. In view of what my own father did to your folks, I don't blame you much." Smiling thinly at Morgan's surprised face, Ryan nodded. "Oh yes, Travis spared no quarter. I learned the whole nasty, painful truth last night. But I'm not my father, Devereaux.

"When all this comes out in Bennett's paper, there are going to be a lot of people eating crow and I've got to say it couldn't happen to a nicer bunch of folks. With what I overheard outside those doors about a journal, I'd be safe in saying that Owen McCandless' good name is about to take a serious beating.

"The only question now is what to do about you..and this pair of jail breakers," he added thoughtfully with a meaningful look at Amber and Cooter.

"It was all my idea, ranger," Cooter growled defensively. "Miss Amber went along with it against her better judgment."

Ryan chuckled aloud at the old man's instant defense of the

girl. "I don't think that'll be necessary, Cooter. In view of the fact that the two of you prevented that blood thirsty pack from doing McCandless' dirty work, I have a feeling the decent people in town will be pretty grateful.

"Which brings me to you, Devereaux," Ryan mused with a nudge of the shotgun barrel in Morgan's direction. "I've been studying you over the past couple of months so I think I can understand now what's made you the man you are. Still, you've been convicted and sentenced to hang so it's my duty to take you back. I know the rape charge was McCandless' idea," he interjected before Amber could speak.

"Still, the law is the law and I'm sworn to uphold it. On the other hand, if I were to kill Morgan Devereaux here today and bury him in the prairie next to his folks, who's to say that in, say four or five months some tall, good-looking fellow wouldn't ride in here and ask Miss McCandless for a job. Why, who knows? Maybe in a few months this fellow and Miss McCandless might discover they had a yen for each other."

Morgan's face was a mask of confusion as he stared at the ranger. Amber's fingers clutched in his shirt and he felt her body tremble violently while they both stared at Ryan in amazement.

Ryan smiled slightly. "Course this fellow would bear a striking resemblance to a dead gunfighter, but since his name would be completely different people would have to chalk it up to coincidence and pretty soon they'd stop wondering about him altogether. Especially after he married Miss McCandless and they had a couple of children."

When Ryan paused, Morgan and Amber exchanged glances, then Morgan found his voice. "What the hell kind of game are you playing, Tyrell?" he demanded.

"No game, Devereaux," Ryan replied. "It appears to me that you and the lady have something pretty special going for you. I'd hate to think she'd be a widow before you could marry her, or worse, spend the rest of her days trailing from one town to another, wondering when you were going to get a bullet in the back.

"So I'm making you a proposition, Devereaux. You hang up that gun and promise to go straight and I'll take a shovel out to that spread of yours and bury Morgan Devereaux in the prairie next to his kin."

"How do you know you can trust my word?" Morgan asked cautiously.

"The same way you know you can trust mine."

"What do you get out of all this?"

"Maybe a home cooked meal once in a while when I'm up this way. Maybe have one of your children named after me since I'm not likely to have one of my own."

"That's all?" Amber asked in a hushed little voice that held both great hope and even greater doubt.

"And the chance to do for someone else what was done for me once. What's it going to be, Devereaux?" Ryan asked. "Does Miss Amber mean enough to you to take the chance on going straight?"

"You already know the answer to that question, Tyrell. If you didn't, you wouldn't have asked it."

"Then I suggest you get your butt headed someplace safe for a few weeks until this blows over and folks get the word that Morgan Devereaux is pushing up sagebrush," Ryan said with a pleased smile as he lowered the shotgun.

He put Morgan's pistol in his own holster and pitched Morgan his weapon. "Might look suspicious for an ordinary cowboy to be toting a gun with all these notches in it and a cut-away trigger guard. Somebody might get the idea you know how to use it."

"Will it work, Mr. Tyrell?" Amber questioned anxiously. "Will Morgan be free?"

"As long as he minds his own business and stays out of trouble," Ryan assured her with a grin. "Course it wouldn't hurt if he grew a mustache or a beard to help change his looks some. If he learned to smile a little, well, that would be nice too. Who knows, Miss Amber, he might even learn to tell you how he feels without acting like you're pulling teeth to get it out of him."

A faintly embarrassed tinge came to Morgan's dark cheeks.

Ryan walked toward him, extending his hand. Morgan took it in a firm grip and met the big ranger's steady gaze.

"I don't know what to say, Tyrell."

"Then, don't try," Ryan replied. "If you want to thank me, just keep your nose clean and don't give me reason to regret this moment of weakness."

"You can rest assured of that," Amber said with a confident expression as she glanced up into Morgan's face.

Ryan turned to Cooter with a grin. "Cooter, why don't you and I find a couple of shovels and take a little ride. A gunslinger is about to be put to rest and I know the perfect spot to plant him."

"I'll take care of that, ranger," Cooter grunted. "You just get rid of this."

Ryan grinned at the motion the old wrangler had made with his head toward the crumpled heap that was all that remained of Owen McCandless. As Ryan lifted the shotgun to his shoulder in preparation to walk from the room, Amber threw herself into his arms and stood on tiptoe to plant a wobbly kiss of gratitude on his cheek.

Ryan blushed so profusely it made Amber giggle while she held his free hand for a moment.

"Thank you, Mr. Tyrell," she whispered, tears spilling down her cheeks.

"It's my pleasure, ma'am. Just my way of making up in part for what my father helped rob him of." Then looking at Morgan as he moved toward the door, he added, "Take care of her, Devereaux, and keep in touch. You're a lucky man to have a woman like that fight so hard for you. But I've got a feeling by the time she's through with you, you may just be worth it. If I were lucky enough to be in your boots, I'd sure try not to disappoint her."

As he left the room with Cooter following behind, Amber felt Morgan's arm slide around her waist, drawing her slender body against him. Her gaze moved up his strong, masculine frame to lock on his face, and she smiled at the glow that leaped from the depths of those inky black pools. For such a long time she had been unable to look behind the veil of control he kept over his emotions, but now, seeing the love he had such difficulty putting into words, she knew it had been worth waiting for.

"I have a feeling he's right," Morgan said with a hesitant smile. "I can't make any promises, Amber, except that I'm willing to give it one hell of a try. It may not last. There's always the chance that someday I'll be found out. Are you willing to risk that?"

She nodded emphatically, encircling his waist with her arm. "Whether it lasts for a week or a lifetime, Morgan, even if someday you have to resurrect your past, I want only to be with you. God has given us a chance, Morgan. With His help we'll make the very most of it," she said confidently.

Morgan smiled at her assurance and breathed a long sigh. He savored the sight of her golden beauty with a softness that was still new to him, still awkward and strange.

"With you to keep telling me that you love me, Amber, I may be able somehow to bury Morgan Devereaux and be the kind of man you deserve," he said cautiously as he bent his head to kiss her.

"You already are, Morgan. You're everything I ever dreamed of," she murmured against his lips.

She smiled softly at the doubt and concern in his handsome face. It would take time for him to learn to trust other people, time to feel secure in his new found identity without the necessity of always looking back, time to learn it wasn't weakness that made him love her enough to turn his back on the past, but strength.

For now it was enough that his arm was safely in place around her as he led her from the hollow specter of the past toward a future filled with promise and nurtured by their deep, abiding love.

Edwards Brothers Malloy
Thorofare, NJ USA
January 31, 2013